## ALSO BY ALAFAIR BURKE

The Ellie Hatcher Series

*Dead Connection*
*Angel's Tip*

The Samantha Kincaid Series

*Judgment Calls*
*Missing Justice*
*Close Case*

# 212

## A NOVEL

## ALAFAIR BURKE

**HARPER**

*An Imprint of* HarperCollins*Publishers*

www.harpercollins.com

HarperCollins books may be purchased for educational, business, or sales promotional use. For information, please write: Special Markets Department, HarperCollins Publishers, 10 East 53rd Street, New York, NY 10022.

FIRST EDITION

*Designed by Eric Butler*

Library of Congress Cataloging-in-Publication Data has been applied for.

ISBN: 978-0-06-156122-1

10  11  12  13  14    ID/RRD    10  9  8  7  6  5  4  3  2  1

*For Philip, Mary, and Anne-Lise Spitzer*

212

# CHAPTER ONE

Tanya Abbott noticed the quiver in her index finger as it pressed the three silver buttons in the rain—9 . . . 1 . . . 1. Listening to the ring, she found herself mentally calculating the number of days that had passed since she had first arrived in New York City.

Tanya had put the number at twenty-six by the time the dispatcher answered the call. It had been three full weeks and another five days.

"Nine-one-one. What is your emergency?"

She'd taken the Amtrak to Penn Station three Thursdays ago, and now it was Tuesday night. Twenty-six days in New York. Twenty-six days since she had started over again. Twenty-six days, and already she was calling 911.

"Hello? Is anyone there? What is your emergency?"

Tanya cleared her throat. "The penthouse apartment at Lafayette and Kenmare."

"That's your location, ma'am? Tell me what's going on there."

The corner of Lafayette and Kenmare was no longer Tanya's location, but twenty minutes earlier, she had been inside the luxury penthouse perched on top of the white brick building on the corner. She'd sipped Veuve Clicquot from a crystal flute while leaning against the black granite bar. She had lounged on the low white-leather sectional sofa with her legs crossed modestly as her host pointed out the panoramic SoHo views, temporarily obscured by cascading sheets of rain. She had followed him into the master suite. She had cleaned herself up with a washcloth in the gleaming marble bathroom when it was all over.

"A shooting. There's been a shooting." Tanya used her palm to wipe away the drops of water from her eyes, tears mixed with rain. Her attempts were futile, serving only to smear mascara across her clammy cheeks.

"You heard gunshots?"

"Inside the apartment."

"Ma'am. I need you to use your words. You heard gunshots from inside the apartment? Could you tell what direction they were coming from?"

"There was a shooting. Inside the apartment at Lafayette and Kenmare."

"I've got your location as Lafayette and *Bond*, ma'am. Did you mean to say Lafayette and Bond? . . . I need you to speak to me, ma'am. Can you tell me if you're okay? Are you hurt?"

Tanya hadn't realized that she had run five full blocks before finding a pay phone. She couldn't even remember crossing Houston. Maybe her heart was pounding because of the running. She found comfort in the thought of some distance between her and the apartment.

"Lafayette and Kenmare. The penthouse."

"Can you tell me your name, ma'am? I've got an ambulance on the way. Just keep talking to me. My name's Tina Brooks. Can you tell me your name?"

Tanya returned the handset to its cradle and sprinted south on Lafayette toward the subway station at Bleecker. She hadn't given her name to the dispatcher, and she hadn't used her cell phone. She could move swiftly without prompting attention from the other pedestrians who were also rushing for shelter.

At the same moment Tina Brooks had dispatched an ambulance

to the penthouse, she had no doubt sent a police car to the pay phone on the corner of Lafayette and Bond to search for the anonymous caller who had dialed 911. But before either vehicle reached its intended destination, Tanya Abbott would be long gone, drying her face against her damp sleeve and catching her breath on the 6 train.

# CHAPTER TWO

**D**etective Ellie Hatcher and her partner, J. J. Rogan, were soaked. Not damp. Not soggy. Soaked. The rainfall that poured onto Manhattan's streets that night felt like the kind that meteorologists might measure in buckets per second.

Ellie should have been grateful for the storm. It was the first break in a week-long, record-setting late-May heat wave. For seven consecutive days, the mercury had approached triple digits. Those kinds of oppressive temperatures were never cause to celebrate, but in New York City, atmospheric heat led to an altogether different kind of swelter. Thanks to the combination of heat-retaining concrete and still, breezeless air, the entire city reeked of a unique potpourri of body odor, garbage, and urine. The streets and subways were crowded. People were sticky. People were cranky. People drank more. They stayed out later. And people got dangerous.

In New York City, heat begets violence.

Ellie and Rogan had hoped that the rainfall might wash in their first quiet night of what had been a hectic week. They should have known better.

Their first callout was to the scene of a reported homicide in SoHo. A couple huddled beneath a restaurant awning had made out the image of a man's prone body in the backseat of a BMW 325 parked on Grand. By the time EMTs found the track marks and Ellie pulled the eighteen inches of rubber tubing from the back passenger footwell, Ellie and her partner were soaked.

They had just reported clear and were looking forward to drying out back in the squad room when the second call came in, this time to a penthouse apartment at Lafayette and Kenmare. As they drove up Crosby, Ellie noticed a small pile of flowers propped up against a stoop at the corner of Broome, a rain-battered memorial to the late Heath Ledger. It had been more than four months since the actor's accidental overdose; today, the media had announced the death of Sydney Pollack from stomach cancer. When celebrities died, everyone cared, even though the public knew those stars no better than whatever sad sack Ellie and Rogan were about to open a new case file for.

The address at the condo turned out to be 212 Lafayette, but the blue glass sign on the bright white exterior marked the building merely as 212. Whereas builders had co-opted the American West a century ago with names like the Dakota, the Wyoming, and the Oregon, the latest flavor was minimalist titles that managed to evoke images of urban perfection with one discreet word: Cielo, Onyx, Azure. And what could be more quintessentially New York than Manhattan's famous area code—212?

Dishwater gray puddles had pooled at their feet by the time the elevator reached the seventh floor. The doors parted to reveal a narrow hallway occupied by a uniform officer standing between two slate-colored doors. The officer nodded in the direction of the open one.

"Not technically a penthouse," Rogan observed as the elevator doors whispered shut behind them. "In a real penthouse, you walk directly from the elevator and into the apartment."

The foyer alone was twice the size of Ellie's entire apartment. "I don't care if a realtor would call it a shanty," she said. "I'd take it."

Rogan unbuttoned his trench coat and let it fall to the foyer floor. Ellie did the same with her black slicker. The last thing they needed was a waterlogged crime scene.

As they made their way to the sounds of voices beyond the living room, Ellie took in the apartment's condition. Beneath a single built-in shelf, books were scattered haphazardly across the floor. The empty drawers of a credenza in the dining room were flung open. Kitchen cabinets, also open.

A pyramid of unlit logs rested picturesquely beneath a mantel sporting a single crystal-framed photograph: a handsome middle-aged man shaking hands with the former president. The man looked familiar.

The person in the picture was not, however, the man they found splayed naked on the white sheets of a king-size bed in the master suite, a used condom knotted neatly on top of the nightstand beside him.

Bullet holes riddled the corpse, the bed beneath the corpse, and the wall behind the bed. The nightstand and dresser drawers were open, as were the doors to two double closets. All empty. By comparison, the adjoining bathroom looked relatively peaceful, with only a stack of towels toppled onto the floor.

A voice from the living room interrupted their inspection of the disarray.

"Robo? Robo! Where the hell is he?"

"Detectives. I think the apartment owner's here." A uniform officer stood nervously in the doorway of the master bedroom.

"Who called him?" Rogan asked.

The officer shrugged. "We called the super. The super must've called the owner."

"Did someone ask you to call the super, Officer?" Above Rogan's clenched jaw, a vein pulsed at his temple. "Did *we* ask you to do that?"

"I'll deal with it," Ellie said, brushing past the uniform as he muttered a halfhearted apology. She turned in the living room to face a trim, middle-aged man in a black tuxedo and white bow tie. He had closely clipped silver hair and intense green eyes. She recognized him as the man from the photograph on the mantel.

He eyed her up and down, clearly trying to determine how a barefoot woman in a turquoise linen shirt and black pencil-legged pants fit in among an apartment full of uniformed police officers.

"Who are you?"

"Detective Ellie Hatcher. NYPD." She flipped open the badge holder that was clipped to her waistband.

"I take it from your bare feet that two of these many shoes on my Ryan McGinness belong to you."

"You mean on your rug?" Ellie looked at the patterned area rug separating her from the man in the tuxedo.

"It's art," the man said, "but you apparently don't recognize that. Robo, get this cleaned up. Robo—I called him forty-five minutes ago to deal with this shit. Robo—"

He headed toward the bedroom, but Ellie held her hand up. "I answered your question, sir. Now it's my turn. Who are you?" She still could not put her finger on where she'd seen him before.

"I'm the man who owns the apartment you all have apparently commandeered. Robo—"

"Is Robo a well-built guy? Brown hair? Sleeve tattoo wrapped up his right arm, leprechaun tat on his left hip?"

He blinked at her. "I don't even want to process what you're insinuating."

"I wasn't *insinuating* anything. Assuming you have never seen the tattoo on the man's hip, the rest of the description fits?"

The man nodded. "Where is he? I don't appreciate getting called away from an important event by some building superintendent."

"Unfortunately, sir, the man you're calling Robo is dead. He was shot in what is apparently your bed. And he was naked in your bed, in case you were wondering."

The man stared at her for three full beats before the corner of his mouth crept upward. "You're going to regret this conversation, Miss Hatcher. I won't ask you to clean up the mess you've made lest you accuse me of sexism, but please have one of these lackeys standing guard on taxpayer dollars remove your soggy shoes from what you so eloquently called my *rug*. It's worth more than you make in a year."

"First I need a name and some identification, sir."

"Samuel Sparks." He didn't even feign a reach for his wallet.

"And who's Robo?"

"His name is Robert Mancini. He's one of my protection specialists. I've been calling him ever since I was beckoned down here about some kind of police emergency."

"A protection specialist. You mean a bodyguard?"

The man nodded, and Ellie suddenly matched the name to the face: Samuel Sparks was *Sam* Sparks. *That* Sam Sparks. Before she scored a rent-stabilized sublet of questionable legality, she had perused countless real estate listings for units in Sparks's buildings that she could not afford. This was the man who had been rumored to be purchasing the 110-building Stuveysant Town to convert into condos before a rival tycoon outbid him. He was the mogul who had been photographed with so many A-list women that he himself had become fodder for the tabloids and paparazzi, including some who speculated about the sexuality of the self-declared "permanent bachelor." Ellie assumed those rumors might explain Sparks's response to her mention of the victim's exposed hip.

Sparks's smirk widened into a full-blown smile. "You can apologize after these shoes have been picked up."

Needless to say, Ellie did not apologize.

"Mr. Sparks, your apartment is now officially a crime scene. I need you to leave."

"Excuse me?"

"Did you hear my request, sir?"

"Of course I *heard* you, but—"

"Then I'm ordering you, for the second time now, to leave the premises." Ellie intentionally used the kind of I-get-high-on-my-authority tone that made a person want to disobey.

"I am not leaving my own—"

"Sam Sparks, you're under arrest for disobeying the lawful order of a police officer." Ellie used her index finger to signal to a uniform officer who'd been observing cautiously from the front doorway. The officer removed his handcuffs from his duty belt.

"You want to do the honors, or should I?" the officer asked.

Sparks sucked his teeth and squinted at the officer's nameplate.

"Officer T. S. Amos. I'd warn against taking another step in my direction unless you plan to spend the rest of your NYPD career on parking patrol."

Ellie snatched the handcuffs from the uniform's grasp. "Not to worry, Amos. This one's all me."

# PART I

---

**YOU CAN'T LET THIS GET TO YOU.**

# CHAPTER THREE

**FOUR MONTHS LATER . . . WEDNESDAY, SEPTEMBER 24**

**11:00 A.M.**

Ellie Hatcher raised her right hand and swore to tell the truth, the whole truth, and nothing but the truth.

But the testimony she gave before Judge Paul Bandon was not *really* the whole truth. It was a dry, concise recitation of the basic facts—and only the facts—of a callout 120 days earlier. Time: 11:30 p.m. Location: a penthouse apartment at a building called 212 at the corner of Lafayette and Kenmare. Nature of the callout: a report of shots fired, followed by the subsequent discovery of a bullet-ridden body in the bedroom. The dead man: Robert "Robo" Mancini, bodyguard to Manhattan real estate mogul Sam Sparks.

Ellie allowed herself a glance at Sparks, who sat at counsel table with a blank-faced stare next to his lawyer, Ramon Guerrero. According to her police report, Sparks was fifty-five years old, but looking at him this morning, she could understand why he enjoyed the serial companionship of the various models and aspiring starlets who graced his side on the society pages. It wasn't just the money. With his square jaw, bright green eyes, and a permanent Clint Eastwood squint, Sparks exuded the kind of chiseled intensity that was catnip to a certain kind of woman.

Ellie was surprised that he had bothered to make a personal appearance. It was probably the man's way of signaling to Judge Bandon that this hearing was just as important to him as it was to the police. The only spectator on the government's side of the courtroom, in the back bench by the entrance, was Genna Walsh, the victim's sister. Ellie had told her there was no point coming into the city for the hearing, but she could not be dissuaded. Perhaps Sparks was not the only one trying to send a message.

Assistant District Attorney Max Donovan continued to feed Ellie the straightforward questions that would lay the groundwork for today's motion.

"Did the decedent reside at the apartment in which his body was found—the penthouse in the 212 Building at 212 Lafayette?"

"No, he did not. Mr. Mancini's personal residence was in Hoboken, New Jersey."

"Did he own the apartment where his body was found?" Donovan asked.

"No."

"Who does own the apartment?"

"Mancini's employer, Sam Sparks."

"In your thorough search of the crime scene, did you find any evidence to suggest that the decedent was staying long-term at the 212?"

"No, we did not."

"No suitcase, no toothbrush or shaving kit, nothing along those lines?"

"No." Ellie hated the formal back-and-forth that was inherent in testifying. She'd prefer to sit across a desk from Judge Bandon and lay it all out for him. "In fact, Mr. Sparks himself told us that very night that the decedent was only using the apartment for the evening."

Again, Ellie reported just the facts. According to Sparks, he had completed the development at 212 six months earlier and kept the penthouse for himself as an investment and as a place to host the European investors who increasingly preferred downtown's modern lofts to the more conventional temporary housing stock in midtown. To further justify the space as a corporate deduction, he allowed his personal assistant and security officers to make use of the apartment when the calendar permitted.

Max Donovan had pinned photographs from the crime scene on a bulletin board next to the witness stand. Moving through the sequence of photos, Ellie described the disorder in the apartment—the open cabinets and drawers, the relatively few possessions in the apartment tossed to the floor like confetti.

"From the looks of it," Max said, "only the bathroom was spared?"

In the final picture on the board, a single cabinet door in the otherwise tidy master bathroom was flung open, a pile of towels splayed on the tile floor beneath the sink.

"That's about right," Ellie responded.

"I guess extra rolls of toilet paper and back issues of *Sports Illustrated* aren't the usual targets of a home invasion."

Max's comment wasn't especially funny, but the bar for comedy in courtrooms was notoriously low, and the remark drew a chuckle from Judge Bandon.

The point of the testimony was simple: the violent home invasion on May 27 of a seventh-floor condo overlooking Lafayette Street had nothing to do with poor Robert Mancini until Robo got caught in the crossfire. The bodyguard's relationship to the apartment was too inconsequential—too tangential—for the dead man to have been the premeditated target of the four bullets that eventually penetrated his naked torso that night.

No, the crime had nothing to do with Mancini. The real target was either a robbery or Sam Sparks himself, and robbery seemed unlikely. Despite the expensive furnishings—two flat-screen televisions, a top-of-the-line stereo system, the rug that doubled as art—nothing was missing from the apartment.

So now the police wanted to know more about Sam Sparks.

From the witness stand, Ellie eyed a silver picture frame behind the bench. In the photograph, a smiling Paul Bandon beamed alongside a perfect-looking wife and a teenage boy in a royal blue cap and gown. Outside this courtroom, underneath the robes, Bandon was a normal person with a real life and a family. She wondered, if she cut through the bull and laid it all out for him, whether Judge Bandon would understand how the series of events beginning on May 27 had led her to the middle of a battle between the district attorney's office and one of the most powerful men in the city.

Maybe he would understand how she had felt when Sparks had sauntered into the crime scene, in his custom-cut tuxedo, somehow dry and picture-ready on that rain-soaked night, so put out by the disturbance at his pristine penthouse. Maybe he could imagine the disdainful looks Sparks had given to the police officers sullying his spotless pied-à-terre, the very officers who protected the appearance of order that allowed Sparks to earn billions in Manhattan real estate. Maybe he would realize that she hadn't even meant to arrest Sparks and had immediately kicked herself for doing it. All she'd wanted was to wipe that smug look off his face, just long enough for him to give more of a rat's ass about a dead man in his bedroom than the area rug in his foyer.

If Ellie were telling the whole truth, she'd tell Judge Bandon that there was something about Sam Sparks that got under her skin. And she would try to explain that the only thing that bothered her more than that something was her own inability to maintain control in the face of it.

Sparks's rigid refusal to cooperate with the police investigation— all because of their first ill-fated encounter, an encounter in which she had played no small part—had contributed to a four-month investigation that led nowhere.

"So, in sum, Detective Hatcher, would access to the financial and business records we are requesting from Mr. Sparks assist you with your investigation, Detective Hatcher?" Donovan asked.

"We believe so," she said, now looking directly at Judge Bandon. "Mr. Sparks is, as we all know, an extremely successful man. A break-in at one of his showcase personal properties would send a message to him. If he has financial or business enemies, we need to look into that."

"And to be clear, is Mr. Sparks himself a target of your investigation?"

"Of course not," Ellie said.

If she were revealing the whole truth, she would have told Judge Bandon that at one point they of course had looked at Sparks as a suspect, but had quickly cleared him.

"Is there anything you'd like to add to your testimony, Detective Hatcher?"

In polite courtroom discourse, ADA Max Donovan referred to her as Detective Hatcher. But this was not the whole truth, either. If courtrooms had anything to do with the whole truth, he would call her Ellie. And one of them might have to disclose the fact that, just that morning, the testifying detective had woken up naked in the assistant district attorney's bed.

"No, thank you, Mr. Donovan."

# CHAPTER FOUR

**M**egan Gunther rolled her fingertips lightly over the keyboard of her laptop computer. It was a nervous habit. If her typing fingers were positioned at the ready, she had a tendency to keep them moving—tiny little wiggles against the smooth black keys.

She remembered begging her mother to teach her to type at the age of six. Her parents had just purchased a home computer, and Megan would eavesdrop as they sat side by side at her father's desk, marveling at the wonders on the screen, all attributable to something called the Internet. But Megan had marveled at the speed of her mother's fingers as they flew across the keyboard.

She glanced at the round white clock that hung above the blank blackboard behind Professor Ellen Stein. Eleven forty-five. Fifteen more minutes. Thirty-five minutes of class had passed, and the only words on her laptop screen were "Life and Death," followed by the date, followed by a single question: "Are all lives equally good?"

Megan had enrolled in this seminar because the catalog description had piqued her curiosity: "Is life inherently worthwhile, or only if the life lived is a good life? Is death necessarily negative? Is a life not lived superior to a life lived in vain?"

Megan was no philosophy major—she would declare biology

next year, and her curriculum was designed specifically for premed. But that course description had grabbed her attention. She figured that it could only serve the medical profession well if a future doctor took the time to contemplate the larger meaning of life and death in addition to learning the science that could extend one and forestall the other.

She should have foreseen, though, that a philosophy seminar with no prerequisites would devolve into a series of free-floating chat sessions during which unfocused undergrads—the ones who would eventually wind up behind a Starbucks counter, or perhaps in law school—attempted to show off their mastery of the most reductionist versions of the various branches of philosophy.

Today's class, as was often the case, had held momentary promise when Dr. Stein posed the question that was still staring at Megan from the screen of her laptop: "Are all lives equally good?"

Unfortunately, the first student to respond immediately played the Hitler card. As in, "Of course not. I mean, who here mourns the death of Hitler?" After just three weeks of a single philosophy course, Megan was convinced that the quality of the national civic dialogue would be noticeably improved by a voluntary prohibition against all analogies to Nazi Germany.

Poor Dr. Stein had done her best to steer the conversation on track, but then the girl who always wore overalls and patchouli oil had set off another frenzy of mental masturbation by wondering aloud whether the mentally disabled enjoyed their lives as much as "regular" people.

Megan found herself contemplating her fingers jiggling on the keyboard again. Not her fingers as much as the keyboard itself. The layout. She understood why the Q and the Z belonged to the whim of her left pinky; Hitler analogies were more common than the use of those letters. But what criteria had been used to determine the keys that would qualify for "home base," as her mother had called it during her early touch-typing training? A, S, D, L—those she understood. But F and J? And the semicolon? How often did anyone use semicolons?

She forced herself to tune back into the conversation around the seminar table. She gathered that the patchouli girl's comment about the mentally disabled had set off a larger conversation about the value of knowledge when a guy with a paperboy hat and a beatnik soul patch retorted, "Please, go read more Ayn Rand. You're asked about lives without value, and you pick on the retarded? Of much more questionable value is a life spent absorbing knowledge but then doing absolutely nothing with it."

At that, Megan thought she noticed a twitch in Dr. Stein's left eye. Twenty minutes later, the class was still debating whether knowledge was worthy for its own sake, or merely as a means toward practical ends.

"But even to differentiate between knowledge for its own sake and for its pragmatic import is a fiction," the patchouli woman insisted. "It assumes an objective reality that stands alone, independent of our own cognitive responses to it. We have no measure of reality other than through our own thoughts, so what precisely do you mean when you say 'knowledge standing alone'? Knowledge *is* reality."

"Only if you're an epistemological idealist," the soul patch argued. "Maybe Kant would agree with that kind of logic, or even John Locke. But a realist would maintain that there is an ontological reality that is independent of our own experiences. And if we can set aside our narcissism for thirty seconds and accept that premise, then it's not a lot to ask of the privileged elite that they use their knowledge to make a concrete, objective difference in that reality."

"This might be slightly off topic—"

Megan felt her eyes rolling involuntarily away from the speaker, the decent-looking guy who always wore concert T-shirts.

"This might be slightly off topic, but has anyone else wondered why John Locke on *Lost* is named John Locke? It explains the inconsistencies in the various narratives. The writers are telling us to take all those flashbacks and flash-forwards with a grain of salt; they are each filtered through the lens of the characters' personal experiences."

"Oh, my God. Did he really just say that?" The whisper came from the student sitting next to Megan, a guy in a Philadelphia Flyers jersey with a serious case of bed head. "I should have saved my trust fund and gone to Penn."

"Okay, people, time out." Stein rapped her knuckles against the tabletop to call the class to order. "Let's get back to the original question."

Megan wished she had a dollar for every time Dr. Stein had taken them "back to the original question." The woman no doubt knew her shit, but she had to stop treating these morons as intellectual equals. If this group could be trusted with the amount of guidance provided by the original question, they wouldn't be talking about Hitler, the mentally disabled, and a television show about island castaways.

She finally caved to temptation and opened Internet Explorer on her laptop. Almost all of the university's buildings were equipped with wireless Internet access, but a serious professor like Dr. Stein certainly expected her students to refrain from partaking during class time. Barely veiled surfing ran rampant, however, and to Megan it was no surprise. The university's current regime was, in her view, no different from cutting lines of cocaine on the desktop in front of addicts and telling them not to snort.

She moved her right hand onto the laptop's mouse pad and checked her Gmail account while making a point of periodically looking up from her screen to deliver a pensive nod. From there, it was on to Perez Hilton's site for the celebrity gossip. Then to Facebook, where it was her turn in the Scrabble game she was playing with Courtney. She knew that at some point Courtney's decision not to attend NYU would cut back on their socializing, but for now they remained in daily online contact.

Megan noticed that her neighbor with the bed head was eyeballing her computer screen. She was about to deliver her best warning glare when he nudged his notebook an inch in her direction.

Beneath a series of doodled boxes and circles, he had jotted, "You missed HAYSEED for a bingo."

She turned to her game and confirmed the mistake. Switching the laptop back to her blank class notes, she typed a sad face—a colon, followed by a dash and a left parenthesis.

Her neighbor scribbled another note: "campusjuice.com."

Megan clicked back to her browser, typed the Web site name into the address bar, and gently hit the enter key. "Campus Juice." White bubble letters against an orange background, followed by a slogan that said it all: "All the Juice, Always Anonymous."

In the middle of the screen was a text box, labeled "Choose Your Campus."

Megan typed in NYU and hit enter. Up came a message board consisting of a list of posts, each with its own subject title.

**Craziest Person in Your Dorm**
**WTF?!: Did Brandon Saltzburg drop out?**
**Freshman Fifteen (Plus Another Fifteen)**
**Who's Sluttier: Kelly Gotleib or Jenny Huntsman?**
**Hottest profs.**
**I've got a sex tape**
**Michael Stuart gave me the clap**

Megan dropped her right hand beneath the seminar table and flashed a thumbs-up at her neighbor, who doodled an exclamation point in the margin of his notebook.

She clicked on the link to pull up the thread concerning Michael Stuart and his supposed STD. The message had been posted an hour earlier, and two people had already responded—one alleging that Stuart lived in her dorm and was a rampant meth fiend, the other claiming to be Michael Stuart himself with some not-so-kind words about the original poster's cottage cheese thighs.

Megan scrolled through the next three pages of posts. The entire site was devoted to on-campus gossip, insults, and attacks—all naming real names, and yet capable of being posted with complete anonymity if the author so chose.

She had just finished perusing one of the more respectable

threads—speculation about the identity of this year's commencement speaker—when the title of another post grabbed her attention.

She stared at the two words on the screen:

**Megan Gunther.**

Moving the cursor to the hyperlink, she could not bring herself to click on the text. Something inside of her—whatever instincts humans possess for emotional self-preservation—told her that one click would change everything. She didn't want to read whatever had been written there for the entire world to see.

Megan jerked at the sound of a book being dropped on the table. She looked up to see Ellen Stein's eyes directed at her, along with nineteen younger, conspiratorial faces smirking at her embarrassment.

"I'm sorry, Ms. Gunther. Are we interrupting your computer research?"

# CHAPTER FIVE

Ellie had barely made her way from the witness chair to her seat on a bench behind Max Donovan before Judge Bandon opened the floor to argument. As Ellie had predicted, and as Max had warned, Sparks's lawyer was casting her as some kind of rogue cop on a single-minded anti-Sparks mission: Mark Fuhrman minus the race stuff.

The lawyer's name was Ramon Guerrero. According to Max, Guerrero was a hard-line anticommunist from Miami who had first applied to law school to help other Cubans apply for political asylum but, as lawyers often do, had since forged another—and more lucrative—path. Now he was one of the few corner-office partners at a five-hundred-plus-attorney law firm who had actual trial experience. He was the charismatic guy the eggheads brought in when the documents had been reviewed, briefs had been filed, depositions were over, and it was time to talk to a judge or a jury.

And on this particular afternoon he found himself in Paul Bandon's courtroom, demonizing Ellie Hatcher.

"Your Honor, the only reason the NYPD hasn't made more progress investigating the tragic murder of Mr. Mancini is that the lead detectives, most notably Detective Hatcher, decided early on that wherever Sam Sparks appears, Sam Sparks must be the story. Rather than fully investigate the possibility that someone out there wanted to see Robert Mancini dead—someone violent, someone who's still at large—they want to pursue a fishing expedition through confidential business and financial records."

"With all due respect to Mr. Guerrero," Donovan said, rising from counsel's chair, "this is not the kind of contractual dispute that he and Mr. Sparks are used to dealing with. This is a murder investigation. And, as you and I both know from the myriad of murder cases we have seen, murder victims—and the people close to them—lose their privacy as a result of the violence directed against them. You have signed countless search warrants for victims' homes, offices, cars . . ."

As Donovan continued to hammer away at the list, Ellie's gaze shifted from the Bic Rollerball braced in his hand to Guerrero's Montblanc. "Police pore over every document and cookie stored inside a victim's computer. We review every bank record, phone log, and credit card bill. And it's all a matter of routine, Your Honor. We're only here because Sam Sparks is . . . well, he's Sam Sparks."

"The problem with your analysis, Mr. Donovan, is that Sam Sparks was not the victim of this crime. Robert Mancini was."

"Sparks *was* a victim, Your Honor. It was *his* eight-million-dollar apartment that was stormed into. It was *his* apartment that was riddled with bullet holes."

"But it was not his body in the bed," Judge Bandon replied.

"No, but the police believe it was intended to be."

"Precisely. That is what the police *believe*. And usually when we talk about what the police believe, we subject that belief to a standard of probable cause. I don't see probable cause to search through the personal records of Sam Sparks."

"Exactly," Guerrero chimed in.

"But, Your Honor, Mr. Sparks is not a suspect. If that's his concern, we can work out an immunity agreement to placate Mr. Guerrero."

"Immunity?" Guerrero asked. "*Immunity*? The last thing Sam Sparks needs is for some newspaper to report that he has received

*immunity* in a murder case. As the police themselves have acknowl-
edged, he had nothing to do with the events at his apartment on
May 27. Because he's at no risk of criminal charges for those events,
immunity from prosecution is worthless to him." Guerrero pressed
his weight into his hands on counsel table and leaned forward for
emphasis. "The government fails to appreciate importance of public
opinion and the privacy of information to Sam Sparks's significant
net worth. His real estate holdings are valuable, yes. But as we all
know, the real value to the industry that is Sam Sparks lies in his
reputation as a businessman. The fact that someone was shot at one
of his properties is not great PR. But if the police are actually investigating Mr. Sparks—even as a potential target—then, before you
know it, people are speculating about improperly financed debt, the
Mafia . . . who knows what? And of course the risks of disclosure of
information regarding pending deals cannot be understated in this
kind of market."

Ellie found herself tiring of the invest-in-Sam-Sparks-for-your-
future sales presentation and began doodling on the notepad she had
removed from her purse. She let her gaze move to the left, where
the head of what Sparks Industries called its Corporate Security
Division, Nick Dillon, sat on a bench behind Sparks and Guerrero.

Before Dillon was associated with either Sparks or Mancini, he'd
been a member of the NYPD. After a stint working for a private
military contractor, he'd moved on to Sparks. Now he was one of
those lucky former cops who collected both a city pension and a
private paycheck. Dillon had been Mancini's immediate supervisor.
He had also been his friend.

Ellie and Rogan had spoken to Dillon at least once a week since
that initial callout four months earlier. He had done his best to play
mediator, but they'd nevertheless wound up here in court. Dillon
nodded along with Guerrero's argument, but Ellie knew from earlier
conversations that Dillon would like nothing more than to elbow
his boss in the throat for his refusal to cooperate with the police. She
liked the image.

"Your Honor," Max protested, "counsel's argument assumes that any information disclosed as part of this investigation will become public. The suggestion is an insult to the fine detectives who have worked—"

"Which brings us back to Detective Hatcher," Guerrero jumped in. "Our background information shows that in the short time she's been in the homicide division, her name has appeared in forty-nine newspaper articles in a LexisNexis search. Prior to that, she granted various interviews to outlets like *People* magazine and *Dateline NBC* about her own family background—"

Ellie looked up abruptly from her notepad. Dillon glanced over with a barely perceptible shrug. The thought of his coaster-sized elbow crushing Sparks's windpipe was growing more appealing by the second.

"Counsel's comments are wholly inappropriate," Max said.

*Complete and utter bullshit.* She continued to scribble as she listened to her boyfriend's voice rise half an octave. "Two of the NYPD's biggest collars in the last year. A Police Combat Cross for rescuing another officer in the line of duty. Personal interviews granted only at her peril and only to help her mother, who was widowed in Kansas when—"

Judge Bandon cut him off. "I've been known to read the occasional *People* magazine myself. I'm familiar with the circumstances of her father's death."

"My point," Guerrero continued, "is that Detective Hatcher is relatively inexperienced, and although she has created quite a record for herself in a short period of time, she also has a knack for finding herself in the public eye. She also made it clear with her outrageous arrest of my client that she has a personal grudge against him."

"I would hardly call it an arrest," Max argued. "She placed him in loosened handcuffs after he twice disobeyed a request that he leave the crime scene. Once he was out of the apartment and in the hallway, she immediately removed the cuffs and gave Mr. Sparks another opportunity to stay out of the way, which he wisely took advantage of. Any other citizen in the same situation would have spent the night in Central Booking."

Judge Bandon cut him off. "Are you seriously suggesting that Mr. Sparks should be treated just like any ordinary citizen?"

Max had warned Ellie that Judge Bandon might be starstruck by Sparks, but she had never imagined that she would hear a judge admit on open record the favoritism shown to the rich and powerful. She turned to glance at Genna Walsh, who was shaking her head in disgust.

"What I mean to say," the judge said, catching himself, "is that Mr. Sparks was at that point known to Detective Hatcher, both as the owner of the property in question and as a respected member of this community. Those considerations would appear to undercut her decision to arrest him, however briefly. I must admit, I am troubled by what I see here."

"As well you should be," Guerrero added. "That same obsession with Mr. Sparks that caused her to jump the gun on that first night has distorted this investigation from the outset. Your Honor, we are outsiders to this investigation, and even *we* are aware of at least two far more credible theories as to motive for Robert Mancini's murder."

Guerrero ticked off his theories on two stubby fingers. "First, the police still—four months after the murder—have not identified the woman who by all appearances had sexual relations with the victim prior to the murder. Second, and separately, we have recently learned that the NYPD is conducting a drug investigation of the apartment directly next door to the apartment where this murder occurred."

The movement of Ellie's pen against her notebook stopped.

"Could this have been a home invasion at the wrong address?" Guerrero continued. "Have the police looked into that possibility?"

Home invasions were often the m.o. of choice in drug-related robberies, so one of the first steps she and Rogan had taken was to look into the possibility of a mistaken entry. Immediately after the murder, she had personally checked the department's database of ongoing drug investigations. They even reached out to Narcotics to be certain. They found no addresses that might have been confused with Sparks's apartment, let alone one on the very same floor.

"With these two very important unanswered questions, Your Honor, it strikes us as quite audacious indeed for the police and the district attorney's office to stand here demanding private information from my client as part of a fishing expedition while a killer runs free."

"I don't like it either," Judge Bandon said, settling back into his overstuffed leather-backed chair. "The court is granting Mr. Sparks's motion to quash the state's subpoena—"

"But, Your Honor—"

"I've heard enough, Mr. Donovan. Interrupt me again, and there will be consequences. Under *Zurcher v. Stanford Daily*, the prosecution does have a right to obtain evidence from nonsuspect third parties, but only upon a showing of probable cause that the party has actual evidence to be found. There has been no such showing here. A written order will follow."

Max lowered his head momentarily before he began packing his hearing materials into a brown leather briefcase. It was a subtle movement, but Ellie noticed. He was disappointed, and not merely about the court's ruling. He'd warned her that morning that their chances weren't good. But that small motion suggested a fear that he had let her down.

He glanced over his shoulder in her direction. His brown curly hair was bushier than usual; for a week he'd been trying to find time for a trim. His gray eyes looked tired, but when she lifted her chin toward him and winked, they smiled back at her.

The private exchange did not last long.

"Your Honor!" Guerrero's exclamation was quickly followed by an audible sucking of air from Sam Sparks. They were both staring at her notebook, still open on her lap beneath her pen.

She felt Judge Bandon's eyes follow their gaze.

"I take it there's more to see than tic-tac-toe boards and vector cubes?"

Silence fell across the courtroom.

"Your notes, please, Detective Hatcher." It took him only the briefest glance before he called her back up to the witness stand. "I have a few questions of my own, Detective."

# CHAPTER SIX

**Megan Gunther**

The twelve letters formed just two words—one name—on a screen filled with many other words about scores of other people on the NYU campus. But those two words—her name, as the header on a subject link of the Campus Juice Web site—had made the last three hours the longest one hundred and eighty minutes of her lifetime.

Megan had closed her laptop the second that Professor Ellen Stein busted her. But that hadn't stopped Stein from instructing her to stay late after class—an example to all the other seminar students who might have been tempted to ignore the class discussion in favor of more interesting online material.

By the time Stein had finished lecturing her on the importance of group discussion and the empirical research demonstrating the deleterious effects of multitasking on learning, Megan was running late for her biochem lab. She would have blown off a lecture, but the labs counted for 60 percent of her grade and couldn't be made up. And med schools would care about her biochem grade. No, the lab couldn't be skipped. And it was impossible to juggle her computer while titrating liquids and triggering chemical reactions over a Bunsen burner.

Now she had finally made it back to her building on Fourteenth Street, three hours after first seeing her name posted on a Web site that promoted itself as the home of the country's juiciest campus gossip. She walked quickly through the lobby, pressed the elevator call button, and then pushed it several more times as she watched the digital readout on the elevator tick down to the lobby level. As she rode up to the fourth floor, she pulled her laptop and keys from her bag.

She slipped a key into the doorknob—she never bothered with the other locks—and turned. Once inside the apartment, she glanced at what had once been the empty bedroom, the one that now belonged to her roommate.

Megan's parents had originally justified the purchase of this two-bedroom condo as both an investment while Megan attended college and also a place for them to stay when they visited the city. But with the economy down and Manhattan rents still sky-high, the prospect of additional cash flow outweighed the Gunthers' desire for a room of their own in the Big Apple: Megan had to tolerate a roommate after all. Heather called the first day the ad hit Craig's List in May. She was transferring into NYU in the fall and seemed pretty normal, so Megan went with her gut.

The truth was, Heather was easy to tolerate. Today, as on almost every other day, Megan returned home to find Heather's door closed and the apartment quiet and in exactly the same condition she'd left it. Whether Heather was out or at home, this was the usual state of their shared home. Sometimes Megan wished Heather would come out of her shell and start treating this as her apartment, too, but today she was grateful that her roommate kept to herself.

Inside her own room, she closed the door, flopped down on top of her pale yellow bedspread, and opened her laptop. The connection to her wireless network seemed to take forever. Once the signal was finally established, she opened Internet Explorer, clicked on her history bar, and scrolled down to www.campusjuice.com.

She navigated her way to the NYU message board. All of the posts on the first page were new, entered within the last three hours. She clicked through the board, searching for her name again. What had once appeared on the fifth page of the forum was now on the seventh. The site was clearly getting some use.

She moved the cursor to her hyperlinked name, took a deep breath, and clicked.

**11:10 AM—noon   Life and Death Seminar**
**12:10–3 PM   Bio Chemistry Lab**
**3–7 PM   Break: Home to 14th Street?**
**7–8 PM   Spinning at Equinox**

The schedule was hers, down to her five-times-weekly cycling classes at the gym. Whoever posted the message obviously knew her comings and goings. They also knew where she lived, or at least which street. The short message was detailed enough to convince her that the final line of the post was no exaggeration:

**Megan Gunther, someone is watching**

# CHAPTER SEVEN

Rogan snatched a gallon-size Ziploc bag from the grasp of the booking clerk at 100 Centre Street.

"I'd get that smile off your face real fast, son."

The clerk lowered his eyes and continued to complete the release form Ellie would sign as the official termination of her sentence for contempt of court.

" 'What if Sparks did it?' " Rogan asked Ellie in a hushed voice. "How about, what in the big bad fuck were you thinking?"

*What if Sparks did it?* It had been a little more than twenty-four hours since Judge Paul Bandon read those words in Ellie's notebook. She had scribbled them next to a cartoon drawing of a stick figure with stubbly hair and a striped jumpsuit, standing behind prison bars.

"Apparently I was thinking that we'd been too quick to give Sparks a pass." She removed her tiny gold hoop earrings from the plastic bag and began looping them through her lobes.

Rogan held the bridge of his nose and shook his head. "Like jewelry's gonna do anything for you looking like that."

Partners were like families that way: the booking clerk had best keep his mouth shut, but for Rogan, the subject of her incarceration was fair game.

Ellie had been replaying the scene in the courtroom for twenty-four hours, and she still couldn't believe Bandon had pulled the trigger on her. She was convinced that until that moment—when Bandon had said, "Your notes please, Detective Hatcher"—she hadn't even been aware of the words and images that were forming in her scribbles.

Her mistake had been trying to persuade Bandon of that fact. If she had simply admitted to carrying vague suspicions that she hadn't disclosed on the stand, she probably would have gotten off with a lecture.

But instead Ellie had tried to explain. And Bandon, instead of understanding, had accused her of being "cute." And then when she argued even more insistently, as Max tried to quiet her down, Bandon had concluded that she was lying. To him. Personally. And *that*, no judge would tolerate.

And now because Bandon thought she was a liar, she had spent the night in a holding cell.

"No bo-hunk boyfriend to bail you out?" Rogan asked.

"You didn't *bail* me out. I was released after fully serving my twenty-four-hour sentence."

"Whatever. Where's your man, Max?"

"I didn't want to chance Bandon finding out about us. I'm obviously on his shit list now. No need to add Max to that picture. Besides, you're the one who insisted on picking me up. I could've gotten back to the precinct on my own."

"What? And miss the opportunity of you doing the walk of shame in your jelly slippers?"

Ellie looked down at her black leather flats, happy to have her own shoes back. "Please tell me that smell in my nostrils is just the memory of my overnight sojourn at the lovely Centre Street inn."

"Sorry, *chica*. I'm afraid you absorbed the permeating funk of your surrounding atmosphere."

"I'm so happy that my personal and professional misery has brought you such happiness."

"So are you going to explain those notes that landed you in this shit pile?"

"My mind was wandering in court. We both get some of our best ideas when we aren't even trying."

"Are you forgetting that we looked real close at him early on? *Real* close." Rogan's arms were crossed, fingertips tucked beneath his underarms. Always well dressed, today Rogan wore a black wool suit, a crisp lavender dress shirt, and an Hermès tie worth more than Ellie's entire outfit. He might have a cop's blue-collar values, but, thanks to a grandmother who married well late in life, he could live beyond a cop's salary.

"Look, you mind if we talk about this in a slightly less depressing environment?"

Ellie led the way out of the holding floor onto the street, and Rogan didn't stop her. By the time they reached the fleet car that Rogan had parked on Centre Street, she was ready to talk.

"So we took a look at Sparks and cleared him."

Rogan glanced back at the building from which they had just exited. "Pretty sure I was the one saying that back there a couple of minutes ago."

"Keys." She held up her right hand for the catch. In the six-plus months they'd been partners in the homicide task force of the Manhattan South Detective Borough, Ellie was usually happy to leave the driving to Rogan, but after the last twenty-four hours, she wanted control over her own movements. Rogan obliged, tossing the keys across the hood.

"We've had this case four months now," she said, turning over the ignition as Rogan climbed into the passenger's seat. "We checked out the obvious angles first: sex and money."

A guy gets filled with bullets after leaving his semen inside a knotted condom on the nightstand, and the first theory is sex. But when it came to sex, everyone who knew Robert Mancini said he was uncomplicated. Thirty years old. Unmarried since a starter marriage to a high school sweetheart had ended eight years earlier. No children. If he had a girlfriend—and he didn't at the time of his death—he was with that woman, and that woman only. If he didn't have a girlfriend, he hooked up and made it clear that hooking up was all he was interested in. Apparently there was no shortage of women willing to play by those ground rules.

Unfortunately, they'd been unable to locate the woman who played the game that particular night. The 212's overnight doorman had no memory of either her or Mancini, and had since been fired for routinely leaving his post to play video games with the teenage son of a tenant. Without a video recorder, the building's monitoring system was useless, and Mancini's phone records and e-mail messages had also led nowhere.

Then there was money. But again, with money, the picture seemed equally uncomplicated. Mancini had been working at Sparks Industries for almost a year before his death. Prior to that, he'd served in the U.S. Army, where he met a private contract worker named Nick Dillon in Afghanistan. When Dillon hung up the Middle Eastern travel and became the head of the corporate security division of Sparks Industries, he offered Mancini a job back home, which Mancini accepted as soon as his military commitment was up. His salary was in the low one hundreds, a figure that Rogan and Ellie had confirmed as the going rate for a decent corporate security gig.

He owned a two-bedroom condo in Hoboken, only two and a half miles from the childhood home where his sister's family still lived. He was up to date on a moderate mortgage. He had no unusual debts, no irregularities in his bank records.

"Sex and money didn't get us shit," Rogan said. "And when sex and money and gambling didn't get us shit, we took a close look at Sam Sparks and cleared him. I think that's now the third time we've agreed on that."

But the notes Ellie had scribbled during the motion hearing were asking them to revisit that determination. And Rogan wanted to know why.

As she drove up Centre Street, Ellie hit the wigwag lights on the dash to cut through the standstill traffic that was blocking the intersection at Canal through Chinatown.

"We looked at Sparks before he decided to stonewall us. Now that we know just how much he wants to be *off* our radar, we have to look at him again."

"Holy crap, Hatcher. Rogan told us you got into some shit at the courthouse, but we didn't think he meant literally."

John Shannon was a portly detective with light blond hair and ruddy skin. He sat directly behind Ellie in the squad room and had a bottle-a-week Old Spice habit.

"I got two hours of sleep on a mattress thinner than the layer of fat around your neck, Shannon; haven't eaten since I bit into the mystery meat burger they handed me for dinner; and spent the last twenty-four hours in city-issued underwear approximating the consistency of eighty-grit sandpaper—"

"And she's still better looking than anyone you ever dated, Shannon," Rogan interjected.

"I'm just saying, cut me some frickin' slack."

Rogan draped his suit jacket on the back of his chair. As he took a seat at the gray metal desk that faced Ellie's, he threw Shannon a look that sent the detective's attention back to his own work.

"Just because the man's stonewalling us doesn't mean he's our guy." Rogan reached for a tin of Altoids on his desk and popped a mint in his mouth. "Rich assholes shit on us all the time. They usually aren't murderers. You don't think this has something to do with Bandon throwing you in the clink?"

She gave him her middle finger and her friendliest smile. "Did I say anything about investigating Bandon? I'm talking about Sparks. All we wanted was a closer look at his financials. Just a way to check on his enemies. Why go to court over something like that?"

"Donovan said going into it that we were probably going to lose. We didn't have PC."

She opened her top desk drawer and removed a jar of Nutella. She'd long ago given up offering any to Rogan. "So?" she asked. "Most innocent people cooperate with us even when we don't have squat."

"Like I said, not the assholes."

"No, but even the jerks usually have a reason. I was sitting in the courtroom watching Guerrero bill four hundred dollars an hour to fight us. Sparks even showed up personally, and his time's got to be worth way more than Guerrero's. Why?"

Ellie's father had always told her that the key to good police work was to scrutinize people's motives. "Find the motive," he used to say, "and the motive will lead you to the man."

She understood why the innocent citizens of Bushwick didn't cooperate when some Trinitarios took out another banger. In a neighborhood run by gangs, a conversation with the police could be followed by a knock on the door in the middle of the night by a machete-wielding messenger. She even understood when some corporate bureaucrat wouldn't open the company records without a warrant. Regular people had jobs to protect.

But Sparks wasn't a regular person. He was the boss. He was a billionaire. This was his call, and he'd made the wrong one.

Rogan leaned his weight back in his chair and rested his palms on top of his closely shaved scalp. "Sparks showed up personally, huh?"

"Yep."

"Shit," he said, letting his weight bring his chair back to the floor. He pointed a finger at her across the desk. "You know I never liked Sparks for it."

From the very beginning, Rogan had firmly believed that a man as savvy as Sam Sparks wouldn't eliminate a threat inside an apartment he owned. She, however, had believed it was just the kind of reverse psychology that someone as arrogant as Sparks would employ. *Me? But why would I draw attention to myself by having the man killed inside my own apartment?*

"J. J., you know as well as I do how quickly we eliminated him as a suspect. All that mattered to us was the time line, the call records, and the personal assistant." The same assistant was in charge of both Sparks's personal calendar and the schedule for the 212. According to her, Mancini hadn't asked to use the apartment until 2:30 on the day of the murder, and she had never mentioned it to Sparks. She insisted that Sparks could not have known that Mancini would be at the apartment that night.

And because they had scratched Sparks from the list of possible suspects, they had never scratched beneath the surface of Sparks's public persona to unearth whatever secrets Mancini could have stumbled on.

"You win," Rogan said. "We look at Sparks again."

Ellie smiled as she took another bite of Nutella.

"You go tell the Lou, though. She was on the warpath yesterday."

"At me or Bandon?"

"A little of both. A lot of both, actually. She'll want to know you're back."

"Yeah, okay."

She started toward her lieutenant's office, but then turned again to face Rogan. "Do me a favor?"

"Burn those clothes you're wearing?"

"Track down that guy we talked to in May at Narcotics. Tell him to expect us at about"—she looked at her watch and calculated the time she'd need for another stop—"five o'clock."

"Any hint as to why?"

"In court, Sparks's lawyer claimed we've got an investigation running on the apartment next door."

"And how would he know that?"

"We figure that out after we see if he's right."

# CHAPTER EIGHT

Ellie rapped her knuckles against the glass window that separated Lieutenant Robin Tucker's office from the cramped detective squad, packed as it was with unmatched desks, dilapidated chairs, and the chaos of eighteen homicide detectives working out of a single room. She swept her bangs to the side as she watched through the glass. Tucker's head tilted ever so slightly toward her office door.

"It's open," she called out, still reading whatever report she held between her fingertips.

"Afternoon, Lou. Rogan says you wanted to touch base?"

Tucker set the document down on her desk. "Did you really need your partner to tell you that, given what happened in court yesterday?"

Ellie had finally won over her former lieutenant three short months before he was demoted due to an internal affairs investigation, the details of which were still wholly unknown and therefore rampant fodder for the NYPD rumor mill. When she found out that her new lieutenant was called Robin Tucker, she had assumed that the gender-ambiguous name belonged to a man. Statistical odds. But when Ellie learned that this particular Robin was of the female variety, she was optimistic. Maybe her luck would be better with a woman as a supervisor. Unfortunately, though, Ellie's problems were with authority, not men.

"No, Lou. Just making sure Rogan got credit for keeping me in check."

"If you were in check, you might not have spent the night in jail for contempt of court."

Ellie pressed her lips together. Explanations had done nothing to help her with Judge Bandon. She wasn't going to waste her breath attempting to persuade Tucker that the judge had overreacted.

Tucker looked Ellie in the eye during the silence. Ellie knew from asking around that her lieutenant was forty-eight years old, but her makeup-less skin was clear and bright. Her wavy hair had probably been shiny and blond years before turning to its current wiry mix of gray and light brown.

She gave Ellie a nod. "Actually, a little bird already told me that the judge teed off on you for no good reason."

Ellie shut her eyes and thought about the ribbing she was going to get in the house if Max called her lieutenant in an attempt to protect her. Then as quickly as the idea had come to her, she rejected it. Max knew better.

"You know Nick Dillon." The way Ellie said it, it wasn't a question. As an ex-cop, the head of Sparks Industries' Corporate Security Division would know more than a few former colleagues at the NYPD.

"We were both in the Seventh when I was just a rookie. He called this morning looking for your Lou. I guess he wanted to save you from a month's worth of desk duty. Anyway, we recognized each other's names from back in the day."

Tucker's affect changed as she spoke about Dillon—her eyes softened, the corners of her lips raised into a slight smile—and Ellie noticed for the first time that with a little effort her lieutenant could be attractive.

"He's been pretty decent to Rogan and me."

"He's a good guy. When he called, he gave me a heads-up that Sparks may go back to court to get access to our evidence."

"On what basis?"

"Given where you spent the last twenty-four hours, do you really think Sam Sparks considers himself bound by the usual rules?"

"Valid point." A week earlier, Ellie had read online that Sparks was in negotiations for a reality show in which contestants would show off their eye for potential real estate jackpots. Sparks would supervise their work, like Donald Trump on *The Apprentice*, but meaner and with better hair.

"Dillon knows it's futile. No court will give Sparks what he wants, no matter how much he pays his lawyers to go through the motions."

"But Dillon does know you from back at the Seventh."

"Exactly. A guy like Dillon doesn't chat up someone like me just for shits and giggles. Someone who looked like you? Now that would be different."

Ellie was used to her fellow cops making remarks about her looks. She would probably always look a little bit like the girl who was once the runner-up in the Junior Miss Wichita pageant. But what she usually chose to take as a compliment sounded like a dig coming from Tucker.

"So Dillon was sniffing around to see what he might turn up?" she asked.

"Yeah, I actually felt sorry for the guy. You can tell he thinks Sparks is a schmuck. I guess Sparks wants everything we know about the missing girl. He figures that if he can find her, we'll work that angle and forget about him."

"That's a dead end. We've got the latents from the champagne flute and the DNA on the outside of the condom, but no hits on either one. She's a mystery woman."

Ellie hadn't been particularly surprised. In a criminal justice system dominated by male perpetrators, and with a DNA database consisting almost entirely of sex offenders, striking a hit on a female subject was rare.

"I guess when you've got enough money, the sky's the limit," Tucker said. "He wants Dillon to work the case from beginning to end with his own people. You know, Dillon spent ten years between homicide and special victims before he went private. I got the impression the work in the private sector was pretty high-speed—corporate kidnapping prevention. He's a good cop."

"Except he's *not* a cop. He's been a ten with me and Rogan, but he's still a guy making four times what you're pulling in, doing half the amount of work, for some rich prick who thinks he's entitled to more safety than regular people."

"Tell me how you really feel, Detective."

"I just did. Because for a second there it actually sounded like you wanted us to share our evidence with Sam Sparks."

"No, I don't. I was, however, suggesting that a cop with those kinds of years under his belt might catch the sort of details that a less experienced detective—someone who got promoted too early, someone who was the brass's darling—might miss."

"Seriously, I've got to defend Rogan here. He paid his dues."

Tucker was unamused. "So what's the next move?"

"Rogan and I were thinking we'd take another look at Sparks." She set out her theory that Sparks's resistance to their investigation could have more to do with his role in Mancini's death than any concern for privacy.

"For what it's worth, I told Dillon we wouldn't be giving his boss special treatment."

"So we're a go?" Ellie asked.

She nodded. "But I also told him you'd continue to work every angle. Don't just focus on Sparks. And I don't want to hear from anyone in the house that you're shucking off new cases, either. We stopped pushing full-time on this two months ago."

"We know."

"And watch your back, Hatcher. You already spent one night in jail. I'd hate to see what Sam Sparks could do if he was really pissed off."

# CHAPTER NINE

Megan Gunther stood in the lobby of the Sixth Precinct, fighting back the tears that were pooling in her eyes and threatening to roll down her reddened cheeks.

"What do you *mean*, there's nothing you can do?"

She had never seen her father like this. Jonas Gunther was an insurance man. That wasn't to say he was weak—quite the opposite, in fact. He was a man of principle, who valued character above all else. At work, he expected others to live up to their word. In his personal life, he expected people to do what was right. And he did not hesitate to stand up to those who failed to deliver on his expectations.

But Megan's father, however forceful he could be about making a point, was always in control. Strong, but subdued. Emotions, he would tell her, got in the way of an effective argument.

Today, though, Jonas Gunther was emotional.

Megan's mother, Patricia, placed a comforting arm around her daughter's shoulder and gave her a squeeze. She stroked her straight blond hair and told her that everything would be all right.

"We don't *know* everything will be all right, Patty. That's why we're here. Things don't become *all right* just because we hope for them to be. They become *all right* when the men and women who have sworn to protect and serve us pay attention when someone is threatening another citizen."

Megan noticed a woman and her young son seated on a bench on the other side of the lobby watching them, alarm registered on their faces. The child dropped his gaze and burrowed his cheeks against his mother's abdomen.

"Mr. Gunther, I understand your frustration, but I need you to lower your voice right now."

According to the metal nameplate affixed to his uniform, the desk sergeant trying to calm Megan's father was called Martinez. His words did nothing to mitigate Jonas's anger.

"When I told my daughter to call the police two and a half hours ago, I expected an officer to go to her apartment to start an investigation. Then she tells me she's required to come into the precinct, so her mother and I drove into the city from New Jersey, expecting something to be done about this. My daughter has done everything one could ask of her. She missed a biochem lab today. She found each and every mention of her name on this disgusting Web site. She printed out copies for you." He shook the quarter-inch stack of paper for emphasis. "And now you tell us there's nothing you can do to protect her?"

"Sir, I've tried to explain, we have received more than our fair share of calls in this precinct from other NYU students, all complaining about what people are saying about them on this very Web site. And we've run our options past the district attorney's office, and the same problems are going to apply here. First of all, the site doesn't require users to give a name, address—anything. It's totally anonymous."

Jonas was already shaking his head. "That's not true, that's not true. I called the IT person at my company, and they tell me there are options. There's a way to track—you can track the IQ or something like that. What's it called again, honey?"

"IP address, Dad."

"Yes," he said, pointing to Sergeant Martinez. "The Web site should have that information. You can use it to—"

"And that's the second problem, sir. This company is not willing to release that information without a subpoena—"

"So go get a fucking subpoena."

Megan flinched. Except for the time her cousin had head-butted her father with his first catcher's helmet, she couldn't remember ever hearing her dad use the F word.

"Let the man talk, Jonas. Please."

Megan's father set his jaw. He was clearly angry, but at least he was being quiet. For now. Sergeant Martinez gave Patricia Gunther an appreciative glance.

"We can only get a subpoena if we have cause. And, as difficult as I'm sure it is for your daughter—for you, Megan—to read something like this on the Internet, the posts are not directly threatening."

"But my schedule. Someone's watching me."

"You said yourself that everyone who knows you knows your class schedule and your workout routine. Unfortunately, messing with someone's head isn't a crime. If you've had any disputes with anyone lately—a former friend, a boy—"

"There are no disputes, Officer." Jonas was interrupting again. "My daughter has no idea who would do something like this. You have to listen to us."

"That's true, sir, and I have. I have listened now for more than twenty-five minutes. And I'm sorry, but that's all I can do for you today. If it's of any consolation, you might want to take a closer look at the other stuff on that site. A whole bunch of it is even worse than what your daughter's going through." He looked directly at Megan. "You can't let this get to you."

"You can't just make us leave," her father said. "You must—"

With just the placement of her hand on her husband's forearm, Patricia Gunther silenced him. "Do you have a daughter, Sergeant Martinez?"

Martinez cleared his throat and then looked Megan's mother in the eye. "I do, ma'am. She's fifteen years old. So pretty, it scares me. And if you ask me as a father, I'd say the scumbags who run this Web site should all find Molotov cocktails in their cars tomorrow morning. But if you ask me as the desk sergeant of the Sixth Precinct, there's nothing more I can do for you folks. I'm sorry."

As Megan led the way out of the precinct, she reread the final page she had printed about herself from campusjuice.com. She had printed not just the original posts, but also the comments that had been posted by other users in reply:

**POST**
> **11:10 AM—noon   Life and Death Seminar**
> **12:10–3 PM   Bio Chemistry Lab**
> **3–7 PM   Break: Home to 14th Street?**
> **7–8 PM   Spinning at Equinox**
> **Megan Gunther, someone is watching**

**COMMENTS:**
Seriously, Dude, what is up with you? I'm in Math 210 with her and she's not even hot. Go have your rape fantasies on someone else.

Both the original comment and the reply were obviously posted by a couple of virgins who need to get a life, and some respect for womyn.

Got stalk? Yo, this site is whack.

Not to kill the party, but does this chick know about this? Maybe someone should notify campus security? Looks odd to me . . .

**REPLY TO COMMENTS:**

Good luck with security. You're all anonymous, and so am I. They'll never find me.

And neither will Megan.

As Megan left the overhead fluorescent lights of the Sixth Precinct and stepped into the gray overcast of West Tenth Street, she stopped fighting the wave of emotion that had been building in her since she had first spotted her name on that vile Web site. She did not try to choke back the sob in her chest. She let the tears begin to roll.

# CHAPTER TEN

Katie Battle rang the doorbell first, just to be safe, and then slipped the key into the lock. She enjoyed a mental sigh of relief when she felt the familiar tumble of the interior pins. She couldn't count the number of times she had schlepped a client to a showing, only to learn that the seller had left the wrong keys with the doorman.

"Hello?" she called out through the cracked door. Another annoyance avoided; the sellers were out of the apartment, as promised. "So this one's just over eleven hundred square feet, which means you could easily convert it to a two-bedroom."

Her clients today were Don and Laura Jenning, who were looking to purchase their first New York City apartment. Some clients came to Katie with a sophisticated understanding of the market, formed through countless hours perusing the *New York Times* real estate section and the plethora of Web sites devoted exclusively to property listings.

The Jennings were not that type of client.

"Wow," Laura said. "This is so much nicer than the other ones."

"I wanted you to see it, just to give you an idea of the difference it can make if you're willing to stretch."

Katie, of course, was not surprised that the apartment—a large one-bedroom condo just off of Madison Park—was more impressive than the six other properties she had already shown the Jennings earlier in the day. After all, the entire purpose of this day's viewing tour was to lead them to this apartment. Today was what Katie called a We Can Do It tour.

Like many of her clients, the Jennings had leaped into the fluctuating New York City real estate market with unformed and unrealistic expectations. "We don't really know what neighborhood we want to be in: downtown ideally, but the Upper West Side's fine, too, or even the Upper East." Already, that first sentence from Laura had been a giveaway. To a person who considers downtown her "ideal," the Upper East Side is definitely *not* fine. Either Laura didn't know Manhattan—unlikely, given she'd been renting in Chelsea for six years—or she just wasn't being honest about her preferences.

And then there was the budget. "We want to stay under 700. We'd love to get a two-bedroom, but know we may have to get by with a one-bedroom-plus to start."

It was a so-called compromise that Katie heard all the time. The reality, though, was that a true "one-bedroom-plus"—a one-bedroom with a separate space for an office or a crib—was the same square footage (and price) as a small two-bedroom. And neither could be had for anywhere near seven hundred thousand dollars, no matter what people heard about so-called bargains in the down market.

If Katie believed the Jennings' budget cap to be real, she would not have wasted her time on a We Can Do It tour. She instead would have arranged a Come to Jesus tour. In a Come to Jesus tour, Katie would drag a couple like the Jennings to six nice (and, ideally, overpriced) two-bedroom apartments. When the clients finally realized they could not afford apartments of that size, she would lead them to a nice, reasonably priced one-bedroom. It would be time for the clients to Come to Jesus: either get into the market with a small place or rent for the rest of their lives.

But the Jennings didn't need a Come to Jesus tour. They needed the We Can Do It tour, designed not to persuade the clients of what they could *not* afford, but instead to convince them of what they *could* afford.

Katie knew from the Jennings' mortgage application that quiet, petite Don pulled in a quarter mil a year as a "director of credit risk policy," whatever that was. Since shacking up with Laura, he was living month to month, but in the decade before he'd met her, he'd managed to save an entire year's salary. Laura was a jewelry designer who sold her wares at open fairs and to a few small boutiques. Lucky, *lucky* Laura—whom Katie tried not to resent—had never made more than twenty thousand in any individual year from her craft, but had her father—and now, Don—to fall back on.

The Jennings could afford more than they knew. They just had to put away their existing notions of a dollar and to start thinking, We can do it.

Katie knew that this generously sized one-bedroom would be a good candidate for convincing the Jennings to "stretch," as she liked to say, but the apartment was even more impressive than she had imagined. The seller had followed all of the rules: clean surfaces, no unnecessary clutter, even the welcoming fragrance of a warm pan of brownies, still cooling on the stovetop. And absolutely no photographs; the apartment should feel like it already belongs to the potential buyers.

"Now this one's one-point-one-two-five," Katie said, as if the extra four hundred and twenty-five thousand dollars was chump change, "but my guess is that there's some softness there."

Don winced at the number, but his wife did not. "Wow, Don, look at this kitchen. We could actually cook if we had this kind of kitchen. Think of the money we'd save in the long run."

And then Katie knew she had an ally. Crossing the million-dollar threshold would be a leap for Don, but now Katie could see that Laura had been there all along. She felt a twinge of animosity toward the woman for so willingly spending her husband's hard-earned money, but then reminded herself that she needed the commission. Given Katie's standing in the hierarchy of her agency, it wasn't often she had a shot at selling above the million-dollar mark.

"Feel free to open the cabinets," Katie urged. "They're Italian. High-gloss lacquer, top of the line."

Katie checked her BlackBerry while the Jennings made their way through the apartment. She preferred to give buyers privacy so they could imagine life in their new apartment, without the watchful eye of a broker, but last year a couple posing as buyers made off with a hundred thousand dollars of jewelry and collectibles at various open houses across Manhattan. Now Katie kept one eye on her clients, even while she read her e-mail.

She could have used some good news. Instead, the incoming messages brought her more headaches with no corresponding revenue. The purchaser of a Tribeca studio under contract was bickering over a hundred-dollar difference in the negotiations over a built-in wall unit. Katie used her thumbs to type her most comforting words, even as she rolled her eyes in frustration.

Another e-mail delivered far worse news on the business front: a client who had been on the fence about making an offer for a West Village one-bedroom had climbed down on the wrong side. That he delivered the news to her electronically was not a good sign. On the phone, she had a chance of persuading him otherwise, or at least lining up the next showings. A terse e-mail like this one told her that the guy had written off not only this particular apartment, but his commitment to purchasing anything at all.

The message she received from Marj Mason, a caretaker at Glen Forrest Communities, was even more upsetting. Katie had seen the assisted living center's telephone number pop up on her vibrating BlackBerry as she had stepped into the elevator with the Jennings. As Katie had requested a few months earlier, Marj had followed up with an e-mail. It was easier for her to check written messages than voice mails when she was with clients.

Katie's mother had fallen again. According to Marj, there were no breaks this time—only bruises, and of course even more fear now of walking on her own. There was no way around it: Katie was going to have to increase the intensity of her mother's care.

And then there was the final message: a text message that Katie had noticed first on her BlackBerry, but read last. She felt a knot form in her stomach as she took in the abrupt instructions.

As she replaced her BlackBerry in her red Coach purse, she prayed her mother would never find out about that final message, or what Katie would be doing the following night because of it.

# CHAPTER ELEVEN

Rogan was waiting for Ellie at his desk when she emerged from the locker room, freshly showered, hair still damp.

"We cool with the Lou?"

"Icy. Did you get hold of our guy in Narcotics?"

"Yep. He wasn't real happy about sticking around for a five o'clock arrival. I told him we'd do our best."

Ellie looked at her watch. It was nearing four. "Our best will be five o'clock."

"Are you going to bother telling me why?"

"We'll have to work our way through traffic going uptown."

"*Uptown?* The Fifth Precinct's in Chinatown."

"We're making a pit stop. You'll see."

Twenty minutes later, Rogan peered through a glass storefront window on Eighty-ninth and Madison and flinched.

"Is that woman doing what I *think* she's doing?"

"Um, that would depend on what exactly your imagination might be doing with the input being processed by your visual cortex."

"I have no idea what you're talking about, but I think if my brain's doing anything, it's trying to forget what I just saw. That shit should be illegal."

"It's called threading," Ellie said.

They watched as an Indian woman with smooth dark skin and burgundy-stained lips moved her head back and forth, using the grip of her teeth and the movement of her head to maneuver a thread across the face of a young blond woman seated on the other side of the glass window.

"She's using a *thread* to pull that woman's eyebrows out?"

"It's called threading," Ellie repeated.

"Should be called torture. What the fuck are we doing here?"

"You could use a little tidying up around there," Ellie said, reaching for his brow line.

Rogan swatted her hand away.

"This is Perfect Arches," she said. "It's Thursday, ten after four. You don't remember?"

"If you've some personal woman business to take care of, Hatcher, you really didn't need to drag me along."

"Perfect Arches? Thursday at four p.m.? Kristen Woods?"

"Kristen Woods is Sparks's assistant."

"The timeline, Rogan. When we first tried to track down Woods about the timeline, she was out of the office. She said she's got a standing appointment every Thursday at four p.m. to have her eyebrows threaded. I asked her—"

Rogan snapped his fingers. "You asked her where. Then you went on and on about how perfect her eyebrows were. I was tempted to reach down and check my anatomy to make sure I was still a man, the two of you blathering like that in front of me."

"I was *bonding*. Like the way you talk up sports to every doorman we ever need information out of? Pretending you're a Mets fan? So I pretended to care about eyebrow plucking. Kristen loves me."

"So if Kristen loves you so much, why are we bombarding her at this dungeon of torture?"

"If we want to see Kristen without popping into the Sparks building, this is the place to do it. Look, there she is."

Rogan followed the line of Ellie's fingertip and spotted a woman with straight strawberry-blond hair down to her shoulders, leaning back in a salon chair, another Indian woman working her magic with a string of thread above her.

"She dyed her hair," he observed.

"Did she?"

"Yeah. It didn't have any red in it before. It was more your color."

Ellie dropped her gaze. "You might want to check that anatomy after all, girlfriend."

Rogan flexed his bicep and gave it a little kiss. "One hundred percent Afro-American Manly Man, sweetheart. Don't you forget it."

He tapped her with the back of his hand. "Heads up," he said, his tone more serious.

Inside the salon, Kristen Woods checked her eyebrows in a handheld mirror, nodded her approval, and then walked to the front desk to pay.

"You ask me, the money should be going the other direction," Rogan muttered.

Woods nearly ran into them as she exited the salon, and then turned back as a glimmer of recognition crossed her face.

"Ellie Hatcher, from the NYPD. My partner, J. J. Rogan."

"Yeah, sure, I remember. I hear you and my boss had quite the run-in yesterday in court."

Ellie was glad to see that the rapport she'd previously developed with Kristen had not been affected. "Mr. Sparks shares those sorts of colorful details with you, does he?"

"Are you kidding? He doesn't tell me squat. I heard him yelling about it in his office yesterday. I think I got the gist."

"I'm sure your boss was heartbroken by my brief period of incarceration."

"Uh, yeah, if what you mean is that it only lasted a day. Sorry, you probably aren't laughing about this yet."

"Would you be? I couldn't even keep my own underwear with me."

"Eeewww."

Rogan tapped one heel, his gaze affixed upward.

They both took the hint, and Kristen changed the subject. "You're wrong about him, you know."

"Wrong about what?" Ellie asked.

"About Sparks. He can be a prick in his own way, but he's actually a decent person. There's no way he'd kill anyone."

Ellie smiled. Everyone was capable of killing someone. It was just a question of whom, and under what circumstances. But the last thing she wanted was to advertise their agenda to Sparks's personal assistant.

"Really," Ellie assured her, "he's not a suspect. I tried explaining it to the judge. The whole thing got blown out of proportion."

" 'What if Sparks did it?' A cartoon showing him behind bars? It's kind of funny, I guess, but you're wrong. I swear."

"It was just doodling. Totally unprofessional, but not at all a reflection of where we are in this investigation. Your boss is not a suspect."

"Right. And that's why you tracked me down here, where Sam wouldn't know? But you know what? I don't care. When cops ask questions, I answer. And if Sam asks me point-blank whether you came to me, I'm not going to lie to him either."

"No one's asking you to lie, Kristen."

"Yeah, okay, but whatever. He's not going to ask. I'm sure that was your intention in coming here instead of the office. I was just saying, there's no way he'd hurt Robo, if that happens to be what you're thinking. So go ahead and ask whatever you want. I've got no problems with you guys."

She was about as straightforward a witness as two detectives could ask for. Loyal to her boss, but not so loyal that she'd want to lie.

"We're going back to the very beginning," Ellie said. "Making sure we didn't miss anything. We wanted to talk to you again about Mancini reserving the apartment for that night."

"Okay."

"So the way you explained it to us, you keep a calendar for the 212?"

"Right. Sam offers the penthouse to various business associates when they come to town. More impressive than a hotel. I keep track of it all so I can make sure the maid service comes and cleans up after guests, changes the linens—that kind of thing. And that requires knowing when people are there and for how long."

"And then Sparks lets employees use the place, too?"

"Yeah. Not a lot, but, you know, it's the occasional little perk. I told you, he's not the evil shit you think he is. Everyone knows not to take it for granted."

"And who's everyone?" Rogan asked.

"Not corporate employees, but more of just the personal staff. Me, the bodyguards—I mean, *protection specialists*," she said, smiling. "I think he even lent it to his contractor once."

"And none of these people has a key, right?" Ellie was pretending that she needed to hear all of this information again.

"No one keeps a key. There's a coded key compartment that hangs from the apartment door. You flip the digits around to match the code. The box pops open, and the apartment key's inside. One of my responsibilities after someone stays is to reset the code."

The night of Mancini's murder, they had found the door unlocked and the key inside on the kitchen counter. Mancini had not locked the door behind him.

"So when someone wants to use the apartment, they contact you to reserve their spot on the calendar and get the code."

"Exactly."

"Okay, and when did Mancini reserve the apartment for the night of May 27?"

"May 27 was the night of—the night he died, right?"
Ellie nodded.

"He called me that day. I think I told you before it was around two, but I wasn't sure."

In fact, Ellie and Rogan had pulled Kristen's call records from the cellular phone company used by Sparks Industries. Mancini had placed a call to her at 2:32 that afternoon.

"And it was just for that night?" Ellie asked.

"Yeah. It's always just one night when we're using it. Like I said, we don't want to take advantage."

"And did you tell anyone that Mancini would be using the apartment?"

"No," she said, shaking her head.

"Not even a housekeeper to get the place ready?"

"Nope. The apartment had been cleaned two weeks earlier. For the CEO of General Electric, I would have had a fresh cleaning. Robo could live with a little dust."

"And where were you after two o'clock?"

*"Me?"*

"Like I said, we're covering all the bases. Sorry," Ellie said, offering her best supportive head-tilt.

Ellie had no interest in Kristen's whereabouts, but focusing on the assistant's schedule gave them a back door to talk about her boss's timeline. And if Kristen was on the defensive, she might not notice the maneuver.

"I was in my office taking care of a ton of details for a party Sam was having the following week. Finalizing the bartenders, the catering menu—I swear I wish the man would get married so his wife could take over his social affairs."

"Married?" Rogan interjected. "I'm surprised you even mentioned the possibility, given the rumors."

"Which ones?" Kristen asked. "You listen to the local tabloids, and he's either an irrepressible playboy or the most popular ride at Big Gay Al's homosexual theme park."

Ellie coughed. "We hadn't heard it put in quite those terms."

"Well, I have. And the rumors aren't true. He dates a lot, but mostly to avoid the rumors that come about when a wealthy bachelor is by himself too often. Hasn't done him much good, though."

"So the party planning," Ellie said, pulling Kristen back to the timeline. "That was enough to keep you busy the entire afternoon?"

"Pretty much. I'm sure I worked on other stuff as well, but I'd have to go back and try to reconstruct it all from my e-mails, and—"

"But you were in the office working? You didn't have to leave, perhaps with Mr. Sparks?"

"No," Kristen said, apparently not noticing the pointed direction of Ellie's comment. "He was in the field with his architects that whole afternoon, touring the properties under construction. And after that he had to run straight to a fund-raiser for the Conservation Voters. I remember because I knew from his calendar that I had a big chunk of time to get some work done and then get out early for the day."

"Did you speak to Mr. Sparks at any point that afternoon?"

Again, Kristen shook her head. "I even teased him the next day that he'd made remarkable progress in his independence. Not a single call, e-mail, or text message."

Kristen's recollection was consistent with the information she'd given them nearly four months earlier. And Ellie and Rogan had confirmed it against her phone records: there had been no contact between her and Sparks from the time Mancini booked the apartment to the time of his murder.

Ellie thanked Kristen for her time. "You want a ride somewhere?" she offered.

"No, thanks. Sam's done with me for the day, so I'm meeting a friend up here."

As Ellie led the way back to the Crown Vic, she ran through the timeline in her head again. If Sparks had known where Mancini was going to be that night, he had not learned it from Kristen Woods.

It would be three more days before Ellie realized her mistake.

# CHAPTER
# TWELVE

The Fifth Precinct of the NYPD is located on Elizabeth Street and Canal. Forty years ago, the spot would have been at the dividing line between Little Italy and Chinatown. But when the federal government changed its immigration laws in 1965, allowing more Asian immigrants into the country, the population of Chinatown exploded. Now Mulberry Street, with its tourist-trap restaurants and sidewalk vendors hawking Bada Bing and Fuggedaboutit T-shirts, was the last remaining enclave of what had once been a real Italian neighborhood. And the Fifth Precinct now stood at the epicenter of an ever-expanding Chinatown.

Rogan parked the car on Elizabeth, just south of Canal, and began making his way north to the precinct.

"Hold up," Ellie called out as she pulled open a glass door stenciled with gold Chinese lettering. She emerged sixty seconds later with a roasted pork bun wrapped inside a napkin, the first real food she'd seen since shunning the slop masquerading as lunch at the jail.

"A buck twenty-five," Ellie said, popping a piece of the doughy ball of marinated meat into her mouth. "You can't beat China-town."

By the time they turned the corner to reach the sky-blue door of the white-brick building that housed the Fifth Precinct, Ellie had finished her makeshift lunch. A civilian aide with a round Charlie Brown head sat at the front service desk.

Rogan pulled back his jacket to reveal his detective's badge. "Narcotics?"

The aide gestured toward a staircase just beyond the entrance. "Next floor up."

A few years earlier, police assumed that all home invasions were drug-related. Teacher? Priest? Hero landing an airplane in the Hudson? Wouldn't matter. Home invasion victims were always and automatically labeled as drug dealers. But in recent years, police had seen an increase in both home invasions and the number of tragic cases in which innocent people had found themselves targeted by the most predatory and violent offenders, simply because their address was one digit away from a reputed drug house.

On the second floor, Rogan asked a second civilian aide to see Sergeant Frank Boyle.

"The sergeant had to leave. Are you Detective Rogan?"

Rogan nodded. "And Hatcher. I called Boyle a little more than an hour ago. He was expecting us."

"Something came up."

"Like maybe five o'clock?" Rogan said, glancing at his watch.

The aide smiled politely. "Perhaps. He said to see Detective Carenza over there." He pointed to a refrigerator-sized man standing over a desk toward the back of the squad room.

As they walked toward the man who was apparently called Carenza, Ellie noticed that his tanned, veiny biceps were challenging the seams of his fitted black T-shirt. The rest of the ensemble consisted of faded blue jeans, pointed alligator shoes, and a heavy gold chain.

"Ellie Hatcher," she said, offering her hand. "Your sergeant left word to see you?"

"Tony Carenza." The detective gave her a firm handshake and then turned to Rogan to offer the same. "Then you must be Rogan, because Boyle told me some guy from Homicide was coming."

"You heading out on an undercover?" Rogan asked, eyeing the wardrobe.

Carenza glanced down at his own clothing and shrugged. "Nah, man. Just wrapping up some paperwork here, and then I'm audi."

Rogan was nodding politely when Carenza broke out laughing. "Gotcha nervous there, didn't I? Nah, my stuff might not be quite up to what you got going on here," he said, pointing at Rogan's three-button Canali suit, "but this getup's definitely for the job. The mod's running some buy-and-busts tonight at some of the clubs." In addition to the teams of stop-and-frisk uniform cops that had made New York's zero-tolerance policing famous, the narcotics division used so-called investigatory modules to run undercover operations.

Carenza pulled at the diamond-encrusted dollar sign dangling from his gold chain, most likely a trophy seized during a prior bust. "Too much?"

"Fierce," Ellie said.

"Yeah, I thought so. So what can I do you for? My sergeant made a point of instructing me to be helpful, so consider me your most helpful helper."

Rogan scratched his cheek while he spoke. "We're still chasing a case from May—dead body left behind in a home invasion on Kenmare and Lafayette."

"Yeah, I know that case. The 212. Should be called the 646. Last time I checked, no one could get a 212 number anymore. The place belonged to Sam Sparks, right?"

Rogan nodded, and it struck Ellie that Sparks might be better known to the general public than she had realized, even without the assistance of a reality show.

"We checked with Boyle at the time to see if we might be looking at a case of mistaken identity. He came up with nothing. Now Sparks's lawyer says he hears otherwise. He claims you're running an operation on one of Sparks's neighbors."

"I wouldn't call it an operation," Carenza said, handing Ellie a DD5, the departmental form used to report on ongoing investigations. This one related to for Apartment 702 at 212 Lafayette.

"It's directly next door," she said.

Rogan glanced at the sheet of paper over her shoulder. "The only other apartment on that floor, as I recall."

The DD5 contained entries for three events—two in March, one in June.

"Two neighbors came to our front service desk in March, complaining about a drug dealer who had just moved into one of the luxury condos on the top of the building. You've seen that building?"

They both nodded.

"Okay, so you know the deal. It's this old building, been there forever. Most of the tenants are rent-stabilized. Also been there forever. Then Sam Sparks buys up the roof space, stacks a few multimillion-dollar apartments on top, and calls the place 212. Two totally different kinds of tenants, now sharing one elevator and one lobby. You get your culture clashes."

Ellie felt her cell vibrate against her waist but let the call go to voice mail.

"And where did these two neighbors fit into the clash?" she asked.

"The old ladies who eat dinner at four thirty at the corner-diner side. They'd lived a good century and a half between them. And I'm telling you, they were a hoot. Watched *Law and Order* and *CSI* reruns all day long on 'the cable,' as they called it. They had the lingo down: skels, perps, mary jane, CIs, gun run. I mean, you name it, and they knew it. They were ready to sign up as CIs themselves. But let's say that as confidential informants go, they weren't the most reliable profilers when it comes to detecting drug dealing. Dirty old men? Not pushing the garbage all the way down the chute? That, I would trust them on. But they were the kind of sweet innocent citizens who think anyone who's got friends coming and going at all hours of the night must be up to no good. Let's call it a generational divide."

"So why do you have a DD5 on the apartment?"

"Because the sweet biddies wouldn't go away. God love 'em, they kept coming in and harping to the front desk with all their cop slang, cracking up everyone in the house but also being a major pain in the ass. So eventually the poor sacks in the community policing unit got dragged in to calm them down. You know what those guys are all about—it's appeasement. So finally they put the old birds to work on a citizen-driven search warrant."

"How come Boyle didn't tell us about this when we called you guys at the end of May?"

"Because half the time when we start a citizen-driven warrant, the oh-so-concerned citizens get lazy and let it drop. We don't bother logging anything onto a DD5 until they come back with all their paperwork. In this case, that didn't happen until June."

"What exactly is a citizen-driven warrant?" Rogan asked.

"No time in Narcotics, huh?" He said it as if no qualified cop could make it into Homicide without pulling duty in the drug squad. Given that Ellie made it to her current position after only five years in uniform and one as a detective in general crimes, she was thankful the question hadn't been aimed at her.

"Major Case Squad, then SVU," Rogan said.

"Okay, so a citizen-driven warrant is this thing we came up with, but it's really a community policing tool. You know, after nine-eleven, we've got these ads all up and down the MTA, telling people, 'If you see something, say something.' "

"But we're not always talking about the next Zacarias Moussaoui."

"No, knock on wood, not in most cases. Instead, we get these nosy neighbors convinced that someone's up to something. So the citizen-driven warrant puts them to work. They write down every suspicious thing they see. They turn in the pages to us. If it adds up to probable cause, we ask for a warrant. If not—"

"You assure them you did everything you could, and then tell 'em to pound sand."

"Pretty much. So that's what we've got here on the DD5. The two ladies walk in to the help desk in March. A couple weeks later, after a few more streetwise Laurel and Hardy routines downstairs, they hook up with the community policing liaison, who tells them about the citizen-driven warrants. We take a look at it after a couple months, and there's nothing there."

"You're sure?" Ellie asked.

"No doubt. You work drugs a little while, and you get super-honed spidey senses. Homeboy's getting his party on like any other single man with that kind of money in Manhattan. And so we could say we did everything we could, my partner and I even did a little knock and talk with the guy. That's the entry in June there. Truth be told, I just wanted to score a peek at the place."

"And?" Rogan nudged.

"The condo was sweet. Marble floors. Floor-to-ceiling windows—"

"The *resident*. Drugs? Dealing?"

"Nah. Dude's Eurotrash, buying up Manhattan real estate while the dollar's in the toilet. Goes clubbing every night. Picks up bridge-and-tunnel skanks looking for a short-term sugar daddy, a place to party for the night. Had no problem letting me search. The place was clean but for some personal-use marijuana in the nightstand. He didn't seem fazed that I found it, and I really didn't want to process him for it, so he flushed it. No hard stuff. No paraphernalia. No packaging materials. No cash or books."

"No dealing."

"No dealing."

"You got a cell number in case we need you to nail this down for court?" Ellie asked. "Sparks's lawyer made it sound like Pablo Escobar lived next door."

She jotted down the number in her notebook, and they began to make their way out of the squad room. Guerrero had been blowing smoke with his claims of a drug operation going down across the hall at the 212, but she still wondered how the lawyer had even known about it. Then she realized the likely source.

She turned toward Carenza. "Hey, you don't happen to know Nick Dillon, do you?"

"Sure. My brother's on the job, too. He and Dillon were in the Major Case Squad before Dillon sold out to the man. We play cards sometimes. Takes my money big-time."

"Any chance you mentioned this whole citizen-driven warrant thing to him?"

"Yeah. He used to work Narcotics, too, you know? I thought he'd get a kick out of his boss's neighbors practicing their slang over mah-jongg. Hey, that didn't cause any problems for you, did it? I mean, there was nothing to it, so—"

Rogan waved him off. "Don't sweat it, man."

Rogan caught Ellie's eye on their way out of the precinct. "The man's got ears, right? That guy makes a friend, he keeps a friend."

"Well, being his pal didn't save me from a jail cell. Maybe next time you can be the one who does our time."

"Would never happen," he said, holding open the precinct door for her to exit. "I'm way too pretty for central holding on some chippy contempt rap. Someone like me goes down, it's got to be major. I would need some serious federal corrections facility—golf course, croquet . . ."

"Rogan, you were raised in Brooklyn. Do you even know what croquet is?"

"I know it involves a round thing called a ball, which means it's yet another sport a brother could dominate if we only gave it a shot."

"When you're done, you think you might get around to letting me in?" Ellie tugged on the Crown Vic's locked passenger handle to make her point.

Inside the car, she flipped open her phone and saw a new voice mail from Max Donovan. Opting to wait for some privacy, she clipped the cell back to her waist.

The drive from Chinatown was slowed by end-of-day traffic. Even with the assistance of wigwag lights, they didn't pull up in front of the Thirteenth Precinct until nearly six o'clock.

Ellie was about to log onto her computer when she caught sight of Max Donovan through the open slats of the blinds that covered

Lieutenant Robin Tucker's office. Tucker stood, walked to her office door, and poked her head into the squad room.

"Good timing, you two. A quick word?"

Rogan shot Ellie a look that made her wish she'd checked Max's message in the car. "This can't be good."

# CHAPTER THIRTEEN

"**A**DA Donovan has an update for us on the Sparks case." Robin Tucker leaned back in her chair and smiled in Ellie's direction. "We should thank him for the special attention he's shown by coming here in person to deliver the news."

Ellie knew it was a dig from her lieutenant about her personal relationship with an assistant district attorney—a relationship that was undoubtedly behind Max's decision to make the trip from the courthouse.

"Apparently yesterday wasn't a big enough win for Sparks. I got papers delivered to my office this morning from Ramon Guerrero."

"What more could they possibly want? Our motion for access to Sparks's files went down in flames. I got smacked with a contempt charge."

"They fucking slaughtered us," Rogan said.

"Well, Guerrero wants another pound of flesh. His motion demands access to all evidence gathered by the NYPD in relation to the death of one Robert Mancini."

"That's ridiculous," Ellie said.

Rogan chimed in. "Tell them to take their motion and stick it up—"

Robin Tucker made a T sign with her hands. "Will you two let the man speak? He's trying to tell you where things stand."

"Well, of course the motion's frivolous," Donovan said. "The mere fact that Sparks has a connection is insufficient to give him any claim to access to the investigation. And they can't rely on public records laws because it's obviously an ongoing investigation."

"So is this just a big-firm lawyer trying to run up his bill?" Rogan asked.

Max ran a hand through his already tousled brown hair. "No, or at least, that's not the only reason. Guerrero's good. He knows he's got a judge who wants to please him."

"But supposedly Bandon's solid," Rogan said. Judges earned reputations with law enforcement. Bandon was known as a straight shooter—tough on crime, but fair to both sides.

Max nodded. "That he is, but for a reason. Bandon's not the kind of guy whose career ends with the state trial court. He was a major player in DOJ in the nineties, then got a sweet special counsel hookup at a major law firm. He's only pulling duty as a local judge to perfect his resumé for the federal bench, and rumor is, his name's finally coming up. No more elections. Better cases. Higher prestige. It's basically every lawyer's dream gig. So, yeah, for three years, he's been as solid as solid comes. But for our purposes, on this case, at this particular time, he might be a little *too* solid. Someone like Sparks's got the ear of the machine that pulls those political appointment strings."

"So he's just going to turn over our entire case to Sparks? That's blatantly illegal."

Max shook his head. "No. Bandon knows there's no merit to Guerrero's motion. In fact, his clerk called me this morning right after the papers were served and basically said the whole thing is bullshit. But then something must've changed his mind, because Bandon's clerk called back again about"—he looked at his watch—"a little under an hour ago."

Rogan threw Ellie a worried look as she was already picturing a loose-lipped Kristen Woods, with freshly arched brows, dishing to her boss about this afternoon's surprise fishing expedition.

"So what exactly are we looking at?" she asked.

Max frowned. "Bandon wants to throw Guerrero a bone. I figure he's trying to send a message to Sparks that he did all he could."

"Which is?" Rogan asked.

"Bandon wants a briefing, under oath, about where things stand. And then from there he wants updates on the case."

Ellie and Rogan were only two people, but from the cacophony in Tucker's office, they could have been the entire studio audience of *The Jerry Springer Show*.

"Can he do that?" Rogan finally demanded.

"Not typically," Max said. "There's a separation of powers issue. We're the executive. He's the judiciary. He has no claim to a general right to access information that we possess in an investigation."

"Okay, so once again, tell them where they can stick that motion."

Max looked at Ellie, and she knew what was coming. "He says this isn't a typical case. He says there's at least a colorable claim that the NYPD is harassing Sam Sparks—"

Rogan was already shaking his head, but Ellie held up a hand, wanting to hear the rest of the explanation.

"Bandon says it's a colorable claim, that's all. And that in light of the jurisdiction he has over the matter given Guerrero's demand for discovery, he's ordering this process as temporary relief. It's basically a middle ground. The way he explained it to me, he's essentially protecting us—you, really, the police"—he looked again at Ellie—"from a harassment suit by intervening."

"Tell him to bring it on," Rogan said. "He's gotten kid gloves compared to anyone else who'd be in his position. Bring it the fuck on. Let him sue."

Rogan looked to his partner for validation, but Ellie just stared at the speckled earth-tone linoleum of Tucker's office floor. If Max was here, instead of the courthouse, it was because he had already tried to fight on her behalf.

"I already ran it up the chain," he said, confirming her suspicions. "Knight thinks it's best if we play along." Knight was the chief prosecutor of the trial unit at the district attorney's office and was also Max's boss. "It's just a matter of meeting with Bandon in chambers—in camera—no Sparks, no Guerrero, not even a court reporter—and then I'll informally notify him of any further material developments. Like I said, it's really just for show. Bandon comes out looking good to Sparks. Nothing on the record shows he's doing some rich ass a favor—"

"And we're going to play along," Rogan said. He didn't bother to hide the sarcasm.

Ellie finally spoke up. "Donovan's right. Bandon's probably helping us out."

Robin Tucker looked at Ellie with raised eyebrows. It was a look of surprised approval.

"And Rogan should be the one to do the in camera session with Judge Bandon."

"What? So I can serve some time, too?"

"So I won't be an issue. So Bandon will see we've dealt with Sparks on the up-and-up."

"That's a good idea," Max said quietly. "Thank you."

"Okay, so we're all done here?" Tucker said. "Happy campers all around?"

No one looked happy, but no one was protesting. "That was easier than I thought. Now get out of here. I've got a kid waiting at home for dinner."


Rogan didn't bother waiting until they were back to their desks before reconstructing the events that must have led to Judge Bandon's phone call to Max Donovan that afternoon.

"Your girl Kristen Woods gave us up," he said once they had both crossed the threshold of Tucker's office.

"I assumed the same thing."

"So much for the sisterhood of the traveling pantsuits," he said.

"Well, Woods is more of a miniskirt and stiletto heels type anyway." Ellie tried to muster a smile as she lowered herself into her worn vinyl-upholstered desk chair. "Given the timing, she must've called Sparks the second we left her on the street."

"And then Sparks makes a call to Bandon."

"Or, more likely, he calls his lawyer, and then Guerrero calls Bandon. That way it at least *looks* like an actual legal process."

"Instead of the bullshit rich-boys club that it is."

Ellie felt a hand on her shoulder and looked up to find Max Donovan smiling down at her.

"I'm gonna get my gear from the locker room," Rogan said.

"You okay?" Max asked once Rogan was out of earshot.

"Yeah, I'm good."

"I know this has to be hard on you."

"Really, it's fine. I'm actually grateful that Rogan will be the one to deal with Bandon this time. I probably need some distance."

"I've got another couple hours of work at the courthouse, but meet at my place when I'm done?"

"I'm sorry, Max. I'm really tired. Last night wasn't exactly the Ritz-Carlton, you know?"

"That's fine. Why don't you go home and get some rest, and I'll come to you."

"I don't think I'll be very good company."

"That's all right. I'm used to doing all the talking while I watch you chew," he said, smiling.

Ellie knew she should be grateful for his response. She should be thankful that he wanted to support her, to comfort her, to watch her sleep the way she'd sometimes catch him in the morning. And she wanted to accept his offer. She wanted to be the kind of woman whose first instinct was to run to a man who cared about her when she was under pressure.

But one of the things she loved about Max was that he seemed to understand her, even when she had trouble understanding herself. And he was comfortable and confident and took everything in stride. Unlike other men she'd dated, she never had to worry about

Max making it all about him. It was all the more reason to wish she could give him what he wanted.

"I'm sorry. Tomorrow, okay? I promise. Tonight I just need to kick the blankets, squish the pillows, drool onto the sheets, and snore like an old fat man. And I really don't want you to see me like that."

"Might kill the magic."

"Exactly." She held his gaze and brushed his forearm.

"Tomorrow."

"Tomorrow."

"I'm holding you to it."

"You better."

"Well, get some rest, all right? You've earned it."


Outside on Twenty-first Street, to the west, Ellie spotted a familiar figure leaning against the white stone of the building, smoking a cigarette. Jess.

She smiled at her older brother as she imagined all of the one-liners he must have come up with at her expense since she'd called him the night before from jail.

"Hey, you." She caught a whiff of smoke and wondered when she'd stop missing it.

He removed an unopened pack of Marlboros from his faded jean jacket and handed them to her.

"I quit, remember?" She had, for the most part.

"I hear they're currency where you're from."

"Funny."

"I'm serious. Anything you want. Soap. Candy. Porn. A shiv. Reefer. The white pony. These bad boys can get you anything on the inside." He shook the cigarettes for emphasis.

"Is that all you got?" she asked dryly.

"Of course not. I figured I'd go with the prop comedy first. Let the rest of my lines trickle out over the next few days. Weeks. Months, if necessary."

"Oh, good. Something to look forward to."

"Are you up for a drink, or are you too jacked up on bootleg hootch from your time in the joint?"

"Oh, I think I can stay awake long enough for a drink."

"You know I only treat at one place."

"You know the torment that awaits me in there?"

The bar in question was Plug Uglies, a classic old watering hole around the corner on Third Avenue. Thanks to its proximity to the precinct and an absurdly cheap happy hour, one could always count on finding a row of cops drinking there at this time of day.

"C'mon. Cheap drinks. A little darts. Some shuffleboard. You've got to take your lumps from the house sometime, or it's only going to fester."

"*The house.* Listen to you with the cop talk."

"Jesus, I've been spending too much time with you."

Ellie and Jess had been raised in the same home, with the same intense homicide detective as a father, but had dealt with their police-dominated environment in opposite ways. Jess had rebelled, shunning any kind of hierarchy or ordered regime that might even begin to resemble a law enforcement culture. Ellie, on the other hand, had breathed it all in and had allowed it to define her.

She pulled the wrapper from the Marlboros. Just one drag. She'd earned it.

# CHAPTER FOURTEEN

Inside the tiny efficiency studio that Glen Forrest Communities called her mother's "apartment," Katie Battle filled a green-tinted glass with water from the sink and placed it on the small rosewood table that doubled as both nightstand and end table between the empty bed and the chair that her mother currently occupied. Once she received the e-mail about her mother's latest fall, she'd wrapped up the tour with the Jenning couple and made it to the assisted living center as quickly as she could.

Katie sat on the bed and watched as her mother slowly raised the glass to her lips with a quivering hand.

"Don't you . . . even . . think . . . about grabbing . . . one of those . . . ridiculous children's toys . . . on top of my icebox."

Katie had purchased a box of plastic straws for her mother four months earlier, but they still sat unopened on top of the refrigerator. "Those are for children," her mother had said. "I start using one of those, and the next thing I know, you'll be trying to feed me with a miniature spoon passed off as an airplane."

Katie noticed that her mother placed her right hand on her chest during the three-second gaps between words. She knew that the falter in her mother's usually strong voice was the byproduct of doctors tinkering with her heart medication again. They'd assured Katie that the occasional skipped beat wasn't itself a danger, but she could tell that the irregularities in something we all took for granted—our beating hearts—scared her mother, causing the pauses in her speech.

None of this was easy for Katie's mother. Phyllis Battle had always been a woman who had known what she wanted. When her first daughter, Barbara, had been killed in a car accident in 1974, she had known—and insisted to her husband—that they would adopt another, even though they had each already celebrated their fiftieth birthdays. And she had known—and insisted to her husband—that they would name the girl Katie, after the confident and independent woman who leaves Robert Redford behind in *The Way We Were*. And when her husband passed away ten years ago, leaving behind debts he had never mentioned to his wife, Phyllis had known—and insisted to her daughter, Katie—that she would continue to live in the family home alone.

The highest hurdle Katie had ever faced had come a year ago when she told her mother she needed to move. For the first time, someone for once was insisting on something to Phyllis. Katie had eventually won that initial battle between the Battle women, but that didn't mean her mother was going to forfeit what might remain of the war. No plastic drinking straws. No arts and crafts in the common room with the women whom her mother called the "pathetic old biddies." None of the loose, maintenance-free cotton housedresses that were practically a uniform at Glen Forrest.

And definitely no wheelchairs.

"Mom, I know you don't want to hear this, but another fall could be really bad."

"I can . . . take care . . . of myself."

"I know. But you'd find it's a lot easier if you'd take advantage of some of the things they have here to help you, like a chair, Mom."

Katie leaned forward and rested her hand gently on top of her mother's. At eighty-two years old, her mother had maintained her full cognition and spirit, but her hand had never felt so thin and frail, her blue veins bulging beneath the loose and wrinkled skin.

"You mean . . . a wheelchair. I'm not . . . an invalid."

"We could ask for a really crappy one if that would make you feel better. None of this high-speed electric power stuff. You'd wheel yourself. Think of the upper-body workout you'd get. I can even request a bum wheel so it would be like a bad shopping cart if you want."

Katie was happy to see her mother smiling, but then the smile turned into a laugh and her mother wheezed and then coughed. Her hand moved reflexively to her chest again.

"Shhh," Katie said soothingly.

Her heart. The stroke. The falls. Keeping track of her mother's ailments required Mensa-caliber mental juggling.

The second her mother caught her breath, she was back on message. "No wheel . . . chairs."

"You scare me, Mom. I know you like to think it's just a fall. But this isn't something you can play around with. Falls in the elderly—"

Her mother shot her a look of darts.

"Falls now can be fatal. Do you know how stupid it would be to survive everything you've survived, just to go out by *falling down*? Phyllis Battle is way too tough—and much too smart—to allow that."

Her mother set her jaw, but she at least wasn't arguing anymore.

"I've asked Marj to bring a chair up tonight." Now her mom shook her head, but still no verbal resistance. "Just for you to experiment with. She'll work with you out in the hallway when the others are listening to a music group that's coming in tonight."

"Horrible, *horrible* . . . they call themselves singers. Like someone threw . . . a cat . . . in a washing machine."

"OK, so when all the old biddies are down there clapping along with the terrible music, you be nice to Marj. I'll check in with her tomorrow about how it went, and we can go from there."

Still, her mother said nothing. Progress.

Katie rose from the bed, picked up her purse from the floor, and leaned over to place a kiss on the top of her mother's head.

"Good night, Mom."

Katie had already opened the apartment door when she heard her mother's quiet voice behind her.

"I'm . . . sorry, Katie. For . . . falling. For . . . being old."

"Don't you *ever* apologize. Just be nice to Marj tonight. I want you around for a long, long time."

On her walk to the F train, Katie retrieved her BlackBerry from the depths of her oversize black leather satchel. Pulling up a phone number, she hit the dial button, only to hang up after one ring. She wanted someone to take her place tomorrow night. With Mom's latest fall, the last thing she wanted to deal with was tomorrow night.

Ironically, though, it was her mother's situation that required her to handle this appointment herself. It was only a few hours. She'd get through it, just like she always did.

# CHAPTER FIFTEEN

If there was a bar in the East Twenties that epitomized the drinking side of the law enforcement culture, it was Plug Uglies. Where glass-walled martini bars soaked in ubiquitous lounge music had begun to dominate even Murray Hill, Plug Uglies was still a dark wood pub adorned with black-and-white photographs of old New York, dartboards, and a well-stocked jukebox.

The comments began the moment Ellie opened the door.

"Look alive, Officers. We've got a hardened ex-con in our midst."

"Call the probation department. Make sure she's checked in."

More jokes about the need for a shower, despite the fact that she'd cleaned up hours earlier.

Ellie took a mock bow in recognition of the attention, and someone playing shuffleboard in the back broke out in a round of "For She's a Jolly Good Fellow."

And then it was over.

"See, not so bad," Jess said, ordering a Johnnie Walker Black for her and a Jack Daniel's for himself.

Ellie took a seat on the bar stool next to his. "So how was life without me last night?"

After briefly shacking up with a self-described exotic dancer for two months last summer, Jess was back on Ellie's living room sofa again, where he always seemed to spend the largest bulk of his residency.

"Quiet."

"It's not the first time you've been trusted at home alone without a watcher."

Ellie and Max were taking things slow. Casual. Dating. No relationship talk yet. But she did spend the night with him about twice a week, enough to justify a second toothbrush at his place.

"Quieter than that," Jess said. "I was worried about you."

"I think you got our roles switched. I'm the worrier. You're the worri-ee." She smiled, picturing her usually stress-free brother alone in her apartment fretting over her.

"Oh, shit," she said, her momentary inner calm destroyed. "Did Mom call? I totally spaced."

With rare exceptions, Ellie called her mother in Wichita every single night. The routine dated back to her first days in New York, where she'd followed Jess more than ten years ago to assuage her mother's concerns about her only son, and most reckless child, living on his own in a city where a person like Jess could find more than his fair share of trouble. Ellie would call her mother each night because she knew her mother would sleep better once she heard her two children in the big city were safe.

Then slowly what had begun as a sweet habit had become a requirement—minimal validation to lonely, widowed Roberta that the children who'd abandoned her at least missed her from afar.

And now Ellie had forgotten to call. She knew from experience she would pay for it the next time they spoke.

"You didn't tell her where I was, did you?"

"Are you kidding? I didn't pick up the phone."

"Jess."

"Sorry, sis. That drama's your department."

"I assume she left an epic message?"

Jess nodded, knocking back a toss of bourbon.

"Don't tell me. She did her whole passive-aggressive, I-know-you've-got-more-important-things-to-do speech."

"Something like that. I believe she may have said something about spending all your time with a man she still knows nothing about and has never met."

"Jesus. I never should have mentioned Max to her."

"Uh, duh? Don't ask, don't tell, is my motto. Tie me to a water board at Gitmo. Call out the dogs. I say *notzing*," he said in his best Sergeant Schultz impersonation.

"You know the only reason you get away with that is because I tell Mom what's going on with you."

"No, you tell her what she wants to hear about what's going on with me. The dude featured in the fictional tales of those phone calls is a complete and utter tool."

Ellie did have a tendency to convey to their mother a brighter version of her and Jess's lives. In the fairy-tale world that Ellie had created for her mother's benefit, Ellie was a well-adjusted woman who just happened to be a cop, who had girlfriends, dates, and hobbies. She was nothing like the father, and her mother's husband, who had given everything to the job. And in these stories Jess's band, Dog Park, actually got paid to play standing-room-only gigs, and a lucrative record contract was waiting for them around the next corner.

"You should have picked up, Jess. Just to make her feel better."

"And you should stop coddling her, and allowing her to hold you hostage with your daily calls. But that's not up to me."

Instead of responding, Ellie took another sip of her drink.

"So," Jess said, filling the silence, "I may have met the stupidest woman on the planet yesterday."

"Hmm, I don't know. The competition in that arena can be pretty stiff."

"I was walking down Fifth Avenue to meet this girl at Park Bar when I notice this kid—couldn't have been but four years old—sitting in the passenger seat of this parked car. And I noticed because I was thinking that's how we'd ride when we were kids—just plunked down in the front seat like that—no child seats, no seat belts, whatever. Then I notice the windows are down and there's no one else in the car. Then I see there's a purse sitting on the console, and the keys are hanging from the ignition."

"Brilliant."

He took in another gulp of bourbon. "So then I see this lady stroll out of the deli with an arm full of flowers, carefree as can be, and she starts making her way over to the car. I said, 'This is your car?' 'Oh yeah,' like nothing's wrong. And I told her she couldn't be leaving her kid alone in the car like that. She's all, 'But I could see him the entire time.' "

"Idiot."

"Right. So I say, 'I could've hopped into that front seat and been gone in a second. Your car, your kid, your shit, would be gone.' You know what she says? 'I don't worry. I'm a woman of God.' Like everyone in the world who has bad crap happen to them must have turned their backs on God."

Ellie found herself smiling. "Aren't you the one who usually says 'Live and let live'?"

"Even *I'm* not such an apathetic sack not to notice when some little four-year-old's at stake."

"No, but getting in a woman's face like that? Trying to convince her to be a better mother? Jess Hatcher, you actually tried to change the world."

"Shit. I really *have* been spending way too much time with you. I'm turning . . . *earnest*."

"Poor you. You know you're welcome to vacate Chez Hatcher whenever you feel like it," she teased.

"And give up the best-priced sofa space in Manhattan? And with cable, no less? Not a chance."

Ellie spun the bottom of her glass—down only to the remnants of ice—in a circle against the bar. There had been a time when she'd been annoyed by Jess's repeated periods of tenancy in her living room, each one a sign that his most recent job and/or roommate situation hadn't taken. But he had now held the same job for more than six months—a new personal record. It happened to be at a strip club called Vibrations, but Ellie had long stopped worrying about that. To know that he was staying with her by choice changed everything.

"So, El, when are we going to talk about what happened?"

"What happened when?"

"Don't try to play this cool with me. Yesterday. In court. Getting a judge mad enough that he put you in a *jail* for a night? That doesn't sound like my well-behaved team player of a little sister."

"I already told you what happened. The entire thing got out of control."

"You don't get out of control, Ellie. It's not your nature. You are the most controlled person I have ever known."

"What are you saying?"

"I've seen how you work. Even at home, when you're reading cold case reports, you hunch over your documents and create this private world that no one else can penetrate. That little notebook of yours? You treat that shit like the gold at Fort Knox. So you tell me: How'd that rich prick's lawyer wind up sneaking a peek?"

"You think I did this on purpose?" She shook her head and laughed. Catching the bartender's eye, she pointed to their empty glasses to signal for another round. "Maybe we should take this conversation home so I can lie on the couch while you tell me what other Freudian tendencies I have."

"I'm not saying you did it intentionally. I'm saying you did something that's not you, El. You're usually the chick who can talk her way out of anything."

They sat in silence while the bartender set down two fresh glasses. Ellie gave the guy an awkward smile as he cleared away their empties, extricating himself from what he clearly sensed was a private conversation.

"I can't believe you're blaming me for this. Do you have any idea how much last night sucked? It was filthy, and awful, and lonely, and terrifying. And totally humiliating."

"You're misunderstanding me," he said, his voice softening. "I'm not saying you wanted this to happen. All I'm saying is that it could only have happened if you were off your game. And I'm sorry, El, but that scares me. For your own whacked reasons, you are totally committed to doing the same crazy work Dad did. This time you got twenty-four hours of hell, but next time, you might really fuck up. That's the kind of shit that can really get you hurt."

"I'm fine."

"You're not," he said, holding her stare.

Her brother was rarely serious, let alone stern. As she looked at his concerned face, she felt her defiance begin to melt away. She didn't want to talk about this. She didn't want to think that Jess had seen something in her that she was completely unaware of.

"I don't know what happened. It's Sparks. It's this feeling in my gut that I missed something, and now he's getting away with it. Because of me. And no one else cares because he's who he is. And that poor man, Jess." She thought about Robert Mancini's body, laid out naked and bloody against the crisp, clean white cotton sheets. God, she was tired. And the whiskey on a near-empty stomach was taking its toll. "It's been four months. He has a sister, and two little nieces, and they don't have any answers. And Sparks. He doesn't even care. And his lawyer had the nerve to bring up the *Dateline* thing and *People* magazine, as if I had done any of that for myself."

Media interest in her father had briefly landed Ellie in the national spotlight. Back in Wichita, Jerry Hatcher spent the better part of his career as a detective—close to fifteen years—hunting the infamous College Hill Strangler. When he was found dead behind the wheel of his Mercury Sable on a country road north of town, the department labeled it a suicide, but Ellie had spent the length of her father's search and then some convinced it was not. The media became momentarily fascinated with Ellie when the Wichita Police Department finally captured the killer, nearly thirty years after his first murder. Ellie thought the attention would pressure the WPD to honor her father's pension.

That was all in the past. Six months ago, she had begun to accept the truth about her father's death. Sometimes fathers killed themselves. Ernest Hemingway. Kurt Cobain. Jerry Hatcher. She'd never understand it, but she had finally stopped fighting. But then Sam Sparks's lawyer tried to use it all against her in court.

"I let him get to me," she said. "I hate him. I hate him, and I let it show. I let him get to me."

She felt her brother's arm around her shoulder and saw him throw crumpled bills from the front pocket of his jeans onto the bar. He managed to shuffle her out of Plug Uglies, away from the view of her fellow officers, before she began to cry.

# CHAPTER SIXTEEN

Eight-fifteen a.m. on Friday.

Two days had passed since Megan Gunther had discovered that hideous Web site, Campus Juice. Day one had been spent reading and rereading the posts, trying to digest the fact that someone out there apparently despised her. Day two had brought her parents and a trip to the police station, but nothing had changed. She wondered whether day three might finally be the end of it.

She laid belly-down on her double bed, kicking alternating calves against the bedspread while she read her next biochemistry assignment and listened to Death Cab for Cutie on her iPod. With a neon pink highlighting marker, she traced a sentence in her textbook about the biosynthesis of membrane liquids. She had an exam in a week and was going to have to set the curve to have any shot at an A after missing lab yesterday.

She had e-mailed her lab TA with a polite explanation for the absence, but had not received a reply—at least not when she'd last checked her e-mail twenty minutes ago. She thought about logging in again but didn't want to go online. She didn't want the temptation of reading those horrible messages about herself again. She didn't want to think about the possibility that there could be newer postings.

As impossible as it seemed, she was trying to follow Courtney's advice to ignore the Web site altogether. She and Courtney had practically grown up together in New Jersey. When they had both accepted college admissions in the city—Courtney at Columbia, Megan at NYU—they had celebrated the fact that going off to school was not going to separate them. But now they were sopho-mores, and the reality was that the six miles between Courtney's Morningside Heights apartment and Megan's Greenwich Village place may as well have been a train ride between Chicago and Philly. Between classes, homework, and making new friends at their re-spective schools, they were lucky to see each other once a month.

But Courtney had dropped everything when Megan had called her yesterday. And Courtney had proved more helpful than either Megan's parents or the police. Courtney was a volunteer at a do-mestic violence hotline and had some experience dealing with stalking—or at least its victims.

According to Courtney, Megan would be best off ignoring what had been written about her on the Web site. They were merely words in cyberspace. The first post she'd found went back three weeks, and until she came across her name two days ago, the words had sat online—stagnant, black and white, incapable of harming her. She simply needed to erase the problem from her mind—forget she'd ever seen the posts, and force herself to go back to normal.

Easier said than done.

She kept replaying Sergeant Martinez's words in her mind. *Mess-ing with someone's head isn't a crime. . . . There's a whole bunch on there that's way worse. . . . You can't let this get to you.*

She reminded herself that there were thousands of posts on that Web site, millions if one were to count all of the many anonymous chatboards and blog comments that were on the Internet overall. She couldn't let a couple of sentences—among all of that garbage—get to her.

Still, instead of learning more about how the molecules of life were synthesized, she found herself running through a host of possible suspects. Her father had immediately brushed off the sergeant's suggestion that Megan might know the author of the notes. That's the kind of father he was, the kind of father who instinctively leaped to his daughter's defense. Of course he had sought to protect Megan against the notion that she might have made herself an enemy. Of course he hadn't stopped to wonder.

But he had reacted so quickly that Megan hadn't stopped to wonder, either. Even standing for half an hour in the precinct, she had never paused to really think through the question of who might be in a position—or have a motive—to "mess with her head," as Sergeant Martinez had said. Or, as Courtney had put it more bluntly, "pull a mind-fuck on her."

There was that guy outside their apartment last month. He was at the bus stop when she ducked inside Jamba Juice. She initially noticed him because he was cute, but by the time she had her Mango Mantra, the 3 bus had come and gone without him. Instead, he stood at the entrance of her building, and as she approached, she could have sworn that he'd been reading the list of names posted at the entrance, his finger resting close to her buzzer. She'd blown it off once the lobby door shut securely behind her, but now she wondered if there was some possibility she'd seen him before on campus.

As hard as she tried to remember that man's face, her mind kept pulling up another image. Keith.

They were still together when she picked her fall classes, so Keith knew her schedule. Keith would know how much something like this would distract her from school. Keith was addicted to the Internet. He would know about a site like Campus Juice, and he would know that the site provided anonymity. And Keith could be vindictive when he set his mind to it.

But they had broken up back in June, and the online posts didn't start until the beginning of September. Would he really stew for almost three months before carrying out a full-on assault of terror against her that continued to this day? It was hard to imagine.

But as she wrapped her necklace—the thin silver chain dangling the heart pendant that Keith had given her—around the tip of her right index finger, she couldn't help but wonder.

Over the quiet distraction of the background music flowing through her headphones, she heard the clang of a pan against the electric stovetop in the kitchen. Heather had emerged from her cave for a feeding.

Megan had hoped that the one upside to getting a roommate would be a new friendship, a girlfriend to talk to late at night. And when Heather first moved in, she wasn't particularly cold. In those initial weeks, she joined Megan in the living room for a couple of episodes of *Project Runway*, one of the only shows Megan ever made time for. They also formed a habit of piggybacking their takeout orders so they could share dinner at the table.

Then one night in June, after Heather caught Megan crying in her room after officially calling it quits with Keith, Heather had actually opened up to her. She said she'd gone through some rough times—a boyfriend, someone older, someone who really fucked with her head. She said she was pretty screwed up until she went through counseling for it, and now she was getting a fresh start. But then Megan had made the mistake of asking her what had happened between her and the guy to make it so bad, and all of a sudden, Heather was gone. She had a paper to write or something, excused herself from Megan's room, and never mentioned the conversation—or any other one, for that matter—again. She was just a tenant renting a room.

Then, yesterday, when she got home from the police station, for just a second, Megan had felt something like a bond again when Heather noticed how upset she was and asked what was wrong. But when Megan told her about the Web site, all Heather had said was, "Wow, I'm sorry to hear that. That must be really stressful."

Megan supposed it was a polite enough response. But it wasn't the kind of thing a real friend would say. Courtney had spent nearly an hour with her on the phone yesterday, helping her pull herself together and put the entire situation into context. "The big picture," Courtney kept saying.

Then later, when Megan was hanging her coat in the closet out-side Heather's room, she heard Heather on the phone saying some-thing about "threats" on a Web site. She hadn't asked Heather to keep it a secret. And she probably should have expected Heather to gossip to whomever it was she spent most of her time with when she wasn't home. But she didn't want anyone else talking about it. About her.

And she didn't need to hear that word. *Threats.*

Megan looked at her watch. Eight forty. She should be at her morning spin class, pushing through a sprint to spike her heart rate. But Courtney had advised her to deviate from her usual schedule, just in case.

She turned her attention back to a paragraph about steroid bio-synthesis in rat cells, and realized she was actually starting to feel better. She had gone a full hour without crying. Maybe in the after-noon, after classes, she'd go to the gym and use the elliptical trainer for a little while.

As she turned the page, she heard a knock on the apartment door. She pulled one bud from her ear to make sure Heather was going to respond. Maybe she would finally meet one of Heather's friends.

"I'll get it," Heather yelled from the kitchen.

Megan readjusted her headphones and turned back to her book just as she realized she hadn't heard the security door buzzer.

"No, wait," she yelled, pulling off her headset.

Jumping from her bed and lunging toward her bedroom door, she heard voices in the living room, then a loud groan, followed by the sound of something heavy hitting the floor.

Megan should have stayed in her room. She should have jumped out the window to the street below if that's what it was going to take.

But she didn't think. She acted on instinct. And her instinct was to help Heather. Heather. Poor innocent Heather. In the wrong place at the wrong time.

She opened her bedroom door to see her roommate sprawled on the floor next to the breakfast table. A man in a black-wool ski mask was plunging a six-inch blade into her torso. As he pulled the knife from Heather's body, he looked up, saw Megan, and charged toward her.

Following instinct again, she slammed her door shut. She found herself grasping at the doorknob, but there was no lock on the bedroom door. She pressed her back against the door, trying to hold it closed with the weight of her body, but it was no use.

As she felt the door spring open and push her forward to the ground, Megan knew she would die. She knew she would never see her mother, father, or Courtney again. She would never graduate from college. She would never become a doctor.

She wished she could have saved Heather. She wished she knew why this was happening. And she wished she could have said good-bye.

# PART II

_____

**"GO AHEAD. LIE TO ME."**

# CHAPTER SEVENTEEN

Despite two large coffees and a cherry Danish, Ellie still felt like she'd been hit over the head with a sledgehammer and then strapped to an all-night merry-go-round.

She had gotten the tears under control by the time she and Jess made their way back to her apartment last night, but the emotions that had led to the outburst were still raw enough that she'd made the mistake of adding two Rolling Rocks at home to the two rounds of whisky she'd already consumed at Plug Uglies.

And then of course there had been the telephone call to her mother.

Her nightly calls to Wichita were never what she'd call the highlight of her days. At best the calls were short, just long enough for a telephonic kiss good night. At worst, they were hour-long reminiscences, with Ellie's mother lamenting her status as a widowed bookkeeper whose happiest days were long behind her. Last night's call fell on the crummy end of the spectrum.

And whether it was because of the whisky, the bad jail memories, the conversation with her mother, or a combination of the three, Ellie had slept in fits and spurts for a second consecutive night.

The case certainly wasn't doing anything to help her stay awake.

She was poring over Robert Mancini's financial records and telephone logs while Rogan was at the courthouse briefing Judge Bandon.

Ellie looked up to see Lieutenant Robin Tucker standing next to her desk, hands on hips in a tailored white shirt and black pantsuit.

"Rogan's not back yet?"

Ellie glanced at the readout on her desk phone. Ten-fifteen. Rogan was supposed to meet Max in the judge's chambers at nine.

"Should be done soon," she said.

"Good. Call him. You two are up." She handed Ellie a piece of paper with an address on it. East Fourteenth Street. Somewhere near Union Square Park.

Ellie scanned the squad room and saw several other teams of detectives working away in paired sets of desks.

"Rogan and I were hoping to take a new look at where we are on the Mancini case."

"I told you two you're not protected. New callouts just like everyone else."

Ellie scouted out the squad room again, this time less subtly. "I'm not sure when Rogan will be done, Lou."

"You're a big girl, Hatcher. Your partner will find you soon enough. Now scoot. Your body's a dead college girl. Right up your alley. Who knows? If she's from Indiana, you might just earn yourself another medal."

Her lieutenant's quip referred to the murder last spring of a midwestern college student. The case had earned Ellie a Police Combat Cross for what the commissioner had called her "extraordinary heroism while engaged in personal combat with an armed adversary under circumstances of imminent personal hazard to life." At the ceremony, Ellie had known the commissioner was simply reading the standard language that defined the award itself, but she had committed the words to memory anyway. They provided a palatable description of that case's unflinching violence, both in the killer and ultimately in Ellie when she had taken his life. Robin Tucker could mock the recognition if she wanted, but Ellie knew that the finest thing she'd ever done in her life was to bring some measure of justice to that Indiana family.

The address that Tucker had handed her turned out to be on the southwest corner of Union Square Park. Ellie approached the address from the east, hit her dashboard emergency lights to flip a mid-block U-turn, and then pulled the Crown Vic in front of a fire hydrant on Fourteenth Street. Around the corner on University Place, she saw three patrol cars, an ambulance, another unmarked fleet vehicle, and the medical examiner's van. The gang was all there.

The apartment building itself was a new condo, erected like so much new construction on top of a bank branch. On the other side of double glass doors off of University, she spotted a young Asian patrol officer with a crew cut inside the tiny lobby, his gaze apparently fixated on the abstract painting that filled the wall opposite the building's elevator. She pulled on one of the doors. It was locked, but the sound of her attempt caught the patrol officer's attention, and he pushed the door open for her.

Ellie flipped opened the badge holder clipped to her waist. "Apartment 4C?"

With a silent nod, he pressed the call button. She stepped inside and watched the digital readout track her trip to the fourth floor. The quiet of the elevator was immediately disrupted when the doors parted.

"God damn it, how the fuck did the EMTs wheel the other girl out of here?"

Ellie turned to see a short, heavyset man with a dark mustache and thick neck struggling with a gurney in the narrow hallway. She quickly counted four apartment doors—three closed, one held ajar by a uniformed patrol officer who was still staring at the black heavy-grade plastic body bag flopped on top of the aluminum gurney.

"Coming through," the man said. Short of breath, he pushed the gurney farther toward Ellie and the elevator. "No one's supposed to be up here anyway. Damn it," he cried out to no one in particular, "someone call that stupid fuck in the lobby and remind him his one and only fucking job this morning is to serve as a human shield between these apartments and any more people to get in the way."

"Looked like he was doing his job to me." Ellie flashed her detective's shield to the harried technician. "Besides, what's the rush? Doesn't look like you've got much hope of saving her."

"Hey, sorry about that." He offered a gloved hand on instinct. "Gabe Berry. ME's office."

She wrinkled her nose at the sight of his extended hand, and shook her head.

"Oh, yeah, right." He wiped the perspiration from his brow with his palm. "You're from Homicide?"

"Yep. You said the EMTs took a girl out of here already?"

"Yeah, now *that* was a rush. They were hauling ass out of the lobby when I pulled up. Taking her to St. Vincent's, I think."

"She supposed to make it?"

"No clue. From what I could see, there was big-time bleeding. She managed to crawl to the phone and dial 911, but it didn't look so good. They found a pulse, but it was slow and weak. Could still be a DOA."

"Anyone else we need to keep track of?"

"Nope. Just this unlucky one and the other less unlucky one."

"And you were going to take my body before I got a look. How could you do that to me, Gabe?"

He shrugged. "A lot of detectives don't give a sh—don't care. We bag and tag. They get the details later from the ME."

"Not me. I want to see her."

Plenty of detectives were content to leave the technical aspects of a case—the inspection of the body, the crime scene analysis, the collection of physical evidence—to the teams of specialists assigned those tasks in any large police department. But seeing the victim's body wasn't just a matter of science. It was the first—and often, only—introduction to a human being whose life had been taken. This was Ellie's chance to see the person before all color was gone.

Before a forensic pathologist cut a Y incision into her torso, removed her internal organs, and sawed open her skull. While there was perhaps still some lingering sign of the spirit that had been lost.

"I want to see her," she repeated.

"Here?" He looked at both sides of the narrow hallway. The idea of him navigating his broad body on either side of the gurney was clearly unimaginable.

She turned sideways and wiggled herself around the edge of the aluminum cart, careful not to place any pressure on the side of the body, and then pulled the bag's zipper halfway down. She peeled apart the covering of the plastic to reveal the girl's face.

She was young. Early twenties, max. Perhaps even still a teenager. Tucker had told Ellie to expect a college girl, so it made sense that she was young.

She was plain, at least in this condition. She had long, straight, blond hair, and Ellie could tell that this seemingly rushed technician had taken the time to arrange it around her shoulders, away from her eyes and face. Her skin was the color of Silly Putty, marred by streaks of dried red blood, but Ellie could tell that the girl's complexion had been clear and clean. This was a girl who had taken care of herself. A few freckles darkened the bridge of her nose.

"Who is she?"

"Ask them." Berry looked over his shoulder toward the apartment. Ellie noticed that the patrol officer who had been holding the door ajar was no longer there. "Like I said, I bag and tag. Some college chick, from what I heard."

On another day, Ellie might have told the guy to show some respect—this woman didn't deserve to be called "some chick." But then Ellie looked at the girl's shiny hair, so neatly straightened inside the body bag. Berry's demeanor came with the territory, but he had treated this girl as a person, even in death.

She unzipped the bag farther to reveal more of the body. Ellie looked past the damage that had been inflicted by the knife, forcing herself to focus first on the person, not on the violence.

The girl wore a ribbed cotton V-neck T-shirt and a pair of dark blue jeans. She was in good shape, with slim arms and a flat stomach. The jeans hit her just beneath the belly button, not the kind of pelvis-revealing denim for which so many young, fit women opted these days.

No jewelry except for a dainty chain holding a tiny heart that rested just beneath her collarbone. It was the kind of necklace a girl this age would have been given by either a mother or a boyfriend. She made a mental note to find out which.

She scanned the body one more time and swallowed a lump forming in her throat. Someday she'd get past this. One day she might complete this ritual—this need to be introduced to the victim at the beginning of a new case—without letting it get to her. But she honestly didn't know whether she'd still be the same person when that day came.

For now, she did her best to hide her emotions from Berry and gave a silent nod to the girl in the bag. Now it was time to take a more analytical look at the body.

What had been the girl's bright white T-shirt was soaked through with near-black blood. Beneath slashes in the cotton fabric, Ellie saw several deep gashes in the abdomen, sides, and chest. She counted at least six. Some of them appeared to be long but shallow slices, perhaps inflicted in a struggle. But one wound in her chest and another near her liver evidenced deep, forceful, and, most likely, the fatal stabs.

Ellie's inspection was interrupted by the cheerful *ding* of the elevator beside her. The doors opened, and J. J. Rogan stepped into the hallway.

"You were gonna let them cart away our body before Double J got here?"

"Christ," the technician said. "Let me guess. This is your partner?"

# CHAPTER EIGHTEEN

Inside Apartment 4C, Ellie counted three officers from the crime scene unit. One was photographing copious blood patterns—a combination of spatter, drips, and pools—on the bleached bamboo floors in a small dining area just inside the apartment's entrance. Another stood in the galley kitchen, carefully placing a drinking glass inside a plastic evidence bag. A final CSU officer was on her knees, dusting a door leading from the right side of the living room for fingerprints.

The apartment itself was luxurious—floor-to-ceiling glass windows, high ceilings, stainless steel kitchen appliances—but its furnishings were not much different than what one would expect for a college student, or at least one who could afford new purchases instead of the Goodwill merchandise that Ellie still depended on. Past the dining table, the main living area was just large enough to house a brown upholstered sectional sofa, a glass coffee table, and a television stand. Ellie was fairly certain that she recognized at least some of the furniture from an IKEA catalog she had browsed the previous week before throwing it into the recycling bin.

The patrol officer who had held the door for Berry and his gurney stood awkwardly near the dining table, on the opposite side of the blood. He had dark, wavy hair and a prominent nose. The sleeves of his uniform pulled against biceps that had clearly seen some time at the gym. According to a nameplate on the left side of his chest, his name was A. Colombo.

"Did he finally manage to get the meat cart into the elevator? I thought that dude was going to stroke out from the physical exertion. Geez, jog a mile or something, dude."

Ellie gave him her best deadpan look. Rogan wasn't going to let it go with just a look.

"Did someone ask you for your stand-up routine, Bob Saget?"

"Just offering some levity, Detectives. You know, comic relief. They say it helps with, you know, the morbidity."

"Laughter cures diseases, does it?" Rogan asked.

"Huh?"

"You said it helps with the morbidity, which refers to the rate of a disease or illness. It does not mean a mood that is morbid, which is the concept I believe you intended to convey, Officer."

"I'm sorry. Huh?"

"Forget it. You know the backstory here or not, Colombo?"

"The victim's parents called the precinct this morning wanting us to check in on her."

"They're sisters?" Rogan asked.

"Who?"

"The victims. You said the victims' parents. Are you saying they were sisters?"

"No, sorry. At least, I don't think so. The one victim's parents— the one who died—"

"She have a name?"

"Um, yeah." He stole a glance at his notebook and then tucked it back into his chest pocket. "Megan Gunther, according to the super. Anyway, that vic's parents were trying to call her, and she wasn't answering the phone. They got the brush-off from the dispatcher, so then they called the condo's super. He used the building's keys to enter and found . . . well, you can get the picture. Turns out the other vic had crawled her way to the phone to call 911 after the bad guy left, and paramedics showed up right behind him. Me and my partner responded, too."

Ellie jumped in before Rogan could correct Colombo's grammar. "Your partner's posted downstairs?"

Rogan wasn't usually so critical. Either this officer had done something to earn a place on Rogan's shit list, or something else was bothering her partner. She had a bad feeling his mood might be related to his trip to the courthouse that morning to brief Judge Bandon on the Mancini case.

"Yeah. Making sure no one's coming up except authorized personnel."

"And you're keeping a log of who's going in and out of here?" she verified.

He patted the pocket that held his notebook. "Just need to add the two of you."

"Good man," she said. "Got to keep track of the crime scene."

"Hey, you look pretty young. How long'd it take you to make it to Homicide? Cuz, you know, that's basically my dream. I mean, with a name like Colombo, you just got to go for it. I'd get the tan trench coat and everything."

"Just keep the log. Detectives Hatcher and Rogan. Manhattan South Homicide. In at eleven-oh-two a.m. Write it down."

Maintaining the crime scene log was not the only thing that Officer Colombo had done right that morning. He had also instructed the building's superintendent to return to his office on the building's second floor.

Ellie knocked on the office door. She detected a European accent in the voice that instructed her to come in.

"You're Gorsky?"

"Yes. People around here call me Andrei." The man's eyes were red-rimmed.

"Ellie Hatcher. I'm a detective with the NYPD's homicide unit. It's not easy walking into a scene like that upstairs."

"No. It was not easy."

"My understanding is that one of the girls' parents asked you to check up on her? Megan Gunther?"

"Yes, that is right. The tenant's name was Megan. My phone was already ringing when I walked into the office this morning. It was Megan's mother saying her daughter was not answering her telephone. She wanted me to check on her."

Ellie glanced at her watch. "So this was what time?"

Gorsky stared at the black cordless phone on his desk. "The first time, it was probably just before nine o'clock in the a.m."

Ellie let silence fill the room, knowing that the superintendent would eventually explain what he meant by the first time.

"I try to tell her that it is not up to me to check on the residents. This is not a college dormitory, you know. If they want someone to be the guardian to their children, they shouldn't buy them their own apartments."

"All right, Mr. Gorsky. I think I understand. But you went upstairs to check on Megan?"

"Eventually, yes, I said I would do it. But I have workers here this morning to install a new cooling system. I have another resident locked out of her storage unit crying in the lobby that she will lose her job if she doesn't get it open and find a very important file of some kind that she is missing. I have to find another resident's keys for a realtor who is coming but I cannot find them. And at first, you know, Mrs. Gunther wanting me to check on her daughter did not seem so important."

"So she called more than once."

"Four times she called me in twenty minutes before I went upstairs. We are not even supposed to go in. The parents, they pay for the apartment. But the legal resident is the daughter. I am not even supposed to go—"

She knew where the man's thoughts were taking him. Police and paramedics had shown up right after he entered the apartment.

The phone call from the parents had given him a twenty-minute head start. Twenty minutes might have made the difference.

"You couldn't have saved them, Mr. Gorsky." She wasn't convinced, but said it anyway, for his sake. "And it's possible you could have gotten yourself hurt instead."

His eyes remained fixed on his telephone, but she assumed all he was seeing was a replay of the scene he had encountered when he opened the apartment door. He'd see it tonight in bed before he slept, and again in his dreams. He'd continue to see it forever. It was just a question of how frequently and how vividly.

"She was a good girl, Megan was. We have more young people in this building than you would think. The parents, they buy, like an investment. Then the kids live on their own. Megan was a good girl, not spoiled like a lot of them. She always said hello. She used my name to talk to me like a human being, not a servant. She would even bring fresh coffee sometimes if she saw me working in the lobby."

"There was a second girl in the apartment."

"She was the roommate. Just moved in a few months ago."

"Was she the same kind of 'good girl' as Megan?"

The cordless phone on Gorsky's desk broke out into a loud chirp. Even though he'd been staring at the phone, the noise clearly startled the man, but after a quick flinch, he jumped back into the conversation.

"She seemed like a nice girl. Quieter than Megan. Not as outgoing."

"Do you need to get that?" she asked, looking at the ringing phone.

He shook his head just as the phone finally silenced.

"And what was the roommate's name?"

"Heather. I'm not sure if I ever knew her last name."

"Don't you need a name for her to live in the building?"

Again, the phone began to ring. And again, Gorsky ignored it and continued to speak.

"As a matter of technicalities. But the Gunthers were responsible financially for the apartment, and I trusted Megan. She told me she was getting a roommate, and that was the end of the conversation. Some of these other people, I would've wanted credit checks, a deposit . . . don't get me started." He waved a hand at the thought.

"Do you know if either of the girls had any problems recently? Boyfriends? Drugs? Money?"

"Megan would come in and out of the building with the same boy for a very long time, but he has not been here since, well, since around the time the roommate came."

"A breakup?"

Gorsky smiled and nodded his head. "I don't keep this job with the same management company for so long by talking to residents about their romances. Could be breakup. Could be he doesn't get along with the new girl. I have no idea."

"You know anything about him? Name? Address?"

He shrugged. "I wish now I had asked. Tall, skinny. Had these things, you know, through his—" Gorsky pulled at his lower lip.

"A pierced lip."

"Yeah, but in two places. On both sides. Now *that—that* I noticed."

"Anything else? Hair color? Eyes?"

"Dark brown hair. Probably brown eyes, I guess. I don't know, kind of like mixed looking. Maybe he was part ethnic of some kind. He hasn't been around."

The phone was ringing once again.

"I'm sorry, sir, but if you're not going to answer that, I'd appreciate it if you could turn off the ringer. It's a little distracting."

He fumbled with a button on the phone, and the chirping quieted to a subtle jingle. "I do not know how to turn it off."

"No, that's much better," she said. "Thank you. Now, the lobby entrance was locked when I came in. Is that twenty-four/seven?"

"Yes. You have to call up to a resident and be buzzed in by them to enter."

"Do you have any way of knowing who buzzed people in this morning?"

He shook his head.

"What about cameras? Any film from the lobby or the elevators?"

Ellie had not spotted any cameras in the building, but with security advancements, the equipment might not be visible.

Gorsky shook his head again. "In the bigger buildings, our company uses cameras. Not one of this size. I am sorry I cannot be more helpful. You know, right before nine o'clock, there's a lot of foot traffic on the street. People coming and going. It's not hard to walk in after someone leaves."

"What would really help is if you could give me whatever you have in the way of a file for Megan's apartment. I assume her parents' contact information will be there?"

He handed her a manila envelope from the top of his disheveled desk. "Already done." He stared at his phone, which had finally gone silent. "I have been sitting here for over an hour staring at this telephone. I have lost count how many times it has rung."

"Given the tenacity of whoever's on the other end of that line, I'd suggest you either answer it or leave town."

"I do not want to answer it, because I know it must be her. Mrs. Gunther. I am afraid to speak to her and tell her what I saw." He sighed quietly. "I am a coward. It is the girl's mother. She should know."

"You're not a coward, Andrei. You don't need to be the one to tell her. I will tell them. I will tell Megan's parents what happened and what you saw. It is my job, not yours."

He finally took his eyes off of his phone and looked up at Ellie. "After today, I will never complain again about my work."

As it turned out, Ellie was going to deliver the news sooner than she realized.

# CHAPTER NINETEEN

She found Rogan leaning over the desk in Megan Gunther's bedroom. He was scrolling through a cell phone that was not his usual Motorola, his notebook open in front of him.

"Is that the vic's?"

"I'm assuming. It was on a charger beneath the desk."

"How's it look?"

"She's got a mess of friends in her directory, almost all of them listed only by first names. I'm writing down the outgoing calls—we've got her parents, a few different girls, mostly one named Courtney—"

"Got a boyfriend yet?"

"Two calls to someone named Kendall?"

"With their generation, that's probably a female."

"I thought the same. Then we've got a bunch of other outgoing numbers that weren't in her contacts list." He tapped his pen against his notebook, indicating that he was jotting them down. "Unfortunately, it looks like her parents have been hitting redial over and over this morning trying to reach her, so it wiped out her entire incoming call list."

"The super says the roommate's name was Heather, last name unknown."

"She's Heather Bradley. I found it on a political science paper that was on the desk in her room—'Two Views of American Federalism.' "

"Your detecting skills are profound, J. J. Rogan."

"As is your affectionate sarcasm, Hatcher."

"Well, between your discovery of the cell phone and my trip to see the super, we're pretty much tied for who found the parents' phone number first. You want to call, or should I do it?"

"You mind?"

"Yeah, no problem. You all right?" Ellie could tell that whatever had caused Rogan to snap earlier at Officer Colombo still had him in a mood.

Before Rogan could answer, they heard the loud crackle of a police radio in the living room outside of the bedroom.

"Colombo, it's Eng. You still Code 11?"

"Copy. Did you *see* me walk out of the building? Yeah, I'm still here."

"We got a problem downstairs."

Ellie poked her head out of the bedroom to better hear the exchange between Officer Colombo and the man she presumed was his partner posted in the building's lobby.

"I've got a Mr. and Mrs. Gunther here—first names Jonas and Patricia. I've explained that we are controlling access to the fourth floor because of a police inquiry right now, but they say their daughter lives in 4C? They're getting pretty animated."

Ellie made out another male voice on the radio, this one in the background. And considerably angry. Something about owning the apartment. About how they couldn't ban him from entering his own property. About how this better not have anything to do with their daughter. In that final sentence, despite his vocal force, Ellie heard more desperation than anger.

"Megan's parents are in the lobby," she said to Rogan.

He looked at the bloodstains smeared across the white cotton bedspread, the pale wood floors, and the back of the bedroom door. "No way they can walk into this."

"I'll go down," she offered. "Colombo, tell your partner to grow a pair. He'll be pulling tunnel watch duty for the next year if he lets those people up here."


The mother's eyes.

As soon as Ellie locked eyes with Patricia Gunther, she was certain that the woman already knew what was coming. She knew her entire life was about to change. She knew she was going to learn that her daughter was dead.

Ellie quickly looked away toward the dignified but surprisingly brawny man standing beside the woman. His long face was somber, his brow furrowed. He was worried. Worried and sad. And royally pissed off. But he didn't know. Not yet. Not like his wife.

"Mr. and Mrs. Gunther?"

"That's right," the man said. Next to him, his wife's head fell forward as she cried out.

"I'm Ellie Hatcher. I'm a detective with the New York City Police Department. We've responded to an act of violence in your daughter's apartment."

As she delivered the news—two girls, one critical, one who didn't make it (their daughter, according to the super)—Ellie tried to recite the facts in just the right way. No false melodrama. Enough compassion not to appear cold.

When she was finished, she turned away to allow them a moment of privacy. She went so far as to close her eyes when she spotted their embrace in the reflection of the lobby's glass door—the strong, tall father crying into his wife's hair, the mom sobbing against her husband's chest. She blocked out the sound of their cries by evaluating her own performance.

She had done her best, but she nevertheless knew that Jonas and Patricia Gunther would always remember this scene—Ellie in her black turtleneck and slim gray skirt, this antiseptic lobby with its reproduced abstract art and fake marble floors, Officer Eng posed awkwardly outside the elevators with his hands clasped behind him—as the very worst kind of collision between the impersonal and the intimate.


Once the Gunthers were ready to talk, Ellie borrowed Andrei Gorsky's office on the second floor. Before the couple was even seated in the two metal folding chairs crammed between the superintendent's desk and the wall, Mr. Gunther made no secret about where he placed the blame for his daughter's death.

"This is your people's fault. We tried to tell you. Just yesterday. We begged you for help."

"Who, Mr. Gunther? You begged who for help?"

"*You.* The police. There must at least be some kind of report. We were there for nearly an hour."

Patricia placed a calming hand on her husband's forearm. "She doesn't know what you're talking about, Jonas. She'll understand better if we just explain it to her."

"Fine. You explain to her what we tried to tell them yesterday, while our daughter could still be protected."

"We went to a precinct yesterday. On Tenth Street."

"The Sixth Precinct," Ellie clarified.

"Right. The Sixth. We spoke with a Sergeant Martinez. Our daughter was being stalked on a Web site. It's called Campus Juice dot com. They told us they'd already talked to the district attorney, and they couldn't do anything about it."

"Megan was terrified," Jonas added. "Whoever was posting that . . . filth, knew her schedule. He said he was watching her. And you people wouldn't do anything."

"The sergeant said they'd had complaints about the site before," Patricia explained. "Some kind of First Amendment thing that the police couldn't touch."

"It was threatening. It was stalking. What are the police for if they—"

"I am very sorry, Mr. Gunther. I'm not going to defend what took place yesterday because I simply don't know anything about it.

I take your word on what occurred, and God knows you're entitled to be furious right now and forever. But the faster I can figure out who we should be talking to now about what happened in your daughter's apartment, the sooner I can give you some answers."

Jonas nodded sternly. "Campus Juice dot com. I assume that today, unlike yesterday, you will be able to make the Web site tell you who was harassing Megan."

Ellie wrote down the name of the Web site.

"Wait," Patricia said. "I still have the printouts we showed the sergeant."

She opened a large brown leather shoulder bag, removed a thin stack of folded white paper, and handed it to Ellie. Ellie skimmed the pages.

"We will definitely contact the Web site to track down whoever wrote these things about your daughter. But did Megan have a sense of who the author might be?"

Jonas shook his head. Patricia quickly followed suit, but Ellie noticed the short pause.

"Mrs. Gunther? Were you going to say something?"

"No," she said, shaking her head once again. "Megan didn't have any enemies."

"Sometimes we have enemies we don't think of in that way. A boyfriend, maybe? An ex? I noticed she was wearing a heart-shaped pendant."

"Our daughter was premed," Jonas said. "She was focused on school."

Patricia said nothing.

"I see. Because, you know, if there was anyone, *anything*, you can think of—no matter how far-fetched—it could prevent us from wasting time chasing down false leads. You never know . . . even someone who was just a friend might have noticed something unusual. It could really help."

"There was a boy," Patricia said. Her husband turned quickly in surprise but said nothing. "His name was Keith. I don't know all the details, but he wanted more from Megan than she was in a position to give. He was clingy, I guess you could say. Last I heard, Megan broke it off a few months ago."

"Did he give her any trouble about that?" Ellie asked.

"Not that I know of. But, you know, before the breakup, it was on and off, here and there. Megan didn't tell me much, but I could see she was stressed. I was worried it would get in the way of school, so I was relieved when she finally cut the cord."

Ellie recalled what the superintendent had said about seeing a guy with a pierced lip accompany Megan to and from her apartment.

"Did Keith happen to have a pierced lip?"

"I'm not sure," Patricia said. "Wait. Maybe. I don't know. Megan said something once about how we wouldn't approve of him, even at first sight. Something like that. So maybe."

"Do you know anything else about this Keith? A last name? Where he lives? Is he a student?"

Patricia shook her head. So did her husband, but for a different reason.

"You knew this? Why didn't you say anything yesterday? The sergeant—he was on our side there at the end, but he said there was nothing he could do. If we'd known this boy's name, he could have called him. Scared him. Told him to back off."

"Don't, Jonas. Don't say that."

"Why didn't you say something? Was I that hard on Megan? You couldn't even trust me enough to let me know she had a boyfriend? Even yesterday? Even with those messages?"

"I'm very sorry," Ellie said, interrupting. "It would be helpful if you could make a list of some of your daughter's friends. We can follow up with them."

She pushed a pad of paper and a pen across the desk toward Patricia, who looked relieved by the distraction.

When Ellie finally escorted the Gunthers back to the lobby of their dead daughter's apartment complex, she noticed that they did not hold hands on the way out of the elevator, as they had on their way up to the superintendent's office. As she watched them walk into the sunlight of University Place, she wondered if that meager oversight—the failure to grab a spouse's hand—was just the beginning.

For the next few months, they would be grateful to have another person who cherished Megan. But as time passed and they began to long for at least one hour during which they did not think about what they'd lost, Jonas might begin to wish that Patricia's nose wasn't pointed at the tip the way Megan's had been. And Patricia might look away when Jonas jutted his jaw out, the way Megan had.

And Ellie wondered if she had witnessed the beginning of the transformation: that moment in Gorsky's office. Jonas asking why Patricia hadn't spoken up yesterday. Patricia thinking, but not saying, that she would have—Megan would have—if Jonas hadn't been so overbearing.

Resentment. Fault. Blame.

She wondered if whoever killed Megan Gunther had also destroyed the very best of what she had known in her parents.

She had shoddy reception inside the building, so she stepped outside to call Max. He picked up after just one ring.

"Hey, you."

"Hey."

"I hear you got another callout."

"You've got spies tailing me? We may need to have a little chat about boundaries."

"No spies," he said with a chuckle. "I was with Rogan this morning when he got your message."

"Yeah, how'd things go with Bandon? J. J.'s been a little jumpy since he showed up."

"It was fine. Just Bandon pretending to be principled, thorough, and objective. Of course, that didn't stop Rogan from going on a tear both before and after we were in chambers."

"But he was on good behavior for the middle part at least?"

"Yeah, he held it together. What have you been up to?"

"New callout. Still figuring out who's who."

"Which means you probably weren't calling me to whisper sweet nothings in my ear."

"Sweet nothings."

"Wow, *so* hot."

"What can you tell me about Web site postings?" She gave Max a quick summary of what she had learned from the Gunthers and the complaint they had made yesterday about Campus Juice.

"Sounds like the cop they talked to at the precinct had it about right, although he should have filed a report to build a record."

"We don't like being told to write stuff down that's never going anywhere. If that sergeant had been told by the DA's office that nothing could be done, that's the only part of the discussion he's going to remember."

"The DA's office was involved?" he asked.

"According to the parents, that's what this sergeant told them."

"You just need to know any identifying information for whoever posted those messages. Is that right?"

"Yeah."

"Okay, give me the dates, times, and titles of the posts."

Ellie flipped through the printout the Gunthers had given her and recited the information Max had requested.

"All right. Let me look into it, and I'll call you right back."

"Thanks."

"It was the sweet nothings that did the trick."

Ellie was on her way back to the apartment building when Rogan stepped outside.

"Got word from the hospital. The roommate's conscious."

"She's going to make it?" Ellie asked.

"Yeah. At least one of them had luck on her side."

As they turned the corner onto Fourteenth Street, Ellie could see that the lunch-hour rush at the Union Square green market was under way. The skateboarders who transformed the south park steps into stunt ramps dodged shoppers juggling canvas tote bags filled with organic greens and heirloom tomatoes. Dog walkers tugged on leashes, pulling their hopeful charges past the enticing displays of fresh food. Only a few passersby even stopped to glance at the gathering of official city vehicles that had descended upon the corner of Fourteenth and University.

"Your ride or mine?" Rogan asked, looking at the two identical fleet cars.

"The usual."

As she hopped into the passenger side of the Crown Vic, she overheard a woman who was walking into the bank tell her friend, "Oh, I'm sure it's nothing. Crime's so low, the police show up for anything these days."

# CHAPTER TWENTY

The half-mile drive to St. Vincent's was a straight shot west on Fourteenth Street, then a quick left turn on Seventh Avenue. Rogan swerved around the two layers of ambulances stacked on the west side of the hospital and took another quick left on Eleventh Street, pulling the car to a halt at the curb.

As they exited the car, a bicyclist pedaling west on Eleventh yelled out, "Wrong way on a one-way, idiot."

"NYPD," Rogan hollered. "And you're not wearing a helmet, so who's the idiot? I'd give you a ticket, but I guess you'll learn your lesson when your brains wind up on the dash of a cab."

The cyclist flipped them the bird as he sailed through the light at Seventh Avenue.

"Picking fights with boys on bikes?" Ellie asked.

He threw her a dry look and opened the hospital door. Ellie flashed her shield at the front information desk. "We need to see Heather Bradley. She was admitted about two hours ago with multiple stab wounds."

She turned back to Rogan while the clerk tapped away at her computer keyboard. "Are you going to tell me what's up or not?"

"This morning, that's all."

"Bandon put you through the ringer?"

"Detectives, Heather Bradley is in the ICU. You'll find it—"

"Eighth floor," Ellie said. "Got it."

As they made their way to the intensive care unit, Ellie nudged Rogan again. "So, Bandon gave you shit?"

Rogan shrugged. "It was nothing specific."

"Max said it wasn't too bad."

"Max, huh?" Rogan said with a smile.

"ADA Donovan. Whatever. So it was bad?"

"Just the whole damn thing was messed up from the get-go. Bandon making us brief him so he can schmooze his ass all the way to the federal bench on Sam Sparks's back."

"The thought of his ass on Sparks's back is pretty disturbing."

"Damn, you are pissing me off right now. I thought you hated these two knobjobs at least as much as I did."

"I don't think *anyone* hates a single person on the planet as much as you seem to hate Sparks and Bandon today. I mean, hate groups are calling for lessons on how to hate more deeply."

"Yeah? Well, some lame-ass-joke group has been calling for you."

"Seriously, did it go all right or not?"

Another shrug. "Yeah, it was fine. Your boy Donovan made it cut-and-dried."

"Hey, you managed to walk out of chambers without handcuffs and jail scrubs, so you clearly did better than me."

"Sorry I'm PMSing. I'll get over it. You run the show with this girl upstairs? You always do better with the young white girls."

"That's not what you said yesterday about Kristen Woods."

Ellie immediately regretted making any further reference to the Sparks case. When the elevator doors opened, Rogan had one more comment. "You think Tucker gave us this callout to keep us from bothering Sparks?"

"Yep."

"Any thoughts about what we can do about that?"

"Find out who the hell killed Megan Gunther and then get right back up Sparks's ass again."

Even in a hospital bed, with an IV in her arm and bruises on her face and neck, Heather Bradley was objectively attractive. Her sable-colored hair fell in loose curls past her shoulders. As a resident pointed a pen-size flashlight into her pupils, she blinked her almond-shaped green eyes, dark lashes contrasting against flawless pale skin.

"Excellent," the resident announced. "Hard to believe that an hour ago we were worried whether you'd make it."

Ellie tapped the open hospital room door.

"Yes?" the young doctor asked.

"We were told Ms. Bradley might be ready for a few questions?"

He looked to his patient for guidance, and Heather nodded. "Unless you think it's better that I not."

"It's totally up to you," he said.

"I want to help," she said.

"Be quick?" the doctor said quietly as he passed them. "She's a lot better off than we feared at first, but she's still in shock and needs some rest."

"Hi, Heather. I'm Ellie Hatcher with the NYPD. This is my partner, J. J. Rogan."

"It's almost funny," Heather said. "I was about to say 'Nice to meet you' out of habit, but—"

"I know. Not exactly nice circumstances," Ellie said. "How much do you know about what happened in your apartment this morning?"

"I know that Megan didn't make it. I know that some crazy person forced the door open with a knife and began attacking me."

*Some crazy person.* Ellie had hoped that Heather would be able to give them the name of someone she recognized, someone the girls knew.

"How did he force the door open?" Rogan asked. They had seen no damage to the girls' apartment door.

"There was a knock. I just assumed it was for Megan. As soon as I opened the door, he pushed his way in."

"Just one person?" Ellie asked.

"Yes."

"Do you have any idea who it was?" Ellie already knew the answer to the question, but it seemed natural to ask. Heather shook her head. "What did he look like?"

Heather paused. "I don't even know. He was wearing, like, this black ski mask thing. I'm pretty sure he was white. At least that's how I'm picturing the skin beneath the mask."

This was not good.

"What about his clothes?" Ellie asked.

Another pause. "Jeans, I think. And a long-sleeved shirt," Heather said with more confidence. "That, I remember, because I tried to scratch at his arms, but all I got was fabric. I'm sorry. It just happened really fast, and I was thrashing around trying to fight him off. I didn't see very much."

"Did he say anything to you?"

Heather shook her head again. "He just came at me. It was . . . totally crazy. He was cutting at me and slicing me, and all I could do was try to get away or push him off of me. Then I decided to play dead, but then Megan opened her bedroom door."

"And you—"

"Just laid there." Tears welled in Heather's eyes, and she dropped her gaze. "I knew I couldn't help. I could barely get to the phone after he left. But I should have—"

"No, you shouldn't have," Ellie said firmly. "You did exactly the right thing. You *survived*, Heather. Don't ever regret that."

"But it feels so . . . wrong. Maybe if—"

"Did Megan talk to you about this problem she was having with a Web site called Campus Juice?"

Heather reestablished eye contact with Ellie and nodded. "Just yesterday. You think this had something to do with those postings?"

"We don't think anything yet," Ellie said. "We're just running through all the possibilities. Did Megan have any idea who might have posted those things about her?

"No. She seemed really thrown off by the whole situation. And really scared. It seemed totally out of the blue, you know?" She seemed even more disturbed by the thought that she and her roommate might have known someone who would do this.

"How so?" Ellie asked.

Heather paused. "Like, you know, Megan was just the kind of person who minded her own business. School. Exercise. A couple girlfriends. She didn't really seem the type to have, you know, trouble."

There was something soulful about Heather Bradley's face. If it hadn't been for the high voice that depended on the word "really" like oxygen and ended most sentences with a question mark, she might have seemed older than her young age.

"What about boyfriends?"

"Megan? No, not really. I mean, there was a guy right when I moved in—Keith something—but that was a few months ago. They were already on the outs, you know? Like Megan told me a couple of times at the beginning that he wasn't quite getting the hint, but that was it. At least as far as I know."

"Did you ever meet him?"

"He came around a couple of times, but I never got to know him."

"Any idea where we might find him? Was he also at NYU?"

She shook her head. "Definitely not. I think that was part of the issue. He was like some really funky musician type. He'd wander around the city recording weird noises on his laptop and then mix it into dance music and stuff. It was a little whackadoo. Oh my God, you don't think it was him, do you?"

"Like I said, we're just considering the possibilities. What about you?"

"Me?"

"Yeah. Anyone on your end we should talk to?"

"Gosh, no. Wow, I didn't even think about that. I just assumed this was some crazy person. It happens, you know?"

"So you don't have a boyfriend? Even an ex?"

Heather shook her head. "No, I just transferred here from Arizona, and NYU's been kicking my ass, you know? I haven't even had a date. I can write down my schedule or something if that would help."

"Yeah, sure, if you're up to it. Anything you can think of."

"Is everything all right in here, Heather?"

Ellie turned around to see the young doctor lingering in the doorway.

"Detectives, I can make sure that any notes Heather writes get to you, but if you're about done—"

Ellie felt her cell phone vibrate against her waist, flipped it open, and saw a text message from Max Donovan: "Call me about Campus Juice."

"How much do you love me?"

Max used a four-letter word that had not quite been uttered yet between them, but Ellie knew he hadn't meant *love, love*. She plugged her free ear with her finger to block out the sounds of approaching sirens outside St. Vincent's on Seventh Avenue.

"I take it you've got good news?"

"How soon can you get to the courthouse?"

"We're in the heat of this thing right now."

"Trust me. It'll be worth your time."

Max's office was on the fifteenth floor of 100 Centre Street, home to many of Manhattan's criminal courts and most of its five hundred assistant district attorneys. Ellie and Rogan breezed past the receptionist for the homicide investigation unit and headed directly to Max's open door, adorned by a bulletin board plastered, as usual, with the various news clippings and cartoons that Max had found sufficiently amusing to earn a spot on his office mural of humor.

As Ellie rapped her knuckles against the fake wood grain of the door, she noticed the board's latest addition—a story in this morning's *Post* about a fleeing felon who'd lost a race against Seventy-ninth Precinct officers when his baggy pants fell to his knees, causing him to trip over a dozing homeless person's open jar of urine.

Max rose from his desk and shook Rogan's hand. "Good to see you back here, man. After this morning, I thought we'd soured you on this building for at least a month."

"I was tempted to wait in the car, but Hatcher swore you said this would be worth our time."

"It will be. You want a Coke or something?"

"Max," Ellie said. "We're in the hunt."

"Just a few minutes. I promise. In the meantime, take a look here." Jiggling the mouse on his desktop, he awakened the computer screen. "This is the Campus Juice Web site you were telling me about."

He clicked on a menu bar that read "Choose Your Campus," and then scrolled down a long list of university names until he reached "New York University."

"Typical format for a message board. A big list of topics, which are the titles of original posts, and then anyone can click on a subject and reply."

"We got the gist." Rogan pointed to Ellie. "She's got a verbatim printout of the posts about our vic from the girl's parents."

"Right," Max said. "But you probably didn't see this."

He clicked on a link labeled "Privacy and Tracking Policy." "This site knows precisely the kind of harassment it's inviting with these kinds of terms. Look here, in bold letters: 'Campus Juice does not require identifiable information from users who read or post messages to our Gossip Board.' And down here, again in bold to make sure no one misses it among the legalese: 'We share aggregate traffic information with advertisers and potential advertisers, but this does not identify individual users.' And you'll love this."

He scrolled down the screen farther, to a heading entitled "IP Addresses."

"That's what we need," Ellie said. An IP address identifies an individual computer's connection through its Internet service provider. It was their best shot at determining the author of the posts about Megan.

It was only then that she read the fine text beneath the subject header: "If you are particularly concerned about your online privacy, there are several services that offer free IP cloaking. Just do a quick search on Google and find one you like."

"This is beyond belief."

"Like I said, whoever set up this site did it in a way that invites cowards to stay in the shadows."

"So now what?" Rogan asked.

A young, slender woman in high heels, a fitted navy dress, and a sleek black ponytail slipped into the office and handed Max a stack of papers. Ellie caught herself watching Max to see if his eyes followed the woman out of his office. She was unsurprised, but still pleased, when they did not.

"Perfect timing," Max said, flipping through the pages of the printout. "So here's the deal: I ran the domain name registration for Campus Juice, and the owner lives out in Long Island. That means I've got subpoena power."

"And is that what I think it is?" Ellie asked.

"Signed, sealed, delivered," he said, handing the document to her. "I tracked down the ADA who researched this issue for the Sixth Precinct. Your vic wasn't the first NYU student to complain about the Web site. Apparently there were enough reports last year that we finally took a closer look. The Web site's not a company as much as just some dude working out of his basement. The ADA who called him said he's a total prick who prides himself on all the pain he's causing. Payback for all the spitballs hurled his way on the playground."

"And you were able to get a subpoena?" Rogan asked.

"We didn't stand a chance when it was just a vast graffiti board of anonymous insults. But your homicide nails it down to one specific person and the people who posted messages about her. Judge Jacob agreed that was a narrow and compelling enough request to sign on the dotted line."

Watching Max beam, she remembered what had initially drawn her to him when she'd first met him here six months earlier. The broad shoulders, curly dark hair, and cute smile probably helped, but there was more to it than looks. Max had an ease about him that showed in his every movement.

The Columbia law degree could have opened any career door he had chosen, but the diploma hung in a simple wooden frame on a wall that hadn't seen a new coat of paint for a decade. Before she moved to New York, Ellie had once dreamed of a life different from her parents'. Taking prelaw classes in Wichita, she imagined herself in a firm like Ramon Guerrero's, with all the attendant perks. When she'd briefly lived with an investment banker, she had enjoyed the six-course meals and occasional tickets to Lincoln Center. But for reasons she might never understand, she always found herself uncomfortable with people who occupied that world she would never be a part of.

But Max never let any of it faze him. The son of a shoe salesman and a dental hygienist, he never seemed tempted to cash in on his education, but was never a martyr about it either. Supremely confident and unflinchingly modest, he would never let a man like Sam Sparks get to him. And Ellie saw the way women looked at Max, even the one who had handed him the subpoena. But Max being Max, he never seemed to notice.

"Thanks, man," Rogan said, extending his fist for a friendly tap.

Max called out to them as they left his office. "Enjoy the drive to Long Island."

# CHAPTER TWENTY-ONE

**2:45 P.M.**

Like every other Web site on the Internet, campusjuice.com was required to register its domain name and address with the Internet Corporation for Assigned Names and Numbers. According to ICANN, a thirty-seven-year-old man named Richard Boyd had registered the Web site name two years earlier using a residential address in Huntington, one of a chain of towns that comprised Long Island's North shore.

As Rogan pulled to the curb in front of Boyd's house, Ellie took in the surrounding area. The split-level ranch had probably once been part of a neighborhood not unlike Ellie's own working-class street back in Wichita. But Long Island, unlike Wichita, had changed. Most of the homes like Boyd's had been replaced, torn down to make room for McMansions that sprawled to the edges of their small lots. Ellie noticed the three extra inches of grass and the unkempt edge along the walkway as they made their way to the front porch. She could picture the neighbors complaining about the worst house on the block.

Rogan clanked the front door's brass knocker three times. An elderly woman wearing a crimson velour housedress opened the door.

"We're police officers with some questions for a Richard Boyd," Rogan explained. "Is he here?"

"Oh, sure. Richard's down in the basement where he works. Come on in."

Ellie was immediately struck by the smell of mothballs and mildew as they followed the woman into the dimly lit house. It reminded her of her Gram Hatcher's house, where she had always been afraid to fall asleep.

"You say you're from the police?" the woman asked, leading the way past a small kitchen with bright orange laminate counters and wallpaper with yellow sunflowers.

"Yes, ma'am," Rogan said. His tone was considerably more polite than Ellie had heard from her partner that entire day, and she realized that she was not the only one who might have been reminded of a grandmother. "Are you Richard's mother?"

"Practically, but, no, I'm his aunt. Nearly fifteen years ago, Dick needed a place to stay. They say middle-aged women can't land a man, but my sister ran off to California with the love of her life when she was fifty years old. Dick's been here ever since."

"You're a pretty generous aunt," Ellie noted.

"I'd always been on my own, so it's nice to have the company. I don't see a ring on that finger of yours, honey."

"Nope."

"Well, don't wait forever like I did. Not everyone's got the same luck as my sister."

"Okay, I'll keep that in mind, ma'am."

She opened a door leading to a narrow basement staircase, leaned against the oak handrail, and then thought better of it. "These are a bit steep for me."

"Don't even risk it," Rogan said. "We'll find our way down just fine."

"Well, all right then. There's no problem now, is there?"

"Not at all," he explained. "Just something we think your nephew can give us a hand with."

"Okay. Because Dickie's a good boy. A little unusual, and not exactly a looker, but he's good."

When the basement door swung closed behind them, Rogan turned his head toward Ellie and winked. "This Dickie guy sounds like a winner," he whispered. "Maybe we'll kill two birds with one stone and have a ring on that little finger of yours before you know it."

"I liked you better when you were pissy."

"Joanna, is that you?" A voice echoed up from somewhere in the concrete-walled basement. "I told you not to take the stairs. If you need something, I'll bring it up."

They took the final step and turned to find a large, unfinished room lined with crammed metal bookcases. Old newspapers, boxes, and magazines were stacked from floor to ceiling in every available space, leaving only a narrow pathway winding through the basement toward the man's voice.

"Dick Boyd?"

"It's *Richard*. And who's here?"

"NYPD," Rogan said. "We're here for information about Campus Juice."

They took another turn and came face to face with Richard Boyd, who was now standing behind a disheveled sectional desk that contained three separate computer screens.

"I told some lawyer before, I don't turn over private customer data without a subpoena."

"Which is why we've brought you one." Rogan wound his way through the clutter, then muttered under his breath to Ellie, "As if we could find anything in this Collyer mansion."

The reference was to two infamous brothers, hermits and hoarders who were eventually found dead among their eclectic possessions. By the time police removed more than a hundred tons of detritus from the Collyers' townhouse, New York City law enforcement had added a new term to its lexicon.

"I heard that, you know. And I'm not a Collyer brother. Everything in here, I need. And I can describe for you every single piece of paper, the purpose it serves, and its filing location."

He peered at them with small, dark eyes from behind a curtain of greasy dark bangs. Folds of fat surrounded his acne-pocked face. His aunt had been generous in her description.

"Well, where do you think you might file this, Dick?" Rogan handed Boyd a copy of the subpoena.

"I told you. It's *Richard*." Boyd sucked his front teeth while he reviewed the document.

"Copies of the posts we're interested in are attached to the subpoena. 'Incorporated by reference,' I believe is the legal term."

Boyd plopped himself down in a battered chintz-upholstered office chair, wheeled it over to the far side of his desk, and jiggled a computer mouse. He tapped away at his keyboard, shook his head, tapped away some more, and shook his head again.

"Nope. I can't help ya." He tried to return the subpoena to Rogan, but J. J. held up a hand.

"You could at least try to hide your glee. What do you mean, you can't help? Give up the guy's IP address, and we'll take it from there."

"Whoever posted these messages used an IP cloaker, which is precisely what it sounds like. If you're spooked about privacy, you can download free software right off the net to mask your IP address."

"And, gee, I guess it's just a coincidence that your Web site tells people that if they want to hide their trail from the police, they can get themselves one of these IP-cloaking devices."

"I'm just helping people protect their privacy."

"Privacy?" Rogan said incredulously. "Doesn't seem like the kind of privacy you need unless you're doing some sick shit that's going to land you in trouble."

"Just like a cop to say that. It's about *rights*, man. I admire this dude for being smart. Besides, these posts are pretty tame compared to some of our content. This bird must be high-fucking-society to bring you guys all the way out from the city with a subpoena."

"No, Richard," Ellie said, "that *bird*'s not part of any society, at least not now. She's dead."

"Oh, shit." Boyd dropped his eyes to the subpoena.

"Very eloquent," Rogan said. "You still admire this guy and his cloaking software?"

"Hell, man. I didn't know, okay?" He tapped away at the keyboard again before pushing it away. "Really, I tried. The dude knew what he was doing."

"Yeah, thanks to your advice," Ellie said. She looked at the string of dates and numbers on Boyd's computer screen but couldn't make any sense of it. "You mean to tell me that anyone can just post whatever they want to your Web site? They don't need to register, or have an account, or tell you who they are in any way?"

"It's sort of the point, you know? The Web site's slogan is 'All the Juice, Always Anonymous.' "

"I don't get it," Ellie said. "Why in the world would you create something like this? You knew weeks ago when the district attorney's office called you how much damage you were causing."

"It's words. There's no damage in words. And why do I do it? Two words: Muh-knee. I get a grand a month for a single ad on that site. I've launched probably a dozen Web sites since the nineties, and I finally have one that's bringing in cash."

"And what about now, Richard?" Ellie said. "A girl is dead, and it started with words. There's damage. And you had a role in it."

Boyd shook his head and tried to hand Rogan the subpoena again.

"That's your copy," Rogan said. "Ponder it a little while longer before you file it away in your perfect system here."

Ellie followed her partner up the basement stairs to find Aunt Joanna waiting eagerly at the kitchen table.

"Did you get everything you needed?"

"We're good for now," Rogan said.

"Because Dick can be a little ornery at times. He'll listen to me, though, if you need me to intervene."

They thanked the woman for her generosity and then showed themselves to the front door.

"A grand a month times, what, ten ads on there? Not bad cash when you're living in your aunt's basement. You sure there's not the possibility of a little love connection there, Hatcher?"

"With Jabba the Hutt? Don't think so."

As Rogan took the corner at the end of the block, Ellie found herself laughing. "Dick Boyd? You know they called him Dick Boy on the playground."

"Damn. Glad I didn't grow up with the likes of you."

"So Long Island was a bust. Now what?"

"Run Megan's calls through the reverse directory and see what comes up?"

"Or go to her friends. I got a list from the mom. According to her, there's one girl we go to first. She's in the city."

"Okay, you see her, but drop me at the precinct and I'll start working on the phone history. See if our girl was calling anyone her parents didn't know about."

Ellie dialed Courtney Chang's number.

# CHAPTER TWENTY-TWO

Morningside Heights got its name from Morningside Park, which lines the east side of the neighborhood from 110th Street to 123rd. But most New Yorkers thought of Morningside Heights as an academic bastion in the middle of uptown, housing egghead students from nearby Columbia University and Barnard College. The late comedian George Carlin had called his old neighborhood White Harlem, and local business owners had now taken to calling the place SoHa, short for south of Harlem. With gentrification across the entire borough of Manhattan, many saw Morningside Heights as simply an extension of the Upper West Side.

But Ellie and many others had a different cultural referent for this neighborhood. She parked in front of a fire hydrant at 112th and Broadway, looked up at the blue-backed neon sign that read "Tom's Restaurant," and could almost picture Jerry, George, Elaine, and Kramer at a booth inside the window. Courtney Chang lived above the diner that was first immortalized in song by Suzanne Vega and later on the television show *Seinfeld* as the ensemble's daily diner.

Courtney was waiting at her apartment, just as she'd promised when Ellie phoned. She opened the front door and turned away with nothing but a "Come on in," and then plopped herself down on an overstuffed mocha-colored sofa littered with crumpled tissues.

"Sorry." She plucked up some of the mess from the couch and threw it to the floor, making room for Ellie to take a seat. "Whatever, I just can't care about this right now."

"Of course not," Ellie said. "Megan's parents told us how close you two are."

"She's my best friend. Was, I guess. *Was* my best friend. Since junior high school. We used to be inseparable."

"Used to be?"

"Before college." She used her fist, balled inside the overly long sleeve of her Columbia University sweatshirt, to push a shoulder-length strand of shiny black hair from her eyes. "We carpooled to school, took all our classes together, spent the night at each other's houses every weekend. Like I said, inseparable. But now I'm up here, and she's downtown, and, well, it wasn't always easy to find time for each other. I can't believe it's too late." She wiped a tear from her cheek with her sleeve.

Ellie was beginning to wonder whether she'd made a mistake relying on Patricia Gunther's information about her daughter's friends. She was relieved when she asked Courtney if she'd happened to speak to Megan within the last couple of days.

Courtney nodded. "Of course. Probably like . . . ten times. Patty told you about that fucking message board? Sorry—"

Ellie smiled. "No problem. And, yes, we know about the messages. We're trying to determine who might have posted them."

"You're the police. Can't you just—"

"We tried. The information isn't there. Whoever posted this stuff about Megan covered his tracks technologically. I was hoping you'd help me figure it out the old-fashioned way. Did Megan have any enemies?"

Courtney shook her head. "No, that's why the whole thing was so weird. I figured it was just someone from campus trying to screw with her mind. I told her it was no big deal. I can't believe this. I actually told her to *blow it off*. To *forget about it*. What was I thinking?"

"You were thinking what anyone would have assumed at the time. The truth is that ninety-nine-point-nine-nine percent of the time, words really are just words. You couldn't have known, Courtney."

"So poor Megan's the unlucky one out of ten thousand. Because we all just assumed she'd be on the right side of the odds."

"Let me guess," Ellie said, catching how quickly Courtney had translated a percentage into the odds. "Math major?"

"Physics," she said wearily.

"I know this is probably the worst day of your life, but anything you can think of—anything that might stand out—could make a big difference."

Courtney shook her head. "Megan wasn't the kind of person to make enemies. There was no drama with her. She studied. She worked out. She tried to make time for friends."

"Boyfriends?"

"Not lately."

"But before?"

"That was about as close as Megan ever came to having anything close to a scandal in her life. Freshman year she went totally gaga over this guy—"

"Keith."

"Right, Keith." Courtney's expression changed as she realized the significance of Ellie's preexisting knowledge of Megan's ex-boyfriend. "You don't think that . . . Oh, my God, why didn't I figure that out?"

"Don't get ahead of yourself."

"I should have thought of Keith when she told me about those postings. I work a frickin' domestic violence hotline, for Christ's sake. It's all about power and control, and, yeah, Keith wanted both of those. Writing those awful things about her—trying to scare her, and of course through a site read by NYU students, no less."

"You're going a little too fast for me here, Courtney. Take a deep breath, slow down, and tell me what you know about Keith."

"Megan met him at a club first semester of freshman year. He's like a DJ or something. They were crazy about each other right away, but then Keith took it way too seriously. It's like he could never get enough attention from her. He was jealous—not of other guys, because Megan wasn't like that—but of her *life*. Her classes. Her reading. *Me*, when we had the time for each other."

"When did they break up?"

"About three months ago. But they were on and off for a good four months before that. I'd say the tipping point was when Heather moved in—the roommate?"

Ellie nodded to confirm she knew to whom Courtney was referring.

"Last spring Megan's parents told her she needed to find a roommate to share the costs of the apartment. Keith offered to move in and share the rent. It was a ridiculous suggestion for all kinds of reasons. She'd never get her work done if he was around. Not to mention that there's no way he could afford the rent her parents were looking for. Not to mention the fact that she was only twenty years old, for Christ's sake."

"Plenty of reasons not to shack up."

"Right. But instead of fighting over it all, Megan took the easy route and told him that her parents would never allow it. And then he asked whether she had even talked to her parents about it. She made the mistake of telling him the truth."

"She never approached them?"

"Of course not," Courtney said. "It was an absurd idea, but not to Keith. I guess after she found Heather and rented the extra room to her, Keith treated every interaction with Heather—or even remotely related to her—as an excuse to remind Megan that she had rejected him. *You don't even know that girl. Now we never have any privacy. We could have kept that as an extra room. You never took me seriously.* And on that last one, Megan finally had to admit he was right. For her, for her life, the thought of living together was crazy. But for Keith, it had meant everything."

"And that's what ended it."

"Yep. It was hard on her, but he came with too much drama, you know? He was always trying to pull her away from school. It would be just like him to use a message board aimed at college students to get to her."

"But when Megan told you about the postings, you didn't think Keith might be responsible?"

"It never even dawned on me. It should have, though, right? He wanted to isolate her. He knew her routine. Maybe if she was too afraid to live her life, she'd go back to him. It's so obvious."

Ellie was careful not to overvalue Courtney's instincts. She had seen witnesses respond this way before. Once they believed police had homed in on a suspect, witnesses changed their perceptions so that suddenly the suspect's name at the top of the list seemed inevitable.

"All I've got on Keith right now is a first name and pierced lower lip," Ellie said. "You got a last name for us?"

Courtney pressed her eyes closed. "Shit. This is impossible, right? Megan *had* to have told me his last name at some point. I just don't remember. It was always 'Keith this, Keith that.' I don't know. Something Spanish, I think. He said he was half Dominican. Maybe . . . Guzaro, or Guittierez. For some reason, I think it began with a G."

"What about a phone number? Address?" They had already checked Megan's cell phone for a Keith, but she must have erased his number after the breakup.

Courtney shook her head. "He always went to her place. He still lives with his mother. Wait." She hopped up from the sofa, made her way to a dining room table covered with books and notebooks, and flipped open a laptop. "I have a picture."

Ellie rose from the couch and looked over Courtney's shoulder while she clicked through a library of photos. Girls at a bowling alley. Another set on a beach somewhere with tall fruity drinks. On the steps of the Metropolitan Museum of Art.

Courtney sniffled. "Okay, here he is."

Ellie leaned forward to get a better look. Megan was on the left side of the screen, her long blond hair curled softly around her shoulders, a broad smile across her face. The young man with his arm around her shoulder mugged for the camera, replicating a model's exaggerated pout. He had creamy light brown skin and dark brown wavy hair. She could see how his racial identity might appear ambiguous. Nice smile. Round cheeks. He would have been a good-looking kid without the two platinum hoops dangling from either side of his lower lip like metal fangs.

"Any others?" Ellie asked.

Courtney shook her head. "No, I snapped this during one of the few times he tagged along. I doubt you'll find any pictures of him at Megan's either. She deleted them all to prove that the breakup was for good. She still wore the necklace he gave her, though. I noticed that."

"Can you e-mail the picture to me?" Ellie asked. She rattled off her personal Gmail address while Courtney typed, then watched as Courtney hit the send key on a message she had labeled "Predator."

"We should have gone to the same school," Courtney said, thinking aloud. "The original plan was for both of us to go to Columbia, but she didn't get in. I should have gone to NYU with her. Maybe then—"

"Courtney, you don't know me from a hole in the ground, but trust me, I speak from experience: Don't start down that road of maybes. You'll create the kind of demons that can destroy you for years."

When Courtney closed the door behind her, Ellie pictured the girl back at the dining room table, clicking again through the files of old photographs, and knew her advice was useless.

# CHAPTER TWENTY-THREE

Ellie had parallel-parked on Twenty-first Street and was about to open the car door when she spotted Lieutenant Robin Tucker in her rearview mirror. She decided to avoid an encounter and stayed put inside the car, watching as her lieutenant let the precinct door swing closed behind her. Tucker paused just outside the precinct, opened a slim gold metallic handbag, and swept some gloss across her lips. She reached into the same bag again and then clipped her hair into a messy bun at the nape of her neck. As she walked in Ellie's direction, Tucker's tan trench blew open, revealing a dark green wrap dress that played up her pale skin. From the looks of things, Tucker had spruced herself up for something.

Ellie slumped into her seat and continued to watch as Tucker smiled and gave a friendly wave to someone on the other side of the street. As she turned to cross Twenty-first, Ellie lost sight of her in the rearview mirror.

She adjusted the right side-view mirror to get a better look. Browsing the cars parked on the north side of the street, she speculated about which one was her lieutenant's intended destination.

Then her eyes fell on a black Infiniti sedan.

"No fucking way," she said to no one in particular. She adjusted the side-view mirror again to confirm what she had seen. Sure enough, she recognized the Infiniti's driver.

Robin Tucker had spruced herself up for none other than Nick Dillon, the head of corporate security for Sparks Industries.

Ellie found Rogan hunched over a spread of documents across his desktop. She recognized the pages as call logs, most of them from AT&T wireless, and a few from Verizon.

"You got the call dumps already?"

Rogan nodded, but didn't look up from his papers. "Cell phone and landline. A lot more activity on the cell, of course."

Phone companies could produce itemized lists of call activity for cell phones, but for landlines they could provide information only about outbound long-distance calls. Fortunately for this case, young people tended to use their cell phones for most of their calls.

"You happen to see Tucker walk out of here?"

"Hmmm?"

"She was all dressed up."

Silence.

"And guess who was waiting for her outside?"

"Hmmm?"

"Nick Dillon. Un-freakin'-believable."

Silence.

"Find any Keiths yet on those call lists?"

"Nope," Rogan said.

"Anything else in there to get excited about?"

"Nope."

"Any chance I can get a few more words, just so I can pretend you're listening to me?"

"Sorry," Rogan said, finally leaning back in his chair and turning his attention to her. "Maybe I'm in a piss-poor mood after all."

"Gee, you think? If the tables were turned, you'd be on your fifth PMS joke by now."

"All right, so you were saying about the Lou?"

"She just left the building looking a hell of a lot better than I've ever seen her around here, and jumped into a car driven by Nick Dillon."

"She told you yesterday she knew the man."

"Knowing him's different than boning him."

"You think you might be jumping the gun? He called her yesterday to give her a heads-up about your ass being in jail. They go way back to patrol days, decide to get a drink—no big thing."

"Well, you didn't see her."

"So cut the woman some slack. She wants to look decent around a guy like Dillon. I seem to recall you primping your hair and shit when you first met with Max Donovan."

"Yeah, and look where that got me. She's got something for Dillon."

"So what if she does? The dude's been decent to us, right?" He pointed an index finger at her. "You might've been in the doghouse with Tucker if he hadn't schmoozed her and her smitten little ass on your behalf."

Ellie plopped herself down at the desk across from him. "Maybe. So what's up with the call records?"

"We got a ton of calls back and forth with her parents—I guess that's normal for college students these days, can't cut the cord. Local carry-out joints every couple of days. Bunch of girlfriends— the reverse directory listings come back to a handful of girls on that list you got from the mom."

"Including Courtney Chang?"

"Yep, a bunch between her and your girl Courtney. No Keith. No other dudes. No late-night booty calls. This girl was chaste, man."

Ellie shook her head. "Courtney couldn't help us find this Keith guy either. I did get a photograph, though. Figured I'd search records for first name Keith with a lip piercing. See what comes up."

Ellie's phone buzzed at her waist. According to the screen, it was Jess.

"Hey," she said.

"You busy?"

"Always. What's up?"

"Please tell me you don't have something going on with DJ Anus So Hottica."

"Do I even want to know what you're talking about?"

"Your e-mail."

"How many times do I have to tell you to stay out of my cyber shit? There's, like, actually real laws against that stuff. I *am* a cop, if you haven't noticed."

"Can't help it, El. You leave your new-mail alert open on your laptop so your messages pop up and interfere with my porn surfing."

"Nice. That's an image I want in my head all day."

"Oh, trust me, the images I've been working on are so much better."

"So, I'm sorry. What was the point of all this?"

"Your e-mail. I couldn't exactly ignore a subject line like 'Predator,' could I? So I opened the message, and what do I see but that electronica-loving poseur. I'm all for you finding some barely legal boy toy, but that lightweight?"

"Seriously, Jess. Who are you talking about?"

"The picture in your e-mail. He goes by DJ *Anorexotica*." He dragged out the name dramatically.

"What picture? Wait. Are you talking about an e-mail from someone named Courtney Chang?"

"Yeah, I guess. The sender address says ChangBang@macmail. That plus the subject line had me, shall we say, intrigued."

"Jesus, Jess. It's an e-mail on a case. You mean you know the guy in that picture?"

"Duh. What have I been saying? You're not going out with him, are you?"

# CHAPTER TWENTY-FOUR

In the bedroom of her Upper East Side Yorkville apartment, Katie Battle removed a beaded necklace and matching chandelier earrings from the thin top dresser drawer that held her jewelry. She was thirty-one years old and still used the same dresser that she had taken from her parents' home when she moved out after college.

A few years ago, after selling enough real estate to buy a small chunk of her own, she had nearly splurged on new furniture to fill the place. The market had been going strong for three straight years. She had a five-digit savings account. She was feeling confident. She picked out each and every piece herself, circling items in different home decorating catalogs, making sure that everything would work together.

But then, for whatever reason, she had not gone through with the purchases. Had she sensed that the market would slow? Did she know her mother's physician would suddenly conclude that she could no longer negotiate living on her own?

Now the savings account was gone, and Katie got by month to month, barely managing to cover her own mortgage, her mother's assisted living, and the taxes on her parents' Forest Hills home, which she was renting out for some extra income in the hopes that she could get more in a sale once the market turned around. She used credit cards as necessary to cover unexpected expenses and then "saved" as she could to pay down the balances. Just when she thought she might be caught up and could begin building a nest egg again, some other cost arose and she'd be back in the red.

In short, Katie was well into adulthood and still playing financial Whack a Mole.

She threaded the hooks of the earrings through each of her lobes, and then draped the necklace across her bare collarbone and clasped it beneath dark brown, wavy hair that fell just past her shoulders. She closed the jewelry drawer of her dresser, opened the next drawer down, and selected a black lace bra and matching thong bikini panty. She spritzed herself with a lavender-scented body spray that rested on top of the dresser, and then turned to the black cocktail dress already laid out on her bed.

Before walking out of the apartment, she pulled a tube of lipstick from her metallic clutch purse and slid a gloss of berry stain across her full lips. She blotted her lips against each other, checking out her pout in a compact mirror for good measure before locking the bolt on her apartment door.

On the elevator ride to the lobby, she began the transition into another persona. The vestiges of Katie Battle—devoted daughter, dogged real estate agent, incessant BlackBerry fiddler—began to melt away. She ran a dark burgundy fingernail across the beads of her necklace, felt the plunging neckline of her silk jersey dress, hugging the curves of her figure like a second skin. She stood up straighter. Taller. Pushed the locks of dark hair away from her heart-shaped face.

By the time she completed her taxi ride down to 44 East Forty-fourth Street, her mental transformation was complete. Good-bye, Katie. Hello, Miranda.

# CHAPTER TWENTY-FIVE

**J**ess didn't know the real name of the man he knew as DJ An-orexotica, but did know that "An-ex," as he also referred to himself, would be performing that night at a bar on the Lower East Side called Gaslight.

Of course Jess could not bring himself to use the word *performing* to describe An-ex's act without using air quotes. And he couldn't use air quotes without grimacing at the fact that he was using air quotes.

Jess was still complaining about accompanying Ellie on her mission when they emerged from the F train at Delancey and Essex. "You've got his picture. You know where to find him, doing that *thing* he calls performing. Why do you need me?"

"Because you actually know the guy, and you're not expected at the Shake Shack for another three hours." Neither Ellie nor Jess could bring themselves to call the strip club where he worked by its actual name, so they enjoyed making up creative placeholders. "Besides, all you were going to do in the interim was watch that marathon of *Real Housewives of Atlanta* you've had clogging up the DVR for the last two weeks."

"Well, if it's clogging up the machine, I should be at home watching important episodes, shouldn't I?"

"Jess, for me, seriously, quit with the bitching."

Most sibling relationships, like all relationships, involve a certain amount of give-and-take. But the balance of giving and taking between Jess and Ellie was sufficiently off kilter—in ways that both of them recognized—that the words "for me," spoken by Ellie to Jess, usually did the trick.

Ellie had her reasons for bringing her brother along on this trip, and that would have to be—and was—enough for Jess.

The bar was a nondescript storefront with a heavy wooden entrance adorned by a burning gaslight. When Jess opened the door, a discordant blend of Spanish-feeling rhythms and cacophonous mechanical noises set to a techno beat spilled out.

"I see that your scumbag of choice tonight has already begun making his noise," Jess said.

A small crowd of about a dozen people was dispersed loosely across an open rectangular dance floor between them and the stage. Three thin young women with an approximate collective height of eighteen feet who were certainly aspiring models lingered just inside the bar's entrance. A couple stood closer to the bar: she in a turtleneck and plaid skirt, he in wide-wale cords and a pea coat, and both undoubtedly from the Upper East Side. Next to them were a couple of fifty-year-olds in black cotton, denim, and leather who looked like they could have hung out with Deborah Harry and the Ramones during their CBGB heydays.

"Eclectic," Ellie said.

"This is the early-bird after-work crowd. You should come back in seven hours."

"So what's the story on this place?"

"Alternative. Underground."

"Like a rave?"

She heard the group of models chuckle next to her. "Oh my God," one whispered.

"Well, guess I won't be the happy little center of that Glamazon triangle tonight," Jess said wistfully. "Raves, for the record, little sister, are so 1994. This place is a riff off of guerrilla gigs."

"I have no idea what you're talking about."

"It's not exactly easy getting a gig at a top bar in New York, so people go guerrilla, taking over venues that are already staged for another event—usually midtown corporate stuff or high-end Upper East Side fund-raiser shit. Anyway, you sneak yourself in. Leak word online to potential crashers who want to witness the scene. Then you go for it and hope for some attention. Gaslight sort of did the reverse a couple years ago, leaking the rumor that this was a place to be crashed for gigs. Show up and play, draw a crowd, see what happens."

"How can a performance be guerrilla if it's basically invited?"

"Well, it's not. Gaslight's really just an open mic bar with an edgier rep. You know something, El, this proves you haven't been coming out enough since you met that Captain Justice of yours. Dog Park's been playing here every couple of weeks for a few months now."

"And this guy?" She studied the light-skinned DJ spinning records from the elevated stage.

"We hate him."

"I mean, does he play here a lot?"

"Must. I think we've seen him here, like, three times already. This music's shit, right?"

She shrugged. "Interesting enough, I guess. A little weird. I can't even tell what I'm listening to."

"That's because he calls it art. He walks around the city with a computer recording street noises, then mixes it into his whole techno world music blend. It's crap."

Ellie took a look around the half-filled bar. "Decent enough turnout for crap."

Jess made a sour face. "These people aren't all here for him. Maybe those preppy douchebags over there. You only get a half hour at Gaslight unless the crowd gets so worked up that whoever's supposed to take your spot decides it's not such a great idea."

"OK, that's a little guerrilla."

"Well, trust me, no one's going to make a scene trying to buy more time for this Beck wannabe. Unless he's come up with some new aural assault to close out with, I'm pretty sure this is his last song."

They waited while Keith mixed and scratched his way to a crescendo, then abruptly halted the music. The crowd clapped politely, and the DJ flashed a peace sign before starting to pack his turntables, laptop, and other gear into a trunk.

Ellie nudged Jess, pushing him toward the stage.

"Oh, my God. Can you at least put me on the department payroll for this?"

She nudged him harder, and he led the way.

The DJ immediately recognized Jess and greeted him with a nervous smile. "Hey, man." He avoided eye contact by continuing to focus on the packing of his equipment. "I didn't realize you guys were playing tonight."

"We're not. I'm just hanging."

"Hi," Ellie said, offering a friendly handshake and an enthusiastic smile. "I'm Jess's sister. Ellie Hatcher."

"Keith Guzman." Keith's gaze shifted between her and her brother. "Sister, huh? Can't say I can see the resemblance."

This wasn't the first time this observation had been made. Long, lanky Jess with his straight dark hair and angular face, the petite but curvy little sister with blond waves and full lips. And the differences went beyond the physical. Jess was flaky like their mom, Ellie stubborn and determined like their father. Jess, light as bubbles. Ellie, rock solid. Jess, who didn't see the purpose of coming here. Ellie, who now had the elusive Keith's last name.

"So, great music. Jess said you work sounds from the street into your mixes?"

"Yeah, it's kind of my thing. An urban update on *musique concrète*."

"What is *musique coquette*?"

"No, *concrète*. Like concrete. Literally translated, it's concrete music. The original idea was that the components of music didn't have to be singing or instruments. It started in Paris in the forties. The Beatles used it a little, but that was back when they had to use tapes. Now that everything's digitized? It's bananas, man. And I specifically use sounds from the streets of New York City. In theory I'm saying something important about the music of everyday life, like what Marcel Duchamp did for found art in the media of the tangible. It's like found music."

Ellie nodded along with interest. "Yeah, I get it."

"Or," Keith said with a laugh, "maybe it's just a good jam."

"And you play your mixes directly from your computer?" Ellie eyed the Apple laptop that still rested on the table between them and Keith.

"Yeah. The recordings are digitized so I can pretty much do whatever I want with them."

"You can't do all of that with just this one little MacBook though, can you? I assume you have a bunch of stuff at home, too."

"Nope, just this," he said, tapping the thin notebook.

"Really, that's all you've got? Just that one laptop?"

"Yep. Maybe when I hit it big, you know."

"So," Jess interrupted, "you got a girlfriend these days or what?"

Ellie jerked toward Jess with a glare. Guzman apparently mistook her shocked expression. "Wow. Um, I've never seen a brother try to hook his sister up. Uh, I don't know. Maybe you and I can—"

"No, dude, maybe you can stop looking at my sister before you find yourself in a cell."

So much for her plan of flirting her way onto Guzman's computer. She removed her shield from her purse and flipped it open for a quick view.

"I need to talk to you about Megan Gunther."


"Yo, bitch. This is some serious bullshit."

"All right, Li'l Keith, you can drop the street act." They stood on the relatively quiet sidewalk outside the club. Guzman had initially tried to resist, but then Ellie pretended to reach for one of the silver hoops in his lip, and he made his way out the door with her. Now polite and charming Keith Guzman had transformed into DJ Anorexotica, and Ellie could see why Jess had called him an annoying poseur. "When was the last time you had contact with Megan Gunther?"

"I've moved on past her. Couldn't you tell when I was getting ready to make a play on you?"

"Sometimes the best way to move on is to hurt someone. Bad."

"Megan's hurt?"

Ellie was starting to wonder whether this guy had a serious case of multiple personality. The An-Ex 'tude had withdrawn, replaced by a softness to his eyes and concern in his voice that seemed genuine.

"Someone posted some pretty heinous stuff about her online."

A wave of relief washed over his face. "But she's okay?"

"You get information when I get information. What do you know about a Web site called Campus Juice?"

"It's a gossip site."

"So you know about it."

"Sure. People post evil shit about each other on there. Pretty funny sometimes."

"You mean college-student-type people. You're not a college student."

"Boy, you have been talking to Megan, haven't you? She had to go talk about that shit to you? Fine, I don't go to college. I didn't take the three-thousand-dollar prep course for my SATs like Megan and her friends and her snotty-ass roommate. I know a hell of a lot more about life than they do. I can tell you that."

Ellie held up her palms. "All I'm asking you about is a Web site, Keith. You're the one who got all defensive about this college thing."

He pressed his lips together and looked down at the sidewalk. "Let's just say it was an issue between me and her. So, whatever. This Web site. Yeah, I know about it, even though I don't go to college."

"Have you posted on it before?"

"Yeah. About six months ago."

Ellie was wondering if this was going to be easier than she thought. "You have?"

"Sure. That's my target demographic. I did a guerrilla gig last year in Tribeca at a test screening of some artsy-fart indie film about homeless kids on the needle. I leaked the buzz on message boards aimed at college students. Pretty sure I covered NYU, Fordham, and Columbia on Campus Juice."

"Have you posted on the site since then?"

He paused. "Nope."

"You sure?"

"Yep. Why are you asking me this shit?"

"Have you been on the Web site at all since then?"

"Nope. The event was a bust anyway. I got about thirty people there to see me take over the theater, but only about twenty people showed up for the movie. And no press. Sort of defeats the purpose of going guerrilla. Again, why are you asking me this shit?"

"Where were you this morning between eight and nine o'clock?" She had an approximate time of death from the ME.

"At home."

"Anyone with you?"

"My mom was home."

"You live with your mom?"

"Surprised Megan didn't tell you that, too. She didn't believe me that I could afford to pay rent. So instead she gets that Heather bitch to move in. Said it would be nice to have a girlfriend around. And what did it get her? Nothing. Heather's not her friend. She goes out with some mystery boyfriend she didn't even tell Megan about. She even tried to come on to me one night, telling me all about how she started having sex real young and all this other crazy shit. What kind of friend is that?"

"Keith, enough about the roommate and what could've been if you lived with Megan. If I take your laptop in, are my analysts going to back up what you say about not going to that Web site in the last six months?"

"You're not taking anything anywhere. That laptop's my fucking livelihood. That's my *art*. Let me talk to Megan and sort this shit out. She knows I wouldn't say a bad word about her to anyone."

He pulled out his phone and hit the button for his contact list. Megan had deleted all evidence of their relationship from her electronic world, but apparently Keith had not. Ellie grabbed the phone from Guzman's hand and hit the end button. He jerked his hand away.

"First you talk shit about taking my computer. Now you're messing with my phone. You better step back."

"Or what, Keith?"

He stared at her.

"Or what? You gonna stab me? Cut me up?"

"Bitch, you're crazy," he muttered. "Just call Megan, a'ight?"

"Megan's dead."

She watched as a look of confusion on his face turned to realization. He began shaking his head. "No, no. No. No." He spoke that same word over and over again until he bent forward and began to cry.

The front door of the bar swung open, nearly smacking Guzman. He stepped out of the way and tried to regain his composure. Ellie recognized the woman who walked out of Gaslight as one of the attractive group of three from inside. Just behind her came Jess, hands in pockets, guilty smile on his face.

Jess was not the only one leaving with more than he'd hoped for. She headed back into the bar for Guzman's laptop.

# CHAPTER TWENTY-SIX

**6:30 P.M.**

Katie Battle made certain to keep her knees together beneath the short hemline of her dress as she shifted her weight from the cab. A uniformed bellman opened one side of a set of double red doors for her.

"Welcome to the Royalton, ma'am."

She bypassed the hotel lobby's suede sofas, leather-covered walls, and steel tables and headed directly for the wood-paneled Bar 44.

It was six thirty, a bit early for New York City happy-hour standards, but the space had already started to fill. She'd learned that this time of day was popular for married men who could fit in an after-work diversion and still make it home in time to claim a late night at the office.

Taking the last remaining seat at the bar, she ordered a Manhattan from a light-haired bartender, who gave her a knowing look. "You want some bar mix to snack on, or will this be a quick visit?"

The comment was obviously a dig. Or maybe not. Perhaps it was all in her imagination.

"I'm fine, thank you."

The bartender nodded politely and made his way to the other end of the counter, where a barrel-chested man tapped a credit card on the sleek brass bar top.

She had taken two ladylike sips of her cherry red cocktail when the man approached.

"Are you Miranda?"

She gave him her warmest and most welcoming smile. "Very nice to meet you."

"Stuart," he said. "Uh, Stuart—"

"That's okay," she said, with a reassuring nod. "You can be anyone you want tonight."

She gave Stuart a quick but subtle once-over. He was probably just past fifty, but he was still in decent shape. A full head of dark hair, but she suspected the assistance of a toupee. Titanium wedding band. Decent suit and tie. A little shy. Clean.

Pretty routine.

Stuart eyed the bartender nervously. "Um, the bar's a little tight. You want to move over—" He gestured toward an empty brown leather sofa toward the front of the bar, not far from the entrance to the hotel lobby. She led the way while Stuart ordered himself a Maker's Mark neat and dropped cash on the counter for the two drinks.

Once he was seated next to her on the couch, Miranda noticed his left thumb fiddling with his wedding band.

"Are you going to be okay?" She placed her hand gently on him, only at his knee, no higher. The last thing she needed was this guy to succumb to a sudden attack of piousness.

Stuart held his highball glass with both hands and stared at the swirling brown liquid.

"Sorry. Last night was my twentieth anniversary."

She reminded herself she was Miranda and forced herself to keep her hand planted exactly where it was. As if she were comfortable.

"Charlotte was in an accident three years ago. Spinal damage." He wiped at his eyes. "God, I'm sorry. It's, well, this isn't the first time or anything. And I suspect she even sort of knows. But, you know, last night—"

"Sure," she said, giving his knee a reaffirming squeeze. "Maybe another night," she offered, confident that he would decline the offer of a rain check, just like the reluctant buyers who argued with her if she suggested that an apartment might still be available down the road.

He shook his head and downed a sip of his bourbon. "No, I'm good. I'll be fine once we're upstairs." He gave her a sad smile. "Is that okay? If we go upstairs?"

"No problem," she said, rising from her place on the sofa. "And, remember, tonight you're anyone you want. You can be Derek Jeter as far as I'm concerned."

He laughed.

"Go ahead. Lie to me."

He looked at her reluctantly but rose from the couch to face her.

"Really," she repeated softly, almost in a whisper, "go ahead. Lie to me."

He placed his hand on her elbow. "I'm Mike. I'm in town for a convention."

"Yeah?"

"And I'm single."

"Well, nice to meet you, Mike. And I'll be anyone you want in return."

"I do have a favor to ask." He continued to hold her elbow. "Is it possible for you to book the room in your name?"

"I don't usually—"

"It's my . . . well, my wife," he said, looking down at his feet. "It's one thing to do this to her under the circumstances. It's another to flaunt it. A charge on the credit card would—"

"Sure, I understand. It's just I carry a balance, and so with interest—"

"I'll make up for it."

He'd obviously made this arrangement before, as had she. It was a common practice, a way for girls to get some extra cash to themselves on the side. She'd never been ratted on yet.

"All right. Mike."

"Mike's gonna go outside for a smoke. I'll meet you by the elevators?"

She nodded and watched him walk outside.

At the registration desk, she asked the clerk for a single room. While the clerk ran her credit card through the system, Miranda dug her cell phone from her purse, pulled up a number in her list of contacts, and hit the dial key.

"It's Miranda. I just wanted you to know I already sent flowers to Mom, so you don't need to worry about it."

The substance of what she said was irrelevant. What mattered was her use of the word *flowers*. Stuart passed the no-freaks-allowed test, and Miranda was fine.

The word *tight* was another story. One utterance of the word *tight* and help would be on its way. Or at least that's how it had been explained to her.

She understood the need for a check-in system, but she'd been doing this now for six months and still didn't see why they had to be so James Bond about it. She supposed it played into the myth that what she was doing was acting. Role-playing. Fantasy. A "hobby," as some of the so-called providers dubbed it. Something other than what it obviously was.

Stuart (or Mike) was already walking toward her when she approached the elevator, the fading smell of cigarette smoke still on him. She pressed the up button. They waited alone.

"They explained to you I only do what's safe?" she asked. Even some of the tamest men would pressure her to avoid condoms.

He nodded, but his embarrassment about the subject showed in his flushed cheeks. "That's . . . well, of course, that's my preference. I'm . . . I'm definitely safe."

When the elevator doors opened, Miranda stepped inside and Stuart followed. Only minutes later, the fantasy had fallen away, and Miranda was back to being Katie Battle.

And that night, Katie was definitely *not* safe.

# PART III

---

**IT WAS ALL ABOUT MAY 27.**

# CHAPTER TWENTY-SEVEN

With more than a decade passed since the move from Wichita to New York, Ellie was still struck by random reminders of how much her life had changed as a result of that geographic switch. She had grown up in a place where arguments about pizza revolved around the choice between Pizza Hut and Domino's. Now a craving for pizza could spark a thirty-minute debate about the relative virtues of the crispy, charred crusts of John's in the West Village compared to the white pies at Lombardi's. And then there were those who swore that real New York pizza could only be found in Brooklyn.

Fortunately, Ellie had been spared any such discussion. When she'd called Max Donovan to say she was finally ready for a break and could use some pizza, they both knew precisely the place she had in mind.

Ellie pushed her way through Otto's narrow revolving door. The name was Italian for the number eight, reflecting the restaurant's location on Eighth Street, just north of Washington Square Park. If Ellie had been told a dozen years earlier that a craving for pizza would lead her to a crowded Mario Batali wine bar just a block from the famous park arches where Harry had dropped off Sally, she never would have believed it.

But now Otto was Max and Ellie's "place." They didn't have a song or an anniversary or cutesy nicknames for each other, but in the rituals of their relationship, they had developed a well-practiced habit of sitting at the Otto bar, drinking wine and nibbling on small plates of antipasti, pizza, and pasta.

"There she is."

The head bartender, Dennis, wore his usual white oxford shirt, blue jeans, and Buddha-like smile. He was already pouring two fingers of Johnnie Walker Black into a lowball glass, which he set before the awaiting empty stool next to Max Donovan.

"I was just telling the DA here that you must be working harder than him these days. Am I ordering for you, or do you want menus?"

"Your choice tonight," Ellie said.

"And how hungry are we?"

"Very."

"Good. We like hungry people here." Dennis topped off Max's glass of red wine and made his way to the other end of the bar.

"To the end of the day," Max said, raising his glass for a clink.

They had been keeping their relationship casual, but she had allowed Max deep enough into her life that he knew how much she hated the natural pause points in a hot case. You jump from lead to lead, from witness to witness, from the morgue to the crime lab, but at some point, you have to rest. Take a breath. Take a break. Take a fresh look later.

Some cops could turn off during those moments. Close out all thoughts of the case and live their lives until it was time to tune back in. Not Ellie. She'd been moving nonstop for nearly twelve hours on an empty stomach and knew she'd be awake the rest of the night from the lingering adrenaline.

"So what's next on that Web site case of yours?" Max also knew her well enough to anticipate she'd need to talk about the case to transition back into any kind of normal conversation. "Hopefully you'll get something off the boyfriend's laptop."

Ellie had called Max from Gaslight to make sure she had probable cause to seize Guzman's computer. He agreed that she could act without a warrant to prevent Guzman from cleaning out the hard drive. Unfortunately, he also agreed it was premature to haul Guzman in for questioning.

"I dropped the laptop off with the analyst. I swear, that kid looked like he was fifteen years old. And he called me ma'am. But, fuck it, I told him he could call me Grandma as long as he had something for me tomorrow afternoon."

A skinny Italian kid with an apron and ponytail set a collection of dishes in front of them, and Dennis interrupted to announce the contents of their meal. It involved meats and cheeses she couldn't even pronounce, but to her it all boiled down to pizza and pasta and was therefore perfect.

She plunged her fork into a plate of spaghetti carbonara without waiting for Max. "And how was *your* day today?"

"Fine. I had that ridiculous charade this morning with Bandon, of course. Then after you left for Long Island, I spent the rest of the afternoon on a murder plea with Judge Walker. It was like pulling teeth."

"The defendant wussed out?" Exchanging twenty-five years to get out from under a true life-sentence sounded like a good deal until the defendant actually had to seal his own fate in open court.

"No, he got hungry and apparently pretty sick of the prison slop he'll be eating for the next quarter century. He wouldn't plead guilty unless the judge got him some McGriddle cakes and gorditas."

"You're kidding me."

"He wouldn't plead unless we got him his food. And not just any fast food. Two McGriddle cakes and two Taco Bell Gordita Supremes, one chicken and one beef."

"I'm not falling for this." Max had a way of exaggerating or even fabricating entire stories, anything to make her laugh.

He held up his right hand in a mock oath. "I swear to God. After an hour trying to explain why the guy shouldn't waive important constitutional rights in exchange for fast food, Judge Walker finally broke down. Apparently, though, it violates personnel rules for the guards to give anything unauthorized to the prisoners. So then Walker sent his bailiff out on a food run, but he came back without the Mickey D's. I guess McGriddle cakes are a breakfast menu item and therefore unavailable after eleven a.m. I finally schmoozed up a manager and got it done."

Of course he had. Max could talk the archbishop into converting. "Now *that's* power."

"No, real power in the culinary world would involve persuading you to leave me some of that spaghetti."

She shook her head quickly and took another bite, but pushed what remained on the plate in his direction. Just as she felt the tension of the day leave her body, her phone vibrated at her waist. It was Rogan.

"Yeah," she said, cupping her free hand around the mouthpiece to block out the Clash song playing overhead.

"You're with your boy, aren't you?"

"Maybe."

"Well, say good-bye. We've got another body."

# CHAPTER TWENTY-EIGHT

Police presence at the Royalton Hotel was glaring. The streets of midtown had otherwise quieted after the evening commute bustle, leaving the relatively few pedestrians free to gawk at the growing collection of NYPD officers and marked vehicles camped out on Forty-fourth Street.

Ellie's cabdriver, glimpsing the chaos ahead, had refused to turn off Madison Avenue out of fear that he'd be stuck for twenty minutes in a tangle of double-parked city cars and rubber-necking tourists on the cross street. She tried to persuade him with the badge, but finally paid the fare with no tip and hoofed her way east to the hotel.

The uni posted near the elevators paid more attention to the lobby decor than the people walking past him. She rode up to the fifth floor and found Rogan in the hallway, his finger in the face of a young officer in uniform.

"I don't care if you need to call your precinct commander. Someone needs to clear out every rubbernecking uni who's got no business in this hotel."

The officer gave Rogan the appropriate "Yes, sir," but she caught the eye-roll when he turned toward the elevator.

"Who called the cavalry?" she asked.

"Bunch of numbskulled unis want to get a glimpse of how the other half lives. Their usual callout to a hotel's gonna be at some rub-and-tug rathole by the Lincoln Tunnel."

"What are we doing in midtown, Rogan?" He'd given her an address and a room number on the phone, but no details.

"I brought Sydney here for a drink."

"Nice."

"It was till I saw hotel security huddled in the lobby like they'd just gotten a call from bin Laden himself. Sydney made me check what was going on."

"Which was what?"

"Take a look for yourself."

He used a plastic card key to open Room 509. A uniformed officer shook his head silently as he pressed past them on his way out. The gesture didn't begin to convey the disgust Ellie felt when they walked into the hotel room.

The girl had been left hog-tied on her side, her pale skin gray against the bright white sheets as livor mortis set in. Black nylon rope bound her wrists and feet together at the small of her back. Smears of blood on the sheets and on her body suggested the girl had been cut as well.

On the pillowcase next to the woman's head were blots of mascara, face powder, rouge, and lipstick the color of blackberries. Like a makeup mask, the smudged colors created the outline of a face with wide, pained eyes and a contorted mouth. It was a mask of terror.

"Jesus," Ellie said.

"A housekeeper came in for evening turndown service at eight. There was a Do Not Disturb sign on the door when she circled the floor an hour earlier. She probably just missed the guy. She got one look at this and walked right on out and radioed security. I was up here before the first responders."

Two crime scene unit officers scoured for physical evidence, one in the bathroom, one kneeling at the edge of the bed. The one near the bed looked up in their direction.

"The meat truck's here. They were waiting for you before moving the body. We all set?"

Rogan shook his head.

"You know I back you up on everything, Rogan, but my last forty-eight hours have been crap. Do you really need me here to wait for Midtown South DTs to show up?"

"This is our case."

"I don't understand."

"I'll tell you in a sec, but I want your first impressions. I found a business card in her purse. Her name's Katie Battle. She was a real estate broker for Corcoran. She put the four-hundred-dollar room on her credit card."

Ellie was about to press him for an explanation, but could see there was no point. "I don't know. My first guess would be rough sex gone bad. Bondage, pretty typical. A little too much pressure on the neck, it happens. But cutting? Pretty hard-core for the luxury hotel crowd."

She moved closer to the body. "You mind?" The CSU officer kneeling on the floor rose and stepped aside. Ellie took his place, crouching to get a better look. She suppressed a gag reflex. "This woman was tortured."

Rogan stood behind her, and she pointed as she spoke. "Her nipples have been slashed on both sides. And look here, beneath the blood, she's got at least three cigarette burns on her chest."

"Holy shit. Look at her hands."

Ellie rose so she could see the other side of the woman's body where her hands and feet were bound. Several of the girl's fingers were bent at various angles.

"I counted at least six broken fingers here," Rogan said.

"Broken bones. The bondage. Burning. Cutting. This wasn't just a little light S&M getting out of control. She was tortured to death."

"Bingo."

"So now tell me: Why are we here?"

"Because that business card wasn't the only thing I found in the vic's purse. I checked out her BlackBerry. You remember those call logs I had from the Megan Gunther callout?"

"Sure."

"Well, yesterday afternoon, Katie Battle called one of the numbers on that list."

# CHAPTER
# TWENTY-NINE

"Hey, Rain Man. Get around this idiot, will you?"

Rogan swerved his BMW around a minivan with Vermont plates meandering in the right lane.

"How long are you going to keep up this Rain Man shit?"

Ellie looked at her watch. "It's been about thirty minutes. I'm thinking about sixteen more years and I'll be done."

"Really, it's no big deal."

"Yeah, okay. Whatever. 'I'm an excellent driver. Fifteen minutes to Judge Wapner. 82-82-82. 246 total.'"

"Look who's the Rain Man."

"I can't believe, out of all the numbers on Megan Gunther's call list, you recognized a match to Battle's BlackBerry."

"This is coming from the woman who still remembers the date of birth of the first perp she arrested?"

"And I'm pretty sure you called me a freak when I made the mistake of telling you about it."

"You know how long I stared at those call logs trying to figure out who we needed to talk to first? I remembered a call that went from Megan's landline to some number in Connecticut. But it was a onetime call, and four months ago at that, so we didn't get to it yet.

But I looked at the lists long enough to recognize those same digits when I saw them again."

The number belonged to a cell phone owned by a woman named Stacy Schecter. Schecter had a Connecticut area code, but according to AT&T, the bills went to an apartment on the Lower East Side.

"A twenty-year-old-college student and a thirty-one-year-old real estate agent, both making phone calls to the same woman." Rogan pulled the car to a stop in front of a fire hydrant on Avenue B and 4th Street. "So who's Stacy Schecter going to turn out to be?"

Ellie pictured the scene back at the Royalton, thought about the room's four-hundred-dollar price tag, and imagined a possible scenario.

"I've got a guess, but there's only one way to find out."

The brick building stood out from its other brick neighbors, thanks to layers of bright white paint interrupted by red, yellow, and blue accents on what were probably architecturally significant details on the building's exterior. The overall effect was Miami Beach meets Sesame Street.

As they crossed the street, they spotted a man balancing an insulated red pack the size of a pizza box against his hip as he pressed the buzzer next to the building's gated entrance. Rogan stepped up his pace to catch the gate before it closed. The deliveryman was unfazed by the sight of the two of them entering behind him. They followed him up the stairs, breaking off at the second floor.

Ellie recognized the Kate Bush song blasting inside Apartment 2B as a tune she and Jess had enjoyed in high school. She rapped her fist against the door. The music continued, and she tried again, this time harder. "Police. Open up."

The volume decreased drastically, and Ellie pounded on the door again.

A matter-of-fact voice finally spoke to them from the other side of the door. "You don't look like cops."

Ellie held her badge up in front of the peephole, and then listened as three separate locks untumbled. A pair of black-lined eyes peered out to them over a safety chain. "Sorry. He usually waits till ten o'clock before bitching about the noise."

"Who?"

"The misanthrope in 2C. I assume he's the one who called you. It's sort of his thing."

"Are you Stacy Schecter?"

"Yeah, that's me."

"We're not here about the music. Can you open up?"

The girl shut the door before reopening it, this time wide enough for them to enter. The apartment was on the large side for a studio, or perhaps it just seemed large because of its sparseness. The only seating to be had was on a twin mattress that rested in the corner beside a milk crate doubling as a nightstand. The rest of the apartment was empty except for a plastic folding table and two easels. The easels held stretched canvases exploding with abstract smears of primary colors. On the table were a sprawl of painting supplies and an iPod plugged into miniature speakers from which the offending music had blasted.

Stacy Schecter wore a *Flashdance*-style black sweatshirt and skinny jeans, both smudged with paint, as were her bare feet. Her straight black hair hung to her shoulders in a long shag cut, and dark black eyeliner rimmed her big brown eyes. Ellie placed the woman in her mid-twenties.

"I'd offer you a seat, but I'm pretty much the only one allowed in my bed."

"Not a problem," Ellie said. "You're alone here?"

Stacy pretended to glance around the room. "To my knowledge."

"Mind if I take a look around to be sure?"

"Um, no, I guess not."

Ellie opened a sliding door to reveal a cramped closet, while Rogan opened and closed the only other door in the apartment. "Bathroom's clear," he said.

"So this is definitely not about the noise," Stacy said.

"You know a woman named Katie Battle?" Ellie asked. "She's a real estate broker?"

Stacy shook her head. "Not exactly in any position to buy real estate, in case you can't tell."

"How about Megan Gunther? She's a sophomore at NYU. Lives near Union Square Park."

Stacy shook her head again. "I'm afraid I can't help you."

"We think you can."

Silence filled the room until Stacy broke out into a surprisingly disarming smile. "You two clearly know something I don't. And I was kind of in the zone here, so if we could just cut through the usual whatever-it-is-you-guys-do-to-break-people-down, I'd be happy to help you out."

"You got a cell phone call yesterday from a woman named Katie Battle, and we're trying to figure out why."

"No clue. I told you, I've never heard of her."

"You mind if we take a look at your phone, then? If this is some kind of mistake on the part of the phone company, we can take it up with them."

"Um, yeah, I guess I do kind of mind."

"So maybe you've heard of her after all."

"No, but . . . how about I check out my phone and see what you're talking about?"

Ellie looked to Rogan, and he nodded. They watched as Stacy removed a flip phone from a bright blue Pan Am vinyl travel bag on the bed.

"The call came in at 3:15 p.m.," Rogan said.

"Yeah, I see it now. It was a hang-up. I figured at the time it was a wrong number."

Stacy's failure to answer the call didn't explain why Katie Battle had called Stacy's number in the first place, nor why Megan Gunther had called her four months ago.

"What about Megan Gunther?" Ellie asked. "She called you in May from her apartment."

"Last summer? I have no clue how I'd remember that. And I told you, I don't know anyone by that name."

"Why don't you let me take a look at the screen with yesterday's incoming call on it? That would help us sort through this whole thing."

"My phone's private."

Ellie needed Stacy to be the one to spell it out. If Ellie's instincts were wrong and she voiced them aloud, she'd lose all leverage.

"See, that's what's bugging me, Stacy. You let us check out your apartment—your bathroom, your closet—no problem. But one little glance at your cell phone, and now you're all about your privacy. We can straighten this out just by looking at your screen there. We see the digits of Katie Battle's phone number, and we'll know she wasn't listed in your directory. But I have a feeling we're not going to see just her number. We're going to see her name, and then we'll know you're lying to us about not knowing her. And that'll be that."

Ellie saw Stacy's fingers twitch against her phone.

"And don't even think about trying to delete anything right now, Stacy, or we'll pry it out of your hands if we have to, and things will get extremely unpleasant for everyone."

The girl froze, and Ellie spotted a look of panic cross her face before the warm smile returned.

"I really don't understand what's going on."

"That's correct, and you don't have any right to. We came here thinking you could help us out, and you assured us you would. But I've got to tell you that, right now, Stacy? You're about ten seconds away from being taken into custody as part of a homicide investigation."

"A homicide?" Her eyes widened beneath the makeup.

"Turns out your phone number is the single link between two women who were murdered today."

"Murdered?"

"The call to your phone yesterday? The woman who dialed your number was killed tonight."

"Miranda? Miranda's dead?" And with that, Stacy Schecter's black eyeliner began to stream like the cascades of paint on her canvases.

# CHAPTER THIRTY

Stacy Schecter was a different woman without the makeup. The rock-and-roll eyeliner and pale face powder were gone, rubbed away by tears and half a box of tissues. The dry, droll attitude had dissolved as well. She looked at Ellie across the table with the puffy, red-rimmed eyes of a scared and lonely child.

"I don't know why I can't keep it together," she said, wiping her face with the back of her hand. "I hardly knew the girl."

"You knew her at some level. You had her number in your cell phone."

Because her apartment had scarcely enough room for one person to sit, Stacy had agreed to come in to the precinct to be interviewed. It had been half an hour already, and only now had she calmed down sufficiently to get her words out.

"I didn't even know her real name. To me, she was Miranda. No last name, but that would have been fake also."

"How did you know her?" Ellie asked.

"We met last year at a friend's party. We didn't stay in touch or anything. We just hit it off, and so I put her number in my phone."

J. J. stood with his arms crossed behind Stacy in the back corner of the interrogation room. He rolled his eyes when Ellie glanced at him.

"So why was she calling you yesterday?"

"I told you. It was a hang-up. I figured if she wanted to talk to me she'd call back. People pull up the wrong number on their cells all the time."

"We're getting the records from the cell phone company, Stacy. They're going to show any other calls between you and Katie, or Miranda. And I have a feeling we're going to find a lot more calls than we'd expect to find between two women who met at a party a year ago but didn't stay in touch."

Stacy pressed her eyes closed. She was thinking. Hard. She was smart enough to recognize the problem. She needed one more press.

"What are you hiding, Stacy? You obviously cared about this woman."

She shook her head in frustration. "I wish I didn't. Jesus, how did I get myself into this?"

"Into what? Were you and Katie involved in drugs?" It was a classic interrogation technique. Offer the suspect one explanation—a wrong one—so the human need to correct an error takes over. "We can work something out. Finding the person who did this to her is a lot more important than whatever you're holding back."

"We don't do drugs."

"So what was it?"

She closed her eyes again. Still thinking.

"I'm not testifying."

"Whoa, where did that come from, Stacy? We're just trying to figure out why your telephone number was the common link between two women who were murdered today."

"I told you, I don't know anything about that other number. Only Miranda's."

"Fine. We'll talk about the other one later. But right now you need to tell us what you know about Katie Battle."

"You ask me to sign anything, or try to use my name, and I'll deny it all. I'll be out of here, and then I'll bail."

Ellie looked at Rogan, who gave her a look that said the decision was hers. She nodded her agreement.

"I met Miranda last year through a date. Set up by an escort service. We were on, you know, the same date. For the same client. We worked together another couple of times. Since then, we've swapped a few dates. We sort of have the same look." She looked down at her tattered, paint-smeared sweatshirt. "Or at least we have the same look when we're working."

Ellie could see a superficial resemblance. Dark hair. Pale skin. Intense eyes.

"And by working, you mean sex for money."

"You got it," she said. The attitude was on its way back. "You're a cop. I assume you know what working at an escort service means. I was with the service for about six months last year, but now I'm strictly independent. I can find dates on my own, and I get to keep the money for myself."

"It's dangerous working on your own." Before getting her detective shield, Ellie had worked more than her fair share of prostitution decoy operations.

"I'm alive. Miranda isn't. I guess I keep myself safe."

*For now*, Ellie wanted to say. But arguing with Stacy about her idiotic decisions was not the priority.

"Even after I left the service, Miranda and I would occasionally swap dates with each other. It was a no-no for her because of her agreement with the service. I've got an arrangement going with another couple of girls there, too, so that's why I don't want my name getting back to them."

"Who's the *them*?"

"The service."

"And where do we get in touch with them?"

She paused, but didn't bother arguing. "They call themselves Prestige Parties."

"And how often did you and Miranda swap dates?"

She shook her head. "Not a lot. Maybe three or four times since I went out on my own a year ago. When I saw her number on my cell yesterday, I assumed that's why she was calling. But then she hung up, and I guess I wasn't excited enough about working to call her back." Her bottom lip began to quiver. "That could be why she was calling, you know. About her date tonight. She could have been calling to see if I could . . . I could have been the one tonight."

"But you weren't. So stop feeling guilty, and stop feeling sorry for yourself. You and Katie knew what you were doing—"

"So she deserved it? Is that what you're saying?"

"Of course not. No one deserves what she went through. But you were both in this. And to some extent, you were in it together. She wouldn't wish this upon you, just like you aren't happy it happened to her instead of you. Deal with it. You can help us here."

"I'm trying."

"Do you have any idea who her client might have been tonight?"

"No. She didn't have a lot of regulars. She relied on the service to set things up."

"And given how Prestige works, if they tell us they don't know the name of a client, should we be willing to believe that?"

"Actually, yeah, that's believable. They were pretty shitty, you know? They talked a big game about all they were doing for us, but they were no better than any street pimp selling you to whoever happened to call in. Supposedly they took credit cards so you'd have some leverage over these guys, but it seemed like half the jobs I went on, they told me it was a cash deal."

"All right, we'll press them to try to find out who Katie was with tonight. Let's talk about the other telephone number. According to the phone records, an NYU student named Megan Gunther called you in May."

"I don't know anyone named Megan."

"You didn't think you knew anyone named Katie Battle either."

J. J. stepped forward and placed a photograph of Megan Gunther on the table in front of Stacy. She winced at the sight of the dead woman on the metal gurney.

"Take a good look," Ellie urged. "People's appearance can change after they . . . pass."

They both watched carefully as Stacy took in the image for a full five seconds before finally shaking her head. "No, I'm sure. I've never seen that girl before."

Ellie eyed her skeptically, evoking a frustrated chuckle from her witness. "Look, I just got done confessing to whoring myself out. Why would I lie to you about knowing this girl? Maybe it really was a wrong number. Go ahead. Pull up all the phone records you want. You'll find a few calls between me and Miranda, or Katie, or whatever. But this girl? I swear, you're not going to find anything."

Ellie was startled by the buzz of her cell phone at her waist. She checked the screen. It was a text message from Jess. "Just saw U on TV outside Royalton. Thought Capt. America splurged till they said dead realtor. Sorry you're working. But can I have the bed 2nite?"

"Damn it. J. J., they've got Katie on the news already. It's out there. We have to tell the family."

# CHAPTER THIRTY-ONE

Ellie hated nursing homes. They looked like 1972 and smelled like Pine-Sol, bad milk, and lima beans.

Her father's mother had lived in a nursing home in Wichita, but not for long. She'd made it on her own, even after burying her only son, until she was ninety-three years old. Finally, when she couldn't manage getting in and out of the tub by herself, she'd known better than to ask her daughter-in-law for help. Ellie's mother was more a care-receiving type than a caregiver. So Gram had checked herself in to Shady Pines. Six months later, she was gone.

Ellie would have preferred to stick Rogan with notifying the next of kin, but her partner knew Megan Gunther's phone records backward and forward. While she'd been interviewing Courtney Chang and grilling DJ Anorexotica, he'd been studying the details. He knew the dates, the patterns, the numbers. He needed to be the one to work with Stacy. She might not realize she knew Megan Gunther, but she did. Under some other name. Using some other phone number. And that call in May from Gunther's apartment phone to Stacy's cell was the key. She just had to remember.

Taking in her surroundings at Glen Forrest Communities, Ellie could see the attempts that had been made. Individual units with

closed doors lined the hallways, a step up from the limited privacy
her grandmother had found behind cotton curtains. And bowls of
potpourri in the lobby masked the usual smell. But the place still
gave her the heebie-jeebies.

Ellie didn't like to think about what would happen to her when
she was old. No way would she ever be in a place like this. But no
way would she ever do what her father did. There had to be other
choices.

Behind a gray metal desk in the lobby sat a heavyset woman,
her eyeglasses dangling from a rainbow striped nylon cord. A copy
of *People* rested on her ample bosom. Ellie watched the woman's
eyes shut and then snap open as she approached sleep only to have
it snatched from her. After three separate cycles, Ellie held up her
shield and announced her presence.

"I need to see a resident named Phyllis Battle."

"Sorry about that," the woman said, suppressing a yawn. "Grave-
yard shift gets rough."

"Been there."

"Room 127, Officer, but it's very late. I'm sure Mrs. Battle would
prefer that you return in the morning."

"I need to speak with her now."

"Is there a problem? Because, well, at least around here, Mrs.
Battle has earned that last name of hers, if you know what I mean.
You're better off not waking her."

"I'm afraid I have some hard news for Mrs. Battle. It's about her
daughter."

"Katie? She's not in trouble, is she?"

"You know the daughter?"

"I wouldn't call it knowing her. She's good about seeing her
mother. Not all of them are. She appreciates that I get on better
with Mrs. Battle than some of the other workers here, so she makes
a point of making sure I can reach her. She's always messing with
her gadgets, you know, checking her messages and such."

"And Katie pays for her mother's care here?"

"I wouldn't be knowing that for sure. You'd have to check bill‑ing, but yes, my guess is Katie takes care of the bulk of it. She's Mrs. Battle's only visitor. And very regular lately. Her mother had a stroke a few months ago. She and I were watching the television together, and they announced that Sydney Pollack had died. Mrs. Battle was saying that *The Way We Were* was her favorite movie, and then all of a sudden she couldn't talk anymore. It's funny how those kinds of things get filed away in the brain together."

Ellie's mind worked the same way, but her random connections tended to be linked to her cases. She remembered that same rainy day. She and Rogan overheard the news when they ran into a corner deli for some hot coffee. It was the same day they'd found Robert Mancini dead inside Sam Sparks's apartment. Sydney Pollack and Sam Sparks were now forever coupled in her mental library. She hated the fact that she was thinking about the Mancini case. Now. Here. When she had Katie Battle and Megan Gunther to worry about.

"So how did Katie handle the stroke?"

"I think it was the first real scare Katie had about her mother. She dropped everything and came here right away. Even managed to beat the ambulance and rode to the hospital. Since then, she's been real regular with her visits."

"And what are your thoughts about how Katie pays for that care?"

"She's a very successful real estate agent. Busy, busy, busy. Mrs. Battle is so proud. She drives the other ladies crazy, going on and on about Katie."

"And that's her only source of income?"

"What are you getting at, Officer? Has Katie done something wrong?"

"No," Ellie said, shaking her head. "But like I said, I have some bad news."

"Not about Katie."

"It's bad news, ma'am. I need to speak with her."

"Everything's okay though, right?"

"If you could point me to her room."

"I'd better go with you. This will—well, this could kill her, quite frankly."

As the woman rose from her seat, Ellie caught her wiping a tear away from her cheek. Maybe Ellie was missing the point of places like Shady Pines and Glenn Forrest. Katie Battle had not been the only person to care about her mother.


Stacy Schecter stared at the pages and pages of phone records that the good-looking black detective had spread in a layer across the laminate tabletop. She'd initially been skeptical of this enterprise. She did not want to think she was the common link.

But a lot had happened since the blond detective suddenly ran off. Now her partner had more than just Miranda's cell phone and the records of whatever phone number they were so curious about. Now they had *her* phone records, too. Going way back.

And as she focused on the section of the itemized list of phone calls from May 27 of last spring, the detectives' theory was hard to deny. And by the look on this detective's face, he wanted her to make the connections faster than her thoughts were moving right now.

Stacy could feel a chain forming in her brain, but it was as if she didn't really want the sections to come together. She didn't want to believe that the choices she'd made were going to put her in the middle of whatever this was turning out to be.

*Her choices*. As if she'd had many.

Whether out of decisions of her own making, or simply random fate, she was actually here, now, in a police interrogation room, staring at these records and putting together the pieces.

It was all about May 27.

That was the day that someone had called Stacy's cell phone from a landline at an apartment on Fourteenth Street. It was the phone number that Stacy hadn't recognized.

But now that she was reviewing the records of her own cell phone for that day, she saw the significance of the date. On May 27, two hours before she had received a call from that mysterious number, she had also received a call from the woman she'd known as Miranda. Now both of the women who had called her were dead.

Obviously there was a connection, but she just couldn't remember. Four months was a long time.

"Look at the other numbers on the list," the detective urged. "Who else were you in touch with that day? It might help jog your memory."

"This is just a bunch of numbers to me. I don't *know* my friends' numbers. I just pull up their names in my cell phone." She hated the sound of stress in her voice. She hated stress.

"That's fine, then. That's *good*, in fact. If you've got all those numbers stored away in your phone, we just have to find them. We'll work through your entire directory until we match these numbers up. You start from the top of your directory, read off the number, and I'll check these logs for a match."

And with that they started a methodic pattern of cooperation— her reading off the numbers stored in her phone, the detective repeatedly responding with a series of *nopes*, occasionally encouraging her with a "Keep going" or a "We'll find it." Twice they'd matched numbers in her phone to entries on her phone log, but one was to the deli down the block and the other was to her sister in Seattle—nothing to help her remember the specifics of that day, let alone how Miranda fit into them.

After what must have been eighty numbers, the pattern finally changed. She rattled off ten digits, but didn't hear the expected "Nope." Instead there was a pause.

"Got it. There's a match. That's the first number you dialed after Katie Battle called you. It's only a minute long. Ninety minutes later, you got a call from Megan Gunther's apartment."

"It's a number for this girl I know. Tanya something. I only know her first name. Wait, I'm starting to remember now. Miranda— God, I mean, *Katie*—she called me a few months ago. It must have been that day. Her mom was in the hospital, and she needed me to cover a date for her that night. I couldn't do it, but she was freaking out about her mom, saying she didn't know what she was going to do. So I said I'd find someone for her. And then I called Tanya. I'd met her just the previous week; some guy found us both on Craig's List."

She was hoping she wouldn't have to explain the concept of a threesome to the detective, but he waved her on when she paused.

"Anyway, she was the first one I thought of under the circumstances. She called me back later. Maybe that's the call you're talking about."

"Tanya's got a long-distance area code. Four-one-oh."

"It's her cell from wherever she came from, just like mine's from Connecticut. She lives in the city now."

"Wait a second. Wait, wait, wait. This area code. Four-one-oh. It's from Baltimore."

"If you say so."

But she could tell the detective was worked up over something now. He opened a manila folder on top of the layer of records covering the table and started flipping through pages frantically until he finally plunked his index finger down on the center of a document. "Here it is. Here's that same number. An incoming call to Megan Gunther's cell phone at the beginning of May. There's a connection here, Stacy. Between you and Katie Battle. Between you and Tanya. Now we've got Tanya calling Megan's cell phone almost five months ago. And Megan's landline calling you on May 27. There's a connection."

Of course there was. But if this detective couldn't figure it out, Stacy had no clue how she could help.

# CHAPTER THIRTY-TWO

Ellie returned to the detective squad just as Rogan was resting the handset of his phone in its cradle.

"That was quick," he said.

"Didn't feel like it when I was talking to the mom, but I hauled ass on the LIE." The call she'd made to her own mother from the car had made the drive feel even longer. "Where's Stacy?"

He tilted his head toward the interview room. "We've got something." As they made their way to the interrogation room, Rogan walked Ellie through the tangled web of connections he and Stacy had pieced together from the phone records. "We think the call from Megan Gunther's apartment to Stacy was a return call from a girl Stacy only knows as Tanya."

"Who the hell's Tanya?"

"Hold your horses. I'm about to tell you. At the end of May, Katie Battle called Stacy to cover a date for her. Stacy said no can do, but called her friend Tanya to see if she could do it. An hour later, Stacy got a call from Megan Gunther's landline. Her best recollection is that it was Tanya getting back to her. Now, here's the kicker: about three weeks before all of that went down, we've also got Tanya calling Megan Gunther's cell."

"So we know Tanya's connected to Megan. She's calling her and using her landline. So, again, who the hell's Tanya?"

"I did a reverse search on her Baltimore cell phone number. Comes back to someone named Tanya Abbott. I just hung up from Baltimore PD. She's thirty years old. Only prior was a misdemeanor solicitation pop ten years ago. Cited and released. Went through a diversion program and got her case thrown out."

"How in the world could Megan know this Tanya person?"

"Maybe Megan had a side of her no one knew. If she was turning tricks, she might've piled on the makeup."

They found Stacy still in her seat, still staring at the phone records. Rogan placed Megan Gunther's photograph on the table in front of her.

"She might have changed her appearance. Makeup. Hair color. Even wigs. Take another look."

Stacy let out a heavy sigh as she pondered the photograph. "I've never laid eyes on this girl."

"What about Heather Bradley?" Ellie asked. "She's this girl's roommate. Also at NYU."

Stacy looked disheartened as she shook her head once again.

"Her picture. We need Heather's picture." Ellie darted from the interview room and bee-lined to her computer, where she pulled up the New York Department of Motor Vehicles database. Ninety-seven Heather Bradleys. She narrowed the field to college-age women, but still came up with twenty-one hits, with no guarantees that any of them was *her* Heather Bradley.

She looked up the phone number for St. Vincent's Hospital, and dialed it on her cell as she made her way back to the interview room.

"I'm going to have someone at the hospital snap a photo and send it over."

Rogan and Stacy both listened as she navigated her way through the various connections at the hospital until she finally reached a desk nurse on Heather's floor and explained what she needed.

Ellie felt the pace of her heartbeat quicken as the seconds and then minutes passed while she was on hold. The Web site. Campus Juice. The harassing messages. They had immediately assumed that Megan Gunther was the intended target. She, after all, had been the one who died. And once they focused on Megan, their attention narrowed in on the Internet threats like a pinpoint laser.

But Megan Gunther wasn't the only person who lived in that apartment. There was her roommate. There was Heather Bradley— the roommate who said she hadn't had a date since transferring to NYU, but who, according to Keith Guzman, spent all her time with some "mystery boyfriend" she never told Megan about. And she had dark hair, pale skin, and almond eyes. Just like Stacy Schecter and Katie Battle.

"I'm sorry, Detective, but that patient checked out this afternoon."

"How is that possible?"

"You're the ones with handcuffs, not us. I left you on hold for so long because I was asking around. Apparently there was an issue with the insurance information she gave us. Someone went down the hall to inquire about it, and the next thing we knew, she was gone."

As the nurse spoke, Ellie heard a tap on the interrogation room door. She cracked it open to see one of the civilian aides extending a document in her direction. "This was marked urgent for Rogan."

Ellie took the pages from the aide and flipped past a cover sheet from the Baltimore Police Department to find a grainy enlargement of a Maryland driver's license. The name on the license was Tanya Jane Abbott, but Ellie recognized the woman in the photograph. Dark hair. Pale skin. Almond eyes. Ellie had seen this woman in the hospital just that morning. Tanya Abbott was Megan Gunther's roommate, Heather Bradley.

# CHAPTER THIRTY-THREE

**1:45 A.M.**

Ellie knew the moment that she stepped from the elevator into the hallway of the fourth floor that they were too late. It felt like a week, but it had been only fifteen hours since she'd emerged from this same elevator earlier that morning to see the body of Megan Gunther being wheeled from the apartment. Now the door of that apartment was covered with two overlapping X's of yellow crime tape, except for the one edge of a single ribbon that had fallen to the carpet below.

Ellie kicked the loose end of tape with the pointed toe of her boot. "She beat us here."

Rogan slipped the key they'd retrieved from the superintendent into the lock. "We don't know that," he said, even as his tone suggested otherwise.

They both headed straight to Heather's bedroom, the room to which they'd given so little attention earlier that morning. Ellie opened the top drawer of the dresser to find an empty hole in the otherwise overstuffed collection of underwear. From there, she pulled open the closet. The hangers were spaced evenly enough, but the tidy stacks of sweaters on the shelf overhead were separated by a gap just large enough to fit a missing pile.

Ellie slammed the closet door. "She grabbed some clothes in a hurry, and she split. And we were right about the sequence of the calls. Check your cell."

He gave his phone a quick glance. "No signal."

Back at the precinct, they had fit together the final pieces of the story that the phone records had been trying to tell. Nearly five months ago, Tanya Abbott, posing as Heather Bradley, had called Megan Gunther after seeing the ad for a roommate on Craig's List. Less than a month later, Katie Battle called Stacy Schecter to cover a date for her. Stacy in turn called Tanya, who was now living her life as Heather. The call was only a minute long, so Stacy left a short message. But just as Rogan wasn't able to get a signal in this build-ing now, Tanya couldn't use her cell to return Stacy's call from the apartment. She'd used the landline instead.

Ellie began searching the small desk against the window while Rogan opened the top drawer of the nightstand, searching for some sign of who Tanya Abbott was and where she might be.

"Jesus," Rogan said, flipping open a dog-eared copy of John Hart Ely's *Democracy and Distrust*. "Why the hell would a grown woman make up a false identity just to go to college and write political science papers?"

"She got popped ten years ago for hooking. You're tricking already at twenty years old, the idea of being a garden-variety undergrad might sound pretty appealing."

"Getting into NYU with a fake application's got to take some serious preparation. And now just like that, she bailed because the hospital couldn't find a record of her insurance? You'd think a real grifter would try to lie her way through it."

"Guess she figured that once the hospital started asking questions, her whole story would unravel."

"So? Worst thing that could happen are some fraud charges."

"J. J., we need to look at this woman for a lot more than fraud." Ellie closed the final drawer of the desk and moved on to a stack of textbooks propped against the desk on the floor, flipping each one open in case Tanya had stashed any papers inside the books. "Right now she's our best suspect for Megan's murder. We got distracted by Campus Juice. If Megan found out about Tanya's secret—if she saw something, or overheard a conversation she wasn't supposed to hear—"

"But Heather—Jesus, what are we calling these people?"

"Real names. Heather Bradley doesn't exist—or if she does, she's not the woman we care about. We're talking about Tanya Abbott."

"Well, Tanya got cut up pretty good."

"But she didn't die, did she? Passing herself off as another victim is a pretty good way of throwing off suspicion. And it worked. We just assumed the roommate was collateral damage."

"So she kills Megan and then has enough stones to stab herself multiple times? That's hard-core."

"Or she had help. Megan's ex-boyfriend said fake Heather was always running off to meet some mystery man."

"Could have been a lot of different men if she was turning tricks."

"Or she could also have a boyfriend who was in on the con and helped get rid of the meddling roommate when the time came."

"If she had someone helping her, they might also be good for Katie Battle's murder tonight at the Royalton. It's not like a woman to inflict that kind of violence alone."

Ellie reached the final book in the stack, unmarked and cloth-bound. She flipped it open to find two photographs mounted on the first page, both black-and-whites of a woman holding a baby. "I think I found something." She sat on the bed and began turning the pages.

Someone had taken the care to place the photographs in chronological order—from baby to toddler to Santa Claus's lap to a blue ribbon for the fifth-grade relay team. By the time they hit the shot of a dark-haired girl with long hair, full lips, and almond-shaped eyes, beaming from beneath a handmade banner that read "Happy 13th Birthday," Ellie could recognize a young Tanya Abbott.

She flipped the page and found two photographs of Tanya with a young boy, probably only four or five years old. In one, Tanya was seated on the grass next to the standing boy, squeezing him tightly to her chest—apparently too tightly, from the look on the kid's face. In the other, the boy carried an impish expression as he smashed a snowball on top of an unwitting Tanya's wool-capped head.

"Little brother?" Rogan asked, looking over her shoulder.

"Maybe." There was something vaguely familiar about the child's face. He had white-blond hair while Tanya was dark, but plenty of children started out as towheads and then darkened as they got older. Jess had been even blonder than she as a toddler.

She compared the two children in the picture more closely, trying to figure out what was familiar about the boy. Physical similarities could be elusive that way. Although she and Jess looked like polar opposites in all of the most salient ways—coloring, body type, the shapes of their faces—plenty of people had told them there was some indescribable resemblance between them.

Something about that little boy made her feel as if she'd seen him before, and recently at that. There had to be something in his face that reminded her of the adult Tanya, but whatever it was, she couldn't put her finger on it.

After a few more photographs, the pages suddenly went blank. In the final image, Tanya dangled a set of keys and a tiny card that Ellie guessed was her learner's permit to drive. By then, Tanya had discovered makeup, hairspray, and the power of cleavage. But despite the girl's bolder appearance, something else in her had flattened. While the youthful Tanya was radiant, with a broad grin, this older version seemed withdrawn and less secure, as if someone was cajoling her to pose with her newfound driving props.

Only five years later, she'd be arrested for prostitution.

Rogan plopped down on the bed next to her. "Remember that couple in Canada? Those two whack jobs who went on a killing spree somewhere up there."

"You mean the Ken and Barbie murderers?"

"Yeah, it was this dude and his girlfriend. She helped him rape and murder multiple women, including her own little sister. We could be looking at something like that. They had a reason to take out Megan if she realized the scam Tanya was running. Once they killed Megan, maybe the guy developed a taste for it. Went next to Katie."

"Yeah, but why Katie? And why set up a date? If Tanya knew Katie, she wouldn't have needed the ruse. And if she didn't know her, it's a little coincidental that they wound up going after a prostitute who just happened to be friends with Stacy."

Rogan shook his head and then flopped backward on the bed. "I don't know, but I'm so fucking tired, I could fall asleep right here." He shut his eyes, and for a moment Ellie thought he might have actually nodded off until he muttered one word: "Tomorrow."

"What's tomorrow?"

"Tomorrow we find Tanya Abbott."

"How? We have no idea what she's been up to in New York. She could be on her way back to Baltimore. She could be on her way to Mexico for all we know. And she's got a head start."

"You're right. We have no idea where to look, which is why there's no point trying to chase her ass down now. But tomorrow we won't be exhausted. Tomorrow we'll figure it out. We'll find her, and we'll get some answers."

"Tomorrow."

"Tomorrow."

Ellie grabbed Tanya's photo album before they left. "If we ever catch up to her, this might be useful."

Ellie returned home to find Jess sprawled on her sofa. A pint of Ben & Jerry's ice cream rested on his slumped chest as he took in an episode of *The Hills.*

She unholstered her Glock and threw her jacket on a chair in the corner. "I thought you worked tonight."

"Called in sick after I met that girl at Gaslight."

She nudged him with one knee and found a place for herself next to him. "I can't believe you watch this vacuous garbage."

"Hot girls juggling work, school, and boys, all in sunny southern California. What more could a guy want?"

"One little ounce of testosterone?"

"Just ask that girl from the bar if I've got a problem in that territory."

"Ugh," she said, snatching the pint of ice cream while the spoon was resting in the carton. "And here I thought I might actually get some decent sleep tonight."

"What about your juggling of work, school, and boys? No Captain America tonight?"

"No. We were off to a good night, and then I wound up at the Royalton. The victim's a realtor for Corcoran—a frickin' *realtor*, and she's whoring herself on the side. Oh, excuse me—she worked for an *escort agency*. Prestige Parties."

"Classy. My employer could take a lesson from them."

"Well, unlike the fine gentlemen's establishment that employs you, these escort services are always, without exception, a cover for prostitution. I really don't get it. This woman had a good job. A roof over her head. How can a woman with options do something like that to herself?"

"It's more common than you'd think."

"Oh, God, don't tell me—"

"Relax. I'm talking about the girls at work. They're doing dry humps in the VIP lounge for a hundred bucks. Fifty of that goes to the house. Another twenty-five gets tipped to the waitresses and people like yours truly who don't have to get groped. By the time those girls are done paying percentages and the flat fee to the house to work, they're lucky if they're not in the hole on a slow night. Inevitably a few of them see customers on the side for a little more action."

"It's not the same."

"Try not to judge, little sis. That's always been your weak spot."

"Kind of hard to be in my business and not have the occasional streak of judginess. You can't be throwing people in a cell if you think it's all relative."

"If you want, I can ask around at the T&A Café about this service. Prestige Parties?"

"Yeah." She handed the ice cream carton back to him, and he growled when he saw the empty bottom. "I'm hitting the sack."

She had removed her contacts, washed her face, and moved on to the brushing of her teeth when she heard the phone ring, followed by Jess's voice saying, "Come on up." She spit out the minty foam before yelling toward the living room.

"Please tell me you didn't invite company for the night."

"I wouldn't say I invited it, but when contacted, I didn't exactly decline the offer."

"Jesus, Jess." She used her hands to make a sipping cup beneath the faucet and rinsed. "You can't just assume I'm not coming home. Now where the hell—"

"Relax, El." He was pulling on his jacket. "The company's not for me. Captain America texted a few minutes ago to see if you were back yet. I guess it was supposed to be a surprise. Gag. And really, I know you two are on the road to being that old married couple at Denny's every night, but seeing how he's trying to be so romantic and all, you might want to put in a little effort." He pointed a scrutinizing finger up and down her general person.

Ellie was no longer in front of a mirror, but looking down, she got the gist. Blue flannel pajama bottoms. Extra-large David Bowie T-shirt. The slippers her mother had given her, adorned with plush green frog heads. Not to mention her hair was pulled back in a red terry-cloth sweatband and her face was slathered with overnight cream. She heard a tap at the door.

"Off with you," Jess said. "I'll buy you some time."

"Wait. Where are you going?"

"Out."

"You sure?"

"Sis, when are you going to figure out that I can always find a place to sleep?"

Ellie dashed into the bathroom and slid the band from her hair while she wiped at her face with Kleenex. She threw the slippers and the sweatpants in the bathtub. By the time she heard Jess say good-bye to Max, she was ready to emerge—just her and her David Bowie T-shirt—for some well-deserved privacy with Max Donovan.

From the look on his face when he saw her, he didn't mind the attire. His smile—and every activity that followed—kept her mind off Tanya Abbott, Megan Gunther, Katie Battle, Sparks, her lieutenant, all of it. She and Rogan had big plans, but not until tomorrow.

# CHAPTER THIRTY-FOUR

S he takes a triangle stance in her stall at the firing range. The sound of gunfire echoes through the cold room. She levels her Glock in front of her, fixes the torso of the paper target in her sights, and locks her right elbow to prepare for the recoil. She pulls the trigger but nothing happens. She tries again but, again, nothing. She pulls the trigger once more, and this time, the weapon falls from her hand.

"Hatcher."

She turns to find Robin Tucker standing behind her.

"You're not ready, Hatcher. You knew you weren't ready, but you came here anyway. And now everyone is pulling their weight except you. Take a look at Nick's work."

Ellie hears a rumble as a paper torso in front of the adjacent stall flies in her direction like a ghost. Six holes form a tight cluster in the middle of the target's chest.

"Excellent shooting."

She turns to see Nick Dillon, the head of security for Sparks Industries. He kisses Tucker on the cheek and gives her a playful tap on the ass. She giggles in delight.

Ellie hears another rumble. She sees another target being pulled in from the end of the firing range. More rumbling. More targets, all with centered shots. She fumbles for her Glock on the floor and makes one more futile attempt to fire. She hears another rumble as her own target moves toward her. She looks at the paper and sees the gloating sneer of Sam Sparks.

"Ellie."

She holds her hands in front of her to keep the paper from swallowing her.

"Ellie."

She feels hands on hers, pushing her arms closer to her body.

"El, your phone."

Ellie opened her eyes to see her bedroom ceiling. In bed next to her, Max let out a tired groan. "You okay? You were waving your arms around. Thought you were going to coldcock me for a second."

She heard another rumble from the nightstand as her vibrating cell phone crept against the maple top.

"Hatcher," she said, not bothering to check the screen before answering.

"This has to be a first." It was Rogan.

"Hmm?"

"Me waking *your* ass up. I've been a busy boy this morning."

"Yeah?" She rubbed an eye with her free hand, trying to knock out the grogginess of sleep.

"I pulled the records for that cell phone number we had for Tanya Abbott. No calls in or out since the night before Megan's murder, and no current signal."

"She must have known to turn it off so we couldn't track her."

"Smart girl. I also checked out the calls she's made in the months since she moved in with Megan. Not a lot of use."

"You found some calls to Stacy Schecter, I assume?" Ellie sat up in bed and pulled up the comforter to cover her chest.

"Yeah. Another familiar name, too."

"Not Katie Battle?" Ellie asked. A call between Tanya Abbott and Katie Battle would bring their mutual connection to Stacy

Schecter full circle. A direct connection between the two would also strengthen Rogan's suspicions that Tanya's sudden disappearance was related to Katie's brutal murder the night before. But it wouldn't be that straightforward.

"Nope," Rogan said. "Someone else."

"You're killing me."

He paused for dramatic effect. "Paul Bandon."

"No . . . way. As in future federal judge Paul Bandon?"

Max turned on his side next to her and whispered a curious "What?" She raised her eyebrows.

"Yep. And it's not just one call. There's a lot of them, back and forth between the two, like almost once a *week*. I didn't think you'd want to miss the chance to ask him about it."

"Hell, no."

Ellie was already pulling on a pair of pants by the time Rogan said good-bye.


Judge Paul Bandon lived in what New Yorkers called a white-glove building on the Upper East Side. White-glove buildings not only have doormen, but doormen in white gloves who hail the cabs, carry the groceries, walk the dogs, and perform whatever other menial tasks are beneath their privileged tenants. This particular white-glove building was prewar, with marble floors and gold-leaf mirrors in the elevators. The woman who came to Bandon's door, with her navy blue tailored sweater jacket and perfectly set, shoulder-length blond bob, looked like she was born to live in such a building.

"May I help you?" she asked. Even through the crack in the door, Ellie recognized the woman from the photograph Bandon kept on his bench in court.

"We're with the New York Police Department, ma'am. We're here to speak with Judge Bandon?"

"If you have a warrant or something for my husband to review on a Saturday, I would assume that could be taken care of by one of the weekend on-call judges. Isn't that usually how it's done?"

"This isn't about a warrant, ma'am. Is your husband home?"

"Is everything all right?" she asked, alarm now registering in her voice. "I knew his handling a criminal docket could lead to something like this."

"There's nothing to be worried about," Rogan said.

"Laura? Where are you?" a man's voice called from inside the apartment. "Are you even listening to me? I thought we were having a conversation, and you just walk away. Oh—"

The judge's voice trailed off as he realized someone was at the door. The woman widened the crack in the door for them to step inside. "Paul, these detectives are here to see you. I'm Laura, by the way. Laura Bandon."

Next to her stood Judge Bandon in a light blue oxford shirt, khaki pants, and shearling slippers. He hadn't gotten to the leather belt in his hands. And he apparently wasn't going to get around to proper introductions. "Well, gosh. Detectives Rogan and Hatcher. This is, well, certainly a surprise, seeing you at my home like this, unannounced."

Along with the smile, he maintained a tone that was country-club pleasant, but the content of the words could not be ignored.

"It was urgent, Your Honor."

"But not so urgent that you could have raised it yesterday morning when you spent a good two hours in my chambers? Or was this a matter that you wanted to speak to me about, Detective Hatcher?"

Ellie returned the pleasant smile. "It's a subject my partner and I both feel is important. And it only arose early this morning, so yesterday wasn't an option."

"And what exactly *is* this pressing topic?"

"We found your—"

Ellie was ready to forge ahead, but Rogan cut her off. "Perhaps we could speak to you in private, Your Honor."

"Well," his wife said, clasping her manicured hands at her waist, "I can certainly recognize when it's time for me to take my leave. I was going down to the corner anyway to pick up some milk.

Paul, we can continue our conversation when you're finished with this . . . *intriguing* meeting."

They waited for Laura Bandon to pull a tan windbreaker from the front closet and make her way out the front door.

"You may as well have a seat," Bandon said, leading the way into a museumlike living room adorned with Persian rugs and Chippendale-inspired furnishings. Ellie perched herself lightly atop an upholstered ladder-back chair. Rogan looked more comfortable as he crossed his legs on a velvet-adorned settee next to her.

"So what precisely brings you here this morning, Detectives? I thought just yesterday we had squared away everything we needed on this Sparks matter, but I have to say, your coming to my home outside of business hours has me thinking about his charges in a different light. There is a line, I believe, between thorough policing and harassment."

Rogan uncrossed his legs and leaned forward. "With all due respect, Your Honor, you haven't given us an opportunity to explain why we're here. Any comparison of this to harassment seems . . . premature."

Rogan's tone was pitch-perfect, yet Ellie found herself troubled by a nagging feeling of guilt. She wondered if the judge had a point. So his name turned up in a missing prostitute's cell phone records. That single fact made the likely scenario apparent. He wouldn't be the first married man of prominence who partook of the sex trade. Coming here would at best confirm their clear impressions. But it wouldn't get them any closer to finding Tanya Abbott or figuring out what role she played in the murders of Megan Gunther or Katie Battle.

Had they jumped too quickly at the tantalizing appeal of confronting this man with his sins? Maybe, but now that they were here, there was no turning back. They had to lock it down.

"What can you tell us about your relationship with Tanya Abbott?" she asked.

"Pardon me?"

"I think you heard the question, Judge."

"I very well did. And I don't appreciate the obvious insinuation."

"If the insinuation is inaccurate, feel free to correct us. You do know a woman named Tanya Abbott, don't you? She also uses the name Heather Bradley."

"I believe you said you were going to explain why exactly you've come here. All I am hearing from you, Detectives, are questions, but no explanation as to why you are asking them, either of me or at my home at this early hour on a Saturday morning."

She gave him a small smile. He was smart. The people they were used to interrogating would immediately lock themselves into a lie. "Never heard of her," they'd say without pausing.

But Bandon was too good for that. Lies to a police officer create presumptions of guilt. Lies could lead to cover-up allegations against a judge who might otherwise manage to survive what some would wave away as just another sex-scandal. So rather than lie, Bandon was using his power and authority to try to intimidate them.

She handed him a printout of Abbott's Maryland driver's license. "Have a look. Perhaps you know her by another name, Your Honor. But we're confident that you know her."

He glanced at the photo for only a second before returning it to Ellie as if it burned his hand. He focused his gaze instead toward the inner depths of the apartment, down the hallway of what Ellie recognized as a classic six. Before the days of her rent-stabilized pad, during the brief shack-up with the investment banker, Ellie enjoyed the spaciousness of an Upper East Side apartment with almost precisely this same layout. With Mrs. Bandon safely outside the apartment on her way to the corner market, she wondered who might remain to jeopardize the seeming privacy of the living room.

"Fine, I know her."

"In what respect?"

"I suspect you already know, and for purposes of today's conversation only, I won't try to correct your assumptions. I won't be affirmatively confirming anything else without consulting a lawyer first."

"When was the last time you saw her?"

"Again, I don't think that's something I want to go on record with before speaking to counsel."

"We know she called you on Thursday afternoon. She called you a lot."

He nodded slowly. "Yes, but I don't believe it's illegal to have telephone conversations."

"Uh, Dad. Um, am I interrupting?"

A tall teenager with floppy blond hair stood in the hallway, looking at his father with a concerned look. He avoided Ellie's gaze, but she got a good look at him. The boy's face had matured and thinned since the high school graduation picture in Bandon's courtroom, but he was the same kid.

"Sorry, Alex. We didn't mean to disturb you. Go back to your studies."

"You sure?"

"Of course. Just the realities of the job. Warrant applications don't always wait for the judge to show up at work." Ellie could see in Judge Bandon's reassuring smile that he appreciated his son's concern.

"Where's Mom?"

"She ran to Citarella for some milk, but you know how she is. You mind going down and seeing if she needs some help with the bags?"

He glanced back to his room, but then nodded and left the apartment.

"That's a nice-looking kid you've got there," J. J. offered.

Ellie wouldn't have dared to comment on the judge's family given the situation, but the remark appeared to soften him.

"Smart, too," he said. "Senior year at Columbia with a three-point-eight. Off to Harvard Law School next year."

It seemed early for a college senior to know his next academic destination already, but people like the Bandons obviously enjoyed the benefits of the insiders' track.

"Thank God he agreed to live at home for undergrad to save the folks some money. The kid reads Plato with his headphones on. I'm surprised he realized anyone was here. In any event, as you can see, I've got a full house here and much to do. And, as you can imagine, your coming here this morning—for the reasons you've come here—well, it's a lot for me to deal with. If you're looking for some sweeping, sobbing confessional to take back to your colleagues, you won't be getting it, at least not today."

Rogan started to rise from his seat but settled back into his chair. "We don't need to go down the road we initially started out on, Your Honor. We are not here to sweat you on your sex life. You've got a wife, a son—we understand the need for discretion, and as you can imagine, we tiptoe around witness secrets all the time in our job."

"I don't need a lecture from you about discretion, Detective Rogan."

Rogan held up his palms in a peace-making gesture. "I didn't mean to lecture. My only point is that we have other priorities. Your number wasn't the only one in those phone records, but it was one of the most frequent, so we didn't come here without reason."

Bandon clenched his jaw and sighed. He was figuring out what the phone records would look like. He was smart enough to realize that, despite his initial instincts, they were the ones with the power in this situation.

Ellie leaned forward with her elbows against her knees. "Honestly, we don't care about the nature of whatever . . . arrangement you might have with Tanya Abbott. We need your help finding her. There was a girl stabbed to death yesterday near Union Square—an NYU student."

"I saw that on the news," Bandon said.

"Well, Tanya Abbott was that girl's roommate."

He sucked in his breath.

"Tanya was also hurt in the assault. She's fine, but she left the hospital and is missing. Her cell phone's off, and she's probably replaced it by now with something untraceable. But she may reach out to you."

"Well, I don't see why—"

"You might not consider yourself a close friend, but she's on the run. She's alone. She most likely needs money. And from what we can tell, you have contact with her almost every week."

He looked down at the Persian carpet beneath his slippered feet, avoiding her eyes.

"If she's still in town, she's going to call," she said.

"And then what?"

"We need you to get as much information as you can without tipping her off that you're cooperating with us. Set up a meet if possible. At least get a callback number for her. Then contact us immediately." She handed him her business card, as did Rogan.

"Okay," he said, slipping the cards into the front pocket of his slacks. "I can do that. *If* she calls. I don't think she will."

"But if she does," Ellie said.

He nodded. "I will help in whatever way I can."

"Thank you, Your Honor. Thank you very much."

They rose to leave, but Bandon stopped them as Rogan reached for the apartment's front door.

"Is there a way to keep this between us?" he asked. "Just the three of us, I mean. My career, my family, I—"

He stopped at the sound of the crack in his own voice, and Ellie looked to Rogan, knowing what her own answer would be.

"Thank you again for your assistance, Your Honor. We'll be in touch."

Outside the apartment in the hallway, Ellie asked Rogan, "Do you think she's going to call?"

"Anyone's guess, but I'll tell you one thing: If she does, he's going to help us. We've got him scared."

# CHAPTER THIRTY-FIVE

As Ellie made her way to the brick walk-up on 128th Street, she reached back to her days on patrol to identify the tags of gang graffiti that marked the East Harlem neighborhood. BBV for the Bronx Bound Vets. The numbers 031, code for "I'm a Blood." CK for Crip Killaz. ADR, short for Amor de Rey, or the Love of Kings, a local offshoot of Chicago's notorious Latin Kings.

She suppressed an involuntary shudder as a rat the size of her purse scurried along the sidewalk near a stack of black garbage bags lining the curb.

The building she was looking for stood out as the best on the block. Brushed bleach stains against the brick walls and concrete steps revealed someone's stubborn tit-for-tat against unwanted spray paint. On the third floor, recently planted begonias popped from a planter outside a window. Still, standing outside Keith Guzman's apartment building, Ellie could see why the DJ had felt so threatened by his ex-girlfriend's world.

Tanya's phone records remained their best hope of finding the missing woman, so Rogan was working those. He was also nudging CSU again about running the latent prints Tanya had left behind in the apartment. If she had a habit of invoking aliases, she could have been arrested under another name that she was using now that she'd left Heather Bradley behind.

In the meantime, Ellie wanted to find out more about the woman Keith Guzman had known as Heather Bradley.

It took five minutes of persistent buzzing on Apartment 3B's bell before she heard footsteps against the wood staircase inside. Seconds later, a disheveled Keith Guzman headed toward the glass of the front door, still buttoning his jeans.

"Yo, it's early, woman," he said, opening the door.

"It's nearly ten in the morning, Keith. I think you'll live."

"I was at Gaslight till four. Good crowd, too. Would've been hot to play, too, if you hadn't taken all my shit. Now get the hell off my porch before you wind up with my TV, too."

He tried to shut the door, but Ellie snuck her black boot inside just in time.

"Now why do you have to be so rude, Keith? Especially when I come bearing gifts."

She reached inside her backpack and pulled out the laptop she'd seized from him at Gaslight. The pressure of the door against her foot eased.


The begonias belonged to Apartment 3B.

"Nice flowers," she remarked as she took a seat in a green uphol-stered chair by the window. She was careful not to let her weight disrupt the linen cloth that had been draped against the chair back, pre-sumably to conceal the tatters that were starting to rip in the fabric.

"My moms likes them."

She placed the laptop on the coffee table in front of her.

"So the geek squad cleared you on the Campus Juice postings. No visits to that site in the last six months, and no sign of the software that whoever posted those threats used to block the tracking information."

"I told you."

"So you said something the other night about Megan's roommate hitting on you one time."

"Well, you know, everyone wants a piece of DJ Anorexotica."

Ellie shook her head and laughed. "You realize that this whole shtick of yours is a little off-putting, right?"

"What shtick, girl? An-Ex is one hundred percent authentic."

"Are you old enough to remember Vanilla Ice?"

"You mean Ice-T? Sure. He's one of the original gangstas."

Ellie smiled. "No, Vanilla Ice. Now that you've got your laptop back, you can Google him when I'm gone. Trust me: someone else has already mined this creative territory pretty thoroughly. Just try, today, this morning, one time only, to talk to me like a normal person. Talk to me the way I know you talked around Megan."

The sound of her name made him pause, but not for long. "You're trippin'."

"I'm serious, Keith. I need to know about Heather. She's missing. And she's not who Megan thought she was. Her real name was Tanya Abbott." She watched as Keith's eyes widened. "She was a thirty-year-old prostitute from Baltimore. We need to find her, and anything you know about her might help us."

"Oh, shit." The language wasn't elegant, but at least she'd gotten through to him.

"Exactly. Obviously we need to find this woman, and you appear to be the only friend of Megan's who ever spent any amount of time around her."

"Not much."

"Well, not much is more than what we have right now. You said something about her having a boyfriend? She told us she hadn't had a date since transferring to NYU."

"I never saw her with any guys, but me and Megan always joked around that she had some secret sugar daddy on the side."

"Why was that?"

"You know, she was always getting dressed up and shit, and when Megan asked where she was going, she'd act all cute and stuff. Like, 'Just a friend,' with this little smile. And then Heather'd disappear into her room and have these long phone conversations. They'd get kind of heated, you know, like Megan and I could kind of hear the tone. One time Megan was like, 'Guess someone ain't puttin' out to-night.' Like we just assumed it was boyfriend–girlfriend stuff."

"Any idea who the guy was?"

He shook his head. "It was only a couple of times, so I don't want to make a big deal about it or anything. It was more like something me and Megan would joke about—this whole secret life we thought Heather had. I guess she had it after all. I tried eavesdropping once. Megan was trying to stop me, but I could tell she was liking it." He smiled at what was obviously a happy memory.

"You get anything good?"

"Not really. Something about New York being expensive and her being broke. Man, she was trickin'?"

"Looks like it."

"No way Megan would have stood for that." Ellie could tell what he was thinking. If he'd known, if he had listened to more of those calls, Megan would have kicked her out. She would have needed another roommate. Megan would be alive, and they might still be together.

"What about the night she came on to you?"

"I might have overstated that. Just a tiny bit," he added, holding his fingers an inch apart.

"I thought everyone wanted a piece of the An-Ex."

He sniffed as he tugged the sleeves of his sweatshirt up his fore-arms. "Well, you know. Mostly."

She shared in the laugh. "So what's the real version?"

"I don't know if she was trying to hook up or what, but it was weird. Megan went to sleep early because, you know, she had classes or whatever. I was in the living room mixing some files on my laptop when Heather came home. And, man, she was lit. At the time, I assumed she was just really drunk, but now that you're saying she's a hooker and stuff, I don't know. Maybe it was more like heroin or something. Anyway, she wasn't herself. She went straight to the kitchen, poured herself a glass of tequila on the rocks, and started asking me what I was doing. We started talking, and eventu-ally we're doing shots together."

"Would you say you were friends before that?"

"I wouldn't say we were friends after. And I wouldn't say she was friends with Megan either. At the time"—he squinted—"I figured she was one of those weak chicks who's more into guys than any female friends. She started babbling about how nice I was and how lucky Megan was to have someone her age who admired her intelligence and her talent. And then she said something—and, yeah, this was why we always thought she had a boyfriend—she said something about always having a guy who takes care of her. She said it was a kind of a sickness, that she even saw a shrink about it. Then this was why I thought maybe she was coming on to me. She said it all started with this guy who popped her cherry when she was young, and that someone like me would be a change. I thought it was weird because she said *I* was young, even though I'm three years older than Megan. I guess if she's actually thirty, that explains it."

"Did she ever mention any of this to you afterward?"

"No way. She avoided me like an STD, you know? I figured she was embarrassed. I tried telling Megan later she was a head case, but she assumed I had it out for Heather because, well, I wanted to live there instead of her."

"This place doesn't seem so bad," she said, looking around the apartment.

"I wanted to be with Megan."

"I know."

"Hey, Detective."

"Call me Ellie."

"Did any of this help? Are you going to be able to find Heather, or whatever her name is?"

"I honestly don't know, Keith. But, yeah, I have a feeling this is going to be helpful."


Ellie found Rogan deep in thought in front of his computer.

"What's so interesting?" She bent to look over his shoulder.

"You want little news first, or big?"

"Save the best for last."

"All right. To start with, I think I figured out how our girl created a little life for herself as Heather Bradley." Ellie caught a glimpse of a Morgan Stanley logo before Rogan switched screens on his computer, pulling up an article from the *Arizona Republic* Web site. The headline read, "ASU Students Mourn," with a smaller tagline beneath the larger print: "Third DUI Fatality This Semester." A black-and-white photograph showed a crashed Audi A4 with a pickup truck firmly lodged against the driver's side.

The date on the article was from last January.

Ellie skimmed the text. Arizona State University students had held an on-campus vigil after a third student this semester—a freshman named Heather Bradley—was killed by a drunk driver on Apache Boulevard. A summary of the accident followed: pickup truck driven by a thirty-two-year-old carpenter who was being charged with manslaughter. A summary of the other two accidents. And then quotes from Heather's friends and one of her professors.

She reread the penultimate paragraph of the article, the quote from the math professor: "Heather was an outstanding student and a brilliant mind. I had only recently written a letter of recommendation for her. She was very happy here close to home but was ready to leave Arizona after all. I was sorry we'd be saying good-bye to her, but I never expected it to be like this."

And then the final paragraph: "After earning acceptances from New York University, Smith College, and several other prestigious schools, Bradley had accepted an offer from Stanford. She would have matriculated there as a sophomore this fall."

Forging a college application would have been extremely complicated, requiring fake transcripts, an SAT report, and phony letters of recommendation. But Tanya Abbott did not have to forge anything. The application had already been taken care of and the acceptance letter already sent in the mail.

"She just picked up the phone and called NYU," she said.

"Correct," Rogan said. "Think about it. The real Heather Bradley had already made her transfer decision. The family would have contacted Stanford to notify them that Heather wasn't coming, but there was no need to call the schools she had turned down.

"All Tanya had to do was tell NYU she changed her mind. She gives them a change of address, and Heather Bradley's family has no idea that their dead daughter's enrolled in school.

"I called the NYU admissions office and learned more than I ever wanted to know about some federal statute restricting their ability to release academic records, but I also got an unofficial, off-the-record confirmation that that's what happened. And homegirl must've been doing some magic sex tricks in the bedroom, because I more or less confirmed that our girl wasn't on any financial aid. The rest of it is pretty standard identity theft. Fake Maryland ID card. Managed to open a checking account from there. And she found the room in Megan Gunther's apartment on Craig's List without the formalities of a credit check and references."

"You call all this the little news?"

"Yep. Here's the kicker. Any doubts we had about Tanya being the one behind Megan's murder and her own stabbing would appear to be resolved by this." He used his mouse to open a new browser window, clicked on his recent history, and scrolled down to campusjuice.com. From there he navigated his way into the recesses of old postings until he found the most recent thread about Megan Gunther. A new reply had been added.

**Don't bother looking for me. You won't find me. And if you look for me, I'll look for you . . . and your families.**

Rogan leaned back in his chair. "We kicked ourselves for getting distracted by this Web site, but we looked precisely where Tanya wanted us to focus. It's like those magicians with the sleight-of-hand tricks. The harder you try to find the quarter, the easier it is for the magician to dupe you into looking left while he's pulling a coin out of your right ear. Tanya knew Megan's schedule, and she used it to make us look left. We saw those posts and just assumed Megan was the target. This woman's coldhearted. She killed a girl she lived with for months, just as a distraction."

"Jesus, Rogan. This message was posted less than an hour ago."

Immediately after they'd caught the Gunther murder, they'd asked one of the computer technicians to track any new comments about Megan on Campus Juice. He assured them he could write a simple computer program that would alert him of any replies posted to the threads containing the threats. Apparently the program had worked.

"I know," Rogan said. "I was notified within two minutes and immediately called Jabba the Hutt out in Long Island for the Internet provider information."

"The fact that we're sitting here tells me that didn't pan out."

"She used that cloaking device again. The chick's out there somewhere, threatening us, but we have no idea where. She's an electronic ghost."

"We've got her picture up all over the city. The news is running it twenty-four/seven. Eventually someone's going to spot her."

The only thing the media loved more than young, attractive murder victims were young, attractive missing women. The story of one who had walked away from a hospital and disappeared after surviving a murder attempt was like the crack cocaine of tabloid crime reporting. Patrol officers throughout the borough were tracking down the wingnut calls that were flooding the tip line, but so far, none of the spottings had panned out. Now Tanya had upped the ante with this threat.

"Rogan, if Tanya had any details about our personal lives, she would have used them, just like she posted Megan's schedule on Campus Juice to scare her. Threatening our, quote, 'families' shows that she doesn't know anything about Sydney."

"Or Jess," Rogan added.

"Or Jess." But even as she tried to convince herself that Tanya would be more worried about disappearing than targeting the family members of police officers, she used the camera in her cell phone to take a snapshot of Tanya's Maryland ID. She e-mailed it to Jess, then followed it with a text message: "Crazy chick making threats. Likely BS, but just in case, photo in your e-mail."

She hit the send button and asked Rogan if she should send the picture to Sydney as well.

"I kept her up late enough watching the news that she knows that girl's face just fine by now," he said. "I'll call her myself to tell her about this latest garbage. She doesn't always take the job in stride, at least not when it comes home with me."

Rogan's phone rang.

"Yeah, this is Rogan."

Ellie's cell buzzed in her hand. A reply text message from Jess: "Crazy chick's hot. Will definitely be on the lookout."

She was about to text a response to Jess when Rogan's side of the phone conversation caught her attention.

"Yeah, the Megan Gunther case. You got a hit?" She recognized the excited look on his face. There was news. Ellie reached across him to hit the refresh button on the Web browser. No new messages on Campus Juice.

"What?" she whispered urgently. "What?"

Rogan shook his head to shush her.

"No shit? . . . You're sure? . . . Sweet. I need you to do me a favor, though. We're going to need DNA to confirm it. . . . No, we don't have a sample. Send someone back to pull hair from the shower drain? . . . Cool. Thanks."

When he returned the handset to the cradle without speaking, she wanted to nudge his words out with a hard elbow to the back.

"That was CSU getting back to us on Tanya Abbott's finger-prints. Guess the girl's not a ghost after all."

"That prostitution bust in Baltimore wasn't her only arrest?"

He shook his head. "They got a hit, but it wasn't from IAFIS." The Integrated Automated Fingerprint Identification System contained fingerprint and criminal history data from crime records throughout the country. "It was in the NYPD's very own collection of unsolved cases. You want to guess what case we got a hit on?"

"Not in the mood for twenty questions, J. J."

"The prints Tanya Abbott left behind in Megan Gunther's apartment match the latents we found on the champagne glass at the Robert Mancini shooting. I've got them pulling hair out of the shower drain at Megan's place trying to find a DNA sample for confirmation, but the print match is solid."

Tanya Abbott was the missing mystery woman from Robert Mancini's last fatal date.

# PART IV

---

## EASY MONEY

# CHAPTER THIRTY-SIX

Usually when a lieutenant summoned detectives into the office for a case update, it was for a quick conversation. Summarize a few witness interviews. Run through the forensic results. An overview of the next steps. But when Robin Tucker beckoned Ellie and Rogan into her office this afternoon, she got more than she could have possibly expected. Rogan used a purple marker and a rolling whiteboard to diagram all the connections.

Tanya Abbott was, as far as they could tell, the last person to see Robert Mancini alive. She was also the last person to see Megan Gunther, with whom she shared an apartment under the alias Heather Bradley. And through Stacy Schecter, they'd also connected her to Katie Battle, murdered two nights ago at the Royalton Hotel.

Tucker's eyes roamed the board as she processed the new information.

"CSU's *sure* about the prints?" she asked.

"Abbott left prints all over her apartment," Rogan said. "They've got fourteen match points to the latent on the champagne glass from Mancini's mystery date. She's our girl from the 212."

"It was right in front of us," Ellie said. "In the phone records. On May twenty-seventh"—Rogan circled the date written next to the

Mancini murder for emphasis—"that's the date Katie Battle called Stacy Schecter to cover a date for her. Stacy couldn't cover it, so she called Tanya Abbott. The client was Robo Mancini. I can't believe I didn't make the connection earlier."

"I didn't think a wunderkind like you missed anything, Hatcher."

Ellie didn't miss the sarcasm in her lieutenant's tone.

"Well, I did. When I told Katie's mother about her death, the caretaker at the nursing home mentioned that the mom had a stroke the same day Sydney Pollack died. I remembered hearing the news the day of the Mancini murder. I should've seen it. I messed up."

"Jeez," Rogan said, "not this again. I never told you the date of those phone calls. All I said was they were four months ago. You would've needed ESP."

"So lesson learned," Tucker said. "Make sure your partner knows everything you know."

"The same could be said for lieutenants." Ellie cursed herself for letting Tucker's comment get to her, but she was still irked about the lieutenant's date with Sparks's head of security.

"Go ahead, Hatcher. Say what's on your mind."

"The only thing that's on my mind is how to find Tanya Abbott."

"And whoever's helping her," Rogan said, spotting an opportunity to break the tension in the room. He placed a check mark next to the Mancini case. "Abbott could've shot the hell out of Mancini as part of some botched robbery, but no way did she kill Megan Gunther on her own." He underlined the name *Megan Gunther*. "Abbott had real injuries. She went to St. Vincent's in a meat wagon. Stabbing herself like that? Possible, but not likely. And then there's the question of the murder weapon. None of the knives at the apartment were consistent with the injuries to either Megan or Abbott. Someone carried the weapon away, and since Abbott was wheeled out to an ambulance, it wasn't her."

He drew another line beneath another name. "Next we've got Katie Battle."

"Tanya covered a date for her on May 27, and four months later

Battle ends up dead in a hotel room?" Tucker was making sure she was following all the connections.

"Correct," Rogan said. "We just heard from the ME. The official cause of death was asphyxiation. She was strangled. But she was also tortured. Her fingers were broken. Her skin was sliced in twenty-seven different places. She was hog-tied. The pressure alone from the restraints would have been—"

"I get the picture," Tucker said.

"But we don't know that she was raped," Ellie added. "Or at least we don't have any medical findings of sexual assault. The ME found no signs of seminal fluids on the body, and so far CSU has none at the scene."

"The injuries Rogan described sound sexual."

"Agreed," Ellie said. "The motivation could be sexual without any physical evidence to prove that."

Forced vaginal or anal penetration usually caused tearing and bruising, but oral sodomy was not always detectable. And violence could be sexually motivated even if not carried out with a sexual assault. The College Hill Strangler in Wichita had masturbated near the bodies of his victims. Whoever killed Katie Battle could have been smart enough not to leave bodily fluids behind.

"So let's assume she's got an accomplice," Tucker said, tucking a pen behind her ear. "Why are the two of them killing these people?"

*Find the motive, and the motive will lead you to the man.*

"We wondered the same thing," Ellie said. "Picture this. Tanya came to New York to start over. Got herself into NYU as Heather Bradley and was trying to go legit. But she couldn't cover all the costs, so she's still turning tricks. She sees the opportunity for easy money at the 212 with Mancini. She assumes an apartment like that's going to have valuables: jewelry, cash, silver, computers. She didn't know the place was just for show. She and her boyfriend plan a robbery, but somehow it turns to shit. Mancini was an army badass; maybe he fights back."

"I can see that," Tucker said.

"Meanwhile, Megan finds out more than she's supposed to know about her roommate— about either Tanya's true identity or her whereabouts on May 27, or maybe it was just the prostitution. She learns enough that she becomes a danger to Tanya's new life. Tanya posts the threats on Campus Juice as a distraction, then she and her accomplice stage the attack at the apartment. But when Tanya gets to the hospital, she realizes that the search for Heather Bradley's medical insurance is going to turn up dry. And if we booked her for the fraud on NYU, her prints would come back to the Mancini crime scene. Now there is a risk that everything would come out."

"What about the real estate agent? Why kill Katie Battle?"

"Our best theory is that Tanya's partner got a taste for killing when he stabbed Megan Gunther. Shooting Robert Mancini was just part of a robbery. No real thrills. But stabbing Megan was different. Up close. Personal. Intimate. He may have even known her. Next time, he books Katie Battle and takes his time."

"And you know for sure that Tanya left the hospital *before* Battle was killed?"

Ellie and Rogan exchanged a glance. They knew their theory rested on multiple assumptions, but now that they were hearing it out loud, they were seeing all of the holes.

Rogan shook his head. "Unfortunately, Tanya walked out of the hospital without telling anyone. A hospital employee asked about her insurance just before five and then left when her shift ended. Based on the entries in her medical chart, we know she got her dinner at five thirty, and she was gone by the time we got there at eleven thirty."

"No one went in her room for *six hours*?"

"Someone went in to get her dinner tray," Ellie explained, "but the covers were pulled up on the bed, and they assumed the patient was sleeping. Tanya had padded the bed with extra blankets. In any event, it's certainly possible Tanya got out in time to go to the Royalton. Katie Battle checked in to the Royalton at six thirty-seven, and her body was found around eight. Even if Tanya missed the action, whoever helped her kill Mancini and Megan could have been acting on his own."

Tucker shook her head. "Been a while since I've seen a woman kill anyone other than a lover or a kid. She strikes you as the type to do all this?"

"According to Megan's boyfriend, a kid named Keith Guzman, Tanya had some kind of secret guy in her life." They had decided to hold off on telling Tucker about Judge Bandon's connection to Tanya for now. "She said something about always having a man who takes care of her, that it started with the first person she ever slept with. She said she even saw a therapist about it. She might have the kind of character that would make her subservient to a violent personality."

"A shrink, huh?" Rogan asked. Ellie hadn't mentioned this fact when she gave him the initial rundown of her visit to Guzman's apartment.

"Supposedly. Why, does that mean something to you?"

He shrugged. "Probably nothing. That pop she took in Baltimore did require counseling to get the case dismissed. There was a doctor's name scribbled on the dispo sheet the DA faxed me from the file. I noticed because, at least up here, that kind of counseling's done by the probation department, not an actual MD."

"Not unique to New York," Tucker said. "No jurisdiction bigger than Mayberry can afford to have full-fledged shrinks doing hand-holding on misdemeanor prostitution cases. If she had a doctor vouching for her, he would've been private."

Ellie took the assumption to the next level. "Which raises the question of how a twenty-year-old street prostitute can afford a private therapist."

Tucker wagged her ballpoint pen in their direction. "Sounds like the wunderkind may have just figured out something important about our mysterious Tanya Abbott."

# CHAPTER THIRTY-SEVEN

S tacy Schecter blew her bangs out of her eyes and swirled a sip of pinot noir on her tongue as she contemplated the painted canvas in front of her. The splotches of muted color on the skin were about right, but there was something about the expression on the woman's face that was still off.

This painting was something entirely new for Stacy. For the last two years, she'd worked on little other than the abstract yet sooth-ing stretched canvases that could fetch her a couple hundred dollars on the street. She had hoped to be featured in solo exhibitions in Chelsea's best galleries by now, but in reality, the only paintings she'd ever sold went to people who cared more about aesthetically pleasing wall decor than actual art.

Stacy hadn't painted anything representational since college. Her parents had sent their troubled daughter to the West Coast believing that four years of open space and fresh air, away from her overly precocious New York friends, might somehow prove transformative. The hippie college in Washington to which they had steered her, just an hour's drive from her older sister's house in Seattle, was supposed to provide an outlet for her creativity and rebellious ways. Stacy figured she'd met all expectations by becoming an art major and had exceeded them by graduating in the top half of her class.

Apparently her parents had some other understanding of whatever transformation was supposed to have occurred during those four years. When she returned home with the same basic attitude and no employable skills, her parents had cut her off.

Stacy tried to be legit, and in the next four years she learned more than she'd ever picked up in college. She applied for design jobs, then marketing, then assistant positions, and then finally moved down to waitressing. But the money was never enough.

She might still be waiting tables if it hadn't been for that night at the Bowery Ballroom. She and her friend Carmen had gone to see Morrisey two decades after a young Stacy first discovered the Smiths and declared to her mother that she was no longer a carnivore because Meat Is Murder. Three cocktails in, still waiting for the show to start, Carmen went off on a slurred rant about a girl she knew who was turning tricks for extra cash. Stacy found herself defending this woman she didn't know and the choice that she had made for herself. And long after Morrisey finished his finale of "There Is a Light That Never Goes Out," she couldn't put the idea to rest.

A little more than a year later, she could pay her bills and still have plenty of time left over to paint.

Stacy certainly didn't boast about the way she earned her money, but she also didn't see the problem. At any expensive club or restaurant, on any given night, countless girls were on first dates with hedge-fund assholes. They spent the night sipping from the bottle service in the VIP lounge or nibbling on a two-hundred-dollar tasting menu with the expectation that they'd put out for the night and never be spoken to again. What Stacy did was no different, but she skipped the bullshit conversation and got to spend the money as she saw fit. If anything, those gold-digging date-girls were bigger whores than she was.

She usually had no problem separating her primary income source from the rest of her life. As Stacy, she scrunched up her shagged hair with molding paste, piled on the eyeliner, sported a wardrobe of black, leather, and denim, and cursed more than a pissed-off ex-con. When she dated, she smoothed her hair with straightening gel, donned clothes that a Long Island housewife might call "classy," and smiled a lot through a thin layer of age-appropriate makeup. And when she was done with the date, she stopped thinking about that part of her life entirely. It hadn't been easy, but that's what she'd trained herself to do.

But now the fake life was bleeding into the real one. And with real blood.

She looked again at the canvas. The facial expression. It wasn't right.

Part of her wished those detectives hadn't shown her the pictures. If she hadn't come across as such a cunt at first, if they had trusted her to cooperate, maybe they wouldn't have felt forced to place those photographs in front of her. Maybe she wouldn't have seen what happened to Miranda. To Katie Battle.

But she had. And now, like those first thoughts after the Morrissey concert about Carmen's friend, she could not stop thinking about those photographs.

She placed her half-full wineglass on the table next to her palette, plopped onto her bed, and opened her laptop. She clicked on her bookmarks menu and pulled up www.TheEroticReview.com. Within seconds, she was looking at her profile on the site. Shunning the faux-glamour pseudonyms so frequent in the trade—Angel, Destiny, Cherry, and the like—she went simply by Ess, short for Stacy, when forced to use any name at all. She scrolled her way down the page, past the description of her appearance, past the list of services offered, and saw that a new review had been posted. A user calling himself Carlo had given her a 9 for both appearance ("model material") and performance ("I forgot it was a service"). She'd take it.

She'd first learned of the site more than a year earlier. When she saw its description of a "community of escorts, hobbyists, and service providers," she was certain it was a sting, some kind of trap by law enforcement. But then some of the other girls vouched for it. "The amazon-dot-com of the sex trade," one girl had called the site. Even Stacy had found herself flinching at the rawness of the language as she clicked *yes* or *no* to the various services one could offer. But eventually the site had enabled her to leave the escort services behind and go out on her own. Between the hardcore hobbyists who found her on this site, and the more casual clients who used Craig's List, she had more than enough business.

Next she checked her Hotmail account, the one that was untraceable, the one she used for her Craig's List postings.

She saw her ads as a form of creative writing—not a particularly challenging form, but a form nevertheless. Like dirty little greeting cards, her online listings all followed the same clichéd storylines—bored housewife looking for adventure, pent-up sales executive needs to indulge her fantasy life, graduate student available for private modeling. In the norms of the sex industry, potential johns saw these ads for what they were—a thinly veiled cover for an illegal offer of sex for money.

The one strain of continuity through all of her ads was the description of herself as an "honest and attractive brunette." Stacy didn't let her dates have her phone number. Being untraceable minimized the chances of getting caught.

But she didn't mind regulars. If someone wanted to date her again, and she wanted to accept, she told them all they had to do was peruse the Craig's List postings. Women Seeking Men. Look for the "honest and attractive brunette."

She scrolled through her in-box on Hotmail, past the inevitable Viagra and diet-related spam, searching for any mention of Craig's List in the subject lines of the new messages. She found one toward the bottom of the page and clicked on it.

Someone had responded to the ad she'd placed that morning.

**I am an honest and attractive brunette. I came to New York for adventure but am having difficulty finding a place to stay for the night and hopefully will find a good man to take care of me. This is for real. Please write back with your phone number if you are interested.**

She opened the reply and immediately noticed the return address: GoodMan@hotmail.com. Someone had apparently created an account specifically for this message. Probably had a suspicious wife who snuck too many peeks at his BlackBerry.

> **I'm sorry to hear that your search for adventure has left you stranded. I think I can help you out if you can meet with me tomorrow night. I'm very generous towards the right kind of woman under the right terms. No phone number to offer, but e-mail me back with a photograph and a place where you'd feel comfortable meeting, and we'll work out the details in person.**

Stacy was accustomed to discovering that she was not the only half of the transaction who required anonymity. She could tell this guy was a repeat player. There were no explicit references to sex for money, lest she be a decoy working a police sting. But all of the not-so-subtle hints were there: veiled references to generosity, terms, details. He knew the drill.

She clicked on the reply button but found herself hesitating as she began to type the text that would finalize the particulars of the date. She rose from the bed and stood again in front of her easel.

This time, she realized what had been bothering her about the woman's face. It was her mouth. It was too relaxed. Too tranquil. Even more than the strangling marks on her neck, what had been so disturbing about those pictures of Miranda had been her lips— twisted unnaturally, the kind of bizarre facial expression sometimes captured in the awkward timing of a bad snapshot. Stacy still could not believe that Miranda had died with her mouth frozen in that state.

She painted over the mouth in putty gray, using the tip of her brush to sketch more angular lines that she would eventually trace over with color.

That blond detective had lectured her about the dangers of what she was doing. She had tried to manipulate her into "changing her lifestyle," as she put it. And she'd used the horrible things that had been done to Miranda in an attempt to persuade her. She could still hear that tough and somehow slightly condescending tone in the detective's voice when she'd told her, "The next time, it could be you." The detective even forced Stacy to add her cell number to her phone so she'd have it any time she needed—"even just to talk, Stacy."

Using her name with her, like they were friends. Ironically, it was a move Stacy used with her dates—or at least the ones who seemed to want some semblance of intimacy.

Well, the detective was wrong. Miranda didn't deserve what happened to her. No one did. But Miranda had never been street-smart. She didn't have that intuition that could tell her right away if a guy was a problem or not. Stacy did. She was a good judge of character. And she was smarter than Miranda.

And she knew the police were full of shit because they also warned her to stay away from Heather. Maybe Heather—or Tanya from Baltimore—had bolted. But there was no way she had anything to do with those heinous things that had been done to Miranda. She probably just got scared when she saw Miranda's picture on the news after she was killed. She probably decided to give up the life and get the hell out of Dodge—sort of like what that blond detective wanted for Stacy.

She walked back to her bed and typed the reply e-mail. She attached a photograph of herself, the one in a bikini and a cowboy hat.

She hit the send key. Easy money.

# CHAPTER THIRTY-EIGHT

Words—tiny, meaningless details scribbled on yellowed sheets of paper—could make all the difference. Beneath fresh light, the trivial can become significant. Cold can grow hot. And thin reeds of data can blossom and expand into indisputable evidence.

Ellie had lost count of the number of times she had come across that one nugget—that one piece of the picture that pulled the entire mosaic together—in some dusty, old, long-forgotten police file. Now she and Rogan were scouring Tanya Abbott's decade-old prostitution file in the hope of a lucky break.

It was only a two-page report from the Baltimore PD and a few pages of notes they had managed to obtain from the Baltimore County State's Attorney's Office, not like the bulky cold-case murder books, so rich in detail, that Ellie had grown accustomed to searching. But this thin stack of fax paper was the one and only piece of Tanya Abbott's history they could count on. They would start with what they knew about her ten years ago and work their way forward.

Rogan was learning what he could about the psychiatrist whose name had been jotted down so haphazardly in the court's dismissal of the prostitution charge against Tanya. "DM'd," the judge had scrawled in large block letters, followed by the cryptic notation, "in counseling, per Dr. Lyle Hewson."

While Rogan was tracking down Hewson, Ellie was trying to get a bead on Tanya's family. When Tanya was arrested, she listed a Baltimore address, as well as a corresponding telephone number. Ellie tried the number first, but the Asian woman who answered managed to explain in broken English that she'd had the number for two years and had never heard of anyone named "Saundra" Abbott. Then Ellie had called Baltimore's Office of Land Records and learned that the address Tanya had given to the arresting officer had been sold three years earlier by the estate of Marion Abbott.

Her next attempt had been to call the new owner of the property. The man who answered knew no more about the former occupants of his home than had the Asian woman who'd inherited their telephone number.

He was also only slightly easier to understand, thanks to a thick southern accent.

"Abbotts? No, can't say that rings a bell, but I can't swear it would. I dealt with some realtor. Lady said the owner bought the farm and the family needed to sell. Had a big debt on the place, she said, so it was a good deal for me—except for the parts that were falling over. You might check with some of the neighbors around here, though. There's some old-timers . . . Names? Nope, can't help you there."

Ellie thanked the man for his time, hung up the phone, and opened Google Maps on her computer. She typed in the old Abbott address and then hit the link for "street view."

Her screen displayed a street-level view of what had once been Tanya Abbott's home. The house was a nondescript single-level ranch. The exterior's beige paint looked fresh enough, but from the aluminum ladder and the loose stacks of roofing tile visible in the driveway, Ellie guessed that the current owner had bought himself a fixer-upper.

She used her mouse to do a virtual walk to the south and then clicked on the house next door to the former Abbott residence. The neighbor's street address popped up at the top of her screen.

After a quick detour to the reverse phone directory, Ellie dialed the number.

She knew that Google used still panoramic photography to replicate her online stroll through Baltimore. Even so, as she listened to the trills through her handset, she caught herself watching the photo on her screen as if she might actually spot the person inside answering the phone.

"Hello?"

.It was either a little kid or a woman with a really stupid voice. She started to ask whether Mommy was home, but thought better of it, just in case she was dealing with a Betty Boop.

"Is this the person who owns the home? I'm calling from the police department."

"The police? Am I in trouble?"

Definitely a kid.

"Nope. I just want to talk to one of your parents. Are they home?"

"I only have a mommy."

"Well, is she home?"

"Yes."

"Can you go get her?"

"She's exercising in her room."

"Okay, well, can you go get her for me?" This kid was one tough customer.

"I'm not supposed to bug her when she's exercising."

"What's your name?"

"Benjamin."

She made a mental note to scold Benjamin's mother for her failure to cover the whole don't-talk-to-strangers terrain. "This is very important, Benjamin. I'll tell her it was my decision to get her, okay?"

"But she has someone in there with her. And she told me never, ever, ever go in there again when she's exercising with someone."

Ellie had a good idea of the kind of exercise Benjamin's mom was doing in her bedroom in the middle of the afternoon, and she didn't want to be responsible for the baggage the little guy might carry around for life if he opened Mommy's door right now.

"How long have you lived in your house, Benjamin?"

"A long time. Like, forever."

"Were you born there?"

"I don't know. I think babies come from the hospital. But my big brother's sixteen and he measured himself on the same door as me, down in the basement, and I'm taller now than he was when he was seven."

So Benjamin's mom had lived in the house for at least nine years.

"What's your mom's name, Benjamin?"

"Anne. Anne Hahn."

"I need you to knock on your mom's door. Okay, Benjamin? Don't open it," she emphasized. "Don't look inside. Just knock. Really loud. And tell her the police are on the phone."

It took another couple of rounds to reassure Benjamin he wouldn't get in trouble, but she eventually heard him comply. And comply he did. The kid had a strong fist and stronger lungs.

"Hello?"

The woman sounded simultaneously worried, exhausted, and pained. Apparently her exercise partner was a very talented trainer.

"Ms. Hahn. My name's Ellie Hatcher. I'm calling from the New York Police Department about your former neighbor, Tanya Abbott."

"Tanya?" The stress in the woman's voice fell away as she caught her breath and tuned in to the conversation.

"Yes, she may be a material witness to a homicide here, and we're trying to find family members who might stay in touch with her."

"I haven't heard a word from the girl since they sold that house—what? It must have been three years ago."

"That was after Marion died?"

"Her mother. That's right. Tanya was, you know. Well, maybe you don't know. She was a troubled girl. In and out of that house, back and forth all the time like it was some kind of youth hostel. I tell you, Marion was a *saint*. She had nothing in life but that daughter of hers, and she worked her tail off for that girl. And Tanya? Well, she was a good little girl back in the day. Even used to babysit my eldest when he was just a peanut. But late teens? I tell ya. You've never seen a girl go so fast from teacher's pet to . . . well, I'll go ahead and say it: a Little Lolita is what she became."

Ellie realized that the one activity Anne Hahn might enjoy more than exercising was gossiping about her neighbors.

"You said Tanya had a habit of coming and going from the house. Did Marion have men going in and out of there as well?" A sudden shift from the honor roll to promiscuity was a telltale sign of sexual abuse, and most of the abuse happened close to home.

"No way. Marion wasn't like that. If she even dated, I surely never saw sign of it. My guess is she got knocked up at nineteen and learned her lesson. Kept her knees shut ever since."

"Tanya was an only child?"

"That's right."

Ellie reached for the photo album she'd found in Tanya's bedroom and flipped through it, stopping again on the page depicting a young, happy Tanya with an even younger blond boy. Something about the boy still felt so familiar. It had to be some resemblance to Tanya, but she still couldn't put her finger on it.

"Are you sure? Maybe she had a half-brother? We found some pictures of a kid who was probably eight or so years younger than her."

"The sperm donor who knocked up Marion could have impregnated half of Baltimore for all she knew, but a relationship with a half-sibling? Huh-uh. Marion made it real clear the dad wasn't around. The kid could have been anyone from the neighborhood—Tanya baby-sat for a whole bunch of us."

"Her mom was pregnant at nineteen and died three years ago? She must have been young."

"Yeah, like forty-seven or something. Cervical cancer. Said she should have just ripped out all the equipment after she had Tanya. Poor thing spent that final year worrying about her medical bills."

"They didn't have much money, I take it."

"You kidding? No one who lives around here does."

"What about Tanya? We got the impression that she might have had a private counselor or a psychiatrist about ten years ago?"

"News to me. Now, she might've *needed* it, but there's no way Marion could've afforded something like that, even before she got sick."

"We got the impression Tanya might have access to some funds. Maybe Marion had life insurance?"

"No, I would've heard about that. I went to see Marion a few times a week there at the end. She was borrowing against everything. If she'd had life insurance, she would've been borrowing on that, too. Marion didn't even have health insurance. She worked as a domestic, you know?"

"A housekeeper?"

"No, like a nanny, I guess. She'd treat those families like her own. Come to think of it, that kid you saw in the pictures with Tanya could've been one of the kids Marion nannied. A couple of the families she worked for along the way were real good about letting Marion bring Tanya around with her, like they were all one big happy family. Shoot—I should be able to remember some names, but nothing's coming to mind. I know one of the guys was some big muckety-muck. She worked for that family for years. Doesn't matter, though. When she got sick, none of them came to take care of her, so it only goes so far. You know?"

"Can you think of anything else I should know?"

"Well, there is one thing, but, well, I probably shouldn't say anything."

*I probably shouldn't say anything.*

Those five words had been the countdown to countless gossip sessions over the decades. Oscar Wilde's downfall could probably be traced to some woman in a corset, sipping tea in a parlor of Victorian London, whispering, "I probably shouldn't say anything."

"It's not catty chatter," Ellie assured the woman. "It's background material for an official police investigation."

Anne plowed ahead. "It's just funny what you said about Tanya having some money. I always wondered about that. I should have figured that girl stashed something away. And to think she let her mother die worrying about hospital bills."

"What made you think Tanya was holding out?"

"Because I talked to her one day, right about the time the realtor put up the For Sale sign outside their house. Must've been just a month after Marion died. I asked her, wasn't there some way she could hold on to the house on her own. She said she tried, but that the money was all tied up."

"What money was that?"

"Exactly. I pressed her on it, and she got real nervous and said she had some money from an uncle but that she had to use it for school. Well, that surprised the heck out of me, because as far as I knew, Marion was an only child, and Tanya's daddy was never part of the picture. So I said, 'Well, you're sort of old to be going back to school, aren't you?' And she said something like, 'Well, that's what the money's for, and you never know.' Then she scurried back into the house, and I never thought it my place to ask her about it again. Tanya moved out not long after that, and I've never seen her since."

Ellie thanked Anne for her time and hung up the phone just as Rogan was doing the same.

"Anything?" he asked.

"More questions than answers," she said. "Tanya's mom was a nanny. Died about three years ago with a ton of debt. The bank sold the house from under Tanya. The neighbor did say Tanya mentioned something once about having some money for school that an uncle gave her, but the neighbor doesn't think Tanya even has an uncle."

"Maybe a sugar daddy?"

"Who knows. What do you have?"

"Dr. Lyle Hewson's still in business. Closed on Saturday, of course, but from the on-call number, I finally got through to his assistant. Big surprise, she was worried about patient confidentiality, but I did ask if Dr. Hewson ever did pro bono work on court cases or anything like that. She laughed and said the doctor wouldn't get out of bed for free. She also said he charges one-fifty an hour."

"Would've been less ten years ago."

"Eighty-five, to be precise."

"Too much for a single mom working as a nanny."

"Way too much."

Ellie tapped her pen against the desk, wondering what it all meant.

# CHAPTER THIRTY-NINE

**SUNDAY, SEPTEMBER 28**

**2:45 A.M.**

"**N**iiicccce."

The meathead in a black leather blazer and too much Polo cologne eyed Ellie's chest as she approached the club's entrance. Apparently in her sleep-deprived state, she had not tugged sufficiently at the zipper of the hoodie she had pulled on as she ran out of her apartment.

"You're not doing so bad yourself," she said, poking one of the man's flabby pecs. "Where's my brother? Jess Hatcher. About your height but eighty pounds lighter."

"As smart-assed as you but a hell of a lot less cute?"

"That's the one."

"Saw him go in the back office with one of the girls about ten minutes ago. Knowing your brother, you might want to knock first."

Against all her better instincts, Jess managed about once a month to persuade her to drop by this place for one reason or another. Given that he'd started working here in March, she guessed this was her seventh trip to Vibrations. For years, Jess had been that guy who couldn't hold down a long-term job. He managed to hang in for three months as a short-order cook at a Garment District diner one time, but only out of guilt, since Ellie had been the one to find him the gig. His average was a few weeks.

But for reasons she might never understand, this cheesy, neon-lit, 1980s hair-band-blasting strip club on the West Side Highway had brought out the best in her brother. Vibrations was the kind of upside-down, backward, bizarro universe where Jess was the sensible adult and the packs of lawyers and money managers whooping it up for a bachelor party were the raging idiots.

Ellie's periodic pop-ins were usually preceded by some promise from Jess of the most amazing display of carnal creativity ever witnessed. Ping pong balls were commonly involved.

But this time Jess had promised her more than entertainment. She found him on a couch in the office, the woman perched beside him eyeing Ellie with skepticism.

"Is that her?"

"Yeah. My sister. Ellie Hatcher. She'll take care of you, Jasmine."

Jasmine's look matched the name. She had dark brown hair with caramel streaks that fell well past her shoulder blades. She had teased and sprayed it just enough to replicate pillow-tousled sex hair. She threw Jess a pout that managed to be simultaneously angry and sexy. No doubt she scored big tips with that pout.

"Your brother has a way of talking people into stuff they really don't want to do."

"Tell me about it. He says you know something about Prestige Parties?"

# CHAPTER FORTY

It turned out that Jasmine was her actual, legal name. Jasmine Anne Harris, twenty-six years old. Her only appearances in the NYPD's data system were ancient history: listed as a witness to a domestic assault against her mother when she was ten; as the complainant in a Rape II when she was thirteen by an assailant who shared the last name Harris; and then four runaway juvenile reports over the next two years. Jasmine's home life had not been a happy one.

But she had managed to keep her own criminal record clean, even as she admitted to Max and Ellie that she'd been on and off drugs for the last eight years—from pot to coke to heroin to meth—periodically turning tricks as she needed to support first her habit and now her three-year-old son.

Currently she sat in a conference room of the district attorney's office, wearing the Columbia Law School sweatshirt that Max had offered her when she'd arrived this morning in a low-cut spaghetti-strap top to detail everything she knew about Prestige Parties.

According to Jasmine, the head of the operation was an older man she knew only as Uncle Dave. According to the articles of incorporation that Prestige Parties had filed with the attorney general's office, the company's CEO and sole shareholder was named

David Taylor. Jasmine knew only a little more about the two sisters who helped Dave find girls and book dates. Their names were Corliss and Cadence LaMarche.

Jasmine suspected she wasn't supposed to know their last names, but Corliss had let it slip once. She'd asked Jasmine if that was her real name, and Jasmine had confirmed that it was and then asked Corliss the same. "Yep. Corliss, Cadence, and our brother Caleb. I guess our mom figured that with the last name LaMarche we may as well double down on trying to sound like royalty."

"She only mentioned it the once," Jasmine said, "but I remember because I kept repeating it to myself. Corliss LaMarche. Really classy. A lot better than Jasmine Harris, you know?"

Jasmine paused intermittently to wonder aloud whether she was "shooting herself in the hip." That was a phrase that Jasmine seemed to favor.

This time when she invoked the saying, it was after she took a big sip from the bottle of Mountain Dew that Ellie had fetched for her from the DA's vending machine. "You know, I keep thinking that I'm shooting myself in the hip." She let out a tiny burp of carbonation from the soda and then covered her mouth and giggled. "Even giving Prestige half the cash, I've been taking home between seven and twelve hundred bucks a night when I work for them. They only use me every couple of weeks, but combined with what I'm making at Vibrations, I've been doing pretty good. I can't go back to hundred-dollar dates with the pricks I meet at the club."

Someone at Prestige Parties had managed to persuade Jasmine that she had earned her way into that elite category of high-class, high-price call girls. They had sold her on the idea of a fantasy world in which smart, beautiful women earned financial independence and a kind of feminist empowerment by taking money from weak but adoring men for something as easy as sexual contact.

But working decoy operations on patrol, Ellie had gotten to know the girls on the corners, the ones with the callused feet, hardened eyes, and faded bruises. And she knew that the line that divided them from the Prestige Party girls of the world was nonexistent.

Just as a lawyer could use his skills to move from job to job and industry to industry—defending gas companies and then drug makers
and then the latest indicted politician—sex workers moved from
stripping to porn to dominatrix dungeons to street corners to three-
thousand-dollar-a-night hotel penthouses.

"You'll land on your feet," Ellie assured her. "Think about it
this way, Jasmine. Are you any prettier now than you were when
you were getting a hundred dollars a date?"

"Hell, no," she said, smiling. "I'm only getting older, and thanks
to my kid, I've got stretch marks on my belly."

"And are you doing anything drastically different for these men
now that they're paying a thousand dollars a night compared to
what you were doing before?"

She shook her head. "No pervs. I strictly cover the basics."

"So if you're the same attractive woman, doing the same exact
thing, why do you think these men are paying more?"

"Beats the shit out of me."

"Because they've been told you're worth it. Tell a guy that you're
worth a hundred bucks, and that's how he's going to treat you. But
force them to pony up a couple grand, they're already convinced
you're the most beautiful girl they've ever seen. They truly believe
you have secret skills to rock their tedious worlds. When Prestige
Parties is over and done with, all you'll have to do is look the next
guy in the eye and tell him what it costs, and that's what you're going
to get."

Jasmine took another sip of her soda. "Damn fucking straight I'm
worth it. A thousand bucks a night isn't even that much in the city.
I've heard of girls who make as much as ten." Her eyes gleamed at
the thought.

"Now tell us again about the women who book the dates."

The truth was, despite Ellie's assurances that Jasmine would find
some way to make the money up, she honestly didn't care. Persuading Jasmine to cooperate was a necessary step to bringing down
Prestige Parties, which was a necessary step to finding Katie Bat-

tle's murderer. If Jasmine wound up broke and desperate again, it wouldn't be because of Ellie.

It took Jasmine another hour to tell them everything she knew. Uncle Dave. The two sisters, Corliss and Cadence. Six dates in the last three and a half months, all involving sex for money. And now she was in the district attorney's fifteenth-floor conference room, eating a package of Hostess Cupcakes from yet another trip to the vending machine, while they conferred in the hallway.

"It's still not enough," Max announced.

"How is that possible?" Ellie asked. "That girl, despite all the old drugs and recent refined sugar flowing through her veins, has one of the best memories I've come across in a witness. She's willing to let us use her name. She's got no criminal history and no apparent motive to lie. Her word, plus what we already got from Stacy Schecter, has to be enough."

"It's the same problem you always have with these agencies. The entire purpose of an escort service is to look legit. She knows this guy as Uncle Dave, which is about as creepy a name as I can think of for a pimp. But on paper, according to the AG's office, he's David Taylor, the CEO and sole shareholder of a legitimate corporation that provides legal and luxurious entertainment. They dot their *i*'s and cross their *t*'s. They're lawfully incorporated. They had Jasmine fill out a W-4 to pay taxes on that income. I'm sure he pays the LaMarche sisters with reported funds, too, as well as paying taxes on all the company's earnings. These people aren't stupid."

"No, but they are guilty of promoting prostitution in the third degree. We get the arrest warrant, hook them up on the felony charge, seize all their assets, and then use the money and the criminal case against them to get some answers about Katie Battle and Tanya Abbott."

"The problem is they've covered their asses. You heard Jasmine. They told her not to engage in sex with the client. They even had her sign a piece of paper acknowledging that any sexual contact with the client was automatic grounds for dismissal."

"And she also said she knew when she signed that document that it was just for show. When Corliss first approached her at Vibrations, she even asked her if she ever dated."

"You and I know that *dating* is code, but Uncle Dave will argue it means innocent companionship."

"We don't need a conviction. I just want the leverage. I want some answers."

They heard the creak of the conference room door. Like most of the doors in any building with a Centre Street address, it could use some WD-40.

"Um, is everything okay?"

"Just fine, Jasmine. If you can wait a few more minutes, we can explain what we're going to do next."

"It sounds like you guys are fighting." Jasmine looked at her with the worried eyes of a child, and Ellie realized that some part of Jasmine's personality would always be frozen in adolescence, suspended in time at that first knock on her bedroom door, the knock that had finally led to the police report when she was thirteen years old.

Ellie assured her once more and waited for the conference room door to close before speaking again in a quieter voice.

"Let's take it to Judge Bandon. He'll do anything for us right now. He'll sign the warrant."

Max shook his head. "That's not right, Ellie, and you know it. We need more evidence."

This wasn't the first time Ellie had butted heads with a prosecutor. Prosecutors were always worried about trying their cases before a jury, having every thread of every last detail knotted and tucked away to create a smooth, impenetrable layer of proof. Police needed enough evidence to know in their gut they had the right guy.

Usually, though, when Ellie didn't see eye to eye with a prosecutor, the prosecutor wasn't a man who shared her bed a couple times a week. That tiny little distinction had Ellie on better behavior than she otherwise might have been.

But she still wanted her answers.

"I'm sorry, Max, but I'll go to Bandon for the warrant myself if you don't have some other suggestion."

Max swallowed and shook his head. She held his stare defiantly but felt one corner of her mouth move upward.

"Damn, you're sexy," he said.

"I'm also right. We can't be this close and just stop."

He stepped toward her. She felt his breath whisper across her forehead. "You know I never stop when we're close. I just might need to take a little detour."

His body was so close to her now that she felt his hand move near his hip. She closed her eyes. Just when she thought he was reaching for her, she heard the creak of a door, followed by Max's voice from the threshold of the conference room.

"Jasmine, sweetheart, I'm afraid I'm going to have to ask you for one more thing."

Ellie pushed past him through the doorway. "You're a tease."

"You said you wanted a suggestion."


The phone rang three times before a woman answered in a professional tone. "Prestige."

"Hi, is this Corliss?"

"I'm sorry. Who's speaking, please?"

Ellie gave an encouraging nod to Jasmine, who was clutching the handset of the conference room telephone so tightly that her knuckles were turning white. Ellie listened to the conversation through a headset plugged into a digital recorder, which was in turn attached to the base of the phone.

"It's Jasmine Harris."

"Oh, hey there, Jasmine." The woman's businesslike demeanor melted into the voice of a girlfriend. "We haven't forgotten aboutcha. I'll give ya a call as soon as we've got some work for ya."

"It's actually that, well, I guess I have work. Or at least a chance to work. One of my dates from last month saw me at Vibrations last night and wants an appointment for tomorrow. Guess his wife is visiting her sister or something."

"Well, I haven't gotten any calls asking for you, babe. Sorry."

"No, I mean, he's just planning to come by the club tomorrow to meet me. I wasn't thinking about it last night, but then it dawned on me that might not be cool with you guys. I don't want to mess up what I've got going with you just for one trick, you know?"

"You mean an appointment, Jasmine."

"Right, an appointment. Sorry."

"It's good you called. The models are definitely not allowed to date Prestige clients except through the company. Every once in a while, we'll have a client get really close to one of the girls and want to see her on a regular basis, but we expect a buyout in exchange for making that initial introduction. Do you think it's that kind of a situation?"

"Nah, he just happened to come in with some of his buddies. Who knows whether he'll even show up tomorrow. If he does, I'll tell him he's got to talk to you guys."

"It's for the best, Jasmine. Uncle Dave's a real stickler about that. If he finds out the models are booking privately, they're gone. He puts the word out to other agencies, too."

Ellie knew that last part was a bluff.

"No big loss," Jasmine said. "Dude was kind of a freak anyway. It was the guy from Labor Day weekend. Kept trying to take the rubber off during oral. I was trying to go down on him and kept winding up with his little dick and his stubby fingers in my mouth. I couldn't tell what was what."

They'd rehearsed the line with Jasmine at least six times before placing the call, but she still managed to deliver it with that silly giggle of hers. It worked, because Corliss laughed and dropped her guard. "I'll look up the name and make a note of it. We tell everyone to keep it safe, but some of the girls still accept bareback on oral. And, don't forget, watch it on the phone, Jasmine, okay?"

"Yeah, sorry."

"No problem. And I'll try to find something for you this week to make up for tonight, all right?"

"Thanks, Corliss."

Jasmine hung up the phone and worked the kinks out of her knuckles. "Was that okay?"

Ellie couldn't help but grab the girl's hands across the table. "That, Ms. Harris, was unbelievable."

But it wasn't Ellie's approval that Jasmine yearned for. She looked up with wide eyes toward Max, who was sitting with one hip against the conference table. "Was that good? Did it sound good?"

"You were perfect, Jasmine."

She removed her hands from Ellie's and used them to pull Max's sweatshirt up over her chin. Ellie knew that sweatshirt would smell good, like a blend of truffles and cedar and lavender and coffee. Like Max. Like home. It was the kind of smell that made a woman feel safe.

For a second, Jasmine looked happy.

# CHAPTER FORTY-ONE

"I don't know how many times I need to explain this to you, Detectives. I'm a business owner." David Taylor tugged at the lapels of his navy sports jacket as if the attire spoke for itself. "I spent what seemed like a lifetime owning a bar on the Upper East Side in the nineties. Check it out. No marks on my license. A good relationship with the boys in the Nineteenth. Call Ed Devlin up there. He might be retired by now, but he'll tell you, I'm good people."

Ellie had been pacing behind Taylor in the interrogation room as he repeated his mantra that he was a legitimate businessman. Now she leaned one hip against the table in front of him. "You don't own a bar anymore, Uncle Dave, and the boys in the Nineteenth don't know bupkes about Prestige Parties. Or, if they do, they're not exactly going to tell me, now are they?"

"The bar"—Taylor pronounced it "Bah," with a northeast accent—"closed down almost ten years ago. Made a mistake not buying the building when I had the chance. Couldn't keep up with the rents, you know. Turned out okay, though. All those hours keeping bar, I saw how things work. Hardworking men with a lot of money but not a lot of time just want someone pretty to spend an evening with. Classy, smart, attractive girls."

"Prostitutes," Ellie said. "And you're their pimp."

"No way, ma'am. I know better than that. I want no part of such a thing. I'm a Catholic, for God's sake. Pretty sure the pope frowns on pimping. I even had a lawyer draw up documents for the girls to sign, just in case they got the wrong idea. No sex allowed. No way, no how, or they're out the door."

She'd had Taylor in this room for twenty minutes now, and his story wasn't budging. Rogan was down the hall in another interrogation room with Corliss LaMarche. The last Ellie had heard, Cadence was rock solid, so Rogan had moved her to a holding cell so he could work on the weaker sister alone.

"We've got your employee Corliss on tape, Taylor." She hit the play button on the digital recorder and heard Jasmine's voice as clearly as if she were sitting in the room with them.

*"Just for one trick, you know?"* Taylor smiled with satisfaction as Corliss corrected her: *"You mean an appointment, Jasmine."*

His face fell slightly when Corliss explained the buyout requirement for private dates. *"Uncle Dave's a real stickler about that."*

"Oh, wait," Ellie said, "here comes my favorite part." She caught a slight chuckle in Taylor's breath as Jasmine described performing oral sex as her date attempted to remove the condom.

*"We tell everyone to keep it safe, but some of the girls still accept bareback on oral. And, don't forget, watch it on the phone, Jasmine, okay?"*

Ellie hit the stop button, and Taylor shook his head. "I can't believe Corliss would stand for such a thing. If she and some of the girls have been engaged in this kind of conduct, it was certainly not with my knowledge. I've been absolutely clear—"

"I know, I know," Ellie said. "No sex. They signed the papers."

"Exactly."

She heard a knock on the door and cracked it open to find Rogan.

"Wait a second," Taylor said. "Don't tell me. This is the part where someone comes in and tells me that that airhead Corliss dimed me up as the big bad boss in charge of the whole operation. Well, guess what, Detectives? I've seen every single episode of *Law and Order*, and I'm not falling for it. Corliss did this on her own. I'm a legitimate businessman, and if you don't believe me, you can talk to my lawyer."

Rogan opened the door ajar. "Actually, Mr. Taylor, I wasn't here to speak with you at all. You have a guest here to see you."

Behind Rogan stood a house of a woman, nearly six feet tall, an easy two hundred pounds, with bright orange hair and green eye-shadow that managed to clash with her multicolored floral silk shirt and thick gold cuff necklace. "God damn it, Dave. What the hell have you dragged my daughters into?"

"This is Mr. Taylor's sister, Karen LaMarche. She's Corliss and Cadence's mother. She'd like to have a word with her brother."

Apparently Uncle Dave was *literally* Uncle Dave.

Fifteen minutes after they left Karen LaMarche alone in the interro-gation room with her brother, they heard a tap against the one-way window. Taylor wasn't lying when he said he'd watched a lot of *Law and Order.*

By the time they opened the door, Taylor's sister was already pressing her way past Ellie. "My son of a bitch brother will tell you whatever you need to hear," she said. "But my girls, my daughters, they get a deal. They walk."

Ellie had already called Max as she'd eavesdropped on the con-versation between Taylor and his sister. He was prepared to grant immunity to Corliss and Cadence as long as they cooperated.

"Only if Dave here agrees," Ellie said. "No deal for him. Just the girls. We need full access to every piece of information Prestige Parties has. All clients. All dates."

"But Corliss and Cadence get a full walk, right?" Taylor asked. "No one can even know I got them into this. Their names can't be on any single piece of paper. Nothing."

"No problem."

"Okay, then, yeah, whatever. I got all of it in the computer. Go to town on it."

"Where?" Ellie asked.

"At home, whaddaya think? But welcome to the twenty-first century, sweetheart. Some tech dweeb—one of those guys who tells you his name is John but you know it's really Sanji—hooked me up so me and the girls could all access the appointments whenever we wanted. Get me online and I can tell you what you need to know. Let's get this over with, for my nieces' sake."

Karen LaMarche gave Ellie a satisfied smile.

"What got into him?" Ellie asked as the woman turned to walk away.

"Would you believe me if I said an uncle's love for his family?"

"Nope."

"Let's just say I've got dirt on him that might not land him upstate, but would cost him big at home."

"Bigger than serving three to five for running a prostitution ring?" Rogan asked.

"Don't ask me why, but my sister-in-law, Carmen? She loves that fat slob. Worships the ground he walks on. She'll visit him every week in prison and won't give a damn whether you take every last nickel from their bank account. She'll find it in herself to forgive him, but not if she knows he brought my girls into it. She loves them like they're her own. It would break her heart. And even though my brother's a pig, he just couldn't live with himself." She stopped and called out to her brother. "You hear me, Dave? You be nice to these detectives, or I'll be here with my cell phone calling Carmen right in front of you."

"Yeah, yeah," he said, waving her to leave him in the relative peace of the run-down interrogation room.

They were interrupted by a knock on the door, followed by the tentative peek of the civilian aide who monitored the front desk. "Detective Hatcher. There's a woman here to see you. She was very persistent but won't give me her name."

Rogan waved her to go. "I think Dave and I are just fine now. Let's see if we can't get a laptop in here."

★   ★   ★

The woman was waiting in the rickety wooden chair next to Ellie's desk. Her perfectly tailored jade green suit and freshly set hair looked out of place among the dinge and dishevel of the squad room.

"Mrs. Bandon." Ellie offering her outstretched hand, Laura Bandon gave it a limp shake.

"Thank you for making time for me, Detective. I hope you'll understand why I didn't want to give my name to the young man up front."

Ellie took a seat across from her at the desk. "I'm not sure that I do, actually."

"I'm aware of the subject of your visit to my apartment yesterday morning. I thought as a woman, I might implore you to treat this as a private matter between me and my husband."

"It's not just a matter of privacy. There are crimes involved. And your husband is a judge. He used to be a prosecutor. I'm sure at some point he has sent someone to jail for doing what he did here."

Laura crossed her manicured hands in her lap. "Paul has plenty of failings as a man, and I suppose being a hypocrite is one of them. But we have a son, and a family, and, if you must know, a certain understanding." She held Ellie's gaze. "I was aware of this woman—not her specifically, but of her existence—if it makes any difference to you."

"It doesn't make any difference as far as the law is concerned."

"Well, it probably should. I'll spare you the details of my own shortcomings, but the truth is, we're both happier if he has his outside activities. He's still very much devoted to me and our son. And if this becomes public, my husband won't be the only one harmed by it. My son will enter Harvard Law School a laughingstock. I will become that woman with the stoic stare during her Stand By My Man moment. You saw what happened to Eliot Spitzer's wife. Here was a woman who had been a successful lawyer in her own right at one of the best law firms in the nation. And just because of a private decision she made with her husband, she's mocked now by the entire city as some brainwashed, antifeminist Stepford Wife."

Ellie had Googled Laura Bandon just yesterday and could understand why the woman empathized with New York's former first lady. Like her, Laura had graduated from the country's top schools, had worked several years at a big law firm, and then served on numerous charitable boards even after she stopped practicing law.

"She was in that sort of spotlight for a moment," Ellie said. "But who knows? She could be secretary of state in a few years."

"It's not worth the humiliation. Please, I'm begging you, Detective. All I'm asking is that, before you decide, please give some thought to the other lives you'll be affecting. This isn't just about Paul."

She rose and walked away without waiting for a response.


"Yeah, here it is. Friday night." On the laptop screen in front of him, David Taylor pointed to a spreadsheet entry for the night of Katie Battle's murder. "She had an initial meet-up at six o'clock at the bar of the Royalton Hotel. She called in safe. That's a nice joint. Went there once in the nineties and saw Bryan Adams, standing right there in the lobby. He was a good guy. Let me take a picture—"

Rogan tapped Taylor on the back.

"Yo, watch it." Maybe it was more than a tap.

"Enough with the reminiscing," Rogan said. "Who was the date, Uncle Dave? Who met Katie at the Royalton that night?"

"Doesn't say."

"What do you mean, it doesn't say? You've got to have a phone number or a credit card or something."

"Well, we usually do."

"So why don't you have it this time?" Rogan asked.

" 'Cause apparently Cadence booked it anonymously."

"I didn't think you did that," Ellie said. "Isn't that the whole reason these girls give you half the money? They figure if the johns are giving you their names and phone numbers, there's a layer of accountability built into the process. They assume they're safe."

Taylor shrugged. "Yeah, well, that's the ideal, but it ain't always realistic. It's like that pregnant girl said about abstinence—"

Ellie shook her head. "Bad analogy, Dave."

"Look, all I can tell you is Cadence booked the date the day before. We usually get some kind of contact information, but some guys are nervous. They got girlfriends, wives. They're afraid of cops. Whatever. So we use our, you know, our *discretion*. My nieces have good judgment. If they sent Miranda out with someone, he presented good over the phone. Rich. Classy. And, like I said, she called in safe."

"Just because someone *sounds* safe, you assume he is? You never heard of a guy named Ted Bundy?"

"Baah, Ted Bundy. If that guy had walked into my bar, I would've known he was wrong. You're a detective. You gotta know what I mean. It's instinct. I probably shouldn't tell you how long we've been doing this, but we go on our guts, and we've never had a problem."

"Sure, until now. I think what happened to Katie Battle qualifies as a problem." Ellie made a mental note to put Katie's mother in touch with a lawyer. With any luck, David Taylor would wind up paying for the care her daughter couldn't quite afford.

"I know, you're trying to make me feel guilty. You don't think I've spent the last day and a half wondering if I could have done something more to protect that girl? I'm not a monster. But you know what? She's the one who made that choice for herself. I don't force anyone to do nothing they don't want to do. Plus, take a look at this. This checkmark right here? That means the guy specifically asked for Miranda. We keep track of that sort of thing in case she can't make it, you know? You can't just send some other girl if he asked for a certain one. And, speaking for Cadence, I gotta think that she figured anyone who already knew the girl had to be one of her former customers. She figured he was all right."

Rogan leaned over to get a better look at the laptop. "If the guy already knew her as Miranda, he might've known her through your service."

"Could be. She'd been working for us for about a year."

"Can you pull up a list of all the clients you ever booked for her?"

"Yeah, no problem," Taylor said.

If they were lucky, they'd find someone whose background over-lapped with Tanya Abbott's. Maybe someone from Baltimore.

Taylor laughed and shook his head as he examined the list of cal-endar entries he'd pulled up on the screen. "Now that one there could've been worth a mint. If I'd really been smart, I should have closed up shop and gotten into the blackmail business before this shower of crap came pouring down on me."

"What are you talking about?" Rogan asked.

Taylor pointed to a charge on a credit card belonging to the SDS Group. "Let's just say the person behind that corporation is someone we've all heard of."

"Names, Taylor."

The glint in Taylor's beady eyes might as well have been dollar signs. He was working through the blackmail angle, wondering whether he might raise some cash for a legal defense fund.

"We can call the state for information about the corporation. That's how we found you, remember?" Rogan raised his hand for another light tap of the back, but Taylor stopped him.

"Okay, whatever. Far as I know, the SDS Group's an arm of Sparks Industries."

Ellie and Rogan stared at each other in silence.

"What? You guys have heard of Sam Sparks, right?"

# CHAPTER FORTY-TWO

"**W**e're missing something." Ellie tossed back the rest of her Diet Coke, squeezed the can into the shape of an hourglass, and pitched it into the recycling bin in the corner, the latest sign of a reformed NYPD.

Their whiteboard had spiraled into a spiderweb of tangled lines in blue, black, and purple marker. Photographs, phone records, and printouts from Prestige Parties covered nearly every inch of the table and floor of the interrogation room.

They were missing something. And it had something to do with Tanya Abbott.

"Separate what we know as fact from what we've been speculating," Rogan said. He rotated the plane of the whiteboard to bring forward a clean slate for notes. "Fact: Tanya Abbott was Robert Mancini's date on the night of May 27."

"Fact," Ellie said, "Katie Battle was originally supposed to be the woman on that date, but when her mother had a stroke, Katie called Stacy to cover for her, who in turn called Tanya Abbott."

Rogan jotted down the facts on the board with a thick black marker. "The date was booked through Prestige anonymously, but the caller asked specifically for Miranda, suggesting he'd dated her before."

"That second part's speculation," Ellie said.

"We'll write it in blue, then," Rogan said, switching pens for the final notation.

"Fact: Sam Sparks's company uses Prestige Parties and, specifically, had previously retained the services of Katie Battle. Fact: Judge Paul Bandon utilized the services of Tanya Abbott. Fact: Judge Paul Bandon took a special interest in our investigation of the Robert Mancini homicide."

Rogan paused. "You really think we can call that fact?"

"Yes, I do. And I'm not talking about my little stopover in lockup. I'm willing to suck that up as my own doing. But hauling you in for a briefing on the status of the case? *That* was not standard operating procedure. So, yes, *fact*. Our *speculation* was that Bandon was trying to kiss up to Sparks so he would grease the political wheels for him. But maybe we're missing an entirely different kind of motive."

"Such as?"

Ellie smiled. "Not to say I told you so, but what if Sparks really did do it? What if he killed Robert Mancini because the bodyguard saw more than he was supposed to?"

"You're forgetting that Tanya Abbott did it."

"That's not fact. That's speculation."

"Fact: She posted all that nonsense about Megan Gunther online to throw us off track. Fact: Shortly after disappearing, she threatened us and our families if we kept looking for her."

"Set aside Tanya and Megan for a second."

"It's a lot to set aside," Rogan said.

"Just hear me out. We've got almost twenty charges in the last year and a half by Prestige Parties onto Sparks's corporate charge card. And we've got Robert Mancini's final night connected to Prestige Parties and to Tanya Abbott."

"But Abbott's date with Mancini was *not* on Sparks's charge card."

Sparks had rung up plenty of business at the escort service, but

Tanya Abbott's date on May 27—like Katie Battle's on Friday night—
was booked anonymously as a cash date. "Just hold on a sec. We've
also got Judge Bandon connected to Tanya Abbott. And Judge
Bandon has been bending over backward to help Sparks."

"And what exactly are you ready to speculate from that?"

"We cleared Sparks on the Mancini murder because we thought
there was no way he could have known that Mancini was at the 212
that night. But we'd been assuming that Mancini lined up the date
on his own."

Rogan finished the thought. "But if Sparks was the one who
hooked Mancini up with a woman for the night, he would've already
known where Mancini would be taking her."

"Correct," Ellie said. "And then his timeline in the afternoon
would be meaningless."

"But Sparks was at a fund-raiser at the time of Mancini's murder.
Showed up in the tux and everything."

"A guy like Sparks doesn't pull the trigger himself. He hires
someone to do it for him. And if Sparks was behind Mancini's
murder, Judge Bandon's special interest in the case takes on a whole
new light. If Sparks knew about Bandon's little visits to Tanya
Abbott—"

"That's a big if," Rogan interrupted.

"Hey, we're in speculation land here. Let me speculate. *If* Sparks
knew Bandon's secret, he could've pressed Bandon to keep us away
from his financials and to keep a close eye on the case for him."

"So now we'd be looking at Bandon not just for prostitution,
but—"

"Bribery," Ellie said. "A quid pro quo where Bandon keeps us
away from the financial records that would have shown a connection between Sparks and Prestige Parties. And in return Sparks
keeps Bandon's extracurricular activities to himself. Maybe helps
him get that plum federal judicial appointment Bandon wants so
desperately."

"You really think Bandon would help cover up a murder?"

Ellie shook her head. "No, but maybe he doesn't realize Sparks is the doer. He threw me in the clink for even thinking about it. He just thinks he's helping Sparks cover up the prostitution stuff. Maybe Sparks put it to him as, 'Hey, I hear we have something in common that would be better kept a secret'?"

"But again, this only makes sense if Sparks and Bandon both knew about the other's connections to these women. How would that happen?"

"I don't know."

"Don't forget that you were setting aside our friend Tanya." Rogan snapped the caps back onto the markers. "How does she fit into all this if Sparks is our guy for Mancini?"

Ellie looked at the facts on the board. "I don't know. We're missing something."

Rogan shook his head. "If I said something that stupid, you'd throw something at me."

Ellie paced the interrogation room, taking in the tiny bites of information laid out like oddly shaped pieces of an enormous jigsaw puzzle. The phone calls. Tanya's fingerprints at the 212 and in Megan's apartment. May 27. The photographs.

And then she saw it.


"It's not Tanya," she said.

"What's not Tanya?"

"Our killer."

"I know, you think it's Sam Sparks."

"No, I mean, *at all*. It's not her. She's not a killer. She's not on the run. Or at least, not from us. She's running from the killer."

"What are you talking about?"

"The photographs, Rogan. The pictures. This one." She plucked one of the color prints of the 212 crime scene from the linoleum-topped interrogation room table. It showed the bathroom of Sam Sparks's apartment on the night of Mancini's murder.

"It's a fucking bathroom."

Ellie flashed back to her testimony in Paul Bandon's courtroom.

Every room in Sparks's penthouse had been torn to pieces—except the bathroom. Max had even made that lame joke: *I guess extra rolls of toilet paper and back issues of* Sports Illustrated *aren't the usual targets of a home invasion.*

But the bathroom wasn't completely untouched. A single cabinet door was ajar; its former contents—a stack of towels—had spilled to the tile floor.

Ellie tapped the open cabinet in the photograph. "That's where she was. That's where she was hiding."

"Tanya Abbott was hiding in the bathroom."

"Yep. She heard the shots—or maybe an argument preceding the shots—and tucked herself into the back of that cabinet behind the towels. She heard it all. And when the shooter was gone, she crawled out, leaving the cabinet open and the towels on the floor behind her. The shooter never realized she was there. Not until Max posted this photograph in Paul Bandon's courtroom."

"Where Sam Sparks saw it," Rogan said.

"Where Sparks saw it and realized whoever he hired to do the job left a witness behind. Whatever Tanya overheard could lead back to him."

"So now Tanya's on the run to get away from Sam Sparks. Or whoever's killing people on Sparks's behalf."

"They came after Tanya at her apartment, and Megan was caught in the crossfire. And then when Tanya saw the news about Katie Battle's murder, she realized she was being hunted and took off."

Ellie interrupted her own train of thought as she realized the flaw in this latest thread of speculation. "But wait. The timing's backward. If Sparks was covering his tracks, he would have started with Katie. She was the one who was supposed to be at the 212 with Mancini. Torturing Katie for answers would have led him to Stacy, who would have eventually led him to Tanya."

"But Tanya was attacked first, not Katie. And Stacy's just fine."

"Damn it." Ellie flopped into the chair next to the table, still holding the photograph of the bathroom cabinet. "She was there, Rogan. I can feel it. Tanya Abbott was hiding inside that bathroom.

And the fact that Sam Sparks saw this picture in Bandon's court-room has something to do with all these bodies."

"If Tanya Abbott's our victim and not our bad guy, how do you explain the posts on Campus Juice?"

She looked up to the ceiling as if the answers might be found there. "I don't know," she finally said.

"Don't tell me," Rogan said. "We're missing something."

"We're missing something. But if even part of what I'm thinking is right, then Stacy Schecter is a link in the chain. We have to warn her. *Now.*"

# CHAPTER FORTY-THREE

S tacy's music was cranked to ear-numbing decibel levels again. This time she was listening to Patti Smith's cover of the Stones' "Gimme Shelter." Ellie had to hand it to the girl, she had excellent taste—just the kind of woman she wished her brother would date, minus the occasional penchant for prostitution.

She knocked on the door to no avail, and then quickly shifted to a pound.

Inside, Patti was howling. *"Rape, murder, it's just a shot away."* Ellie tried to ignore the irony and thumped harder on the door with the butt of her fist. "Stacy, it's Detective Hatcher from the NYPD. I need to talk to you. It's urgent."

Ellie felt eyes on her and turned to see a pair of tired, pale blue ones staring through a crack in the door of Apartment 2C just as the music's volume dropped. "It's about time you people came out here. It's constant. At all hours. And the most horrendous noise."

"Mind your own business, you old—" Stacy halted in the door-way when she spotted Ellie. "Jesus Christ, I gave you an entire night already. I'm totally in the zone. Just let me do my work in peace."

"You really want to talk about your *work* out here in the hallway?" Ellie asked.

Stacy stepped aside to make room for Ellie to pass and then closed the door behind her.

"I know, I know. Sex for money, bad. Law-abiding life of goodness, good. The NYPD has done its soul-saving for the week. Message sent."

"I'm not here to lecture you, Stacy."

"Could've fooled me the other day. And I notice you're here alone. Did your partner realize you were wasting your breath?"

"My partner's finishing some reports the DA's office needed in our case against Prestige Parties. We made arrests this morning."

Stacy looked genuinely surprised. And impressed. "You two didn't waste any time, did you?"

"And we kept your name out of it, just like we promised. You went into the affidavits as a confidential informant. We found another girl who was willing to go on record. Together, it was enough. We've got the head of the company cooperating already. Still no sign of Tanya, though, and still a lot of theories about who might have killed Miranda."

"You mean Katie."

"I do, but you knew her as Miranda."

Stacy wiped a smear of yellow paint from her thumb onto her smock. "Can't really know someone if you don't know their name."

"I've got a couple of follow-up questions, if you can spare the time."

"Yeah, sure. I needed a break anyway." She gestured to her bed and then perched herself on the corner.

Ellie removed two photographs from her purse. One was a snapshot she had pulled from the Web archives of the *New York Post*'s Page Six column. It showed Sam Sparks braving the rain to enter the Metropolitan Museum of Art for the annual Costume Institute benefit. He posed for the camera on the red carpet beside event organizer and *Vogue* magazine editor Anna Wintour while a drenched Nick Dillon held a black umbrella over their dry heads.

The second photograph was Judge Paul Bandon's official head shot from the New York State Unified Court System's Web site, complete with black robe, an American flag in the background, and a gavel in Bandon's right hand. According to the bio beneath the picture, Bandon had served as a career prosecutor inside the Department of Justice until he'd moved to New York as special counsel to one of the country's most elite law firms and then on to his current spot on the bench. It was indeed the perfect résumé for a federal judicial appointment. And all of it would be ruined if his relationship with Tanya Abbott were revealed.

"Have you seen either of these men before?"

Stacy took the printouts from her outstretched hands. She reviewed them carefully before handing them back. "No, I'm sorry."

"You're sure?" Ellie said.

"Positive. I mean, yeah, the one—Sam Sparks—obviously I've seen him before in the paper and stuff. But never in person. What does he have to do with any of this?"

"We don't know. Maybe nothing. Did Miranda ever mention he was a Prestige Parties customer?"

Stacy stifled a chuckle. "Really? That's *awesome*."

"I kept your name out of our case, Stacy. You need to keep the fact that I asked you about these men to yourself."

She waved away Ellie's concerns. "No, it's just funny is all. I mean, the tabloids are always hinting he swings for the other team, and turns out he's a big old horndog. Hey, maybe now that you've brought Prestige Parties down, he's in the market for a new girl." She mimicked a Mae West primp.

Ellie rose to leave. "Not a good idea. I said I wasn't here to lecture you, but I did come here with a warning. These guys are poster children for rich, educated, highly distinguished men, and here I am flashing their photographs as part of a homicide investigation, Stacy. You've got to watch out for yourself."

"Always have, always will." The hardened tone was back.

"I mean it. If you see Sam Sparks or Tanya Abbott, you have got to steer clear of them."

"You think they're in on something *together*?"

"No, not together." Ellie had neither the time nor inclination to explain the competing theories about Tanya. "I can only tell you so much, Stacy, and I'm telling you to call me immediately if you see Tanya, or either of these two men, or anything else you think I need to know about."

She handed the woman a business card. "Just in case you didn't happen to hold on to the last one."

Stacy tried to hand the card back to her. "You made me put your number in my cell, remember?"

"Last time I checked, numbers could be deleted."

"Whatever. Don't let the door hit you on the way out."

As Ellie made her way through the tiny living area, cramped with painting supplies and easels, she noticed a canvas still gleaming with wet oil. She recognized the tortured expression on Katie Battle's face.

"This is really amazing work."

Stacy said nothing but nodded her appreciation.

"I guess there's a part of you that's not brushing this off so easily after all."

She didn't let the door hit her on the way out.


The trip to Union City had taken nearly forty minutes. Genna Walsh was waiting for Ellie on the front porch of a modest white-wood duplex, a baby bouncing on her hip and a cordless phone balanced against her shoulder. She waved at Ellie and then held her fingers an inch apart to indicate that her call was almost completed.

"The lawyer told me he faxed it to you yesterday. . . . Fine . . . I'll ask him to send it again. And then how long does it take? . . . Okay, I'll call again tomorrow to make sure you get it. Good-bye."

She let out a sigh and rested the handset on the porch railing. "I tell you, when all this stuff is over, the first thing I'm doing is getting a will for me and my husband. My brother never wrote one. I'm Bobby's only family left, but I swear, sorting through all the legalities, I'd rather just give the money to charity at this point."

Ellie gave the baby, a chubby thing with black wispy hair topped with a pink bow, a pat on the cheek. "Hopefully it won't be too complicated and you'll get it sorted out."

"Well, I guess you know as much about my brother's finances as I do after all the poking around you did."

Ellie started to offer an explanation, but Genna shook her head. "After what I saw in that courtroom, I understand why you had so many questions about Bobby. My brother wasn't perfect, but he worked hard. Never went to college, but managed to buy that nice apartment in Hoboken and everything. He was a good uncle, wasn't he, sweetie girl?" She bounced the baby on her hip again. "This one was only two months old when it happened. My other one— she's asleep inside—just turned three. Breaks my heart his nieces won't remember him."

"Did your brother ever have a problem with Sparks?"

Genna shook her head.

"No. He was grateful for the money. His only complaint is he might have liked something a little higher up the food chain. He was pretty much a glorified bodyguard, but hey, he knew he was getting paid well for it."

"And he seemed to get along with the man he was guarding?"

"Yeah, sure. Not like Sparks was his buddy, but Bobby said he was a pretty decent guy. I mean, not a lot of rich people would let employees use that apartment and everything."

"Did he ever mention Sparks using an escort service called Prestige Parties?"

"Oh, no. Really? That's crazy. Why does a man like that have to go paying for it? No, Bobby never said anything about that. I would've remembered for sure."

"And, I'm so sorry to have to ask this, but what about Bobby? Did he ever, you know—"

"Go to a *prostitute*? Oh, God, I don't think so."

"Through fingerprint evidence, we finally identified the woman who was with your brother that night. We believe she was hired to be with him."

Genna shook her head. "I just don't understand men. I'll kill Carl if he knew."

"What makes you think your husband would know?"

"Because when Bobby was over the day before he was killed, I caught him and Carl snickering, and they got all secretive when I walked in. Later on Carl told me that Bobby said he had this date the next night and it was a sure thing. I figured he meant the girl was easy and let it drop. I don't need to hear something like that. I can't believe he'd go to a hooker, but honestly? How much can a sister know about that part of her brother, you know?"

Too much, Ellie thought. "And your brother never mentioned seeing something at work that maybe he wasn't supposed to see?"

"No, and even if he did, Nick would've vouched for him."

"They were pretty tight?"

"Nick loved Bobby. He took care of him, you know?"

"In what way?"

"Bobby went in the army to get some skills and a better life. We didn't have a lot, you know? And we both tried to do good for ourselves, but you can only do so much. I got married to a good man, but frankly, we only have this roof over our head because Bobby let us have the house when our parents were both dead. And for Bobby, the army was at least something, but a job like what he had at Sparks? That was all because of Nick. Nick could've hired any one of those fancy guys he knew from the private military contractor. But he didn't. The only guy he hired, from all the people he knew from when he was over in Afghanistan, was an enlisted man: Bobby."

"I can tell you're proud."

Genna gave her a half smile. "So proud. And I never once told him. Like I said, he wasn't perfect. No wife. He liked to party. All I ever said to him was, 'When are you gonna grow up?' I wish he knew how much he's helping his nieces. His life insurance. His apartment. We're going to put it all away for the girls. They'll be able to go to college. Do whatever they want."

"I'm sure your brother would be happy about that, Genna."

Ellie thanked Genna for her time and then watched as she gently opened the front door and stepped inside. As she walked to the car, she wondered whether there had been any point to driving out there.


Her cell rang just as she hit the Holland Tunnel. It was Jess.

"Hey," she said. "Talk fast because I'm about to lose the signal."

"I think I just saw that girl."

"What girl?"

"The one in the picture you sent me. The one you warned me about."

"Where? When?"

"Here. Just, like, three minutes ago. I didn't—"

"Where's *here*, Jess?"

Traffic slowed in front of her, and she immediately slammed on her emergency lights.

"At the apartment, across the street. I noticed her when I walked in and thought she looked familiar. By the time I figured it out, she was gone. I ran outside. I'm out front now, but I don't see her."

"I'll be right there. Do me a favor. Move as fast as you can. Go to Park, then uptown like you're heading for Grand Central." Trying to find someone who didn't want to be found in Manhattan, even with only a three-minute head start, was like trying to chase a single fallen leaf in a tornado, but Ellie was playing the odds. "If you can find her, follow her. Don't try to stop her, but keep your eyes on her, and I'll call you as soon as I'm in the city.

"Did you hear me, Jess?" She looked at the screen of her cell. The signal was gone.

# CHAPTER FORTY-FOUR

**D**espite a natural aversion to his father's profession, Jess turned out to have some cop in him after all. The call to Ellie dropped before he could make out her final request, but his instincts had led him east on Thirty-eighth Street and then north on Park Avenue, the same route Ellie had chosen in the hopes Tanya was heading for Grand Central Station. But he never did spot Tanya Abbott. Neither did Ellie, Rogan, or the team of patrol officers who scanned the streets of Murray Hill and a twenty-block surrounding radius for the next two hours.

By eight o'clock, they had regrouped outside Ellie's apartment complex.

"You sure your brother didn't just make a mistake?"

Ellie didn't know the uni, but could tell from the glance at his watch that he didn't appreciate chasing ghosts.

"He didn't make a mistake." If Jess said he was positive, then he was right. She was certain enough that, for the first time since Tanya disappeared, the Public Information Office had published an immediate press release of a confirmed sighting of the missing woman at the corner of Thirty-eighth Street and Park. The notice had gone out on the live local news updates.

None of it had mattered. Tanya had managed to slip past them.

"So you want us to repeat the drill again?" the uni asked, still looking at his watch in case she'd missed the hint the first time.

"You know, we could expand the radius," another uni suggested, to the vocalized annoyance of his fellow officers.

Rogan placed his hands on his hips and looked up and down Thirty-eighth Street, as if one last scan would do the trick. Finally, he dropped his arms and sighed.

"We got to move on, Hatcher. She's gone."

"So we're out of here?" one of the unis asked.

She nodded. "Good work," she offered feebly, triggering a few groans as they walked away.

"I'm hungry," Rogan said once they were alone.

Ellie's only nourishment for the day had been a Hershey's bar from the DA vending machine and a few fast scoops of Nutella at the precinct. She shared the sentiment but wanted to keep grinding away at the case. "Fine, but we eat fast."

"Girl, you *always* eat fast."


Ellie reached for the cheeseburger before the plate even hit the table and took an enormous bite. Food had never tasted so good.

They had settled in at Molly's, an Irish pub two blocks from the precinct with sawdust floors and arguably the best burgers in Manhattan. She withstood the urge for an accompanying Guinness, knowing they weren't yet done for the night.

"Maybe your brother *did* made a mistake," Rogan said as he picked at a piece of eggplant on his vegetarian sandwich. Ellie knew he was struggling to get his cholesterol down and wasn't happy with the diet Sydney had asked him to follow for a month. Watching her tear into a juicy cheeseburger was probably torture for him, but it didn't keep her from taking another eager chomp.

"He's not like that," she said once she'd finally swallowed.

"Not to be rude, but the man's nearly forty years old and lives on your sofa. He has to have made a few mistakes somewhere along the line."

"Not about this kind of stuff. He's not paranoid, you know? If he saw someone and thinks it's Tanya Abbott, then I'd bet money it was her."

"But Jess said she was by herself."

"Then she probably was."

"Why would she do that? The entire New York Police Department is looking for her. Why would she go after you? And why go on her own?"

"Because she's not after us. She was hiding in that bathroom cabinet, and she's scared. First she was scared of the police, but now she's more afraid of whoever killed Katie Battle and whoever's after her."

Rogan shook his head. "Why do you feel sorry for this girl? She had to be involved in what happened to Megan."

"Why are you so certain of that?"

"Because she posted that threat against us on Campus Juice using that ISP concealer or whatever it's called, which means she also posted the original threats about Megan. And there's only one reason she would've done that."

Ellie couldn't ignore his point, but she also couldn't ignore the feeling in her gut that Sam Sparks's connection to Prestige Parties was not just a coincidence.

"Let's say I'm right and that Sam Sparks had Mancini killed and that Tanya was simply a witness."

"Okay. Then Sparks would go after the woman Mancini was with that night, and that was supposed to be Katie Battle. The problem is, you can't explain why someone went after Tanya first, and *then* Battle."

"So maybe we're both right," she said.

"How so?"

"Maybe Tanya's a victim and a bad guy. She was hiding in the bathroom at the 212. Had nothing to do with that. But four months later, her roommate's a problem."

"That works," Rogan said, completely ignoring his dinner by now. "She uses Campus Juice to create a distraction, kills Megan, and cuts herself to make sure no one suspects her."

"But she'd need an accomplice for that," Ellie said. "There was no weapon in the apartment."

"Or maybe she just hid the weapon really well and went back for it when she left the hospital. I mean, it's not like we looked in the toilet tank."

"Okay, good. And then she leaves the hospital, either because she realizes we're going to figure out who she was, or maybe she saw the news reports about Katie's murder."

"Which, if you're right, could be Sparks cleaning up his mess. And now that Tanya's figuring out that she could be next, she might have been reaching out to you for help. Or maybe the last couple of days have given her time to come up with some story that gets her out from under Megan's murder."

This felt right. The pieces fit together. "It doesn't matter. We still can't find her."

"No," Rogan said. "But we do know where Sam Sparks is."

"But we can't prove any of this, and we don't have PC for an arrest. If we go to him with more questions, he'll just lawyer up and Guerrero will never let us near him again."

"So we won't question him."

"What? We're just going to stare at him real hard and hope he comes clean?"

"No. If we're going to assume we're both right about Tanya, let's assume you were right about all of it. Not just Sparks, but about Paul Bandon doing him special favors. If we go to Sparks and rattle his cage, he might reach out to Bandon again. If we can prove that, we can flip Bandon to find out what he knows, and then we might be in business."

"When should we begin the rattling?"

"I'm still good to go. You?"

"Let's do it."

"You going to finish that?" He pointed to the last piece of burger on her plate, which she promptly stuffed into her mouth.

"You're a cruel, heartless woman, Hatcher."


If working a room were a competitive sport, Sam Sparks would line a wall with gold medals. Wherever he paused in the ballroom, clumps of curious onlookers followed, hoping for a handshake, a quick hello, a look into the glint of those steely eyes, perhaps even a photograph of themselves beside the next American celebrity tycoon.

Tracking him down to what the Four Seasons called its Cosmopolitan Suite had not been difficult. They'd started with a phone call to Kristen Woods. Ellie had hit redial seven times before Kristen finally picked up. Over the background noise of light jazz and cocktail chatter, Kristen had insisted that Sparks was unavailable to speak with them until the morning. He was delivering an address for the Columbia Business School alumni association. With that nugget of information in hand, it took only a quick scroll of the school's Web site to learn that Sparks was delivering a keynote speech that night at the Four Seasons about the relevance of business education in the new economy.

Ellie watched from the ballroom entrance as waitstaff cleared dessert dishes and eager alumni lingered to greet Sparks. "I can't take much more of this."

"There's your girl Kristen." Rogan nodded toward a spot not far from the jazz quartet in the corner of the room. They worked their way through the crowd toward her.

"Detectives, my boss will not be happy to see you here."

"I'm sure he won't. If you could find a way to pull him aside, we can be discreet in the hallway. There's no need for this to be uncomfortable." Ellie said it as if she had any authority to force a confrontation.

"Fine. I'll do my best."

Kristen interrupted Sparks's conversation with an older, well-dressed couple. His eyes flashed toward them as he headed for the exit. They took their cue to follow.

Sparks did not waste any time once they were on the opposite side of the lobby outside the ballroom.

"Give me one reason why I shouldn't call my lawyer right now and enjoin you from having any further contact with me."

"Because we would move to have your favorite judge, Paul Bandon, disqualified from hearing any issues involving you or this case."

"Now what kind of paranoid theory have you come up with?"

"You had to know we'd eventually ask ourselves why Bandon took such a special interest in your case," Ellie said.

"I don't think he had a particularly strong interest until you essentially perjured yourself in his courtroom, Detective."

Ellie steeled herself to accomplish what they had come here to do. For months, Sam Sparks had been under her skin. Now it was their turn to slide beneath his. "We know why you wanted access to the evidence involving Mancini's date the night he was murdered."

"As I believe my attorney explained, I wanted my team to follow through on any steps you might have missed in your zealousness to focus attention on me."

"It's all about the photographs we used during the court hearing. You saw the open cabinet in the photograph of the bathroom and realized there was a witness. Someone knows what happened in your apartment that night, and you don't want us to find her. We know why Bandon was willing to bend over backward for you. We know about Prestige Parties."

Sparks had retained his usual self-possessed demeanor, but at her mention of the escort service, his eyes darted toward the alumni event as if someone there might save him from this conversation. She had been right. Something about Prestige Parties linked him to Mancini's murder and to Paul Bandon.

"You may think you know something, Detective, but until you're ready to put your money where your mouth is and file charges against me, you should keep your theories to yourself. My lawyer could have a field day with you in a slander suit."

"We'll be quiet, Sparks, but that won't mean we're not working. And listening to people who aren't so silent."

"And what exactly is that supposed to mean?"

"You should ask yourself how much you trust the people who've been so eager to help you." She needed to plant doubts. She needed Sparks to wonder how much pressure a man like Paul Bandon could resist. She needed him to think that Bandon might admit he'd been pressured to show preferential treatment. "You should ask yourself if your secrets are safe."

She saw it then. A crack in the effortless facade. A hint of apprehension in that otherwise omnipresent stare of resolved confidence. He was no longer certain he was in control.

"Enjoy the rest of your night, Mr. Sparks. We'll be in touch."

As they took the stairs to the main lobby, she said to Rogan, "You were awfully quiet back there."

"I thought you needed to do that on your own."

He was right. She had. The tables were turned. She had gone toe to toe with Sparks and hadn't broken. Now he was the one with something to worry about.

Outside the hotel on Fifty-seventh Street, Rogan threw her the keys to the Crown Vic. "You sure you want the night shift?"

"Absolutely." She was ready to see where Sam Sparks was heading next.

# CHAPTER FORTY-FIVE

Twenty-two minutes. It had been exactly twenty-two minutes since she took the keys from Rogan.

In what was probably the fourth of the twenty-two minutes, Ellie had ducked into the Borders on the corner. A guard was about to lock the door but made an exception when she'd flashed her badge and pleaded for caffeine. She left one minute later, a large black coffee in hand. Once she was in the car, she took a U-turn and parked on the north, hotel side of Fifty-seventh Street, just west of Park Avenue. Sparks would likely have a driver, and the driver would pull up to the front of the hotel. She was poised to follow.

For the remainder of the twenty-two minutes, her gaze floated between the hotel entrance, her watch, the six awaiting black limos she'd counted between Park and Madison, and—just to help the time pass—the ascending floors of the Four Seasons' limestone exterior. Ellie had counted fifty-two on the way up, and was on thirty-one on the way down when she spotted Sam Sparks leaving the hotel, Kristen Woods at his side.

She looked at her watch. Twenty-two minutes. Not so fast to be proof of a panic. Not so slow that she should write off the possibility.

One of the six limo drivers—this one double-parked not a hundred feet from the hotel—hopped into his car, pulled forward to the curb, hopped out again, and dashed to the opposite side of the car to open the back door for Sparks.

Ellie started the engine and pulled into traffic four cars behind the limo on Fifty-seventh Street. Without signaling, the limo took a right at the light to head north on Madison Avenue. She followed. Traffic was moving smoothly, and the limo made good time in sync with the lights. She maneuvered into a different lane to get a closer position.

They'd hoped that the confrontation in the hotel might trigger a meeting between Sparks and Bandon. As they continued north on Madison, Ellie worried that the only act in which she'd be catching Sparks red-handed tonight was a return to his town house on Seventy-seventh, but she reminded herself that Bandon also lived on the Upper East Side.

At Seventy-third Street, the driver shifted into the left lane. Sparks's place was between Madison and Fifth Avenue. Bandon was farther east on Park. He was definitely going home.

When the limo lurched through a yellow light at Seventy-sixth, she chose to stop at the red rather than risk flagging her tail. She watched as the light at Seventy-seventh turned red. The limo stopped. Still no left-turn signal, but the driver hadn't used his blinker back at the hotel either.

Her light changed to green and she hit her blinker to hang a right to take Park Avenue back to the precinct. But something kept her from tapping the gas. She'd waited twenty-two minutes and driven twenty blocks. She'd stick it out until the limo turned onto Sparks's block.

The light at Seventy-seventh turned green. But the limo didn't turn. It went straight. So did she, maneuvering into the left lane to follow.

She trailed behind the limo as it turned left on Eighty-first, then another quick left, south on Fifth Avenue. Had the driver spotted her? She hung back, pulling into the loading zone of an apartment complex on Eighty-first, just in case. She could pause here and catch up after the turn.

She forced herself to count eight full beats and then made a left on Fifth Avenue, holding her breath until she spotted her target. The limo was turning right into the parking entrance for the Metropolitan Museum of Art.

The museum was dead. Maybe Sparks was turning around in the hope of losing her tail. Or maybe he was meeting someone in the garage. It was open to nonmuseum parking after hours, and if darkened garages worked for Woodward and Bernstein, she imagined they'd work for Sparks as well.

She pulled over on the west side of Fifth behind a southbound M4 bus and watched the museum driveway. No limo. If the driver were taking a U-turn, he'd be out by now. But if Sparks had a clandestine meeting inside, there was no way she could drive through the bottleneck entrance without being noticed.

She waited.

Two minutes later, she was parked in the same spot, but with no bus to cover her, when she spotted the black limo pull out of the driveway. She immediately migrated into the flow of traffic, hoping that the driver wouldn't spot her as she passed and would eventually overtake her so she could resume the tail. She was just about to pass the limo when it pulled forward for its right turn onto Fifth Avenue. As the chauffeur paused beneath the streetlamp at the end of the driveway, she could make out a silhouette of the car's interior.

The backseat was empty.

"Damn it," she said, pulling her car in front of a hydrant in the left lane as the limo flew down Fifth Avenue. She scanned the museum driveway in her rearview mirror. Where was Sparks?

She'd hopped out of the car, ready to cover the parking garage on foot, when she spotted another vehicle exiting the driveway. She ducked back into the driver's seat and watched as Sam Sparks passed her behind the wheel of a two-tone gray Maybach.

She wouldn't have known the name of the car except for a brief stint patrolling Central Park when that famous couple had swathed it with bright orange fabric. The artists had viewed their handiwork from a car just like Sparks's, and one of the other officers racking up easy overtime commented that the vehicle cost nearly four hundred grand. With the real estate market in its current condition, even Sparks had to be feeling the pinch, but he certainly wasn't going to let anyone know it.

But Ellie didn't care whether Sparks drove a Maybach or a Honda or a GMC Pacer. What mattered to her was that it was eleven o'clock at night, and he'd ditched his driver and was on the move.


If Ellie had been asked to bet on Sam Sparks's likely destination as the clock approached midnight, her imagination would have carried her on a luxury excursion through the city: a top-secret avant-garde performance art debut in SoHo, an exclusive club opening in Chelsea, the rooftop bar at the Gansevoort. Instead, she found herself in the burbs. Riverdale, to be exact.

Riverdale was a perfectly decent place. Nice, in fact. Pleasant. Even fancy in parts. And she supposed that it technically fell within the limits of the Bronx and was therefore formally part of the city and not a suburb. But in all the ways that counted, Riverdale was the humdrum boring suburbs.

But something had brought Sam Sparks and his Maybach here as the clock approached midnight.

She had followed him crosstown on Seventy-ninth, and then north on the Henry Hudson Parkway. She had wondered if he was leading her all the way to his upstate country home when he turned off at Exit 22. The winding, hilly residential roads challenged her tailing abilities, but she managed to keep sight of him.

She was one turn behind him when she saw the red blush of his brake lights. He parked on the street behind a blue minivan and turned off his engine. She killed her headlights and backed into a spot at the curb. Despite the angle, she could see his car around the corner if she leaned forward.

With the twists and turns through Riverdale, she had not had a chance to take in the surroundings. Upper-middle-class residential neighborhood. Well-maintained brick Tudors seemed to dominate. Average-size lots. Average-size homes. Not the kind of place she'd expect Sparks to leave a Maybach on the street.

She tried to make out the street names on the perpendicular green signs on the corner, but did not have enough light. Why was Sparks here? And why hadn't he gotten out of his car?

She waited. She watched. Nothing happened.

Ten minutes later, she sensed a brightening somewhere on the street past Sparks's car—a porch light—followed by the faint sound of muted voices. She saw the silhouette of Sparks's head slink down in the driver's seat.

Rogan had mocked her for grabbing a set of binoculars before they left the precinct, but she was grateful for them now. She rotated the lenses until the street came into focus.

She spotted the couple on the lit porch of a house two lots down from Sparks's Maybach. Taller guy. Shorter woman with light-colored hair in a low ponytail, keys in her hand. They were kissing—nothing too passionate, but more than just a friendly good-bye.

The kissing stopped, and she heard their muted voices again. The woman turned to leave. She had a bounce in her step. She looked back toward the porch when she hit the sidewalk and then headed toward a white Toyota Camry parked at the curb. The woman was Lieutenant Robin Tucker.

Ellie swung the binoculars back to the porch, where Nick Dillon was waving good-bye. Tucker pulled away from the curb and returned the wave before driving off. When Tucker's taillights were out of sight, she heard the engine of the Maybach. Sparks pulled forward two lots and turned into Dillon's driveway.

He remained inside his car, engine idling, as Dillon retreated inside his house. Seconds later, she heard a faint electric hum as one door of Dillon's two-car garage rolled open. The Maybach pulled inside and the door rolled closed behind it.

Five minutes later after Tucker had left, Ellie saw the white Camry pass her parking spot and turn again onto Dillon's street. She expected it to pull to the curb in front of the house, but it cruised by, slowing slightly but not stopping.

An hour passed. No one came. No one left. Nothing happened. At one in the morning, Ellie finally gave up and drove home. Something was important enough to bring Sam Sparks to the suburbs to talk to his head of security in the wee hours of the night, but watching Nick Dillon's house wasn't going to tell her what that something was.

# PART V

---

SECRETS

# CHAPTER FORTY-SIX

"Not to be rude or anything, Hatcher, but I think you looked better after that night you spent in the hoosegow."

Ellie tossed her head back to drain the last drops of coffee in her Styrofoam cup and saw Detective John Shannon standing beside her desk, peering down at her.

"Not to be rude or anything, Shannon, but do you mind moving to your right a few feet? The shadow from your stomach has caused a solar eclipse above my work area."

"Lay off," Rogan said. "Hatcher was up late on a stakeout. Hard work, nothing you'd need to worry about."

"What's this I hear about a stakeout?"

Ellie hadn't noticed Lieutenant Tucker heading toward her office, unbuttoning her tan trench coat as she walked.

"Rogan and I were following up on some leads we got from the Prestige Parties bust last night."

"I heard Rogan mention a stakeout."

"That's right," Rogan said.

"Pardon me if I'm mistaken, but 'following up on some leads' is quite a bit more vague than 'a stakeout,' which usually requires a suspect or at least a person or location of interest, neither of which you had the last time either of you bothered to update me."

Ellie spun her chair toward Tucker. "No suspects, Lou. Just some theories we're working on."

"What's going on with you two?"

Ellie looked at Rogan, who shrugged. As far as he knew, they were being evasive because they still hadn't told Tucker that Paul Bandon's phone number was in Tanya Abbott's cell records. Ellie hadn't had a chance to tell him about spotting Tucker at Dillon's house the previous night.

"Maybe we can talk in your office, Lou."


"I am so absolutely mortified, I don't even know what to say to either of you right now."

"Really, it's no big deal. You were on a date. I didn't mean to follow you. It's just that Sparks led me—"

"I'm not talking about my date, Hatcher. I'm talking about the fact that the two of you have known for two days that a sitting judge was engaged in criminal activity and didn't bother to tell me."

"We wanted his cooperation," Rogan said. "We thought we were most likely to get it if he trusted us to keep his confidences."

"So you put his confidences above mine."

"We thought you would feel obligated to report it," Ellie said.

"And why would that be? I care less about solving homicides than you? I'm a ladder-climbing bureaucrat who would sell out your best lead on a case to advance her own career?"

"We didn't want to put you in an awkward position."

"As if this isn't awkward. Finding out two of my best detectives don't trust me. Having one of them catch me making out on someone's porch, for Christ's sake."

"It wasn't really *making out*—"

Rogan stifled a snicker.

"That's quite enough, Hatcher. So let me see if I get this straight.

Sparks is connected to both his dead bodyguard Mancini and the escort agency. Bandon's connected to our missing prostitute, who was Mancini's last date. So now you think Bandon's special interest in the Mancini case is part of some deal with Sparks."

"Right," Rogan said.

She shook her head. "The whole reason Hatcher here got her panties in a bunch over Sparks was his refusal to let you inspect his books to look for enemies. If anything, this connection to Prestige Parties seems to help him. It explains what he was hiding. And Bandon? He wouldn't be the first judge to cozy up to a rich corporate guy in the hopes of currying favor. It is, after all, what we ladder-climbing bureaucrats do."

"We know it's a stretch," Rogan said. "But we don't have anything else."

Ellie defended the theory. "This whole thing started with Sparks's bodyguard, who happened to be in Sparks's apartment, on a date set up through Sparks's escort service. Sparks has been resisting us from day one, and I refuse to believe it was all because of this escort-service business. An experienced lawyer like Guerrero would have told him that he could have quietly cut a deal in exchange for his cooperation."

"But he might not have trusted the two of you to be quiet about it after you hooked him up that first night, Hatcher."

"I still can't imagine obstructing a murder investigation over that. He certainly isn't the first wealthy, successful man to pay for it. Ask our former governor."

"Exactly, and look what happened to him. Maybe Sparks didn't want to be Spitzered."

"He's not a politician," Ellie said. "Or a judge like Bandon. It wouldn't have been seen as a big deal."

"You should have come to me," Tucker said.

"We only decided last night about the tail," Rogan said.

"I don't just mean the tail. I mean everything. Bandon and the girl. All these various theories you hatched yesterday. You should have come to me."

They mumbled their mutual apologies.

"Well, if your plan is to catch Sparks meeting Bandon, why are both of you here right now?"

"I bought us some time this morning by sitting on Bandon until he went to the courthouse. He'll be doing arraignments until at least ten thirty. I'll be on Sparks by then."

"From the looks of this one"—she nodded toward Ellie—"you can't be getting any sleep. More importantly, I can't have you on twenty-four-hour overtime. Hatcher, you go home."

She opened her mouth to protest, but Tucker slapped her desk. "I'm throwing you a bone letting you tail Sparks at all. Rogan will cover him during the day. You can resume your spying tonight."

Rogan led the way out of the office. "I'll be right out," Ellie said.


Waiting for the office door to close behind Rogan, Ellie started with the easy stuff.

"I'm wondering what you make of the fact that Sparks went to Nick Dillon's house so late last night."

Tucker shrugged. "It's not like he was keeping it a secret. Sparks called Nick and said he was on his way. That's why I left when I did, quite frankly."

"Then why did you drive by his house after you initially left?"

Tucker's cheeks flushed, and she threw her head back against her chair and sighed. "Maybe this is proof that I shouldn't date. It's been years since I tried this, and now I know why I gave it up. I go from being a giddy schoolgirl to a nervous wreck to a jealous stalker. I'm embarrassed to say, I drove by his house to make sure that it really was Sparks on his way over."

"Instead of another woman?"

She nodded. "I didn't see his car, but I did catch a glimpse of him through the living room window. Nick wasn't lying."

"Sparks pulled into the garage," Ellie explained. "His ride's worth nearly half a mil. Too good for a driveway in Riverdale, I guess."

"My ex-husband ran around on me like an alley cat on Viagra. Old habits die hard, I guess."

"Didn't it strike you as odd that his boss would come over at midnight?"

"Nick said Sparks is like that. He works until all hours of the night and insists that the people around him cater to his schedule. Why? Wait, you think Nick—"

"I don't *think* anything. I'm asking the questions that anyone in my shoes should be asking, and as the person who was standing right there when Sparks called, you're my best witness to whether we should be looking at Dillon harder. If Sparks hired someone to kill Mancini—"

"Then Nick would be a likely candidate."

"I don't like thinking this about an ex-cop. And a friend of yours."

Tucker brushed her hair out of her face. "You're right. You should be looking at Sparks, which means looking at Nick. But I've got to be honest. I can't see it. You should have heard him go off about Sparks's refusal to cooperate. He was *not* happy with the man."

"But he didn't quit."

"Come on, Hatcher. That's not fair. You know how many times I would've left the force if I walked out every time I had to go along to get along? And, trust me, Nick knows Sparks should have been more helpful in the Mancini investigation, but I'm sure it has *never* dawned on him to suspect his boss of the actual murder."

"Would I be out of line to ask for your assurances that you won't be planting that seed in his head any time soon?"

"Yes, it would. You're suggesting I have a conflict of interest?"

"I'm suggesting that Nick Dillon works for Sam Sparks and might therefore be curious."

"Look: this is more information than you have any right to know, but the truth is, I'm a forty-eight-year-old divorced woman with a twelve-year-old boy at home. Guys like Nick Dillon don't just show up in my office asking me out to dinner every day. He's good-looking, single, and a truly decent guy. Ask anyone on the job who knew him. But maybe you're right. Maybe I'm stupid to think he wants to spend his time with me. Maybe he's only doing this to get an inside track on the case for Sparks."

Ellie started to interrupt, but Tucker held up a hand. "The point is, even if all that were true, it wouldn't mean I'd fall for it. I know you're used to being the smartest woman in the room, Hatcher, but you're going to have to learn to start giving me credit. Nick hasn't gotten one speck of information from me about your case. When he apologizes for Sparks or asks how it's going or even when he defended you after your antics in the courtroom, I've never *once* given him a thing."

"Why have you been keeping us away from Sparks?"

"I haven't—"

"You've got to give me some credit, too. We came to you on Thursday saying we wanted to look at Sparks again, and by Friday, we're chasing the Megan Gunther callout."

"At first, the Sparks angle looked like a waste of time. And the Gunther case really was up your alley."

"And what about your comments? About me? Wunderkind, darling of the brass, promoted too early. Pretty strong hints as to what you think about me."

"I'm what my sister calls a strong personality. You shouldn't take it personally."

Ellie looked at the floor and decided there was no need to respond. She had just risen from her chair when Tucker stopped her. "I can't show you favoritism."

"Excuse me?"

Tucker looked to the sealed blinds that covered the glass between her office and the squad room. "I can't appear to favor you. With them. I'm new around here, but I've done this before, first as a sergeant and now as a lou. I know how it works. You think I don't know what goes through their heads when they find out their new boss Robin Tucker isn't a guy with a gender-ambiguous name? Bitch. Dyke. Affirmative action. I've heard it all, but I know how to get past it. It's all about competence. And I'm good at my job,

Hatcher. And despite some of the shit I've given you, I know you are, too. You fucking *earned* that Police Combat Cross. But if they think I favor you over them, we're both toast. Is that any better of an explanation?"

Ellie nodded, looking up from the linoleum long enough to catch Tucker's eye. "Thanks."

"Now, if we're all through with the girl talk, I'd suggest you get yourself some rest."

# CHAPTER FORTY-SEVEN

S tacy Schecter was wearing new shoes, or at least new to her.

She had spotted the black Christian Louboutin slingbacks last week at Housing Works. She'd found some funky vintage bargains before at her favorite used clothing haunt, but she rarely had the kind of luck to come across anything by an in-demand contemporary designer in like-new condition. Even though they might have been a half size too large for her feet, she nevertheless swept up the three-inch pumps as too good a find to pass up. The shoes might not appeal to Stacy the artist, but they suited Stacy the Honest and Attractive Brunette just fine.

As she made her way west on Twelfth Street, she was cautious with her steps, mindful of the height of her heels and the looseness of the straps behind her ankles. At the same time, she was aware of the minutes passing on the clock and knew she couldn't squander them.

Ideally she should have left her apartment earlier. She liked to arrive at the meeting locations well before the clients. The extra time allowed her to still her mind and get into character. It also permitted her to watch the man arrive. Make sure he was on his own, no backup officers monitoring the conversation. No one waiting to bust her once they'd struck the agreement of sex for money.

But tonight she'd continued painting long past the moment she should have begun preparing for her date, and now she was running late. She suppressed the urge to linger at the bargain shelves outside the Strand Bookstore and scurried across Broadway against the light, provoking a honk from a passing cab.

She was only one block from her destination and her mind was still back in the apartment. She'd been working on the piece she had tentatively entitled *Katie Was Miranda*. She couldn't remember the last time she had felt so confident. Somewhere along the way, she had transitioned from a college student who truly believed she would be the next Lee Krasner or Agnes Martin to an artist who chose palette colors based on the latest trends in yuppie home decor. Her painting no longer had anything to do with her. She had stopped painting for herself entirely.

But her portrayal of Miranda/Katie was different. Some artists painted what they saw in life. It had been a long time since she had attempted even to do that. But with this piece, she was going further, painting not what she saw in those photographs of Miranda, but what she *felt* when she saw them. She had no idea whether anyone would enjoy the piece, or admire it, or even lay eyes on it for that matter.

All she knew was that she had to finish. Every stroke of the brush against the canvas was like its own kind of bloodletting. For the first time in years, her art was personal. It was *art*. And she wasn't going to stop with Miranda/Katie. She was carrying other images in her head—of absence and longing, of love and violence, of masked male faces and exposed female bodies. She finally felt inspiration for a series. If she was going to make her money with her body, she might as well make her art count for something. She'd roll the dice and see what happened. Maybe she'd be the only person ever to see it. Or maybe these would be the paintings that would change her life.

# CHAPTER FORTY-EIGHT

Ellie woke up knowing that something had happened. She knew it not in the way you know the multiplication tables, or the identity of the first president, or the capitals of the fifty states, or anything else learned through study or cognition. She knew it in the way you immediately recognize the smile of a long-lost friend, even before you've placed the face within your past. She knew it in the way you sense the onset of a cold, even before you have any tangible symptoms. She knew it not just with her mind, but with her stomach and her heart and her blood and her soul.

She woke up knowing at a base, cellular level that something had happened. Rogan had lost Spark's trail, or had seen something but failed to recognize the significance. Something.

She reached for her cell phone on the nightstand. No new calls registered on the screen. She pulled up the digest of recent calls to make sure. Nothing. But the fact that she hadn't missed a call did not put to rest the anxiety coursing through her body. Something had happened, and she had slept through it.

The intensity of her agitation was momentarily disrupted by the tickle of a fingertip meandering near her right hip, across the faded appendectomy scar, then up toward her navel.

"You're awake." Max brushed her hair back and kissed her just below her earlobe.

"This time it might actually be for good."

She had called him from the precinct to say she'd been sent home for the day and would be working at night instead. She'd been home only forty minutes when he showed up at her apartment. Now the sun was less bright through the bedroom window blinds, and the cacophony of running engines and car horns below told her that evening commuters were lined up outside the Midtown Tunnel.

Except for a brief traipse to the front door for their delivery tacos, they had spent the last seven hours in her bed, alternating between sleep, naughty stuff, and snippets of *30 Rock* online. Based on the tickle of Max's index finger around her belly button and the warmth of his breath against her neck, he wasn't asleep and had no intentions of watching another sitcom.

"Is everything all right?"

"I want it to be. I hope it is."

"El, I know you have this borderline obsessive-compulsive disorder that makes you grind away at a case until all the layers are gone and you can clear the thing from your whiteboard, but even crazy Howard Hughes occasionally let himself sleep. Since the second you left Bandon's courtroom in handcuffs, all you've done is live and breathe this case—nonstop, jumping from one body to the next, searching for one theory that might connect them. That's got to feel like a nonstop roller coaster, and now that you've stepped away from it, you probably feel like it's still moving without you and you'll never be able to get back on. But you've got to trust someone else to steer the ride for a few hours."

She nodded quietly. When she turned on her side to face him, he wrapped his arms around her.

Ellie's last long-term boyfriend, the banker, always expected her to turn off the job once she took off her uniform, but the fact that Max was asking her to take a breather actually meant something to her. One of the traits that had initially drawn her to him was his shared experience in a job that breaks the heart. They spent their days surrounded by the worst kind of human damage. They couldn't see the cases they'd seen—the pain, the violence, the wholly avoidable infliction of harm by one person upon another—without allowing that world to become some small part of themselves. Immersion in the lives of people who become a part of the criminal justice system infects the psyche. Max shared the virus with her. But now even he was worried that she wasn't coping.

She allowed herself to be kissed initially and then felt herself responding to the feel of his tongue against hers, his hand on her hip, the tilt of his pelvis beneath the sheets.

Then just as quickly as her mind registered the warmth building deep in her abdomen, she realized her thoughts about the case had escaped from their cage. This time it was Max who pulled back. He could tell she wasn't there with him. He reached for her cell on the nightstand.

"You want to call Rogan to be sure?"

She panted like a happy puppy, and flipped the phone open. Rogan picked up after one ring.

"So . . . damn . . . bored."

"Nothing?"

"Sparks was in the office all day except for lunch at Michael's and a couple walk-throughs on new builds. I'm following his town car now, but I reached out to an investigator I know at the DA's office. According to him, Bandon's still on the bench, so who knows where Sparks is taking me."

"I'll call you in an hour to figure out where to make the switch?"

"No problem."

Ellie flipped the phone shut and rolled toward Max. She kissed him, softly at first and then more urgently. And then, before she even realized her mind had been wandering again, she suddenly sat up.

She knew whom she needed to call, and it wasn't Rogan.

# CHAPTER FORTY-NINE

Stacy had instructed tonight's client to meet her at the bar at Gotham. The Alfred Portale restaurant was more upscale than the dives she frequented with friends, but for the business at hand, it offered two clear advantages.

The first were its bartenders, Mark and Jill. Some places would balk about the same woman regularly using their establishment for the briefest of drink dates with an array of strange men. But three months ago, Jill had greeted her with a drink and a comment, both served straight up. The drink was Bombay Sapphire. The comment was, "I hope you know what you're doing, woman. Promise you'll be careful." Mark had followed up with a smile and a nod. From that point forward, Stacy had never worried about getting thrown out, not when Mark or Jill was there.

Of course, Stacy could avoid the risks of being eighty-sixed by simply switching up her meeting places, but few bars offered Gotham's second advantage: the view. Thanks to the bar's proximity to the front of the restaurant, and the front of the restaurant's glass exterior, she enjoyed a clear shot of the street from a seat at the bar. Had she arrived early enough, as she usually did, she could monitor the client's approach to make sure he arrived alone.

But because she had not arrived early, she now stood on the outside of the glass looking in at the crowded bar. Mark was jiggling a martini shaker over his right shoulder, and Jill was uncorking a bottle of wine. She scanned the bar for singles among the couples and foursomes waiting for dinner tables. She spotted two men alone, one at the far end of the bar facing the entrance, another who in profile appeared to be reading a newspaper.

She couldn't get a good look at the face of the man farthest from her, but she could tell he was large. She hoped he wasn't the one. Part of the way she had adjusted to sex with strangers was to think of them not as people, but as objects. Mannequins. Human props. That kind of detachment was easiest with generic bodies. Scars, birthmarks, obesity—those imperfections reminded her of the humanity beneath the skin.

She focused her attention instead on the man with the newspaper. Short hair. Middle-aged. Generic. Unremarkable. He'd be the better choice.

As she reached for the door, he turned to look outside. He noticed her. Raised his eyebrows as if he'd been expecting her. He was the guy.

But before she even realized why she was doing it, she dropped her hand from the door's handle. Something about the man was familiar. She'd seen him before.

He was still looking at her. He knew she was there, but she couldn't bring herself to enter the restaurant. Where had she seen him?

She focused on his face—too light for the ridiculous head of dark hair that was surely a piece. And then suddenly she saw him again, this time in the two-dimensional image of a photograph.

She turned and retreated on Twelfth Street as quickly as she could in her stupid new shoes. She looked behind her, praying that he hadn't followed her. She took an immediate right at the corner, heading south on University.

She knew where she'd spotted the man before. He was in one of the photographs the blond detective had brought to her apartment.

*You've got to watch out for yourself.* That's what the detective had said when she'd shown her the pictures, when she'd tried her best to warn her.

She wound her way through the East Village—south on University, east on Eleventh, south on Broadway, east on Ninth—glancing behind her every half block. Still no sign of the man she'd seen at Gotham, the man she'd seen in the picture.

She stepped off the curb to cross Second Avenue, and the left strap on her new pumps slipped, pulling the shoe from her foot and nearly sending her out into the street, belly-first in front of oncoming traffic. She pulled her shoe from her other foot, scooped up both in one hand, and dashed across the street on her bare feet.

From the corner on the other side, she looked behind her again. No sight of the man on Ninth. No sight of him on Third. He'd seen her, she was sure of that. What troubled her most was that he'd seemed to recognize her. How had he recognized her? She was certain she'd never laid eyes on him before, other than in that photograph the detective had shown her.

Even if he'd somehow discovered her real name—if he was the same man who killed Miranda, he could have gotten it out of her—how would he have known what she looked like? Her number was unlisted. So was her address. But her address was on her driver's license. And so was her photograph. But those records were private. Weren't they? Or was all of it available on the Internet these days? She didn't think so, but wasn't sure.

She tried to convince herself that he hadn't really recognized her. He had looked at her that way because she was an attractive brunette walking into the restaurant alone, and he was expecting an attractive brunette to walk in on her own. Once she'd turned the other way, he probably assumed she wasn't the woman he was waiting for—just some passerby who'd mistakenly grabbed the wrong door.

She stole another glance behind her. No sign of him. He hadn't followed her. He hadn't recognized her. He didn't know who she was and therefore could not know where she lived. She'd never see him again. Her lesson had been learned. She'd close her Craig's List account and live off her savings for a couple of months while she found some other way to pay the rent. If worse came to worst, she'd turn back to her parents.

One more glance to be sure. No sign of the man, but she did spot a yellow cab with its rooftop medallion number lit. She waved her shoes in the air and climbed into the backseat when the driver stopped.

Safe in the backseat, she slipped her pumps back onto her blackened feet. The miniature television installed in the seat back in front of her was muted, but she recognized the duo of anchors from the local ABC affiliate. The display then changed to a photograph of the woman whose face had captured the local media's constant attention for the last three days: Tanya Abbott.

She wished she had never met Tanya. She had no idea what the woman had to do with any of this, but if she'd never met Tanya, she could never have called her to cover that date for Miranda. Maybe then Miranda would be alive. Or, who knows, maybe Stacy would be dead. She didn't know how her life would be different if she'd never known Tanya, but in that moment, she wished Tanya was the one being followed by the man in the pictures. She wished Tanya was the one with police officers coming to her apartment and asking questions. Worse, she wished Tanya was the one who was dead.

She turned off the television so she would not have to see the face of the woman who had to be at the center of all of this. She slipped her cell phone from her leather clutch. The detective had assumed Stacy had removed her number from her directory, but she hadn't. She'd certainly thought about it, but for some reason, hadn't hit the delete button.

She pulled up the number and was about to hit the enter key when the driver turned onto Avenue B. Only five more quick blocks and she'd be home. She didn't have enough time left in the cab to start the call now. She also didn't want to wait.

Instead of hitting the call button, she hit the button to send a text message to Detective Hatcher's cell phone and began composing. "From . . . Stacy . . . Schecter. . . Saw . . . guy . . . in . . . photo . . . Tried to meet me . . . Call . . . when . . . you—"

She felt the cab come to a stop. "Five-eighty."

She reached into her purse, gave the driver a ten, and asked for three dollars back. The driver groaned as if the plucking of three singles from his stack pained his fingers. Tucking the change and her phone into her purse, she removed her keys, stepped out of the cab, and crossed Avenue B toward her building. As she slipped the key into the gate, she heard the cab speed south in search of its next fare.

She turned the key and pulled the security gate open. As she lifted her foot to take the one step up from the sidewalk into the building, her strap slipped again, sending her tumbling onto the concrete, the white gate smashing against her shin. She let out a yelp and grabbed her leg to soothe the pain.

"Let me give you a hand there."

She saw black dress shoes and dark gray slacks and reached on instinct for the hand extended toward her. And then she looked up. It was him. She yanked her hand away and crawled like a crab on the ground, trying to pull her body inside the building to slam the gate closed behind her. He grabbed her by the ankle. She twisted away from him, swatting at his hands to free her leg.

The sight of the gun at his waistband froze her body. She knew she should scream. She knew she should resist. She knew that if she yelled loud enough, that busybody in 2C would call the cops, if not to rescue her then to shut her up. But all she could see was the butt of the handgun. All she could think about was the half a second it would take him to reach for it and put a bullet in her brain. She'd be dead. She'd no longer exist. And she'd never know what happened next. She was paralyzed. He pulled her limp body up from the ground and shepherded her toward the curb.

As he shoved her into the front seat, she slipped her fingers into her clutch purse and hit the send button on her cell phone, followed by the delete button to clear old text messages from her phone. As the man hopped into the driver's seat next to her, she tried not to think about his gun. She tried not to think about what he would do to her. And, most of all, she tried not to think about the expression this man had left on the face of the woman she'd known as Miranda.

# CHAPTER FIFTY

As promised, Tony Carenza was on the southwest corner of Union Square Park. The narcotics officer wore a fitted plaid western shirt, tight white jeans, and cowboy boots. His long dark hair was slicked back in waves across the crown of his head.

Ellie was four steps away when she heard him pawning his wares. "Smoke, smoke, smoke."

"Take a break for a second?"

He looked both directions. "Yeah, but follow me like we're making a deal."

She did her best to look nervous as she walked south with him across Fourth Street onto McDougal.

"What kind of luck do I have? Two times I see you this week, and both times I'm dressed like a cowboy trannie. More UC shit. Doing some pot sales here, but later on I'll hit the clubs and get some felony busts."

That first meeting with Carenza seemed like a year ago. Before Megan and Katie were killed. Before Tanya disappeared. Before she'd ever heard of Prestige Parties. Wednesday morning in court, Sparks's attorney had argued that Mancini could have been killed in a home invasion gone bad. He'd known about the knock-and-talk at the apartment next door. But when Carenza assured them the neighbor was chump change, they'd moved on to other theories. They had failed to ask the important follow-up question.

"When my partner and I first talked to you about Sparks's neighbor at the 212, there's something I never asked you."

"Ask away."

She'd wanted to have this conversation in person in case Carenza was uncooperative, but now she wondered if the trip downtown had been necessary.

"You said you told Nick Dillon about your knock-and-talk because you knew Sparks owned the apartment across the hallway?"

"Yeah. I thought Dillon would get a kick out of the two old ladies downstairs, so sure they'd found a drug dealer on the premises. Sorry if I stepped on any toes mentioning it to him, but I figured he'd been on the job and all."

"When did you mention it to him?"

"A while ago, I guess."

"How long a while ago?"

He shrugged. "I don't really remember. Before the knock-and-talk, because I hadn't gone to the building yet. We were still keeping the old birds busy writing down all their notes."

She had first learned of the investigation across the hall just that week, when Sparks's lawyer, Ramon Guerrero, had brought it up in court. And Guerrero said he had just learned about it himself. They had simply assumed that the knowledge was new to Sam Sparks as well.

"How much earlier than the knock-and-talk?" Ellie pressed.

"Way before. Maybe just a couple of weeks after the ladies came into the precinct complaining about the guy. Why?"

The neighbors had first complained in March. If Carenza mentioned their suspicions prior to the murder, and Dillon had relayed them to Sparks, Sparks could have staged Mancini's killing to look like a home invasion, knowing that a pending narcotics investigation across the hallway would bolster that theory of the crime.

She felt a buzzing at her waist. A new text message:

**From Stacy Schecter. Saw guy in photo. Tried to meet me. Call when you**

The message stopped mid-sentence. Had Stacy simply hit the send key prematurely? Or was Ellie's quickening pulse confirming her worst fears?

She hit the call button on her phone, grateful that Stacy'd had the piece of mind to identify herself in her message. It rang four times before going to voice mail. She tried again. Another four rings. She tried again. This time the call went directly to voice mail, as if someone had turned off the phone's power.

"I've got to go."

She heard Carenza ask her if everything was all right as she jogged east.

The first call was to Rogan. He didn't bother with hello.

"You ready to switch?"

"Where's Sparks?" she asked.

"Right here."

"Where's *here*?"

"I'm parked outside Ouest."

"West what?"

"It's a restaurant. O-U-E-S-T. Broadway at Eighty-fourth. He went inside about twenty minutes ago."

A restaurant Rogan knew, and she didn't. Definitely expensive. "Can you still see him?"

"Not at the moment, but I'm watching the only door."

"Do me a favor, please? Go inside? Make sure you can see him?"

"If I do that, he'll make me. He might not hate me as much as you, but he'll recognize me."

"I don't care. Go check. Please."

"What's going on?"

"There's no time. Just make sure."

She hung up and placed the next call to Paul Bandon's chambers. Given the hour, she was surprised when a secretary answered.

"This is Ellie Hatcher from the NYPD. Is Judge Bandon available?"

"I'm sorry, Detective, but he's not in chambers right now. May I take a message?"

"Where is he?"

"Pardon me?"

"When did he leave?"

"Well, he didn't. He's on the bench. We're all hoping he'll call it a day any minute now."

"But you're sure he's there?" Ellie asked.

"Of course. I'm still here, aren't I?"

"I know this sounds crazy, but can you literally see him from your desk?"

"Well, no, but—"

"Can you please do me a favor and make sure he's physically in his courtroom?"

"Is something wrong, Detective?"

Ellie could tell from the secretary's tone that she was worried about the potential of a threat against the judge. Ellie saw no need to disabuse her of that impression.

"It's very important. Please. Just make sure he's in one piece and accounted for."

The secretary returned to the line thirty seconds later. "Yes, he's still there with the lawyers. Do I need to worry—"

Ellie hung up and dialed Rogan again. He picked up on the third ring.

"Got him," he said. "Pretty sure he spotted me, but—"

"Who was he with?"

"He's with some couple and an absolutely gorgeous woman."

"Not Stacy Schechter?"

"Hello? I think I'd recognize Stacy. What's going on?"

Ellie was crossing Second Avenue. She was almost there. She looked again at the text message: *Saw guy in photo. Tried to meet me.*

Sparks and Bandon were both accounted for. Maybe Stacy had seen one of them earlier in the day and only just got around to texting her. Maybe there was an innocent explanation for the cut-off text message, the turned-off phone.

But then Ellie realized that Sparks and Bandon were not the only men in the photos.

"Forget Sparks. Meet me at Stacy's place. She's missing. We have to find her. And we have to find Nick Dillon."

# CHAPTER FIFTY-ONE

Stacy's apartment was empty.

They had squandered fifteen minutes tracking down the building super to unlock the door, and all they had to show for it was an empty apartment. No break-in. No signs of a struggle. And no Stacy.

Ellie tried her cell again, but once again the call bounced directly to voice mail.

"She was smart enough to text you," Rogan said. "She should know that if her phone was on, we could use the signal to locate her."

Ellie tried to ignore the tormented face of Katie Battle, staring at her from the canvas in the center of the room as if Ellie had failed not only Stacy, but her as well. "I have no doubt Stacy knows that. And so does Nick Dillon. That's why her phone's turned off."

They had already called in to have patrol officers check Nick Dillon's house in Riverdale. She called the dispatcher and asked for a progress report. The car that had caught the call had not yet reported on scene.

"Okay," Ellie said. "I also need to issue BOLOs for two subjects: Nick Dillon and Stacy Schecter." She recited the basic identifying information and waited while the dispatcher pulled up the plate information for Sparks's black Infiniti sedan.

"Better be some major crime wave up in the Bronx tonight," she said, flipping her phone shut. "They're slow as molasses getting to Dillon's place."

"You don't think you jumped the gun with that BOLO?" A be-on-the-lookout request would go out to every area precinct. "Man's got a lot of friends on the job. We better be right about this."

"We are." Stacy's text said that one of the men in the pictures Ellie had shown her had tried to meet with her. Sparks and Bandon were accounted for, but in the photograph of Sparks, Nick Dillon had been standing directly behind him with an umbrella. He was the only other man in the snapshots. "He's got her. If he'd been anyone but a former cop, we would've looked harder at him. He's the one who knew Narcotics was looking at the apartment across the hall from Sparks's. He's the friend who could've lined Mancini up with a girl from Prestige Parties, made sure he'd be at the apartment that night."

"And now he's going after Stacy to find Tanya Abbott?"

"That's got to be it. He's still trying to find the woman who was hiding in the bathroom cabinet that night. She's his one loose end."

As prominent as Tanya Abbott's photograph had been in newspapers and televisions that week, they had never publicly released her connection to the Mancini murder.

"Or maybe he's known who she is all along. If he saw something of hers at the apartment—her purse, maybe, her ID—he could have assumed at the time she'd left it behind. He could've staged the attack at Megan's, and now he's gone after Katie and Stacy, assuming they know how to find her."

Ellie shook her head. "Still doesn't explain those threats on Campus Juice."

"Unless he posted those, too," Rogan said.

"Look. All we know is Stacy's missing, and I'm telling you, Nick Dillon has her."

"So let's do better than a BOLO," Rogan said. "Let's see if we can get a warrant."

She flipped open her cell the second it buzzed. "Hatcher."

It was the dispatcher relaying a message from the officers at Nick Dillon's house.

"I've got a UTL on your two subjects at the address you requested."

Unable to locate.

"Did you tell those officers this guy probably doesn't want to be located? How hard did they look for him?"

She heard the dispatcher radioing to the reporting officer at the other end of the call.

"They're saying they knocked on the door. No one answered. No sounds inside. No lights."

"What about the Infiniti?"

"UTL."

"Did they look in the garage?"

More crosstalk. "The only window's in the back. They'd have to jump a fence to look inside."

"Tell them to jump the fence."

"The detective's requesting that you check the garage. . . . Detective, I've got the officer telling me to remind you of the Fourth Amendment. They're reporting clear on the call."

"Do *not* let them leave the premises."

More crosstalk, and this time Ellie thought the dispatcher had placed a palm over the microphone. "Detective, they're outside the house and will watch until further notice."

"Damnit," she said, flipping the phone shut. "Dillon's obviously got buddies up there in Riverdale. They probably think this is some spat between him and a girlfriend, and they're not doing shit to look for him."

"Can't jump a fence without a warrant."

"Or exigent circumstances. Don't tell me for a second that those same assholes don't claim exigency whenever they don't feel like bothering with a warrant."

"I'll go up there myself," Rogan said. "You get to work on the warrant?"

The image of Katie Battle looked out at her from the canvas.

"No, I'll go."

She could tell he was thinking about arguing, but he must have realized the futility. "Okay."

"Call Max to help. And call Tucker. This is going to crush her, but she needs to know."

"You want to stay here and make all those calls, woman? If not, you better stop telling me what to do and get the hell out that door right now."


She spotted the cruiser around the corner from Dillon's house, just yards from where she'd parked the previous night as Tucker had kissed Dillon on his front porch. She pulled parallel to the marked car and rolled down the passenger-side window. The uni in the driver's seat gave her a how-you-doin' smile, then did a double take at the fleet vehicle and lowered his window.

"You here about Nick Dillon's place?"

"You know him?" Ellie asked.

The officer shrugged. "Just to say hi to. He was on the job, you know."

His partner leaned her way from the passenger seat. "Pulled his full twenty."

The uni in the driver's seat looked away from her. "We about set? It's busy out there tonight. Already heard from some wiseasses accusing us of cooping up here." Cops were always looking for a place to nap in their parked cars.

"Don't suppose you knocked on any doors to check if the neighbors have seen Dillon tonight?"

"No one asked us to do that, Detective."

She nodded in silence, knowing full well what she was dealing with. Dillon was an ex-cop and therefore came with a strong presumption of being stand-up. Without the luxury of time to burst their loyal bubbles, she backed her car against the curb behind theirs. She rested her hand on the open driver's side window of the cruiser.

"If I'm not back in fifteen, call for backup. Shield 27990. Hatcher. They'll have me down as Elsa."

She ignored the driver's chuckle and made her way down Dillon's block, cutting through front yards to keep out of view from his windows. As she approached the perimeter of his property, she ducked low, grateful that the sun had begun its descent. She made her way first across his lawn, over his unoccupied driveway, and then to the outer edge of his garage.

Just as the dispatcher had relayed earlier, the solid brick along the side of the garage prevented her from peering inside. She leaned over an adjacent four-foot-high fence and spotted a window in the garage's rear wall. She braced her hands on the fence top and jumped, wincing at the weight of her body against the pointed boards of the picket fence. If she was wrong about this, no one would ever know she peeked. If she was right, she'd save Stacy Schecter's life and figure out a way to justify it later.

Through the dusty glass of the back window, she spotted Dillon's black Infiniti sedan parked in the spot closest to the interior door leading into the house. The other half of the two-car garage was empty. Sam Sparks had parked his Maybach there last night. Dillon's date, Robin Tucker, had not. She had parked on the street, the way most visitors did.

Not Sparks. He had parked not on the street, nor even in the driveway. He had pulled into the garage. Like a man who was comfortable here. Like a man who stayed overnight. Like a man who practically lived here.

She pressed her ear against the glass. No sounds of a cooling engine, but it had been nearly an hour since Stacy's page. The motor could be long cold.

She worked her way along the glass toward the attached house. The blinds were all drawn. She leaned against the back wall of the house and closed her eyes. A dog barked somewhere down the block. A car started and left. Total silence.

The fence at the other side of the property was higher, too high to jump. She worked her way along the back of the house the same way she'd come. As she passed the garage, she peered inside again. This time, she caught sight of an object just beneath the passenger's side of the Infiniti.

She looked for a way to open the garage window, but it was a solid piece of glass, strictly for light, not air. She craned her neck for a better look, squinting to focus her eyes on the object beneath the car. She finally made sense of the dark shape. It was the stiletto heel of a woman's shoe.

She looked at her watch. Only four minutes since she'd told the uniforms to call for backup in fifteen. She sprinted to the front of Dillon's house, across his front yard, and down the street to the corner where she had parked.

The cruiser was gone.

# CHAPTER FIFTY-TWO

"I had a cruiser here five minutes ago. Where are they?" She felt the pressure of her fingers around the radio handset and forced herself to loosen her grip.

"It's hopping out there tonight, Detective. There was a DV beef a half mile from your location. That car reported clear and caught it."

"They weren't clear. They were standby. I've got a missing person located. I'm going in." She repeated Dillon's address twice. "Suspect is Nick Dillon. Known to be armed. I need felony arrest backup."

Using familiar radio 10-code, the dispatcher relayed the information and assured Ellie that officers were on their way.

Ellie pulled her car around the corner, stopping one house short of Dillon's. Then she waited. She heard the dog barking again, but no sirens. She looked in her side-view mirror. No cruisers.

She imagined the tiny glimmer of hope Stacy must have clung to as she pressed the send button on the text message to Ellie. She saw that spark of hope fading away with each minute Stacy remained alone with Nick Dillon.

Still no sirens. Still no black-and-whites.

Her first homicide case had been on a special assignment with a detective who got himself killed checking out a suspect without backup. But she'd saved another cop's life and earned a Combat Cross by walking into an armed murderer's house without a weapon. And even though the NYPD awarded her one of its highest honors for her work on that case, she knew in her heart that she could have stopped the blood spree even earlier if she had thrown out all the rules and followed her own instincts from the beginning.

This time, she wouldn't hesitate.

She opened her purse, removed a L'Oréal powder compact, and slipped it into her pants pocket. Then she hopped out of the car, popped the trunk, and retrieved the standard black baton from the equipment trunk. She followed the path of her own footsteps on the bent blades of Dillon's grass, across the front yard, along the side of the garage, around the corner to the back.

Behind the garage, she raised the baton with her right hand, shielding her eyes with her left. She waited in the silence until she heard the bark of the neighbor's dog, then swung as hard as she could, hoping that the combination of the riled animal and the wall between the garage and the house would muffle the sound of the shattering glass. She used the baton to clear away the broken shards of glass from the frame and then threw the baton to the grass at her feet. She pulled off her jacket and tossed it across the threshold.

The fabric protecting her hands, she hoisted herself through the window, landing in a crouch on the concrete of the garage floor. She immediately reached for the butt of her Glock and twisted the gun free from her holster.

Holding her breath, she felt a bead of sweat form at her temple and creep slowly down her cheek, but she remained still, ready for Dillon to appear from the house to inspect the sound of the disruption.

Nothing.

The sound of the zippers on her ankle-length boots was deafening in the silence. She stepped out of them in her socks, remembering how she had removed these same boots at Sam Sparks's apartment on the night Robert Mancini was killed. She tiptoed to the interior door and reached for the knob with her left hand, the Glock held firmly in the right. She turned the knob and allowed herself to inhale as she felt the cylinder retract, grateful that Dillon, like most homeowners, had not bothered to lock the door between the garage and his house.

She pushed the door open slowly, inch by inch, and then stepped onto the slate tile floor of a mudroom. She saw two steps in front of her, leading to an empty kitchen. She pulled up a mental image of the exterior of the house: the picture window at the front porch probably led to a living room at the front of the house; the sliding glass doors in back must have been for a family room in the back. Given the size of the house's footprint, Dillon probably had three bedrooms upstairs. Subterraneous windows around the property indicated a basement.

Dillon and Stacy could be anywhere.

She took one step up from the mudroom, preparing for the squeaks and creeks that might come with the transition from tile to hardwood. Silence. She took the second step with more confidence, swinging her Glock to the right at the turn from the kitchen into the living room. Still no sign of Dillon or Stacy.

She had reached a fork in the floor plan. To the right were the living room and a staircase leading from the front door to the second floor. Ahead of her, she saw the remainder of the kitchen, followed by a hallway to what she guessed was the family room.

She took three steps toward the front door when a sound stopped her frozen. Without context, she would have pictured an injured dog. A whimper. Desperation. Resignation. Stacy.

The noise was distant. She allowed herself to close her eyes. To close off all her senses as her mind replayed the sound. In front of her and to the left. And down. Beneath the floor. Muffled. In the basement.

She turned to the left, stepping carefully past the kitchen. A well-appointed sunken family room—sectional sofa, upholstered ottoman, plasma television over a fireplace—sat unoccupied at the back of the house. Still further, down the hall past the family room, was a door—not fully closed, not open, ajar just an inch. She knew it would lead to the basement.

She made her way down the hall until she stood just outside the cracked door. She heard voices.

"Just do it. Please, do it." A whimper. Desperation. Resignation. Stacy.

"May 27. Two-one-two Lafayette. I set it up. Miranda was supposed to be the girl, just Mancini's type. But it turns out she wasn't the girl hiding in the bathroom after all. She called you to cover."

"No."

"Stop lying. Miranda withstood a lot more than this, but in the end, she couldn't take anymore. She called you, Stacy Schecter, the 'honest and attractive brunette.' You were the one who was there."

"No."

"Admit you were there, and I'll do it."

"Fine, I was there."

"Then tell me what you heard. Tell me."

Silence. Then a whimper. "I don't know. I told you. It was Heather. The girl on the news. Tanya Abbott."

This time the sound wasn't a whimper, but a wail.

"I was in Afghanistan, Stacy. I learned these moves from watching men trained by Al Qaeda. Men who worked for the Taliban. Stop lying."

"I'm not lying."

"You are saying that name because you've seen the missing girl on the news. Tanya Abbott's picture has been plastered across the city all week."

"I *swear.* It was her."

Ellie pressed her back against the wall outside the door, trying to process the conversation. She'd been right. Dillon was trying to find the woman from the 212 that night. But he didn't know it was Tanya Abbott. He'd started with Katie Battle. Katie had led him to Stacy. And now he was convinced that Stacy was lying because, as far as the public knew, Tanya Abbott was the girl who'd gone missing after her roommate was stabbed.

Ellie reached into her pocket for the compact and then used her index finger to slowly widen the crack in the basement door. She crouched toward the floor and slipped the mirror into the crack above the stairs, adjusting the mirror to view the activity in the basement below.

The glass was tiny. Four inches at best. She made out isolated images, like the staccato flashes of a strobe light. She saw enough to know it was bad. Stacy on her side, her bent legs pulled behind her. Arms over her head. Her face against the concrete floor at Dillon's feet. Dillon bent over her contorted body. And the whimpers.

Ellie was startled by a sound behind her. Her instincts pulled her to the right one hundred and eighty degrees, her Glock held steady in front of her. The garage door through which she'd entered pushed farther open.

She stepped to her right toward a closed door farther down the hallway and smelled the familiar scent of laundry. She held the mirror in front of her to watch the garage entrance.

But where she expected to see Sam Sparks stood her lieutenant, Robin Tucker, her own Glock at the ready.

Ellie slowly peered around the corner and, when she caught Tucker's eye, raised her left index finger to her lips. Tucker nodded. Ellie watched as her lieutenant took one careful step after the next, making her way down the hall toward her. She pressed her back against the wall on the opposite side of the basement door. She was still catching her breath, but the two of them now had Dillon's exit straddled.

Ellie glanced at her watch. Where was backup? And did she really want it after all? If they stormed the house now, Dillon might panic and take Stacy out immediately. Or they'd be looking at a hostage situation in which Dillon had nothing to lose and nothing to gain either.

The voices continued downstairs.

"I was *in* the NYPD, Stacy. And I still have sources. In fact, I'll let you in on a little secret: I have a near, dear friend in the department who absolutely adores me. Tells me everything I need to know. If Tanya Abbott were the girl I was interested in, I think she would've mentioned it. Think of another story, Stacy."

Ellie stole a glance at Tucker, who swallowed and blinked a couple of times before returning Ellie's gaze. Based on that very brief change in her expression, Ellie guessed that something inside her lieutenant had broken as she realized the truth about her role in Nick Dillon's life.

Her attention was pulled back to the basement by more sounds—sobs followed by a thud and then a moan.

"You might not care about this, Stacy, but I mean it when I say, I take no pleasure in this. I'm not some rapist or sadist or sex-crazed killer. All I want is information."

She heard Stacy's pained voice, but could not make out the words.

"I'm sorry. I don't believe you. How about I show you what I can do with a pair of pliers? I'm walking out to the garage, and when I get back, you're going to start telling me the truth."

In the reflection of the mirror, she saw Dillon turn toward the staircase and tuck his handgun into his waistband. Ellie jerked her arm out of view and pulled her body farther from the basement door, waving two fingers at Tucker to indicate that she should reposition herself farther down the hallway. Tucker took two steps to her left and raised her eyebrows to signal she was ready.

She heard Dillon step onto the first stair. The stride of his feet against the steps continued unbroken. The basement door began to open. Dillon stepped into the hallway.

"Freeze," she yelled. "Down on your knees. Hands up. Hands up."

She'd replay the next milliseconds in her mind's eye countless times. What had she seen? Had Dillon's hands reached for his weapon? Had they reached over his head as she'd commanded? Had they moved at all? The subtle movements of a man's body in less than a second's time, when he was surprised to see her, and when she feared for her safety, could never fully be reconstructed.

She knew with certainty, however, what happened a second after Dillon first spotted her outside the doorway. She heard the blast of gunfire—two shots—and saw Dillon fall to his knees, red stains blossoming at his stomach and on the collar of his light blue dress shirt. She saw him look up to her in confusion as he fell to the ground.

And then she saw his eyes move from her to Robin Tucker, whose Glock was still raised, ready to fire again if necessary. Dillon's own weapon was at his waistband. Ellie bent over his limp and bleeding body and removed it to be safe.

She heard the faint sound of multiple sirens in the distance.

"He reached for his gun," Tucker said, reholstering her Glock. "Don't look at me like that, Hatcher. He reached. You saw it. Didn't you see it? Tell me you saw that. He would've killed us."

Then came the first of the many times Ellie would try to replay that partial second—that tiny gap of time between the opening of the basement door and the sound of Tucker's shots. Maybe Dillon had reached for his waist and Tucker simply had a better view from her position. Or maybe he hadn't, but would have half a second later if Tucker hadn't fired. All Ellie knew was that she hadn't seen his hands move. She also knew that her beliefs about what she'd actually seen didn't really matter.

Dillon was a killer. She, Tucker, and Stacy were alive. Ellie was raised by a cop. She knew how this worked. As far as the official record was concerned, Dillon had reached for his weapon. Tucker would say so. So would Ellie. And, from the looks of the blood beginning to pool on the floor beneath him, Dillon wouldn't be around to give his side of the story.

Her lieutenant still seemed to be processing what she'd just done as Ellie stepped around Dillon's body. "I was outside," she said. "Down the street. Watching. I saw him come with her. I thought—I thought he was fooling around. And then the unis knocked and left. And then you showed up, ran off, and came back again. When I saw the broken window, I realized—Hatcher, what am I going to say?"

"He reached for his gun."

"But I was here. At his house. I was *watching* him."

Ellie was already taking the basement stairs two at a time. She could tell from the approaching sounds of sirens that backup would be there soon. "You were coming over to surprise him. It's fine. Call dispatch," she yelled. "Have them send two ambulances."

Stacy let out a sob when she saw Ellie turn the corner toward her.

"Is he gone?"

Her words were strained as she struggled to control her breath. Her ankles and wrists were bound together at the small of her back in a complex tangle of black nylon rope. Ellie relieved some of the pressure from Stacy's limbs by supporting the weight of her bent legs in her own hands.

"We need a knife. Tucker, can you hear me? Find a knife."

Her lieutenant descended the stairs seconds later wielding a ten-inch chef's knife. Stacy's body stiffened at the sight.

"Shh," Ellie said, reaching for Tucker's extended hand. "It's okay now. He's dead."

She sawed at the rope, freeing Stacy's hands and feet. Stacy's weight dropped limp against the concrete, and she began to cry.

"Thank you," she wailed between sobs. "Oh, my God. Thank you."

Ellie crouched on the floor beside her, rubbing her shoulder as Stacy's breath started to return to normal. She heard Tucker's footsteps on the basement stairs and then in the living room above her, followed by heavier footsteps and the sounds of police radios. The backup had finally arrived.

"The cavalry's here," Ellie said, tugging the hem of Stacy's dress over her bare thighs. "Let's get you put together."

She helped Stacy to her feet. She wobbled at first but managed the steps slowly as she held Ellie's hand for support. Just as she reached the final step, she turned to look at Ellie.

"I know what he did to Katie. She tried not to tell him who I was. She tried to protect me. I tried at first, but I just couldn't do it. I told him about Tanya. I told him she was the girl at that apartment that night."

Ellie gave her hand a squeeze. "You were strong, Stacy. And Tanya will be okay. He's gone now."

# CHAPTER FIFTY-THREE

The Maybach slowed in front of the house. Sparks stepped from the driver's seat just as the EMTs were rolling Dillon's gurney out the front door. The change in his face from panic to absolute devastation told a story about his relationship with Nick Dillon— the secret that Dillon had killed to protect.

"Nick," he cried out. He did not need to see beneath the white sheet to understand the significance of the swarm of police cars and ambulances.

Ellie and Robin Tucker were standing guard over Stacy Schecter as she sat on a bench on the front porch, an EMT wrapping the lacerations on her wrists and monitoring her for signs of shock.

"I'll be all right," Stacy said, clearly sensing Ellie's hesitation to leave. Tucker placed a reassuring hand on the woman's shoulder as Ellie made her way across the lawn.

By the time she reached Sparks, a uniform officer was holding him back from the cluster of emergency vehicles in the middle of the street. Sparks saw Ellie approaching and held her gaze.

"Please. Please tell me he's still alive."

Ellie shook her head, and he seemed to collapse against the uniform officer. The confused cop walked him back toward the Maybach, where he rested his weight on the front bumper.

"No, oh God no." He placed his face in his hands. "It's my fault."

She stood and let him cry. And talk. He wasn't in custody. No Miranda warnings were required. And he was about to give them more of a confession than she could ever get through interrogation.

"I should've known. I should have said something. I didn't know. At first, when Robo was killed, I wondered. But I didn't know."

"He was blackmailing Dillon."

Sparks nodded. "It started when Nick was in Afghanistan. Robo found out about Nick—"

"That he was gay."

"It wasn't about that at first. It was Nick being stupid, shaking down some opium farmer he stumbled on during a security job in Nangahar Province. Robo and his people came through on patrol and found Nick where he wasn't supposed to be. Nick made up some b.s. story, but Robo figured out what was going on."

"You knew about this?"

"Of course not," he said, shaking his head. "Not until later. Nick would tell me old stories about cops ripping off dealers, but he always made it sound like he was talking about someone else. Robo made it clear to Nick that he expected a job when he was discharged. By the time that happened, I had convinced Nick to come back to New York. He wasn't happy about working for me, but it was supposed to be temporary, a way for him to bolster his corporate security credentials without being over in that hellhole. Then he'd move on to another company."

"So he hired Mancini?"

Sparks's eyes remained glued on the ambulance as Dillon's body was wheeled into the back. "For a while, things were all right. But then Robo walked in on us once in Nick's office. It was just a kiss, but still, it was obvious what was going on. Next thing we knew, he was asking for a much better job—well, a non-job really—at an exorbitant salary. I wanted to pay it, but my accounting staff would have asked questions. And Nick, with those cop instincts, said it would never stop. Robo would just keep asking for more. And then May 27 happened."

"You had to know it was Nick."

"I think I was still in denial about the entire situation. When I got the call about a problem at the 212, I made a point to find Robo to deal with it. It's like I was trying not to be intimidated. To remind him who he worked for. I had no idea *he* was the emergency."

"But then we told you he'd been killed. The possibility must have crossed your mind."

He nodded. "That's probably why I came off as such a prick that night. Part of me was happy that Robo was dead, but I was so angry, wondering whether Nick was somehow involved. So I asked him, of course. But he swore he had nothing to do with it. He told me how people get killed in these mistaken home invasions. He said it could've been a robbery attempt. And I'm sure I wanted those explanations to sound plausible. You don't want to think the person you love has it in him to do something like that. Then the next thing we know, you're asking about *me* and *my* enemies and *my* finances. I couldn't cooperate, but I knew it only made me look guilty."

"If we'd opened your books, we would have found the payments to Prestige Parties," Ellie said. "Eventually we would have asked the right question and figured out you were the one client of theirs who really was aboveboard."

"Lots of pretty girls to walk the red carpets with me. Nothing more, nothing less. And I truly didn't think I had any information that would help you, or I would have turned it over. I believed Nick. And then you showed up at the Four Seasons last night."

"We said something that made you realize there was more to it."

"You told me that Robo had been with a woman from the service the night he was killed. It was too big of a coincidence. Robo didn't know about the escort service, but Nick did. I realized that Nick had set him up."

Ellie remembered Genna Walsh's description of her brother and husband snickering about Robo's "sure thing." She imagined

Dillon pretending to cede to Mancini's demands, throwing in all the corporate perks for good measure.

"So you drove here after we confronted you at the Four Seasons."

He nodded. "Nick looked me in the eye and told me all over again that he didn't do it. I could tell something was wrong, but I just didn't want to believe he had that kind of evil in him. I said that to him, you know. I walked out on him and said, 'You better be telling the truth, because whoever would do something like that is evil.' Those were the last words I ever spoke to him. He tried to talk to me today outside the office, but I just got into my car and told the driver to leave. Nick did it, didn't he? He killed Robo."

"We think he also killed a woman named Katie Battle. He brought another woman here tonight named Stacy Schecter, but she made it."

"No. No, he would never—"

"He lied to you. I'm sorry." Fifty-year-old men don't suddenly go from shaking down Afghan opium farmers to murder to torture. Just as Dillon had managed to fool Sam Sparks for eight years, he had hidden inside the NYPD for twenty.

"But, why? Why would he hurt these women? What did they have to do with Robo?"

Ellie explained how Katie Battle was supposed to be Mancini's date the night he was killed, but then the trick had been passed off to Stacy Schecter and then ultimately to Tanya Abbott. "We obviously have some loose ends to tie up, but it looks like Nick was trying to find the witness he'd left behind."

A flash of recognition passed through Sparks's glazed eyes. "Nick was the one who wanted us to press for information about the woman who was Robo's date that night."

"A woman named Tanya Abbott," Ellie said.

"The girl from the news?"

She nodded.

"But she's missing."

"She was attacked earlier in the week. Her roommate was killed, and she's been on the run ever since."

"And you think Nick did that too?"

"We don't know," she said. "Based on some of the things he said to the woman he kidnapped tonight, we don't think he knew about Tanya Abbott."

"And if he didn't know about her—"

"Then he's not the one who went after her and her roommate."

"That's not much consolation."

She watched him fall into silence—leaning against the Maybach's gleaming hood, alone, staring at the ambulance as the engine started and strangers carried away the body of his dead partner. She could feel sympathy for him now, but none of it changed the fact that he had played a role in Dillon's violence. She finally had to speak.

"I'm sorry, Mr. Sparks. Perhaps it's cruel of me to say this right now, but when Mancini blackmailed you, why didn't you just call his bluff?"

He shook his head as he wiped away a tear from his left cheek. "There's more to it than just being outed. People would've started asking questions about the women. The escorts, the money—"

He cut himself off, but Ellie finished the thought for him. "You used a corporate card. And if that had come out, your investors might have asked about other expenses as well. My guess is, they would have found some other creative accounting? The Maybach. Maybe a little too much spending given the current economic climate?"

She took Sparks's sad nod as resignation, his financial concerns now eclipsed by Dillon's death. "My entire corporate existence is linked to this image of unapologetic consumption. The truth is, I don't have as much as the world thinks." He fought the quiver of his lower lip. "Financing? Advertising? All gone if the world knows Sam Sparks is just another overleveraged developer, and a poof at that. And, even so, I was still tempted. I would have let Robo scream all of it from the rooftops."

"But Nick?"

"Nick? I'm not sure which he was more worried about, that mess in Afghanistan or the truth about us. Ex-cop. Ex-military contractor badass. A grown man barely out of the closet to himself. Out of the question." For the first time, she heard real anger in his voice and knew that this must have been an ongoing struggle between the two men. "And it wasn't always easy to argue with him. Ask yourself, Detective: How will your colleagues react when they learn that Nick Dillon was queer?"

Ellie wished she could tell Sparks he was wrong. Even so, Dillon had no justification for hurting Katie or Stacy.

"What about Judge Bandon?" she asked.

"What about him?"

"Did you have a deal with him? To protect you?"

"Of course not."

"You didn't have some kind of connection to him through Prestige?"

"I went there for the girls, Detective, not middle-aged judges." A sad smile worked its way through his pained expression, and he seemed to find some comfort in the humor. "You said something about this last night, and I was telling you the truth when I said you sounded like a lunatic."

"He did throw me in jail for you," she said. "And hauled my partner in for an update on the case. We figured his special interest in the case was to protect you."

"Why in the world would the man protect me? It's fashionable to hate the rich these days, in case you haven't noticed."

"But the rich can still help someone like Paul Bandon become a federal judge."

"Well, Guerrero did tell me he was surprised Bandon was hearing the case."

"Why was that?"

"Because Bandon worked at Guerrero's firm for a couple of years before he went on the bench. He didn't officially have a conflict because I didn't start using the firm until after Bandon left, but Guerrero told me Bandon usually recuses himself from their cases so he doesn't have to check on the timing issues."

Ellie remembered seeing a brief law firm entry beneath Bandon's online picture, just between his stint in the Department of Justice and his appointment to the trial court. She'd known from Max that Guerrero was at one of the city's top firms, but she hadn't made the connection.

"It never dawned on you that Bandon might be trying to work you for support?"

"If that was part of the plan, he never told me. Or my lawyer."

Something didn't sound right, but she believed Sparks was telling her everything he knew. She turned away from him, but he stopped her. "Will I be charged with anything, Detective?"

"That will ultimately be up to the DA." If Sparks's suspicions about Dillon had formed only after the fact, she doubted that he had committed any crime, but she didn't want to make any promises.

"Fair enough. Do you know where they'd take him? The ambulance, I mean."

"He'll go to the Bronx Medical Examiner's Office. It's on Pelham Parkway at Jacobi Medical Center."

"Well, the word will be out now for sure. I will insist on viewing his body and making the necessary arrangements, even as I'm sure someone will tell me I'm a non-family member. That should be fun."

She knew it would not be. She handed Sparks her business card. "You have any problems with the ME, you have them call me."

# CHAPTER FIFTY-FOUR

It was nearly ten o'clock by the time she had a chance to call Rogan. He didn't bother with greetings.

"It's about damn time."

"I was at Dillon's."

"No shit. I finally gave up and called dispatch. All she could tell me was there was a homicide. She at least knew it wasn't an officer down, or I'd be up there myself by now."

She gave him the short version: Tucker shot Dillon, Stacy was fine, Sparks hadn't been involved.

"Where are you?"

"Outside Paul Bandon's apartment. Donovan and I didn't know what the hell was going on, so we kept working on Dillon's arrest warrant. See what happens when you don't call people?"

"I'm sorry. It was total chaos."

"I gotcha. Just be sure to call your boy, Donovan. I could tell he was worried about you. He was the one who sent me up here to track down Bandon. He wanted to make sure the warrant got signed."

"You won't be needing it now."

She flipped the phone shut, seeing no reason to tell Rogan that her first call—back at Dillon's, before she'd even started the engine—

had been to Max. She knew it meant something about her feelings for him. Something good.

As she merged onto the Henry Hudson Parkway, she thought about everything she'd learned in the past few hours and realized how off base she'd been. Not unlike those unis who refused to jump a former cop's fence, she had subconsciously bestowed an irrebuttable presumption of innocence upon Nick Dillon, but he'd been in front of them—guilty—the entire time. He had killed Robert Mancini for threatening to peel away a carefully constructed facade that shielded his most coveted secret—a secret about his very identity, a secret that shouldn't have to be concealed.

And just as she'd assumed the best of Nick Dillon because he came from her world, she'd assumed the worst of Sam Sparks because he did not. She had rationalized her obsession with him, first because of the way he'd treated her at the penthouse and then for his refusal to cooperate with the investigation. But the truth was, more than ten years after she'd moved to New York, people like Sparks still had a way of making her feel like the little girl from Wichita who hadn't known which fork to use until an investment banker boyfriend finally told her. If she had set aside her emotions—if she had looked at Sparks more as a person than a stereotype—she might have seen the truth earlier.

She had been right about one thing: Dillon had been using Robin Tucker, manipulating her obvious desire for companionship in the hope of obtaining inside information about the investigation. But Ellie had underestimated her lieutenant. As much as she must have wanted a relationship with Dillon, she had never told him about the missing girl's connection to the Mancini case, even as Tanya Abbott's photograph dominated local headlines.

Ellie was confident that they could clear the Mancini and Battle cases, but that still left the question of who killed Megan Gunther. If Dillon didn't know Tanya was the woman with Mancini that night, then he was not the man who killed Megan and left Tanya for dead. She'd been so off the mark about Dillon and Sparks. What had she missed about Megan and Tanya?

She thought again about the isolated facts they had gathered about Tanya Abbott. She was an only child from Baltimore. Her mother had worked as a nanny. The family was poor enough that Tanya had lost the house when her mother died but somehow still had money set aside for college tuition. A bright and vibrant preteen, she was busted for prostitution by the time she was twenty years old, when she managed to have access to a private counselor to get her out of criminal charges.

It was as if the girl had a guardian angel watching over her until one morning, when her roommate was stabbed to death in front of her and her life fell to shit.

And then Ellie saw what she'd been missing.

Distracted by the noise of Robert Mancini and Katie Battle and Sam Sparks and Prestige Parties, she hadn't focused on what they'd known about Tanya Abbott. When they'd seen the calls between Tanya and Bandon, they'd been so sure it was part of Tanya's current life—the one that had taken her into the bed of Robert Mancini on his last night. But maybe this wasn't about the present at all. Maybe this was all about the past.

Ellie slowed to a crawl in the right lane as she juggled her cell phone and scrolled down to a Baltimore number she had dialed two days earlier.

"Hello?"

Anne Hahn sounded annoyed but not groggy. The call to Tanya Abbott's former neighbor was late, but at least she hadn't woken the woman.

"Ms. Hahn. It's Ellie Hatcher from up in New York again. I'm sorry to call so late."

"Benjamin, I told you to go to sleep. Now. Before I put you into that bed myself." Her tone lowered an octave. "Sorry about that. Go on."

"You mentioned that Tanya's mother worked for a family of some means?"

"I'm not sure how rich they were, but, yeah, he was some big fancy lawyer."

"Could his name have been Paul Bandon?"

"Bandon . . . Bandon. Maybe?"

"His wife's name is Laura. He has a son named Alex."

"Alex." Anne's voice sharpened in recognition. "Yes. There was definitely a little boy named Alex. Tanya talked about him all the time. She was a few years older and, having been an only child, I think she kind of glommed on to him as a sort of little brother. She was the same way with my older son when she'd babysit him. It was always Alex this, and Alex that."

"Do you remember when this would have been?"

Ellie realized now why she had recognized the towheaded kid in the photographs with Tanya. She had seen an older version of the same kid in the high school graduation picture on Judge Bandon's bench when she testified on Wednesday morning.

"Shoot," Anne said, "probably twenty years ago."

"Tanya would have been about ten years old?"

"Well, Marion worked for them for a few years, I'd say from when Tanya was ten to—um—probably about fifteen or so?"

"And were these the years when you said Tanya was the teacher's-pet type or—"

"The Lolita years?"

"Yeah."

"That period of time would have included both. Tanya started changing when she was about thirteen, if I had to say. At first it seemed like the usual teenage girl insecurities. She got quiet, sort of withdrawn. And then slowly she started acting like someone else altogether—sulky, full of attitude, darn right inappropriate when it came to males."

In other words, all the signs of sexual precociousness.

"Thanks for your time, Ms. Hahn. Sorry again for calling so late."

"That's all right. Now you've got me wondering whatever happened to that guy she worked for. I think he was a big deal with the government. Marion used to tell me, just you watch, someday he'll be on the Supreme Court."

As Ellie flipped her phone shut, she wondered if that had been before or after Marion Abbott found out what Paul Bandon was up to with her daughter. She took the Seventy-ninth Street exit off the parkway. Bandon's apartment was right across town.

She had tried to call Rogan in case he was still on the Upper East Side. He hadn't picked up, but she found her partner sooner than expected.

Turning east off of Park, she slammed on her brakes at the sight of uniformed officers dropping gate-style iron blockades at the entrance onto Seventy-eighth Street. Beyond the stopgap, she spotted two fire trucks, an ambulance, and at least six marked police vehicles, all with lights flashing. Even the NYPD's version of SWAT, the Emergency Service Unit, had sent an armored van. A swarm of medical, fire, and police personnel stood among the vehicles in the street. And they all appeared to be looking upward.

Her gaze tried to follow theirs, but all she could see from the driver's seat was the third floor of Paul Bandon's building and the grimy ceiling of the fleet car's interior. A car horn blared, followed immediately in New York style by several others, each more urgent and sustained than the previous.

She pulled up parallel against the metal blockades to get out of the way of through traffic on Park Avenue, then flashed her shield to the uniform officers as she stepped out of the car. As she walked around the barriers, she saw Rogan at the epicenter of the chaos, speaking intensely to Paul Bandon. Even from this distance, she could tell he was using what she called his military voice.

What had Paul Bandon done to cause this scene?

Rogan looked surprised when he saw her approaching.

"I've been trying to call," she said. He glanced at the bedlam around him and then gave her a look that said he'd been too busy to answer the phone.

"So you know?" she asked.

"Know what?"

"It's him." She pointed at Bandon lest Rogan miss her point. "Tanya Abbott's mother was the Bandons' nanny in Baltimore. That's why he and Tanya were calling each other. He's known Tanya since she was ten years old."

She'd already known in her gut that she was right, but if she'd carried any doubts, the expression on Judge Bandon's face would have washed them away. He'd appeared panicked when she'd first spotted him with Rogan, but now his face fell in that same way she'd seen so many times when a suspect knew it was over. Paul Bandon knew that all of his lies—everything he'd been trying to hide for nearly two decades—had finally caught up to him.

Rogan, however, looked confused.

"This is about Alex. The son. He's on the roof."

Ellie looked to the sky and understood now why the crowd in the street had been gazing upward. She made out the dark outline of a body on the roof of Bandon's building. He appeared to be dangerously close to the edge.

"He saw me," Rogan said.

"Who?"

"Alex, the son. I was parked around the corner. Right after I got off the phone with you, he came up Park Avenue from the south and saw me. He did a double take, so I knew he recognized me from when we were here the other morning. I figured he'd say something to his father, so I stuck around in case to explain about the warrant. I was about to leave when I saw a woman pointing up at the roof. I called in a response team."

"You have to get him down," Bandon said. "You have to save my son."

Rogan resumed an authoritative tone. "Like I said, everyone here's gonna work to do that, Judge, but you need to help us help your son. We've got ESU here. They've got a guy who's trained to talk to ju—to people who are distraught like Alex." He had almost slipped and referred to the man's son as a jumper. "It might help us to know what he's doing up there."

Bandon's lips parted, but no words came out.

"I know what happened back in Baltimore with Tanya," she said. "Did Alex find out about it?"

He shook his head. "No. Well, I mean, yes. But he's known about it for years. So has Laura. Jesus—Laura. She's on a spa trip in the country. I need to call her."

Tanya Abbott had not been the one to post those messages on Campus Juice. And Paul Bandon had not been the one who tried to kill Tanya, taking her roommate's life in the process. It had been his son, Alex.

"You need to help us with information right now, Judge."

"Tanya and I, well, it sounds like you know. We had an affair a long time ago."

"An *affair?*" She pictured herself delivering a solid right hook to his temple. Sex with a thirteen-year-old girl did not constitute an *affair*.

"Nothing happened until she was fourteen. And Tanya was very mature."

She let him continue. This wasn't the time to rid Bandon of the rationalizations he had created during sixteen long years of denial.

"When Tanya's mother found out about us, I told Laura everything. She stayed with me, and we agreed with Marion that we'd help her out financially."

"You bought her off."

"We came to an agreement. Our families were very close, Detective."

*Obviously.* She held her tongue. And that right hook.

"You were the one who got her out of that prostitution arrest in Baltimore," she said.

His eyes were glued to the roof of the building, impatient to get past this conversation but realizing that any attempt to avoid it would only delay turning full attention to his son's safety.

"That and plenty of other problems back then. We set up a college tuition fund, but the money just sat there, since Tanya didn't have any inclination. And for the last several years, things had finally quieted down. I thought things were fine. And then she called me at the end of May, saying she was in trouble."

"After Robert Mancini was killed."

He nodded. "She said she'd witnessed a murder. I had no idea she was in New York, let alone what she was up to with NYU. I tried to get her to come forward, but she was convinced it wouldn't do any good. She never saw the man's face or heard any names, but she remembered hearing him say something to Mancini about blackmailing a cop. She didn't think she could trust the police, and she was terrified of losing this chance to start over."

"So when we filed a motion in the Mancini case, you grabbed it."

"It was a way to keep an eye on the case. Let her know if there were going to be any problems for her. I was trying to keep her at arm's length, but she kept calling to see if I'd heard anything about the case. Plus the account we set up for her wasn't enough. She called for money a few times, and I gave her a couple bucks here and there but knew it had to stop. Then she called Thursday, saying her roommate was being threatened on the Internet. She wanted to know if there was anything I could do. All that dysfunction, all that chaos, that I thought my family had finally put in the past when we moved, it's been one thing or another all summer."

"And your family knew about this?"

He nodded. "Not at first, but yes, eventually. Laura stopped by my chambers last month when I was on the phone with Tanya. She knew something was up, but even then, I minimized it as a one-time cry for help."

"But she didn't believe you," Ellie said. Like Robin Tucker, so suspicious after an ex-husband cheated on her, Laura Bandon was still broken by her husband's deception. She would be the kind of wife who snuck occasional peeks at her husband's phone. She would have seen the calls to and from a Baltimore cell number.

"She looked at my phone and saw all the calls. She was furious. We fought. She said I had to make it stop. Tanya was ruining our lives again. I didn't know what to say. I told her that Tanya was blackmailing me."

"Was she?"

"No, but I was afraid what she might do if I pushed her away."

"When did Alex find out Tanya was back?"

"The same day. It was the end of August. He overheard us fighting. I went to his room afterward and explained the whole thing."

"Along with the blackmail embellishment?"

He nodded. "But I never told him where Tanya lived or the alias she was using."

Bandon was reaching for some piece of evidence that might exonerate his son. If Alex had not known where to find Tanya, then he could not have killed her.

"Have you met with Tanya since you talked to Alex about her? Is it possible he saw you?"

She could tell that Bandon wanted to deny the possibility, but the flash of recognition in his face was unmistakable. "A couple times since then," he said. "I slipped out of the apartment to give her a little cash."

If Alex had trailed his father on one of his outings, he could have followed Tanya home from there. He'd had a full month to nail down her schedule and plant the postings on Campus Juice as a diversion.

"You told us how proud you were of your future Harvard law student. You knew he was disturbed enough to kill an innocent woman, and didn't get him some help?"

"I had no *idea*. He ran into the apartment fifteen minutes ago yelling that the cops knew and were after him and everything was over for our family."

"But Tanya must have told you."

"No. She called me from the hospital. She said the man who stabbed her wore a ski mask. She assumed that whoever killed Mancini had finally tracked her down. The next thing I know, her face is on the front page of the paper as a missing person and the two of you are at my door. I haven't heard from her since."

They'd been so consumed by Tanya's cell phone records that they had never bothered asking for a list of the calls from her hospital room.

"Now, please, do something. Alex is—oh Jesus, he's up there. He's going to jump."

Ellie heard a commotion near the barriers at Park Avenue and turned to find a cameraman jumping out of an NY1 van.

"Jesus," Rogan said. "How the hell do they manage to get here before our negotiator? Hey," he yelled to the unis, "get them the hell out of here."

"Wait," Ellie said, holding out her arm to stop him. "Let them film. But on three conditions: they have to announce the address; they have to say we've got a twenty-one-year-old male Columbia student on the roof; and they need to mention that detectives involved with the Tanya Abbott case are on the scene."

Rogan turned to deliver the instructions.

"What are you doing?" Bandon asked.

"I'm trying to save your son. Tanya doesn't know Alex is the one who hurt her. She still has childhood pictures of him. At least as of last night, she was in the city, and she's probably following the news."

"You think she'll come here," he said.

"She might. And if she does, she could be our best chance of talking your son off that roof."

# CHAPTER FIFTY-FIVE

Tanya Abbott let the paperback drop to the floor beside the sofa. The mystery novel had kept her occupied for the entire day since she'd found it in the nightstand drawer, but now it was over. She wasn't ready to sleep yet either. She was stir-crazy.

She'd walked out of St. Vincent's on Friday night, knowing that once the hospital dug further for insurance information, they'd realize the real Heather Bradley was buried in Arizona. She thought about going to Penn Station and catching the first train down to Baltimore, but she knew herself too well. Once she was back home, she'd crash with Mark. Or Trent. Or maybe Saundra. Either way, she'd fall into her old ways. Drinking too much. Floating bad checks. Taking cheap dates. Feeling lucky not to get busted.

So instead she'd come here.

When she'd moved to New York last spring, it was supposed to be a truly fresh start. New name. New place. New age. None of the same bad habits. She had an entire summer before classes started so she could adjust to her new life.

But the money hadn't been enough. Maybe it would have been fifteen years ago when the Bandons first set up the college fund. But college tuition had outpaced the interest on the account. The fund would barely cover tuition through graduation, not the cost to live in New York.

She thought about going to the Bandons for more, but knew it was no use. They'd always been good about helping her in a jam, but a few bucks here and there wasn't the same as a lump sum. The one and only lump sum had been paid with the college fund. She'd found that out for sure when the bank sold the house. Maybe Paul was willing to do more, but her mother had always made it clear that Laura's family was the one with the real money. Fair enough. She had, after all, made a deal.

And so Tanya had supplemented her income, the same way she always had. Craig's List made it easy to jump back in, even in a new city. It was still a new life, only with a bit of a transition from the old one.

She tried to look at the bright side: but for the dates, she wouldn't have had this apartment to hunker down in for the weekend. Granted, she also wouldn't have been at the 212 that night and therefore wouldn't need this place, but that was another issue.

She'd dated Henri twice a month since May, but still didn't really understand what his job was. An equity something-or-another. He lived with his wife and two children in Paris, but worked in his New York City office every Thursday and Friday and kept an apartment in Hell's Kitchen. Every other week, he delayed his return trip until Saturday morning. His wife thought the extra nights were for business dinners.

They were not.

She'd shown up for their date on Friday as planned, making up an elaborate story about a horse-riding accident to explain the bandages. Henri had been sweet. Even tender. She did find a way of pleasing him, even under the circumstances.

And as the time came for him to leave for JFK in the morning, she'd complained from the shower that the bandages were slowing her down. He trusted her to close the door behind her. Instead, she'd helped herself to the extra key in the top drawer of the kitchen, leaving only for a quick dash to the Gristedes on Eighth

Avenue—and for that one ill-fated attempt to find the blond detective on her own.

Only two more nights until Henri returned. She needed a plan.

When four months had passed after that awful night at the 212, she thought she might have actually pulled through. No cops. No questions. Even after that maniac attacked her and Megan on Friday morning, she had wanted to believe it was whoever wrote those creepy Internet posts. It wasn't until the next day, when the news anchor said that the woman killed at the Royalton had led a double life as a call girl named Miranda, that she realized she was in danger.

She flipped on NY1 to catch the mid-hour headlines. She'd been watching incessantly for anything new—about her, about Megan's death, about any connection to last May's murder.

The correspondent was breathless with the pressing report: a twenty-one-year-old male Columbia student was on a building roof at Seventy-eighth and Park, reportedly threatening to jump. He did not know the source of the man's despondence, but detectives looking for the missing woman Tanya Abbott were apparently on the scene.

By the time he promised to keep viewers apprised of any new developments, Tanya was already out the door.

# CHAPTER FIFTY-SIX

**W**herever Tanya had been hiding, it could not have been far. Twenty-five minutes after NY1 went live, the woman for whom they'd been searching for three days stepped out of a cab on the corner of Park and Seventy-eighth Street.

Her eyes fell first on Paul Bandon and then directly on Ellie. She looked five pounds thinner and ten years older since they'd first seen her in the hospital. She looked her own age.

Ellie waved her past the blockade, and Tanya wasted no time on explanations.

"Where's Alex?"

Ellie pointed to the sky. "We've had a negotiator on the phone with him for forty minutes. Alex hung up at one point, saying he was going to jump, but I called him back and said you were on your way—that he should at least talk to you first."

"I don't understand. Why would he do something like this?"

"Because you came back into their lives."

"But we used to be so close," she said.

"And now you're not. I'm sorry, Tanya, but in the years that have passed, his family has moved on by casting you as a teenage problem child who seduced Paul Bandon."

"But that's not how it was. They've always taken care of me. Paul loved me."

Her eyes searched sadly for the judge, who was now sandwiched between the ESU negotiator and Rogan.

"The man who stabbed you: you don't know who he was?"

"Of course not. He was wearing a ski mask."

"You assumed it was whoever killed Robert Mancini."

"So you know I was there?"

"Your fingerprints were on the champagne glass. We've been looking for you."

"The man who came to the penthouse that night said something about it being stupid to try to blackmail a cop. Then all I heard were the shots. I didn't know who I could trust. I tried to go to your apartment, but I got scared waiting. Some guy was staring at me."

So much for Jess's skills of stealth detection.

"There's something else, Tanya. The man who stabbed you, the man who killed Megan. It was Alex."

"No," she said, shaking her head. "He would never do that."

"I don't have time to argue with you about this. He did it, and that's why he's up there."

Rogan was waving them toward the ESU van. "The kid saw the cab pull up. Wants to know if it's Tanya."

"Talk to him," Ellie said as they made their way toward the van. "Tell him you're not going to testify, that you'll say the person who did it was shorter than him, whatever."

"What about those things?" Tanya pointed to the mattresslike structures that the ESU had inflated beneath the building to break Alex's fall.

"I'm told at that height, they can't be certain of the path he'll take. He's got a knife, too, so there are other ways he can hurt himself. Try to get him down from that roof."

The ESU officer extended the cell phone, and Tanya took it hesitantly. "Alex? It's Tanya."

Rogan leaned toward Ellie and whispered, "Why are we bothering to save this prick's life again?"

"Because after what he did to Megan Gunther, he doesn't get to decide what happens."

Tanya placed her hand over the mouthpiece of the phone. "He says you guys need to move. He doesn't want you to hear."

They looked to the ESU officer for guidance. He nodded, and they all stepped away from Tanya like synchronized swimmers.

They watched as Tanya pleaded. Her eyes to the sky. Him standing at the edge of the roof 150 feet above them. She loved him like a little brother. He hated her so much he'd tried to kill her. So much distance between them, but Ellie could tell that they spoke to each other with the intensity and intimacy of siblings.

She could tell Tanya was crying. She heard her say, "I'm sorry," more than once. She heard something about a promise. She heard the word *please*. "I'll go with you. I'll turn myself in."

And then Tanya flipped her phone shut, as calm as if she'd just ordered takeout, as sad as if she'd just learned about a family member's death.

"He's on his way down."

The ESU officer radioed the officers waiting inside the stairwell leading to the building roof. "Coming your way."

"Oh, Jesus. Thank you." Paul Bandon rushed toward Tanya with open arms, but Rogan held him back.

"He's turning himself in," she said. "He wasn't up there because he was afraid of being arrested."

"I don't understand," Bandon said.

"I promised him two things, though. First, he wants you to know that Megan wasn't supposed to be home Friday morning. He'd watched her all month. He knew her schedule, and she should have been at a spinning class that morning. When she walked out of her bedroom, he panicked. She wasn't supposed to be there."

"And the second promise?" Ellie asked.

Tanya kept her eyes on Bandon.

"I promised him no one would know about us, what happened in Baltimore. He doesn't want Laura to be humiliated. That's what this was about from the very beginning. He says you told them I was threatening to go public."

Bandon opened and closed his mouth like a marionette.

"I have *never* threatened you. I would never do that to you. Or Laura. Or Alex." Her voice—her entire body—was shaking now.

"But that's what he told them, Tanya." Ellie kept her voice low, knowing how much this was hurting the woman. "He said you had forced your way back into his life."

"And so Alex blamed me?" Her words were sharp and fast like hurled daggers. "He thought this was *my* fault, instead of *yours*? And now he and I—our lives are ruined. And Megan, who never did a bad thing to anyone, is dead. She's dead, Paul. She's dead."

Alex Bandon stepped out of the building, ESU officers in Kevlar vests on either side of him. Rogan walked toward them, handcuffs already out. Paul Bandon tried to stop him, but two ESU officers pulled him back. As Rogan recited the familiar Miranda warnings, Alex turned away from his father to face Park Avenue, his wrists behind him to accept the cuffs.

And then Paul Bandon fell to his knees, placed his palms on the dirty concrete, and sobbed alone in the street.

# CHAPTER FIFTY-SEVEN

**TWO WEEKS LATER**

J ust as Laura Bandon had predicted, there she stood, blank-faced and stoic, behind and to the right of her husband as he read from the prepared statement.

Ellie and Max watched from a conference room at the district attorney's office as the network replayed the footage for the umpteenth time. The television pundits could hardly contain their excitement as they pored over the salacious details of the unfolding saga: a rising legal star resigning from the bench, brought down by a nearly two-decade-old sex scandal with a barely teenage girl; the ensuing fifteen-year cover-up in which the Bandon family fell into a bizarre caretaking role with the acquiescence of the girl's mother; the arrest of his seemingly perfect son for murder two weeks earlier; speculation about what would have happened if he'd been confirmed to the federal court prior to the disclosure.

Tanya had said what she needed to get Alex Bandon off that roof, but the NYPD was not bound by her promises. They promptly filed first-degree murder charges, setting forth in the indictment the special circumstance that the murder was intended to silence the victim of a statutory rape committed sixteen years earlier in Baltimore, Maryland.

Given that Alex was only twenty-one years old, the media had begun asking questions about the identity of the parties involved in the original crime. A dogged reporter at the *Post* had traced Tanya's past to her former neighbor, Anne Hahn, and made the connection to the Bandons from there. Now Bandon was resigning from office, relying on a statute of limitations to avoid prosecution in Maryland while Max's office weighed potential charges in New York for official misconduct.

And, just as Laura Bandon had predicted, the coverage came with plenty of questions about the wife. *Why would she stay with this man? How could she have helped him cover this up? How could she have allowed him to pursue a judicial career knowing that this bombshell lay in his background?* Comparisons to Elizabeth Edwards, Hillary Clinton, and Silda Spitzer flew. Such accomplished and complex women, all lumped together under one big Stepford Wife umbrella, just as Laura had predicted. Just as her son had feared.

One of the anchors held a finger to her earpiece and then interrupted the panel of breathless political analysts to report a breaking story. "I'm getting word here that real estate mogul and infamous playboy Sam Sparks has just put out a statement. Let's go to Jeff Baker, who's reporting live outside the Sparks Industries building."

A sandy-haired correspondent swept his hair back against a blustering wind. "Well, the single ladies of New York are going to have to scratch one eligible bachelor off their list today. Billionaire Sam Sparks has issued a statement essentially coming out, as they say. It's very brief, so I'll read it in full:

> *"As a prominent public servant admits that the secrets he has hidden for years have harmed those he loves most and brought horrific tragedy to innocent people, I have come to realize the danger of a life lived in a lie. Accordingly, I am making clear today that I am a gay man. I will continue to run Sparks Industries as I have for nearly twenty years and thank my colleagues and investors in advance for their continued support. I have now said all that I wanted to say, or will say, about this subject."*

"Good for him," Max said.

Paul Bandon's disclosure had been forced by circumstance, but Sam Sparks's had not. As far as the public knew, Nick Dillon murdered Robert Mancini after Mancini blackmailed him. No specifics about the nature of the blackmail. No details such as the Blagojevich-style hairpiece and wedding band they'd found in his car, props Dillon had worn on his arranged dates with Katie Battle and Stacy Schecter. No mention of Sparks.

She looked at her watch. One p.m. on the dot. "Think they're going to show?"

"Yeah, they'll be here."

"How do you think it's going to go?"

"I don't know. I understand what Tanya's trying to do, but it could be an absolute train wreck."

Tanya's lawyer was still hammering out a plea deal, but most of the big-ticket items were in place. She would plead to fraud charges and serve four years probation with intensive psychiatric counseling. A support center for adult victims of child sex abuse was trying to convince one of the local colleges to admit her. Given the stunt she pulled with NYU, she'd be a hard sell, but one of her former professors was vouching for the work she'd done as Heather Bradley.

But today's meeting wasn't about Tanya the defendant; she had asked for an opportunity to apologize to Megan's parents. To Ellie's surprise, Jonas and Patricia had agreed. Maybe now that they had someone else to blame, they might be able to begin to forgive Tanya Abbott.

The upcoming sit-down between Tanya and the Gunthers was not the only case of strange bedfellows to emerge from the aftermath. Stacy Schecter had stopped by the precinct the previous week to thank Ellie and Robin Tucker. She said they'd saved her in more ways than one, and Ellie believed her. The Craig's List account was closed, and the Erotic Review profile was gone.

As she'd left the building, Jess had been smoking a cigarette as he waited for his sister on Twenty-first Street. He commented on her

Boomtown Rats T-shirt. They were still talking when Ellie showed up. She lied and said she had more work to do, and then watched from upstairs as they made their way to Plug Uglies without her.

It wouldn't last. It never did with Jess. But women never seemed to mind.

The unspeakable secret that had plagued Sam Sparks's entire adult life came and went from the television in a flicker as the talking heads bounced directly back to the Bandons. Now the screen displayed a photograph of Laura Bandon, with bullet-point highlights of her bio: Princeton, Georgetown Law School, former associate at Covington & Burling prior to the birth of her son.

"I still don't get it." The female anchor sounded as if she had been personally betrayed. "Why in the world would she stay with this guy?"

"So," Max said, hitting the power button on the remote, "would you stay?"

"Why? Are you planning to scope out the junior high schools this afternoon?"

"You're gross."

"You started it."

"Seriously. I'm a man, and I don't get it. I've had girlfriends—"

"No, you haven't. No one before me."

"Fine. I've had members of the opposite sex throw me in the doghouse for a week just for smiling at someone the wrong way."

"Well, you do have an amazing and unrepentantly flirty smile."

"So much so that it's gotten me in trouble. But then some guy like Bandon gets caught doing the nanny's daughter—and let's set aside the fact that she's a child, for Christ's sake. Seriously, why wouldn't a woman like Laura Bandon take off?"

"Because she loves him."

"It's that simple?"

"Maybe. Love's a powerful thing."

A knock at the door caught their attention. A secretary showed Jonas and Patricia Gunther into the room.

"I'm sorry," Patricia said. "Were we interrupting?"

"Of course not." Max stood and gestured to the unoccupied chairs around the table. "Come on in."

Jonas reached for his wife's hand as soon as they were seated. Maybe Ellie had been wrong about their daughter's death being the beginning of the end for them.

"Is Heather—Tanya, I'm sorry. Is Tanya here yet?"

"I'm sure she will be shortly," Ellie said. "This was very important to her."

Max took a seat at the head of the table. "She'll tell you herself, but I've spent a lot of time with Tanya the last couple of weeks. Her defense attorney suggested it so our office would have a better sense of the person we're dealing with. You'd be perfectly within your rights to be skeptical, but, for what it's worth, I do believe that she never realized she was putting your daughter in jeopardy."

They were interrupted by another knock. The same secretary, this time with Tanya Abbott. She had pulled her hair into a demure knot at the nape of her neck and was dressed in a conservative navy blue skirt and tan turtleneck.

Max handled the awkward introductions. "Mr. and Mrs. Gunther. This is Tanya Abbott."

Tanya stepped into the room with her hands clasped in front of her like a child making a presentation to a class. All eyes were on her, but her gaze was fixed somewhere in the middle of the table. She cleared her throat before speaking.

"Thank you for coming here, Mr. and Mrs. Gunther. I'll admit that I didn't know your daughter well. But she was a good person— to me and to her friends. And she was smart and sweet and, just, a really good person." She was starting to stray from her prepared words. "And I just want you to know, and I swear I mean this from the bottom of my heart, that if I could rewind the clock—"

Her voice cracked, and Patricia Gunther choked back a sob.

"If I could rewind the clock and change places with Megan, I would. I really would."

Ellie blinked back a tear forming in the corner of her own eye as Patricia leaped from her chair. Tanya initially flinched as Patricia grabbed her in a tight embrace, but then returned the hug.

"We don't blame you, Tanya. We forgive you. Our daughter *was* a good person."

Jonas was on his feet, holding on to his wife as she cried. "Megan would want us to forgive you," he said.

As Ellie watched the Gunthers console the woman who set in motion the chain of events that eventually led to the death of their only daughter, she marveled at the ability of human beings to still surprise her. Just as love had kept Laura Bandon at her husband's side, it had helped these two forgive not only Tanya, but each other. It had blinded Sam Sparks from seeing whatever part of Nick Dillon killed Robert Mancini and Katie Battle. It had caused Katie Battle to choose her mother's care over her own security. It had brought a son to kill to protect his mother from public humiliation. And it had kept Tanya Abbott running to the person who abused her as a child, because it was the first feeling of love that she had ever known from a man.

Love was, in fact, powerful.

Powerful enough that for just one second, Ellie thought about the father she had lost, the mother who demanded more from her children than she could ever give as a parent, and the brother who was her best and sometimes only friend, and wondered if there were any limits to what she would do for them. And for just a moment, she held the gaze of the man on the opposite side of the conference table and could believe that the ties of a different kind of devotion might eventually find her.

# AUTHOR'S NOTE

Like all of my earlier novels, *212* was inspired by real-world events. If the revelation of the hidden strings tying fiction to life ruins the magic for you, skip the next five paragraphs and jump forward to the shout-outs.

Many readers will have recognized at least one of the headline-capturing cases that made its way into *212*. On March 12, 2008, then New York Governor Eliot Spitzer admitted during a live press conference that he was the mysterious "Client 9" listed in a federal criminal indictment involving an escort service called Emperors' Club VIP. In the ensuing days, the political career of a man once mentioned as a potential presidential candidate had ended, the public learned more than it needed about seemingly privileged young women who nevertheless sold their bodies for money, and members of the media openly challenged the former first lady of New York's decision to stand by her man.

Governor Spitzer was not the first state governor to be brought down by a sex scandal (nor of course, as the last year has taught us, would he be the last). In May 2004, under pressure from the *Willamette Week*, a free weekly paper in Portland, former Oregon Governor Neil Goldschmidt revealed that he had engaged in a three-year sexual relationship with his fourteen-year-old babysitter while he was Portland's mayor in the 1970s. Once an honor student, the former babysitter grew into a troubled adulthood marked by drug dependency, further victimization, and a stint in federal prison. Several members of the governor's political inner circle were alleged to have known about the so-called "affair" and abetted a thirty-year cover-up. A civil settlement paid to the woman in the mid-1990s came with a confidentiality agreement.

To a plot loosely inspired by threads of these two political sex scandals, I added the role of the Internet in the modern sex trade. Even the quickest scan of Craig's List reveals that scalped concert tickets and used sporting goods are not the only easy scores on the Web. As I perused barely veiled offers of sex for money online, I thought of the danger these women put themselves in. On April 14, 2009, two weeks after I turned in the manuscript of *212*, a New York City woman named Julissa Brisman was shot in a Boston hotel room after advertising her services as an erotic masseuse on the Web site. The media dubbed her alleged murderer "The Craig's List Killer."

Craig's List is not the only Web site in *212* that is real. So is the Erotic Review, where "hobbyists" across the country post book review-like feedback on the "providers" who service them, down to details about appearance, professionalism, restrictions, and promptness. And the Campus Juice site that terrorizes poor Megan Gunther is based on Juicy Campus, which enticed users with the promise of anonymous campus gossip, going so far as to instruct especially cautious posters to use Internet provider cloaking devices to avoid detection. When Juicy Campus went out of business in 2009, its owner blamed the economic downturn, rather than the controversy that led to civil suits, investigations by attorneys general, and spam attacks against the site.

In the final pages of *212*, Ellie marvels at the continual ability of human beings to surprise her. I feel the same way, and for that I'm grateful. The moment I'm no longer surprised by the kinds of events that inspired the plot of this book, it will be time for me to stop writing.

For ongoing assistance in the worlds of technology and law enforcement, I am thankful to Gary Moore, NYPD Detective Lucas Miller, retired NYPD Lieutenant Al Kaplan, retired NYPD Desk Sergeant Edward Devlin, Josh Lamborn, David Lesh, and Deputy District Attorneys John Bradley, Chris Mascal, Greg Moawad, Heidi Moawad, and Don Rees. I thank my students at Hofstra Law School for tethering me to a more realistic and vibrant world than I might otherwise know as a writer and law professor. I thank Lee Child for serving as *212*'s first reader and Lisa Unger for her help with *212*'s title.

I consider myself blessed by the most effective, professional, and supportive team in publishing: At the Spitzer Literary Agency, Philip Spitzer (no relation to Eliot) and his associates Lukas Ortiz and Lucas Hunt; Holden Richards at Kitchen Media; and, at Harper-Collins, Christine Boyd, Jonathan Burnham, Heather Drucker, Kyle Hansen, Michael Morrison, Jason Sack, Kathy Schneider, and Debbie Stier. I especially thank Jennifer Barth for her tireless commitment to my work and irreplaceable editorial eye.

I appreciate the generosity of readers who donated to worthy charitable organizations to see their names lent to some of the characters in *212*. Also making cameos as the *212* bartenders were Dennis, Jill, and Mark, the people who keep me fed and hydrated when I don't feel like cooking (i.e., every day).

I send a special note of thanks to the online friends I've made through my Web site, Facebook, MySpace, and Twitter. Writing is a solitary life, but you have become part of my workplace. Like the constant presence of colleagues, your notes provide community, encouragement, sanity, and—ah, yes—procrastination. OMG, I appreciate it. LOL. If you read my books and haven't yet connected with me online, I hope you'll do so.

Finally, I thank my husband, Sean. Not enough words. Ever.

# ABOUT THE AUTHOR

A former deputy district attorney in Portland, Oregon, Alafair Burke now teaches criminal law at Hofstra Law School and lives in New York City. A graduate of Stanford Law School, she is the author of the Samantha Kincaid series, which includes the novels *Judgment Calls*, *Missing Justice*, and *Close Case*. Most recently, she published *Angel's Tip*, her second thriller featuring Ellie Hatcher.